A LITTLE SALTY

A POISON AND POTIONS LitRPG

KIA LEEP

PULSAR PUBLISHING

Edited by Justine Manzano

Cover art by Vexdye Productions

Typography by Inorai

*Too all the young folk out there
who are facing challenges you shouldn't have to face.
We will persevere.*

CHAPTER ONE

A FRESH START

The familiar orchestra of medical devices gradually fades into the distance as a comforting darkness envelops me. I relax into oblivion, knowing that this is the end. I'm dead.

Finally.

No more pain. No more tests. No more sobbing parents futilely trying to hide their tears from me out in the hallway. I've been ready to rest for a long time now.

Only... nothing really seems to be ending.

I peek one eye open. Then the other. An azure sky fills my vision as painfully white clouds drift overhead like cotton candy. Wind ruffles my hair, sending goosebumps racing across my skin. The air smells of grass and earth and fresh rain.

Well. That's not supposed to be in a hospital room.

I breathe in the sweet air, filling my lungs until they burn, fuller than I could ever manage before, and it feels like I'm taking a breath for the first time.

[New authority recognized,] a voice says. [Populating stats. Processing role.]

"Hello?"

Searching for the source of the voice, I sit up—and it's effortless. It's *easy*. Like it should be. I sweep my hand through the damp grass, reveling in the soft, cool sensation.

I'm alive. And not just alive, but healthy.

Laughter bubbles up out of me. How is this possible? Where even am I? I push myself to my feet, staggering as I stand too fast, and I laugh at myself again, giddy with excitement. I can't believe this. But it's real. It's really real.

I run my hands over my body: two legs, two arms, all the standard female parts. I'm wearing some simple clothes instead of a hospital gown, which pleases me almost as much as having a fully functioning body. My hair is long and black and blowing annoyingly into my mouth and eyes. Black is new: it was brown before. I comb it out of my face, tucking it behind my ears. My ears feel a little different, too. The shape's not quite right. And when I touch my face, the nose feels smaller, the cheekbones less pointy—even my teeth feel slightly off. My skin appears just as pale and sun-phobic as ever, but it's clear this body I've woken up in is not the body I died in.

Should that weird me out? Maybe. But I didn't particularly like that body, and it certainly hadn't liked me. Good riddance.

"I'm alive!" I shout at the top of my lungs, just because I can, just because I have the strength to. Whooping, I pump my fists in the air, spinning in a circle to take in my surroundings. The sun is toward one horizon, a forest opposite. Otherwise, I seem to be alone in this grassy, beautiful, amazing field.

[Designation complete,] the voice says.

I pause. Maybe not so alone after all. Though there's definitely no one around here but me. In fact, the voice doesn't seem to be coming from any direction in particular. Like it's all in my head.

"Hello?" I say again. My voice sounds a little different, too. Lower, and warmer, and louder. "Who are you?"

[This interface is a clone of the interface that has been designated Echo,] the faintly-feminine voice says.

"Uh, Echo, then," I say. "Why are you in my head?"

None of this should be making any sense. It certainly doesn't feel like the afterlife—but I also know it's not a dream. It's all too real and vivid—and my dreams are only full of pain and needles and shadows, anyway. An Echo in my head is exactly the sort of thing I should be questioning, but instead it feels as natural as the sunlight.

[This interface is designed to provide audiovisual guidance to users who fulfill the baseline requirements,] Echo says. [Activate stats?]

"Um. Sure?" I say.

A display of words and numbers appears in front of me.

[Name: Sally]

[Species: Human]

[Class: N/A]

[Level: 10]

[Attack: 20]

[HP: 90/90]

[Mana: 10/10]

[Role: Chef]

"Whoa!" I take a surprised step back, and the words float with me. I turn my head from side to side, and they stay within my field of vision. I mentally will them away, and they vanish. "Wait!" I say. "Bring them back!"

The words reappear. Excitement bubbles up my chest. No way. No way! It's just like a videogame! I really have a stats interface of my own? This is totally wild!

"Kind of short, though," I say. "Is this really it? You don't even have my last name."

[The current display is truncated as a result of a previous user's request,] Echo says.

Previous user, huh? That's interesting. "Well, can you give me more?" I ask.

[Affirmative.]

My vision explodes with words and numbers. [Gender: Female. Age: 18. Speed: 10. Weight Class: Medium]. I stumble back, hardly able to see any of my surroundings as text scrolls through my line of sight. No wonder someone else pared it down to the basics.

"Okay, okay, that's enough!" I say. "Set it back to the default for now. I can tailor it to my liking later."

[Affirmative,] Echo says, and most of the numbers vanish.

Just these few lines are already enough to chew on. I'm a human, which is no surprise. Level 10 sounds like some kind of default noob level, which is fair. Still need to get a class: that should be exciting. Mana indicates I should be able to do magic: the rest seem pretty basic.

Except that Role stat.

"Echo, what does it mean my role is Chef?" I ask.

[The Chef role requires the user to engage in cooking, baking, or elements of food preparation on a daily basis.]

Kind of obvious, I guess. "So, what, it's like my job? Do I get paid if I do my role?"

[Negative,] Echo says.

"Will it level me up?"

[Negative.]

"Do I get bonus items? Loot boxes? Unlock magic abilities?"

[Negative.]

I throw my hands in the air, exasperated. "Then what's the point?"

[The role requires that you meet the requirements of the role.]

"Created by the Department of Redundancy Department," I mutter. Well that seems pretty useless. "What happens if I don't meet the requirements of my role?" I ask.

[Failure to operate within expected parameters would result in strain on the system-user interface.]

Cool. Super helpful.

A grin spreads over my face. Honestly, though, who cares? If I have to slap some ham and cheddar on a slice of bread each day as payment for being reincarnated with magic and a videogame interface, count me in! This is real, and I'm not dead, and there's a world of possibilities ahead of me.

My eyes prickle with tears. I'm so glad I'm here, it hurts. An urge to do something wells up inside me. To jump, to climb a tree, to dive into a river. The excitement is building in me like an expanding balloon, until—*pop*! I take off running.

My boots pound against the ground, sending me racing across the field. Laughter bursts from my mouth as I run, exhilaration pumping through my veins, wind ripping tears from my eyes. When was the last time I was able to run? The last time I felt so free and strong and alive? All those days spent in my bed, dreaming of being whisked away to different lands, with a new body and a better life—and now it's real! I don't know how, but it's the best thing that has ever happened to me.

I was given a fresh start, and I'm not going to waste a second of it.

I skid to a halt, breathing hard, my lungs burning in the best way. The land slopes down into a valley before me. A lake shimmers like a sapphire at the bottom of the basin, birds speckling the air as they spiral down to the water. Forests nestle around the vista on every side but mine, and a stream lazily winds out from the woods to spill into the lake before snaking away again in the opposite direction.

"Hey Echo, have I got supplies or anything?" I ask. "An inventory?"

[The user has no items in their inventory,] Echo says.

My heart leaps. "I have an inventory then?" Awesome. Inventories are broken as fuck. "How do I access it?" Even as I ask, however, a display appears in my vision.

[Inventory: 0/1]

What. Are you kidding me? "It only has one slot?"

[Affirmative.]

"What the hell?" There's got to be an explanation. Maybe it's because I'm still a noob. "Can I upgrade it?"

[Negative,] Echo says.

"What?! Rip off!" I sigh. No, no, beggars can't be choosers. One inventory space is better than none—even if it seems pretty useless. But I have to look on the bright side. I'm sure I'll unlock a lot of sweet spells soon anyway that will make up for it.

"Well, guess I'll be needing supplies," I say aloud, just because I can, just because it feels great for every word spoken to feel effortless. "Water seems like a good place to start. And if you get lost, aren't you supposed to follow the river, because they're supposed to lead to civilization? I think I read that in a book somewhere. Right, Echo?"

[Query unrecognized.]

"I'm not really asking you a question, I'm just talking to you," I say, starting down the hill. "If it sounds like I'm rambling, you can just say 'Okay, Sal.'"

[Affirmative,] Echo says.

"Close enough."

I stroll down the hill, humming a happy nonsensical tune. Where should I even start once I get into town? I bet they have adventure guilds or something. That's what they had in the shows I watched. Since I'm starting out with what appear to be pretty basic stats, and no special abilities that I'm aware of, I'll probably have to do a lot of grinding. Do creatures here drop loot? Well, either way, I'll need to get some money and a weapon.

The birds I'd seen earlier caw in alarm and take flight as I approach the lake. I've never seen birds like them before: green feathers and bright yellow beaks, with long tails like a peacock. I watch them for a moment before crouching down at the bank to splash some water on my face and take a few tentative sips. Hopefully I won't get sick from this, but it's better than getting dehydrated.

The birds continue to caw angrily at me—I guess they don't like that I disrupted their little oasis—and then take off over the forest. Without their clamor it's suddenly quiet, and I feel very alone.

My heart stings as Mom and Dad flash through my mind. If I really died back there, then they're probably mourning me by now. I wish I could tell them I'm alright. I'm in a better place—literally. And now they can finally move on with their lives. They don't have to cater every minute of every day around me anymore. They can be happy again.

I slap my hands against my cheeks, trying to snap myself out of it. Come on, I can't get all sentimental now. Not when things are finally looking up. I stand back up and force a smile on my face. It's time for adventure! I plant my hands on my hips, surveying the two streams that branch out from the lake.

"Now, if I were a city, which direction would I be in?"

As I'm considering this, a distant rumble of thunder rolls over the hills. I squint toward the sky, but the few scant fluffy clouds don't look like rainstorms. And even more strange, the sound seems to be getting louder.

The lake ripples, and the ground beneath my feet starts to shake.

"Uh oh," I say, looking around. "Um, Echo? Any insights? I don't suppose this is, like, a small earthquake or something."

[Negative,] Echo says to my complete lack of surprise. The noise crescendos into thundering hoofbeats, and at the same time, a herd of creatures pours over the lip of the valley and begins racing right toward me. [The sound appears to belong to a stampede of pebblebacks.]

"Fantastic," I say, taking a step back toward the lake. I can't make out what the creatures look like at this distance, but they're big, there's a lot of them, and they're coming my way very fast. There's not enough time to run to the forest or climb a tree. And there's nothing out here to hide behind. I take another step back, and my boot splashes into the lake. When was the last time I took swimming lessons? When I was a little kid?

"You think they can swim?" I ask, ignoring the soul-sucking sensation of wet socks as I retreat into the lake.

[Affirmative,] Echo says.

Great.

"I bet they can't swim better than me, though," I say, hoping to will that truth into existence.

[The user's Swimming skill is level 1,] Echo says.

"Well," I say as the wall of creatures races toward me, threatening to put an end to my rather brief second shot at life. "Crap."

CHAPTER TWO

PEBBLEBACKS

The pebblebacks stampede down the hill, and the water ripples and splashes as their thundering footsteps reach me. I back further into the water, raising my fists defensively in front of me, before realizing how absolutely pathetic and useless that gesture is. Even so, I'd rather go out fighting.

A whistle cuts through the air, and excited cheers and whoops quickly follow. Bright colors flash among the creature's rocky hides—there are people in the herd, running alongside the beasts.

I don't have much time to take all this in before the stampede reaches me. The herd splits in half, each side going around the lake, however some in the middle of the pack aren't able to turn in time and come barreling straight toward me. When the first one hits the water, it's like a geyser erupting right in my face.

I throw myself back as the creatures splash through the waves, their legs crashing through the water all around me. The turbulence slams me against one of their hides. I'm sent tumbling head over heels into the water, and I lose all sense of up and down.

Beneath the surface, everything is quieter. I can still hear the muted grunts and stomps of the beasts, bubbles crackling all around from the swiftness of their stomps, but it's a moment of reprieve. A few seconds of peace. I stop flailing and figure out which direction the sun is in. Spinning myself around, I plant my feet on the pebbly bottom and kick off. I'm not going to die here.

I pop from the water like a cork, gasping in delicious lungfuls of air. The pebblebacks are stomping around, musty smelling like farm animals, eyes wide with alarm as they try to make for the bank. One of the creatures lunges for the shore, and when it drags itself from the water, a person is there in the gap of the pack. They're sitting atop a bird-like steed, something between an ostrich and a dinosaur, covered in ruby-red feathers. It's the rider I can't pry my eyes from, though.

[Check,] Echo says as I instinctively wonder who and what they are. [Terimus: Level 18 Dracid Warrior]

Apart from being human-shaped, he's covered in blue scales, with two ridges of horns curling back from either brow. His snout is long and pointed, almost like a dragon's, and he has claws in place of hands. Slashing a spear at one of the pebblebacks, he hollers for a companion, who answers from somewhere in the press. As I stare, slack-jawed, he turns and looks straight at me. The lizard person pauses, eyes going wide in surprise.

That momentary distraction is his downfall.

One of the pebblebacks whips around, its flat, broad tail smacking into Terimus's steed. The bird cries out and jumps, dumping its rider onto the ground. The lizard person—the dracid—vanishes beneath the herd. His spear rolls toward the shore, where it rocks in the shallow waves of the lake.

I lunge forward, half swimming, half wading through the shallow water, stumbling around the pebblebacks that are still climbing back up the bank. I snatch up the spear, and I'm filled with relief and security. Well just a *modicum* of relief and security. I smack the nearest pebbleback with the blunt face of the weapon, and it blatantly ignores me.

[1 point of Bludgeoning damage dealt,] Echo says.

Alright. That's how it's going to be, huh?

I swing the spear again, this time stabbing and slashing at any pebbleback who gets too close.

[3 points of Slashing damage dealt.]

[4 points of Piercing damage dealt.]

"Not," I pant, stabbing a pebbleback in its thick hide. "Today!" I advance another few paces, spinning to slash another one of the creatures as it lumbers in my direction.

I dart another few feet up the shore, away from the water, and suddenly the dracid is in front of me. One of his legs is twisted at an unsettling angle. My stomach flips, and I try not to think about what's going on under that pant leg. Instead I let out a feral scream and spin haphazardly around, slashing at all the nearby creatures like some kind of inflatable car-dealer tube man. The pebblebacks grunt and groan, then gradually wander away. I'm left standing there panting, spear clutched in a death grip, water dripping off my soaking wet clothes, as the dragon person watches me with surprise.

"Rena!" he suddenly calls, and I jump. "There's a person here! Come quick!"

I spin to point the spear at Terimus, squinting suspiciously down at him. Did he sic this whole herd of monsters on me on purpose? What will his friends make of me? I don't know anything about this world, yet. Was helping him a mistake?

He holds up a hand. "Whoa, there! I'm unarmed. I mean, you have my arms. And I can't do much from down here, anyway."

I hesitate, backing up a pace and out of spear-snatching range, then dart a glance around for his companions. They're already riding up on bird-steeds of their own.

[Rena: Level 19 Dracid Bruiser]

[Layf: Level 17 Dryad Ranger]

The other dracid is covered in red scales, while the dryad, as the species name would suggest, is some kind of treeple with brown bark-textured skin and a short crop of yellow flowers for hair. They pull up to either side of me, sword and staff held in guarded stances.

"Stand down," Terimus says. "Everyone, stand down! This human just saved me."

"She did?" Rena skeptically looks me up and down.

Look, I don't blame her, I'd doubt me, too. I cautiously lower the spear, since I've got Lizard-Guy vouching for me.

"What happened?" Layf asks.

"I fell," Terimus says. "One of the pebblebacks stepped on my leg. I would have been a goner if she hadn't taken up my spear and protected me."

Is that what I did? Huh, I guess so. I mean, I was more acting out of self-preservation, trying to bat back the weird armadillo creatures while making my way out of drown-zone-central, than actively trying to save Terimus. But I also definitely wasn't going to leave him there to get stomped to death. Trying to poke the pebblebacks away from him was instinct—just seemed like the right thing to do. Look at me, already being a hero!

"And what about you?" Rena asks, turning to me. "Where did you come from?"

I stand up straight, resting the butt of the spear on the ground. Not like I could fight these two off anyway, even if I wanted to. "I was just trying to get some water. Certainly wasn't expecting a whole herd of these guys to come stampeding down the hill toward me!"

Rena rounds on Layf. "You were supposed to scout the valley ahead of time!"

He holds up his hands. "I did! I swear! There wasn't anyone here."

Rena snorts. "Well *clearly* there was!"

"This argument is great and all," Terimus says. "But I might have a broken leg. Think we can figure out who's more responsible for near-manslaughter after we get out of here?"

Rena sighs. "Layf, go find his footbird."

"Aye, aye," Layf says with a salute, then reins his bird around to trot off to where a group of pebblebacks have taken to grazing nearby. He turns his head back to shout over his shoulder. "Still not my fault!"

Rena swings down off her own steed and heads over to Terimus, crouching down to check him. Gingerly touching his leg, a small glow of pink light blooms from Rena's fingers, and Terimus sucks in a pained breath.

"Oh, give me a break," Rena says, the light flickering out. "It's not broken, you probably just pulled something." She glances up sharply at me. "Hey, kid. Get over here and give me a hand, would you?"

I hesitate for only a moment, weighing the likelihood of any of this being a trap. Considering I have literally nothing but the clothes on me, however, highway robbery seems unlikely. Besides, I kind of like them.

"Sal," I say, jogging over to help. "Not *kid*." I wrap one of Terimus's arms around my shoulder, while Rena takes the other.

"Sure thing, kid," Rena says with a pointy grin. "Now come on, let's get him over to those rocks."

As Rena patches Terimus up and Layf starts setting up a camp, I ask a lot of questions, and I learn a lot of interesting things.

"You guys really don't know what I'm talking about?" I say, incredulous.

"I can assure you, none of us have a voice in our head called an 'Echo'," Layf says. "Um, do you think you might have hit your head in that fight?"

"I didn't!" I object. "And you guys are *sure* you don't see stats? I mean, it says right here that you're a warrior, and you're a bruiser, and you're a ranger."

"Bruiser?" Rena says with a snort. "What does that even mean?"

"I don't know, I kinda like the sound of *warrior*," Terimus says with a grin. He winces as Rena ties off a bandage with a sharp pull. "Ow! Careful, there."

"Oh, I'm sorry, *warrior,* was that too rough?" Rena smirks.

Layf rolls his eyes. "Get a room, you two."

Weird. *How come none of them can see stats like I can?* I ask Echo.

[The user met the prerequisite as defined for system access.]

And those prerequisites are...?

[User does not have permissions to access said data.]

Perfect. I guess I'll just have to keep asking around until I can find someone more knowledgeable than these guys. I mean, it can't just be me, right?

Echo doesn't give me a lot of time to dwell on this.

[Role Requirement,] she pipes up when Layf pulls supplies out of his pack, setting out some alien looking fruit, a stale hunk of bread, and some dried meat. Oh, right. That dumb Chef Role I have. Hey, now that I'm thinking about it, none of these guys have a role—just me. What the heck's up with that?

[Role Requirement,] Echo says again.

Are you kidding me? *Now?* My fingers tingle with anticipation as Layf begins slicing up the bread. As stupid as this role is, it looks like I need to get my hands on one of his knives.

"Need help?" I ask. It's like an itch in the back of my head. Maybe I can just dice up one of the fruits.

He waves me off. "No, you're our guest. Don't worry about it."

I rub my hands together, as if it would disperse the tingling, and look around the field to distract myself. Now that the stampede is over, the pebblebacks have taken to grazing around the valley; several of them appear to be passed out, laying flat on the ground like a bunch of weathered boulders. "We don't have to worry about any of these guys heading over here for some payback?"

"Nah," Terimus says, wincing as Rena pulls a brace tight around his leg. "They're pretty passive when they're not trying to trample you. Just gotta wear 'em out a bit first." He points to a couple of the sleeping ones. "Those are what we're after. Once they're sleeping, they're down for at least a day, and not even Widengra's Wrath could wake them. That's why we ran them down the hill in the first place. When they're passed out, it's easier to harvest the geodes that grow on the males' hides. They should fetch us a respectable sum back in town."

[Role Requirement.]

"Are you sure I can't help?" The words burst from me. I swear the tingling in my brain and hands are getting worse. I don't wait for Layf to object as I spring to my feet and grab one of the fruits from the cloth he'd set it on. "Here, let me." I hold out my hand for the knife.

Layf arcs a perplexed eyebrow at me, glancing at his teammates.

"Oh, give it to her," Rena says. "If she was trying to pull anything, she wouldn't have given Terimus's spear back."

Shit, I do look suspicious, don't I? "Sorry," I say. "It's the mind voice thing again."

Layf shrugs, handing over the knife. "I was done with it anyway. You really should get your head looked at, though."

Relief fills me as soon as my hand wraps around the hilt, soothing the static from my fingers. I immediately sit down and start cutting into the fruit, exposing a soft, blue interior the consistency of an orange. Juice drips everywhere as a result, and I belatedly realized maybe this sort of fruit is meant to be peeled. Oops. Oh well.

"Anyway," Rena says, breaking the awkward silence as they all watch me butcher this piece of fruit. "We'll probably be heading into town tomorrow, after we've finished with the pebblebacks. Might as well make camp here and give Terimus time to rest his leg. You're welcome to spend the night with us if you've nowhere else to be."

I pause my mangling of the fruit. Instead of two halves each cut into four slices, the scene before me has become a large stain of blue pulp and several bruised peels.

I bet a town would have some sort of Adventuring Guild. Or maybe someone there would know about my Echo and Stat interface. Think there's an Offworld Bureau I could check in at?

"That would be great!" I say. "I don't really have any plans. I'd love to stay with you guys for the night and travel to the town with you tomorrow. Thanks!"

"After how you helped me out, it's no problem at all," Terimus says. "Where's all your gear, anyway?"

"Oh, uh." Well, I've already told them about Echo and my stats. How much weirder could admitting my origin be? "I'm from another world," I say. "Just popped up here a few minutes before the pebble-back stampede."

The three of them stare at me.

"Don't suppose you get off-worlders very often?" I ask.

"Layf?" Rena says.

"I'll get my medicine pack," he agrees.

"Wait—I'm serious!" I object. Is that why I have stats and they don't? "Okay, to be fair, it all does sound a bit crazy, but I can prove it."

"Oh?" Terimus says.

I sit there a moment, thinking. "Okay, actually I can't prove it. But I would appreciate it if you just believed me on this."

Rena shakes her head. "Well, you seem sound in most other respects." She dubiously eyes the fruit I've turned into a pile of pulp. "*Most* other respects. Regardless, you can still travel with us to Fairwood, where you can hopefully find help for your... condition." Somehow, I don't think 'condition' is referring to my being from Earth. "For now, let's break our bread."

I give up on the fruit and sheepishly hand Layf's knife back. As I do so, I feel a sort of mental ping.

[Daily Role Requirement quota fulfilled,] Echo says. [Counter reset. Skill Obtained! Knifework: Level 1.]

Man, this really *is* like a videogame. I sure won't object to that knife skill, though. Maybe next time I won't make an embarrassment out of myself.

Layf passes around the bread, meat, fruit (whole pieces as my pile goes tactfully ignored), and a canteen of water, as the group chats and lazes in the afternoon sun. A pebbleback occasionally wanders by, some of them gleaming with black crystals like what Terimus mentioned, but all they do is grunt, graze, and leave us alone. I eventually find myself laughing along with the group's jokes—Layf seems to be the butt of most of them—and even enjoying the stale bread and dry meat. The fruit and water keep my mouth from going dry, but even without that it sure beats hospital food; something about the salt of the meat and grit of the bread tastes *real* in a way the fruit cups and defrosted waffles never were.

Maybe this Chef role isn't all bad. If I've been reincarnated in another world just so I can make and eat good food the rest of my days, I can't be upset with that.

Our meal is interrupted when a sharp crack like lightning shakes the air. I wince, looking around for the source, while Rena jumps to her feet.

"What was that?" I ask. "Thunder?" I didn't see any light, though, and the skies are bright blue.

"I don't know," Layf admits, shielding his eyes as he glances around the valley as well. "It sounds like it came from—"

The crack happens again, this time only feet away. I fall backward as a shock of air knocks into me, and my ears are sent ringing from the noise. I scramble to sit back up, but freeze when I see the figure standing in the middle of our camp.

The woman is wearing an intricate layer of red leather armor and is holding a giant spear adorned with tassels that flutter in the wind. Her brown hair is braided in decorative loops and swirls, her eyes are a liquid red, like blood, and her pale skin shines like the sun filtering through a cloud. I know with some instinctive certainty she's not human.

Her eyes dart about with an animalistic intensity, and her lips curl in an unnerving smile.

"Rejoice, mortals," she says with a flourish of her spear. My three companions are equally frozen in shock, and only Rena reacts, taking a step back at the weapon's twirl. "The Champion of Widengra has graced you with her presence. Submit yourselves to my god's will, and you may bathe in his eternal presence in the Gardens of Yon."

Layf stumbles to his feet. "Gods' grace," he gasps. "You're the Champion of War."

The woman turns her gaze on him, still smiling. "I have been sent to address the appearance of a creature of another realm. The will of Widengra brought me to these lands, but the demon is slippery, well hidden. Answer me briskly: Have you encountered such an aberration?"

My heart beats so fast and loud in my chest, I swear she can hear it. Creature from another realm. Is she looking for me? I don't move, I don't speak, I don't breathe. I just try to melt into the ground and appear as invisible as possible.

Layf and Rena both glance in my direction, but it's Terimus who pushes himself to his feet, leaning heavily on his spear.

"This creature from another realm," he says. "Why do you seek them?"

The woman's eyes land heavily on Terimus. "It is not your place to question the will of the gods, boy." Then, she tips her head. "You know of what I speak?"

"Perhaps," he says.

My heart spikes with fear. He's going to turn me over. I can't even say why that scares me. I know nothing about this woman or what she wants with me. But something about her, the wild look in her eyes, the tension in her posture, screams *danger* to every one of my instincts.

Terimus looks at me. I shake my head ever so slightly. *Please don't. Please don't tell her.* He smiles faintly before turning back to the champion. "It's me. I'm the traveler from another realm."

"Terimus," Rena objects. "Don't—"

But she stops when the champion laughs. It's a cold, mirthless cackle—the laughter of a child who's pulling wings off a butterfly. It's that unnerving sound that makes the reason behind my fear finally snap into focus: this woman is mad.

"Beautiful," she says after her laughter subsides. "By Widengra's grace, my task is made simple. Many thanks to you." She suddenly bows deeply before Terimus, sweeping a hand off to the side. "My lord, this blood is in your name."

"Wait," Rena says.

I don't even see the champion straighten back up. One moment she's reverently bowed over, and the next she's standing over Terimus, her spear stabbed through the dracid's stomach.

Chapter Three

R.I.P.

The champion yanks her spear from Terimus's gut with a spray of blood. Rena screams in rage, drawing her weapon, and Layf cries out in shock and horror. Blood flecks my face like drops of rain, and my body feels full of static. No. This can't be happening. This isn't real. My mind buzzes and swirls in detached disbelief.

Crazed laughter shatters my horror like a hammer to a pane of glass. The champion cackles with an insane glee even as Rena leaps at her with her sword. The champion doesn't even bother blocking the blow. She grabs the weapon, hand wrapped around the blade, then rips the sword from Rena's grasp. She stumbles forward, and the champion cracks the sword across her back. Rena collapses to the ground with a gasp.

Layf screams, tears streaming down his face, as he snatches up a spear and runs at the champion. She raises a hand, and he feints to the side, slipping around her guard and stabbing his staff into her gut. It skips over the leather armor like it's platemail, sparks showering off with the contact. The champion lets Layf pull back, his eyes wide with terror. She grins.

Her kick strikes Layf in his gut, lifting him off his feet and throwing him through the air—and straight toward me. I have enough time to raise one arm and mouth an, "Oh," before he crashes right into me.

[9 points of Bludgeoning damage sustained.]

The world becomes a blur of color as we crash back into the grass and go rolling, limbs striking flesh and ground without discrimination.

[4 points of Bludgeoning damage sustained.]

[1 point of Bludgeoning damage sustained.]

[3 points of Bludgeoning damage sustained.]

The numbers stream past me as pain lances through my body. But it's only the pain of scrapes and bruises—I've survived worse.

My back hits the ground and I stop rolling. I hurriedly flip myself over, pushing myself to my feet before I've even recovered my balance. I stumble, my head still spinning, as I look frantically for the champion.

Rena has rolled over onto her stomach, bleeding but still alive, and grabbed the champion's ankle, stopping her from advancing on the unconscious Terimus. I watch in horror, wondering why she's doing this, what sort of *monster* she really is, which triggers a familiar tingling in the back of my head.

[Name: Maru]

[Title: Demigod]

[Species: Human]

[Class: Warrior]

[Level: 92]

[Attack: 350]

[HP: 500/500]

[Mana: 1000/1000]

[Allegiance: Widengra]

Level 92? *Demigod*?!

"Bastard," Layf hisses, pushing himself up to his knees next to me. A trickle of green blood is running down his nose and chin. He darts a glance at me. "What are you waiting for? Get out of here!"

The champion kicks Rena in her side, flipping her across the ground, then stomps on her stomach. I want to run. I want to hide. I feel like I'm going to throw up.

I take a step back, then hesitate. "But what about you guys?"

Layf staggers to his feet, hand on his side. He looks at me sadly. "Someone has to warn others what happened here."

His words send a spike of adrenaline shooting through me. No, he can't mean what I think he means. They're not all about to die. We just met—I just got here—I was just reborn! This is too horrific, too senseless to be—

Rena screams as the champion plunges her spear into her chest. Shock spikes through me. My body feels distant and numb. I watch, unbelieving, as Layf runs back into the fight, swinging his weapon at the demigod.

I don't hear the rest of the fight. Maybe my brain is in too much shock to register it. Maybe it's the blood rushing in my ears. Either way, the world feels muted and distant as I force myself stumbling back, as I watch Maru stab Layf, as I watch her end Terimus's life. It's like one of those nightmares where you can't move fast enough. Where you know, no matter what you do, the monster is going to get you.

I turn and run.

I hate myself even as I do it. I'm leaving them to die. These kind people who took me in and protected me. I'm a coward. I'm pathetic. But more than anything, I just don't want to die. Not so soon. I'm not ready to die again. All I wanted was to fulfill this dumb Cook role and make cakes and burgers and enjoy life. Do all the simple things I couldn't do before. Is that so much to ask?

What did I do to deserve this?

Maru's voice appears right behind me. "Now, now. Can't have any witnesses scurrying away, can we?"

Pain explodes across my back. I manage another two or three stumbling steps before a weight on my shoulder topples me over, and I crash face-first into the ground. Echo's stats feel distant.

[52 points of Piercing damage sustained.]

[5 points of Bludgeoning damage sustained.]

[HP: 16/90]

I try to struggle upright, but there's a weight pressing into my back, and pain lances through me when I try to move, and I can't make my arm respond. Heat spreads over my back as the pain statics away. I suddenly feel exhausted, all my fight and energy seeping out of me, as the warmth starts to fade into cold.

Oh. I know this feeling. I'm dying.

I still manage a weak scream when the spear is yanked from my back.

[14 points of Piercing damage sustained.]

[HP: 2/90]

My vision is going dark around the edges. My horror is muted beneath my shock, but there's resignation and disappointment, there, too. It's just not fair. I should have had more time. To have a second chance dangled in front of me, just for it to be ripped away at the last second—it feels like a cruel joke. I'd pray to god, but I guess one of their servants just killed me.

I close my eyes and taste salt as tears run down my face. If I just had another chance... just one more chance...

[HP: 1/90]

The world sinks into a familiar black.

Chapter Four

BLASPHEMY

I fade in and out of pain. Everything comes to me through a fog. Sometimes I try to understand what's happening: Where am I? Why does it hurt? Am I waking up from another surgery? But even as I reach for the memories, comprehension slips through my fingers and I'm absorbed back into the nothingness.

Once, my eyes crack open. The world is a blurred green. Birds chirp pleasantly overhead. I'm lying in something—blood. My blood. I try to focus beyond that, and eventually the shapes resolve into a scene of gore. The three adventurers I met. Terimus. Rena. Layf. They don't move from the pool of carnage that was their campsite. Nothing moves, except the pebblebacks grazing quietly in the fields beyond. That contrast, the foreground of death framed by a peaceful, green vibrant valley, pulls emotions from my half-awake mind. My throat feels tight. My eyes sting. I sob out a single breath, but pain spears through me with the small movement, shocking my mind and body back into another haunted, dreamless sleep.

Maru's face surfaces in my subconscious, summoning a fear that brings me to the edge of wakefulness again. I've never felt such terror. Such helplessness.

Such *hate*.

Why? The word spins around in my head, unable to expand into any thoughts more complex than that.

Why? Why? Why?

A rumbling sound rouses me next. The sun is low. The valley in shadows, the sky burnt orange.

I'm not dead. I'm alert enough to understand that, now. But night is almost here, and once the cold sets in, it'll be over for real.

I consider letting that happen. I'm so tired. And not moving like this, the pain is only an intense, cold pressure—not a searing agony. Living is a lot of work.

But a spark of defiance lights in my chest. Maru. She killed them. She tried to kill me—and if I don't do anything, she'll still succeed.

I summon all the strength I can muster and drag my arm up by my shoulder. Needles stab through my back with the movement, and I let out a gasp as my arm goes slack. I was going to push myself upright, but the idea seems laughable now. It hurts too much, and I don't even have enough strength to roll onto my side. I groan from pain and frustration, squeezing my eyes shut against my cruel, indifferent reality.

A low sound rumbles nearby. The same sound that had woken me up, I now realize. The deep murmurs resolve into a voice.

"Did you hear that?"

The voice is so deep and gentle. It makes me think of a mountain lake, quietly tucked away between the remotest peaks. That sounds nice. The pain starts to fade once more as I relax, my mind drifting into oblivion as I think of forests and clouds and snow...

"I think it came from over here."

There's a second voice. Higher pitched. Sharper. It pulls me from my blissful rest. I wish it would go away.

"Gods' grace, Gugora, this one's alive!"

Something touches my arm, and I scrunch my eyes tight, moaning. Even that brush of sensation is too much, awakening my nerves like razors through my skin.

"Hurry!" the sharp voice says. "Lorata's Light, I don't know how she survived."

I sense the chill of a shadow falling over me, blocking out the last few rays of light from the setting sun.

"Let me," the deep voice says. Gugora, I think.

There are more touches on my shoulder, arm, and forehead, but this time they're faint and careful. I relax. This one won't hurt me.

"We'll need to address that wound first," Gugora says. "She won't make it back if we wait for a healer. Have you got a potion on you?"

"Of course I don't have a potion on me," the sharp voice says. "I wasn't exactly expecting to come upon a murder scene, was I?"

Gugora lets out a rumbling sigh. "Alright. The hard way, then."

Something presses against my back, so sudden, and filling me with so much pain, my tenuous hold of consciousness is snuffed out.

The world rocks back and forth. I'm tipped forward, leaning against something warm, cloth scratching against my cheek. My head is resting on something, and I can feel an arm holding me upright, wrapped beneath my legs, while a second one lightly rests on my arm, keeping me from tipping over. A warm weight surrounds me like a blanket.

I try to pry my eyes open, grit sticking to my lashes. I can make out the profile of a head. Ah. A shoulder—that's what my head is leaning on. I'm being carried like a drowsy toddler. Despite the lance of stabbing pain that shoots through me with every footfall, the careful embrace fills me with a fond sense of security.

"Dad?" I whisper.

The arms shift at my voice, carefully ensuring their grasp is secure. "We'll get you home," the person says, his deep rumble vibrating through my chest.

Not my dad. Gugora.

I feel so small in his grasp.

More snippets come and go as we travel. The next time I open my eyes, it's dark. The time after that, woodsmoke fills my nose and flickering lights stab into my eyes. The sounds of the forest give way to thumping footsteps of boots over wood and the clamor of loud voices, which turn to cries of alarm I can't find it in myself to care about. The air is humid and warm here. It smells of dust and yeast. The raised voices are eventually shut away as I'm eased into a pile of furs, and a sharp pain lances through my back as I'm tipped to rest on my side. I groan, trying to roll over onto my back, but a hand stops me.

"You'll have to lay this way until we get that wound treated." Gugora. The deep voice.

I open my eyes and try to focus on him, but the room is dark. He's only a giant shadow, half bent over me. He holds my shoulder, keeping me from rolling one way or the other, and my arm is swallowed in his grasp.

"Iski, help me with the pillows," he says. "Prop them up behind her."

I feel an impression in the sheets by my feet, like a cat jumping up onto the bed. For a disorienting moment I'm propelled back in time, back to when I still slept in my own bed. We had a cat, Oboe. She was black and white and liked to sleep curled up around my neck, her hairs tickling my nose. I miss her.

"Alright, hold on," the sharp voice—Iski—says. The blankets behind me shuffle around, some of them pressing up against my shoulder and lower back, and I hiss in a breath when one tweak of the blankets sends another stab of agony through me.

Gugora says something, and Iski shoots something back, but by then I'm fading once more, sinking into the soft, musty furs that brush against my face and remind me of a distant home.

When I wake up next, it's daylight. Strange, incomprehensible dreams fade from my mind as I rouse, slipping away from me even as I try to recall them. I was drowning in a black ocean full of stars. Consumed by a great hunger. There was a comforting voice, distant and determined. *"I don't plan to die today."*

I try to bring these thoughts into focus, but they dissolve like a sandcastle beneath the tide. The echoing words linger longest, resonating with something inside me.

Death. Why does death sound so familiar? Pain throbs through my whole torso, somewhat distant, and I know from experience that the best way to keep it distant is to not move. I'm lying on my left side, which means I'm facing where Mom always sits, reading one of her magazines by the window.

"Mom?"

But when I open my eyes and find myself in an empty wooden room, it all comes back to me.

My death and rebirth. Terimus, Rena, Layf. The champion, Maru, who slayed them all. Who tried to slay me. Tears prickle at my eyes, and a hot, angry heat coils in my gut. Why? It was so senseless. There was no reason. Why did she do that?

I start to lift my hand to brush the tears away, but pain stabs through my back and chest when I move, and I drop my arm back into the blankets once more. I was hurt bad. But somehow, by some miracle, I lived. Am I still on the brink of death?

[Check,] Echo pipes up, and stats fill my vision. [HP: 12/90]

It's gone up then. I must have some passive healing ability. Not enough for me to risk moving, though. With little else to do, I blink away my tears and lick salt off my lips as I try to take in my surroundings.

It's a simple, small room, entirely made out of wood like a cabin. There's just my bed, a chest, a rocking chair, and a window. The chair and chest have patterns carved into the wood. From the rough texture, hand-carved, I think. I trace my gaze over the gently looping designs, and the focus soothes me. Eventually the tears stop, and my anger simmers, but the hollow ache of loss and regret remains. I'm not sure if it's the three adventurers or my parents that I'm mourning more.

I don't realize I've dozed off until I jerk awake. The sun is up, the pain in my back is still present. The door to my room rattles faintly with the approach of muted footsteps and voices.

When the door swings open, I can only summon faint surprise to see an enormous orc duck into the room.

[Check,] Echo says as I idly wonder.

[Name: Gugora]

[Species: Orc]

[Class: Hunter]

[Level: 31]

[Attack: 92]

[HP: 200/200]

[Mana: 10/10]

He's massive, hunched over just to avoid hitting his head against the crossbeams; his skin is green, and he has two tusks curving up from his lower jaw in an imitation of an underbite. Black and red tattoos decorate his left shoulder, and his thin, black hair is pulled back in a short ponytail. His eyebrows lift in faint surprise.

"She's awake."

It's the same low voice I remember from before.

Someone pushes past him. "Please, give me space. Iski said it was urgent."

Gugora steps back, as much as his hulking form and the small room allow. "Of course. Thank you for coming so swiftly."

The newcomer has white cat ears and a tail which reminds me of Oboe. I smile faintly.

She bends over me, clicking her tongue in disappointment. "You should have positioned her facing the wall. I could see the injury better if it were facing this way."

"Sorry," Gugora says. "Didn't think of that."

"What happened, anyway?"

A light flickers to life behind me, casting my and the cat-girl's shadow across the opposite wall, tinting everything with a purple hue. A soothing warmth floods into my back, and I let out a relieved sigh.

[Healing spell in effect,] Echo says. [Recovery rate: 1 HP every 10 seconds.]

"Not sure," Gugora grumbles. "Bandits, maybe. Found her like this. Three others similarly attacked, though they were already gone. Took her back here, sent Iski for help. She's taking the City Guards out to the... *scene* now. Maybe they'll have some answers."

I clench my jaw at that. I know what happened, and it was no bandits. Gritting my teeth and taking a pained breath in, I blow it all back out in one word: "Maru."

The cat-girl goes still. "What was that?"

"Maru," I say again, though my voice is barely a whisper. Gugora leans in, frowning. "Killed us. Champion."

"Gods' grace," the healer says. "That's not—I mean, she must be delusional. A champion? They wouldn't..."

"The Champion of War would," Gugora says quietly. He frowns down at me. "Are you certain? Did she say why?"

Fear percolates through me. She did say why: She was trying to kill me, because I'm from another world. But I can't tell them that. What if they betray me? Summon Maru to finish the job?

I try to shake my head, but renewed pain burns through me with the movement, and I go still. "No," I sigh, closing my eyes. Even this much talking is exhausting. I should just let the healer do her magic, but I have to make them understand it was Maru. Even if I can't tell them it was because of me, Terimus, Rena, and Layf still deserve justice. "Looking for something. Couldn't find it. Didn't want to leave empty-handed. Sacrifices."

Even saying all that aloud threatens to bring fresh tears to my eyes, but I stamp the sorrow down, replacing it with my fury and indignation. How dare she. How dare she take their lives like that, as if they were nothing? "I'll kill her." And even as I whisper it, I know it's a promise.

The healer sucks in a breath. "What? No, you don't know what you're saying. Just rest."

Her denial just makes me even angrier. I hiss the words out through gritted teeth. "It was wrong. They didn't deserve it. I'll avenge them. I'll kill her."

The comforting warmth vanishes from my back. "Blasphemy," the cat-girl says. "The gods do not err. Praise Widengra, may you have mercy on this child's soul."

[Healing spell ended. HP: 24/90]

I frown, peeling my eyes open once more as the healer steps away, turning to Gugora.

"I'm sorry. I won't work on her further—not if she continues to incur the gods' wrath. It's too dangerous. The healing's not done, but the worst of it is resolved: She'll survive as is."

I want to laugh. I've already incurred the gods' wrath. But she's afraid of a few words? What kind of god is worthy of worship if they make you fear for your life?

"I understand," Gugora says. "You have my thanks. If there's anything you need..."

The healer hurriedly shakes her head, casting a nervous glance back toward me. "I should be going. It's a long walk back to the city. I'd prefer to reach home before sundown."

"Thank you," Gugora repeats, showing her out. As the healer's footsteps vanish down the hall, he pauses in the doorway, looking back at me. "You shouldn't say things like that. Not out loud, at least." Then he ducks beneath the frame, too, shutting the door quietly behind him.

Wincing, I slowly risk rolling over onto my back. It hurts to lay on the injury, but the pain isn't shooting anymore, reduced to a dull throb. Tingling pins and needles start to crawl across my left arm as it wakes up. I grimace at the sensation, keeping perfectly still as the static rises and falls.

The gods do not err? Bullshit. If it's wrong to speak up against murdering innocents, then I don't want to be right. I don't care what that healer might think: what Maru did was evil.

You can't say that, I hear Gugora say. *Not out loud, at least.* I smile grimly. I think that was him agreeing with me—in his own way. But fine. I get the message: I'll keep it to myself.

I came to this world wanting nothing. Just a simple life. Happiness, good food, a second shot at growing old. But Maru took that from me. She took this new, fragile hope I'd barely dared close my hands around, and smashed it to the ground, shattering it into a thousand irreparable pieces.

If it's blasphemy, so be it. But in her arrogance, Maru messed up. She didn't finish me off. And in destroying my previous dreams, she's left me with a new purpose, one that's fueled by loathing.

Even if it kills me, I'll get my vengeance. Terimus, Rena, and Layf will get justice.

I'm going to kill a demigod.

Chapter Five

ROLE REQUIREMENT

I jolt awake, and it's dark. Ah, this is familiar. Drifting in and out of consciousness in a strange bed while I recover from medical treatment. I've been coming to all day: sometimes Gugora was there, sometimes he wasn't. He gave me water and soup, once. The soup tasted like stale socks. He insisted it was medicinal, but I figure any benefits were outweighed by the desire to barf. He showed me to the chamber pot after that, and I'm not sure which experience was worse.

I don't need to use the bathroom now, though. So what woke me up?

Something's tingling in the back of my head. An intangible itch. It feels familiar yet annoying, like a bug bite.

[Role Requirement.]

The sudden voice makes me jump. I'd forgotten about Echo. Then again, I've been mostly unconscious for the last day. Haven't had a lot of opportunities to explore these new mysterious powers.

[Role Requirement.]

I think I might be getting sick of them already.

"What?" I breathe into the dark. I'm still tired and sore, but I can feel my strength returning to me, bit by bit. "What do you want? It's the middle of the night."

[The user is at risk of breaching their Role Requirement,] Echo says. [The Chef role requires the user to engage in cooking, baking, or food preparation on a daily basis. Time remaining in Day: 4 minutes, 14 seconds.]

"Thanks for giving me enough heads up," I grumble. "Can't you delay it a day or something? I'm sort of busy healing here."

[Negative,] Echo says.

I sigh, squinting over at the table next to my bed. Gugora had left the food there before: maybe I can use that to satisfy the requirement. But as my hand gropes blindly across the surface, I only brush up against a mug of water, which I nearly tip over.

"No joy," I say. "What happens if I don't meet the requirement before midnight?" I'm getting some serious reverse Cinderella vibes, and I don't like it. What, is she going to turn me into a pumpkin for not making a sandwich?

A new display appears in my vision.

[Sanity Level: 100%]

Well that doesn't sound good.

[Any time that transpires beyond the Requirement will result in a reduction of the Sanity Level Stat.]

"What?" I hiss. "This role is going to drive me insane?"

Echo doesn't answer.

I swear. "How much time left before midnight?"

[2 minutes, 49 seconds]

"Crap." I lay there a moment longer, marveling at the absurdity. What's the point of these roles, anyway? Make some soup or you'll be driven slowly mad? That's crazy!

The itching in my brain is getting worse. I can feel it crawling its way into my fingers, now, too.

Realizing the universe is not about to take pity on my circumstances, and the time until me and my sanity are parted is ticking down by the second, I throw the blankets off.

A sharp twinge snaps up my back and arm with the movement, and I suck in a breath. Then, much more slowly, much more carefully, I sit myself up.

I hear my blood rushing in my ears for a moment, and I wait for the sound and dizziness to pass. The room is cold without the blankets. Suppressing a shiver, I feel around on my bed and find a knitted texture. Slowly pulling the fabric around my shoulders, conscious of every twinge in my shoulder, I wait until the dizziness and shivers pass. So far so good. Cautiously, I stand up.

I grimace as my back protests, burning as I straighten up. I sway slightly, and brace myself against the wall. It's fine. I got this. Slow and steady wins the race.

[Role Requirement.]

Well, maybe not this race.

I feel my way over to the door, gaining more confidence in my balance as I go. Cautiously, I pull the door inward, wincing against the creaking hinges, and glance out into the hall.

I don't really remember being brought here, not more than bits of broken memory, so I'm not sure what I was expecting, but a hallway of doors wasn't it. The end is swallowed by darkness, and shadowy impressions indicate where more doors like mine line either side. If this is a house, it's a weird one.

Still keeping my hand on the wall, I creep cautiously down the hallway, trying to ignore the tightness in my back that's increasing with each step. Mentally, I will Echo to Check my health as I walk, not daring to speak aloud, and she happily responds.

[HP: 41/90]

Wow, I'm actually healing up pretty fast. That's good, I think. I wonder if this passive healing is what also saved my life after Maru's attack.

I frown at the memory, hatred and anger bubbling up at the thought. But the Role Requirement is getting itchier, a mental static creeping to the forefront of my mind, making my fingers twitch. I have more immediate concerns to worry about.

[Role Requirement,] Echo says, a little more insistently now.

Yeah, yeah, I can hear you, I think, irritated. I can also see the timer to midnight counting down in the corner of my vision: twenty seconds left.

I pick up the pace as I tiptoe my way down the hall, hoping I won't have to start checking rooms. I have no idea where I'm going or what could be behind any one of these doors, but I'm hoping something will obviously indicate itself to be a kitchen at some point. Emphasis on *hope.*

The timer hits 0:00. The static in my mind grows louder. I scratch at my arm, fingers tingling, itching with nervous energy, and then a new stat starts to move.

[Sanity Level: 99%]

I gasp as the wall beneath my hand vanishes, and I stumble a foot in that direction. I blink rapidly, trying to discern shadow from shadow.

I'm at the top of a staircase. I hadn't even realized I wasn't on the ground floor. Beneath me is an open room, full with long thin shadows: tables and benches, I think. Finally, my surroundings start to make sense.

I'm in an inn. The ground floor is the tavern, and up here are a bunch of rooms. I squint at the ground floor, and think I can make out a bar at the far end. If that's where the drinks are, then the food can't be far.

[Sanity Level: 98%]

I force myself back into motion. The stairs creak as I feel my way down the steps. It's a bit eerie, creeping around a sleeping house in the middle of the night, but with my Sanity Level decreasing by the second, I can't let a little fear of the dark stop me.

Tip toeing as best I can manage, I make it down the stairs and across the floor of the mess hall. Sometimes I pause when a board starts to groan beneath my toes, stopping and slowly drawing my foot away to find a quieter path. After doing this a few times, Echo speaks up.

[Skill unlocked: Soft Step, Level 1. Walking silently comes more naturally to the user, their instincts picking out the quietest path 10% of the time.]

Yes!

[Sanity Level: 97%]

No!

I hurry around the side of the bar, where a doorway leads into a back room. I flex my fingers, as if that would scratch the itch clawing its way from my fingers to my brain. Ducking under the curtain, I step into the back room.

"Bingo," I whisper.

Between my vision adjusting to the dark and some thin slants of moonlight scattering through the wooden beams, I can make out barrels and crates lining the walls. More items are stacked on shelves, leading me to believe this is some kind of store room. A large chimney squats against a wall, inside which a cauldron is hanging over the ashes of a dead fire—probably what made that nasty medicine soup I had earlier. My first instinct is to head there, but I pause. Heating up that giant pot would take time—time I don't think my sanity has—and I'm not sure how I'd start the fire regardless. Instead, I turn to the nearby shelves and crates.

The bready smell of yeast and something sharp and sour is even stronger in this room—as strong as it was out by the bar—so I think a lot of the barrels might have beer or alcohol in them. More things that don't help me. The nearest crate is closed, so I try to pry it open, but quickly find it's nailed shut. I try the others scattered about the room, but they're all the same.

[Sanity Level: 95%]

The mind-static is getting worse. The itching is almost a physical sound now, a hissing that's eating at my hearing and crackling in the edges of my vision. I blink my eyes and nervously rub my hands together, trying to focus.

There's a raised shelf by the fireplace. It's about neck level for me, but would be normal counter level for, say, a giant orc. I grab the lip and stand on my tiptoes, peering over the edge.

"Jackpot!" I whisper. A knife is sitting out, just a few feet away. Unfortunately, a few feet is more than my reach can manage from this angle. There's some other bins and jars littering the surface, and some dried plants hanging on the wall. This must be as kitcheny as it gets.

The problem is, it's all up there, while I'm down here.

I reach an arm over the edge, grimacing as the gesture stretches the muscles in my back and digs up a tight pain from hip to shoulder. I manage to grab one of the jars, but everything else is out of reach. Even so, I bring it back over the edge. Lifting the lid off, I give the powdery contents a sniff, and then stifle a sneeze. Some kind of spice. If I had ever spent a day in my life cooking, maybe I would know what it was. Then again, this is a totally different world, so maybe I wouldn't.

[Sanity Level: 93%]

Crap. I set the jar down and hurriedly glance around the room. Aha! A ladder is leaning on the other side of the chimney. As my sanity level steadily ticks down and my anxiety level steadily ticks up, I quickly go grab the ladder. My back protests as I drag it over to the counter, and I grit my teeth against the pain, but I don't have a choice other than to endure it. Because of this completely stupid nonsensical magic system, my very sanity depends on it.

By the time I start climbing the ladder, I've worked up a sweat and my back is throbbing. Four rungs up, the counter is about the right height it's supposed to be, maybe even a little short. But because I'm exhausted, and because I don't trust myself not to fall off, I shimmy over and sit down on the counter instead. Okay. What have we got to work with?

[Dried woodroot,] Echo suddenly says as I'm glancing over the plants hanging on the wall. My gaze shifts, and she continues to fill me in. [Pixie grass. Blue onion stalks. Dried Torra fruit.] I quickly start tearing through everything else on the counter, pulling out baskets and removing the lids from all the ceramic jars. [Rice flour. Rock salt. Fire peppers. Tomatoes. Beetroot. Swamp weed.]

The list goes on, but it's all pretty much vegetables and dried ingredients. What am I supposed to do with this? How can I cook or bake anything with a bunch of flour, spices, and veggies? I don't even have water I could mix with any of this. I look around the rest of the room in mounting desperation.

[Sanity Level: 90%]

It's starting to hurt now. A pressure in the back of my mind. I try to ignore it, along with my mounting panic.

More crates. More barrels. But from this vantage point, I can make out some shelves at the back of the room that I hadn't seen before, illuminated with a faint blue light. It's so bizarre that for a moment I don't comprehend what I am looking at.

[Loaf of yellowgrass bread,] Echo says, reading off the items. [Boar loin. Boar shoulder. Boar ribs. Herron eggs (4). Cheese round.]

Echo isn't done listing off the items, but I'm already scrambling down off my perch and hurrying over to the other side of the room. Bread and cheese and raw meat just sitting out on a shelf at room temperature? Bizarre. But I'm not about to look a gift horse in the mouth.

I can't see them from the ground, but the food comes into view after I climb up another crate and peek my head over the ledge. A waft of cold air blows over my face. Glistening faintly on the surface of the shelf are blue-white symbols and circles, ice crawling over the glowing lines. Some kind of magical icebox, I guess. Works for me! I snatch the cheese and bread from the shelf, leaving the stuff that would require cooking behind. Until I can figure out how to light the fireplace, the meat isn't much use to me. I hurry back over to the kitchen "counter" and dump my spoils over the surface. Finally, I've got something to work with.

[Sanity Level: 85%]

The pain in my head is starting to feel sharp, my fingers like they're full of bees. I snatch up the butcher knife that's sitting on the counter, and immediately, the sensation lessens. I pause, Checking my Sanity Level again.

[Sanity Level: 87%]

It went up! Okay, grabbing the knife was a good call then. Let's see if I can't do better.

I quickly cut into the bread, partially squishing it as I saw off a couple thick slices. The cheese comes next—it's so hard I have to stand up on my knees and put the full weight of my upper body into cutting through the round. Eventually, though, I'm able to cut a crumbly piece of that away as well.

[Sanity Level: 91%]

Good! We're getting there. The tomato next, then. I'm not a big fan of tomatoes, but given the limited options I have to work with, I guess I should be happy this world even has one thing I'm already familiar with. Cutting up the tomato goes extremely poorly, and I basically just mash it into the counter top, but do manage to scrape something resembling a hunk of pulp onto the bread.

[Sanity Level: 92%]

I pause at the spices and dried veggies. The fire peppers smell nice and make my eyes water, so I sprinkle a bit of that on. The swamp weed has a slightly mildewy scent to it, and when I nibble the end it equally tastes a bit fishy, but it's also crisp and fresh, and probably as close to lettuce as I'll get.

The end result is a cheese, tomato, and swamp weed sandwich with a sprinkle of fire pepper and rock salt, which looks like it might have been assembled and then sat on by a toddler. Not exactly Michelin star, but it's *mine*.

My brain tingles, and the static abruptly vanishes.

[Role Requirement satisfied,] Echo says. [Sanity Level: 100%. Knifework Skill Level Up!]

I look at my sandwich and the ruined tomato with skepticism. If my Knifework has improved at all, Echo is being extremely generous.

So I guess that's it, then, I don't even have to eat the thing, I just have to make it. Despite my questionable choice of ingredients, it seems like a waste to just leave it there. Besides, the earthy smell of the tomato, the warm heavy scent of the bread, and the sharp salty bite of cheese are making my stomach grumble. Apart from a few sips of that soup Gugora gave me—if it actually qualified as soup—I haven't had anything to eat all day. Tucking my legs up onto the counter, I settle in, carefully pick up my dripping, awkward mess, and take a bite.

I chew for a moment, then freeze. My stomach lurches as the mix of flavors hits me. My mouth waters and my throat clenches—and I keep it down. No way am I going to puke up this hard-earned prize!

It's not even really *bad*. I mean, okay, it's not great either, but it's a decent first attempt! It's just something different—not what my tastebuds were expecting.

I think it's the swamp weed. The swamp weed was definitely a bad call.

I'm in the middle of picking the slimy green leaves out of my sandwich when the light turns on. Or I guess, more accurately, the room is filled with light, since they don't really have light switches here. Whatever the cause, the sudden burst of color stabs into my eyes and I flinch back with a hiss, squeezing my eyelids shut.

I hear a startled intake of breath. "Thief!" a sharp voice cries.

"No!" I object. I mean, I guess, technically, yes, but these are extenuating circumstances. I shield my eyes with the sandwich, trying to squint at the small figure and bright light at the other end of the room.

"Don't move!" the person cries.

Their voice is familiar, and their stature is incredibly small, but it's the ball of fire they're holding in their hands that I can't tear my eyes away from. Woah. Is that real magic?

They tense up. "Set the weapon down!"

"Weapon?" I ask, giving my sandwich a confused look. "It's not *that* bad."

But the figure doesn't give me a chance to explain my pitiful sub, as in the next moment, the ball of fire is flying my way.

CHAPTER SIX

COMPLETELY UNEQUIPPED

I tip back with a shriek, throwing my sandwich up in front of me in self-defense—for all the good a few pieces of bread will do to save me from getting cooked alive. A wave of warm air rolls over me, and I tense in anticipation.

Nothing happens. Cracking an eye open, the fireball is floating above me, providing ample illumination and a lack of fiery death. I stare at it in wonder, even as it starts to burn holes in my vision.

"Who are you?" my attacker asks. "What are you doing in here?" There's a pause. "Is that a sandwich?"

I squint at the person in the doorframe. Or, at the bottom of the doorframe might be more accurate. The gremlin-like creature before me is two feet tall, has green skin, long pointed ears, and braided brown hair. Even as I'm wondering what it—she?—might be, Echo fills me in.

[Iski: Level 21 Goblin Forager]

Iski. No wonder her voice sounds familiar; she and Gugora were the two who found me. Who saved me.

She seems to recognize me at the same time. "Hey. You're that kid. I thought you were hurt?"

"A healer—" My voice is raspy from disuse. I guess all that mumbling to myself didn't help. I cough and clear my throat and start again. "A healer came. Today? Yesterday, I think. She didn't heal me all the way, though."

"Oh yeah?" The goblin waves her hand, and the ball of fire backs out of my face.

Wait, *is* that even fire? Two small white eyes shimmer from inside the flame's depth, blinking at me. Then it zips over to the fireplace, setting the logs alight.

[Check: will-o'-the-wisp,] Echo says. [This elemental is a summon of the goblin Iski.]

I'm still staring at the wisp as Iski continues talking. "Why'd she stop?"

"What?" I ask, tearing my eyes away.

"The healer," she says. "Why didn't she heal you all the way?"

The reminder of why kindles fury in me once more. "Because I'm going to kill Maru, Champion of Widengra, God of War," I hiss.

Iski gapes at me. The fireplace now sufficiently crackling, her wisp shakes itself from the fireplace, scattering ash and embers about the hearth like a dog shaking off the rain, then flies back to hover over Iski's shoulder.

The goblin, for her part, starts spluttering. "You'll—you'll do *what?*"

A new figure appears in the doorway behind Iski, filling up the frame.

"What's this?" a now-familiar voice says. Gugora pauses, taking in me, the mess of food I've left on the counter, and the general state of his storeroom. "What did you do to my kitchen?"

"Um," I say. "I got hungry?"

"She wants to kill a god!" Iski cries.

"Demigod," he grunts. "Yes. I know. Was hoping that was just the fever talking."

"Why?" Iski asks, looking between him and me.

"Because she killed them." My throat seizes up and my eyes start to burn. I angrily rub at them and swallow the tears down, trying to drown the pain in my anger. "Terimus, Rena, Layf. She killed all of them. And she tried to kill me. There wasn't even any reason for it. She just killed them."

Iski looks shocked.

Gugora lets out a long sigh. "Come on," he says. "You're up, so might as well settle all this now, too. Come out into the tavern. I'll fix us something..." He eyes my mess dubiously. "...*proper*. Then, we'll talk."

I look at my soggy excuse for a sandwich and wilted greens. I drop it on the counter. "Something proper sounds amazing."

Iski and Gugora sit across from me as I consume a crusty loaf of bread and salty broth, served in a bowl meant for the likes of Gugora. The broth isn't half bad when it's eaten with the crust, and it's even better when Gugora returns with a platter of strange greens with melted cheese bubbling on the top, which I slather on the bread. I slowly consume everything placed in front of me. Guess I was more hungry than I thought.

"Where are you from, kid?" Iski finally asks.

I pause, bowl lifted halfway to my mouth. "Sal," I say. "My name's Sal." Why is everyone calling me a kid? I thought teenagers were considered adults in medieval times. Not that I really know this society is medieval, but I've yet to encounter a flushable toilet.

"Sal," Gugora repeats. "Same question."

I'd sort of been hoping to deflect that one. I was nearly just murdered for being from a different world; I can't tell them about my real origins. Even if they don't believe me, that information getting out could cost me my life.

Just like how it cost the others their lives.

Instead of answering, I take another bite of bread and shrug.

"You won't tell us?" Gugora says. "Or you don't know?"

"I don't know," I lie, because that sounds like the better of the two options.

"Where are you heading?" he asks.

"I don't know," I repeat. That, at least, is truthful.

"Have you got friends? Family you can go to?"

I shake my head, trying to ignore the sting in my chest at the reminder of my parents. They're beyond my reach now, anyway.

"Do you know what country you're in?"

"No."

"Amnesia?" Iski wonders.

Gugora grunts. "You do remember how you ended up here, though?"

I nod. "Maru."

"But you can't remember anything before that?"

I hesitate. I guess my injuries could be a good excuse for my supposed amnesia. It's the best lie I can think of on the fly, at any rate. "No. Nothing."

"Sounds like amnesia to me," Iski says. "Shame. Healers don't mess with head stuff."

Gugora is still giving me a calculated look. I try to hold it without squirming. Then he blows air out his nose, shaking his head.

"Iski's right. I don't know if anything can be done for your memories. They might come back in time."

"Oh," I say, not sure how I should respond. Should I appear sad? I'm not sure I could convincingly fake it, so instead I keep my gaze down at the last few dregs of soup left in my bowl. I don't really have to fake anything, though: Thoughts of my parents are starting to seep back in, unbidden, poisoning my appetite. I set the bowl down.

"You can stay here," Gugora says. "While you figure things out."

"Really?" Iski says, giving him a sharp look. "Is that wise?"

He shrugs.

I hesitate. It's not that I don't appreciate his hospitality, but this isn't what I want. Getting stuck in some remote inn in the woods, when I should be out there tracking Maru down? No way.

I shake my head. "I have to get stronger. I need to learn to use magic. I need to learn how to fight!"

Gugora snorts, which only makes me more irritated.

Iski looks similarly skeptical of my abilities. "You aiming to work for the Adventurer's Guild or something?"

A spark of hope ignites in me. "Yes! That's perfect. I'll join that."

But Gugora is shaking his head, and now it's Iski who's chuckling. "Kid, you wouldn't last a second," she says.

I flush with indignance. "I can learn!"

"The Adventurer's Guild isn't where you go to learn," Gugora says, "it's where young naive fighters go to die. But alright," he adds before I can object. "Let's say you want to do that. Where do you find them?"

I hesitate. "I thought maybe you guys would tell me."

"Closest town is Fairwood," Iski says, nodding toward the door. "About a six hour walk due North of here. Can't miss it."

I squint at the two, suspecting some trap. "Then I'll just go there."

Gugora nods. "So you show up at the Adventurer's Guild. Sign up. Pick a job."

"Yep," I say, jutting my chin at him stubbornly.

"And then you get some dinner," he says.

I shrug. "Sure."

"With what money?" he asks.

I pause. "Um. I guess I'll need to finish a job first."

He nods, still humoring me, but I can feel the heat of an embarrassed blush creeping up the back of my neck. "Alright. And that job requires you to hunt a direwolf that's been bothering the city. Or retrieve eggs from a razorbeak's nest. Or fight a pack of—"

"Okay!" I say. "Okay, I get it, it's dangerous."

"And more importantly, you're completely unequipped," Iski says. "Not even basic armor or a weapon."

"And those cost money," Gugora agrees.

"Takes money to make money," Iski adds.

I groan, reluctant to admit they're right. "What am I supposed to do, then?"

The bench scrapes back with a low rumble as Gugora stands, grabbing my empty bowl and plate. "Do the same thing as the rest of us. Get a job."

I look from him to Iski as he disappears into the back with my dirty dishes. "Here?" I ask, skeptically.

"Don't look at me," she says. "I think it's a terrible idea. The Starlight Inn can barely afford to stay running as is. The last thing we need is some maniac bringing the wrath of gods down on our establishment."

I frown. "You really think they'd do that?"

"You really wanna risk it?" she counters.

"If their egos are so fragile that me being mad about my friends' *murders* is enough to cause them to smite us, then they deserve to be taken down," I shoot back.

Gugora returns from the back. "Didn't take long to get back on this subject."

I glower at him. "You saw what Maru did, didn't you?"

He and Iski exchange a weary look. "We did."

"Then you know they deserve revenge," I say. "It's not right what she did to them. It's not fair."

Gugora sighs as he heavily sits back down. "It's not."

"Neither is life," Iski adds.

I roll my eyes. "Oh please, like I haven't heard that one a thousand times." I know it deep in my soul. I know it better than most people twice my age. "Just because it isn't *fair* doesn't mean we should do nothing about it. What about justice?" I look between them. "Shouldn't I *try?* Is this normal? The gods just trample over people and, what, we take it lying down?"

"Demigods," Iski corrects. "It's the champions that tend to leave ruin in their path. The gods don't often leave the heavens. At least, not much anymore."

I shake my head. "God, demigod, whatever. The point is, why can't I fight back? It won't do anything? I'm not *allowed* to?"

"Because you'll get killed," Gugora says bluntly. "And, yes, none of us would stand a chance. Trying to stand up to a demigod is a death wish. Maybe only a handful of the world's most powerful mages could go poking that dragon and survive. For the rest of us, we just have to keep our heads down, hope we stay out of their line of fire, and focus on surviving. The champions are nearly immortal."

I perk up. "Nearly?"

"Effectively," he says, shaking his head. "Look, kid—"

"Sal," I hiss. I wish everyone would stop seeing me just as some weak kid.

"Sal," he says, looking at me levelly. "She already almost killed you, and I suspect she wasn't even trying. Tell me to my face you think you stand a chance."

I hold his gaze, defiance flaring within me. But then the panic of that moment returns, the helplessness, the agony and despair. I drop my gaze, rubbing my shoulder. "I don't."

Not today, at any rate. But I don't intend to stay this weak forever. First, I need to finish recovering from my injuries. Then, I need to save up some money. Start training with magic and swords and whatever else Echo can give me. Even if it takes me years. Even if I have to force every tiny step forward.

I won't die lying down on my back, weak and waning. Not again.

I look back up at Gugora. "So... does the offer to stay here still stand?"

Gugora offers me a small smile as Iski sighs. "You're too soft," she says. "This will be trouble, mark my words."

"Of course you can stay," he says.

"And work?" I ask. "Paid?"

"Hey now," Iski starts to object, but Gugora waves her down.

"Payment would only be fair," he says, and I shoot a victorious grin at Iski. "Of course," he adds, "we'll need to deduct room and board from your wages."

"What! That's highway robbery," I say.

"I seem to remember *you* were the one sneaking into our stores in the middle of the night to take our food," Iski says.

"We're just two innkeeps trying to get by." Gugora says it seriously, but there's a flicker of amusement in his eyes.

"Clothes," Iski pipes up. "Wage deduction for taking our clothes, too."

"Hey," I object. "That one's not fair. I haven't taken any of your clothes!"

Iski jabs a finger at the blanket still draped around my shoulders. "Oh yeah? Then why are you still holding onto Gugora's scarf?"

I look down at the blanket. Now that she mentions it, it *is* a scarf. Black and oversized, all wrapped up around my shoulders like a shawl. I guess for an orc, this would be normal-scarf sized.

"Sorry," I say, a little embarrassed as I start to peel it off. "I didn't know."

He stops me with a gentle hand. "No, no. Keep it. You need it more right now. Don't let Iski's teasing get to you."

"For the record, I'm entirely serious," Iski says. But even she's quirking a smile.

"Thank you," I say. "Both of you. You saved my life—more than once, I think." Finding me in the forest, taking me back here, getting the healer, and now offering me shelter, food, and money. They're being more than generous.

Which stings me with guilt, knowing I'll just be using this place as my first steppingstone to get to Maru.

"Of course," Gugora says. "We would have done the same for anyone. Maybe in time your memories will come back and we'll help you find a way home."

"Yeah," I say, trying to force a smile. "Maybe."

I've only known these people for less than an hour, and already the lies are stacking up.

It's for the best, though. My true origin is dangerous information, and what they don't know can't hurt them. As Iski helps clean up the last of the plates, I take my guilt, box it away, and feed it as kindling to my growing fire of revenge.

CHAPTER SEVEN

RIP OFF FANTASY WORLD

"Alright, Echo," I say. "It's time to spill your guts."

[Command not recognized.]

I snort, scrubbing at the table. Seeing as I was well enough to raid his kitchen, Gugora decided I was well enough to clean the tavern, too. He'd given me the night to sleep, the morning to eat, and then immediately set me to work. I can't believe I got lucky enough to get reincarnated into another world, and then immediately unlucky enough to get stuck doing chores. I should be off adventuring. Getting stronger! Learning magic!

At least that last one I might be able to do something about while wiping down tables.

"You know what I mean," I growl.

A human eating a large breakfast at the table I'm cleaning looks up at me in surprise. "Sorry?"

"Er, I said, I found a bean." I swipe the rag over an imaginary bean and rapidly scrub down the table in the other direction. *The stats,* I think at Echo, before too many patrons can label me insane. *Levels. Classes. Tell me everything!*

And when I ask for everything, boy does she deliver.

I fumble the rag as hundreds of lines of text fill my vision, listing all the stats I have available. It's ridiculous—and not just the sheer number of them. There's your standard gaming stats like Health, Strength, Intelligence, Dexterity, and whatnot, but then there's also a bunch of more obscure stuff like Bravery, Appetite, Humor, Empathy, and Allure. Allure? Really? Why, though?

Finishing the tables, I retrieve a broom from Iski and start sweeping the floors. At least toward midday there are less people around, so less chances of getting caught staring off into space while I talk to Echo. *Okay, let's take this piecemeal. Tell me about Levels first,* I think.

[A level is a quantifiable representation of qualifiable growth. It is increased by gaining experience,] Echo adds, stating the absolute obvious. [Experience is gained through various activities, such as taking damage, dealing damage, and consuming mana through spell use.]

What about doing skills? I ask. *Does using a skill also help me gain experience?* I've already gained the thrilling skill "Housework" just from cleaning the tavern, so I might as well put this mundanity to use.

[Negative,] Echo says, and I frown. [Exception: Skills used to fulfill the user's Role may count toward level experience.]

Hm. I'm not sure what to make of that. Chopping up vegetables with my Knifework skill might help level me up, but it also sounds boring as hell. Grinding still sounds like my best bet, be it with magic spells or finding a mob of low-level monsters to hack up.

But that's alright. *What about magic?* I excitedly ask. *What spells do I know?*

[The user currently knows no spells,] Echo says.

Really? Not even something basic? Disappointing, but I guess I am starting from square one. *How can I learn some, then?*

[The user is currently incapable of learning spells.]

My jaw drops. No way! What kind of rip off fantasy world is this? *Come on,* I plead. *There has to be a way I can learn!*

[The user currently has no affinity for any field of magic,] Echo says. [An affinity must be achieved in order to obtain access to that school of magic.]

I try to calm down. Okay, not all hope is lost. *How does one gain an affinity?*

[Most commonly, affinities are genetically inherited at birth,] Echo says, producing another scowl from me. [However, an affinity may also be obtained through intense practice or traumatic exposure. For instance, someone repeatedly burned by a flame may develop an affinity for Fire type magic, although the method is unguaranteed.]

I must have frozen, and my face must have been betraying my horror, because Iski snaps her fingers at me. "Hey. You okay over there?"

I quickly go back to sweeping. "Yep! Just dandy."

She snorts. "Here." She beckons me over, holding out her hand for the broom. "That's enough indoor work for one morning. You're still healing up and could use the sunlight. Why don't you head outside and help Gugora with the garden?"

I gratefully pass over the broom. "Thanks!" Getting out of here is just fine by me; I hate being cooped up inside, anyway.

But this affinity thing still poses a problem. I'd really, seriously, love not to suffer through repeated 3rd degree burns just for the *chance* to get access to fire magic. Then again, I wouldn't necessarily say that's off the table. It's *magic* after all. How far wouldn't I go to get my hands on some?

Besides fire, what other kinds of magic are there? I ask Echo as I open the back door to the inn. Sunlight spills over me, and I stand there blinking for a moment, basking in the warmth.

[There are countless specialized fields of magic that one could study or gain an Affinity in, depending on the granularity of the arcana school. Generally speaking, magic is often sorted into the following categories: Storm, Earth, Life, Ocular, and Null. These groups can be further decomposed into more specific fields of magic. For example, Storm magic encompasses water, air, and lightning based magic. Anyone with an affinity in one group is more easily able to train themself to access other arcana fields within that same group. Someone with Air magic, for instance, may learn Lightning magic more easily than necrotic magic, which falls under the Life school.]

I drink up the information like I'm dehydrated: it's not nearly enough. *Can those fields also be broken down?* I ask. *Like, are there subsets of Water magic?*

[Affirmative,] Echo says. [Specialties in Water magic might include ice or steam, while specialties in Stone magic might include sand or glass. If an affinity is formed with an umbrella arcana, like Water, then all types of these specialties can easily be learned. However, if an affinity is formed at a lower level, such as ice, then it will be more difficult to move back up the hierarchy, such as to learn Water or other Storm arcana.]

Better to form a broad affinity than a narrow one, then. Of course, I'd be happy with *any* affinity at all. I ask Echo to provide me with an overview of all the fields she just mentioned, and a tree structure pops up in my vision, which I start to sift through.

Storm (Arcana source dimension: The Gyre)

- Water

- Air

- Lightning

Earth (Arcana source dimension: The Pith)
- Fire

- Metal

- Stone

Life (Arcana source dimension: The Lull)
- Nature

- Healing

- Necromancy

Ocular (Arcana source dimension: The Abyss)
- Illusion

- Light

- Shadow

Null (Arcana source dimension: The Between)
- Void

- Mind

- Summoning

There also seems to be a strange sort of progression through the tree, with elements in one arcana field related or almost bleeding into the next. I start mentally tapping on each field of magic, eagerly digging down into the specialties, when I'm startled out of my research as someone clears their throat.

"Sal," Gugora greets, and I realize I've been standing silently in the doorway, staring off into space, for at least a couple minutes now. He's kneeling in a patch of earth, between two, wide, orc-sized troughs of plants. "You alright?"

"Yeah," I say. "Sorry. Iski thought I could use the fresh air."

He smiles wryly. "Wonder why."

I'm going to need to get better at multitasking with Echo in my head. "How can I help?" I ask.

He gestures to a basket beside him. "Come help with these. I'll show you what's ripe."

Happy it seems mundane enough to not involve much talk, I join Gugora in the vegetable garden and mentally turn back to Echo. As I pick through some green bean-like stalks (except they're yellow and orange and a bit fuzzy like a caterpillar) Echo shows me a bunch more specialties of magic to consider. None of them strike me as something that would be easy to force an affinity for, though. Traumatic exposure examples include asphyxiation, getting struck by lightning, and getting lost in a cave and driven to the brink of madness by the dark. Not particularly ideal.

Disappointed, I switch topics. *I don't have a class either,* I note. *Is that at least something I can change?*

[Upon leveling up, the option to pick a class will become available.]

I brighten at that. I'll just need to force a level up somehow. But with magic currently off the table, that leaves... I grimace. Taking damage, dealing damage, and chopping vegetables.

Obviously, playing into my Role Requirement and leveling up cooking-related skills is the easiest path. But based on the tiny fraction of my EXP bar that has barely started to fill in the corner of my vision, that approach will take forever on its own. Taking damage should probably be avoided if I can help it—at least until I finish recovering.

(And happily, that seems to be going pretty quickly on its own. I'm up to 47/90 now!) So that leaves dealing damage, which might be tough without a weapon. Not to mention, what even is there to fight?

"Are there any monsters around here?" I ask Gugora as I pick some more caterpillar green beans to add to the basket.

He stops to look at me, suspicious. "Why do you ask?"

"Uh, no reason," I say.

"You're not looking for trouble, are you?"

Wow, he reads me like a book. "I just wasn't sure if it was safe for me to go wandering around the area."

He grunts, but doesn't appear convinced. "Safe enough."

Damn.

"But don't go too far," he says. "There's wild animals in any forest. We're a short walk from the city, so it's not so bad here, but we're the last inn for miles around. The farther south you go, the more our territory becomes theirs." He eyes me critically. "Which is not an invitation to start exploring the woods south of here."

"I wasn't!" I object.

I was.

Gugora stares at me for a moment longer, then lets out a sigh. He stands up, and his joints crack in low tones like stones knocking against each other in a rockslide. "Come on."

I hop up—then wince a little as my back twinges at the sudden movement—and follow him as he begins to head away from the inn.

"The vegetables?" I ask, glancing back at the abandoned basket.

"We'll just be a minute," he says, waving me off. "Won't go anywhere."

There's a faint footpath on the ground that Gugora is following; nothing paved or official, but packed earth from countless trips. It's also heading south, if I'm not all turned around.

"I thought you said we shouldn't go this way," I say.

"Our butcher hut is a little ways from the property," he says. "The smell can attract predators—want to keep them away from any customers. We aren't going too far, though. Besides, there's nothing to worry about right now." He glances down at me with a small smile. "You've got me."

Despite a lack of any apparent weapon, I don't doubt his confidence for a second.

"Why are we going to a butcher hut then?" I ask.

"You sure ask a lot of questions," he observes.

"Yeah, well, I don't know much of anything about the world," I shoot back. "Can't blame me for wanting to learn, huh?"

He chuckles. "Suppose not."

The hut comes into view, although it looks more like a cabin to me. Echo identifies some skins and drying meat hanging outside on some tanning equipment, but Gugora passes them by to unlock and then duck inside the cabin's door.

I pause in the doorway, my eyes immediately going to all the apparent torture equipment hanging from the ceiling and walls. Terrifying hooks and chains, more types of knives than I can count. Gugora ignores all this as if it's normal—which, for a hunter, I suppose it is—and stops at the closest wall, which happily places me near the exit.

Look, it's not that I think he's a serial killer or anything, but my first impression of this world hasn't exactly filled me with an abundance of trust.

"Here," he says, pulling a knife from the wall. It's only about as long as my hand, and sheathed in leather. "Keep this on you. If you're going to do anything rash, at least have a way to defend yourself."

"Cool!" My stomach flutters as I take the weapon. It's a fraction of the size of the butcher knife I'd used in the inn's kitchen, but it's better than nothing. My eyes trail over the other tools on the wall. "Hey, can I borrow the bow and arrows, too?"

"No." He grabs my shoulders, spins me around, and pushes me out the door before I can even make my case. The keys jingle as he locks the cabin back up.

"Aw, come on!" I beg.

He nods to my knife. "Tell you what. You keep from cutting yourself on that thing for two weeks, I'll teach you how to use a bow. But, as soon as you hurt yourself, the counter resets."

"Sweet!" I say. "Two weeks? No problem." I could just keep it in the sheath for that long and guarantee I make it.

He smiles wryly. "I give you two days."

Chapter Eight

NOT WORTH IT

According to Echo, I make it exactly eight hours and twenty-four minutes before I nick myself with the knife.

[1 point of Slashing damage self-inflicted.]

[HP: 48/90]

"Shit." I drop the knife on the kitchen counter and stick my finger in my mouth, filling it with that coppery sour taste of blood.

Iski watches me passively from where she's stirring the huge cauldron of stew in the fireplace. "You're really terrible with a knife, huh?"

I take my finger out of my mouth to look at it, a small smear of red spreading through the ridges in my skin like ivy over bricks.

"I'll get better at it," I say. "Just need more practice." And some skill level ups. The faster I can pick a class, the better.

Muted, from somewhere out in the tavern, a bell chimes; at the same time, a rune on the wall—invisible until now—lights up orange.

"Well here's another opportunity for practice," Iski says. She knocks the spoon against the lip of the pot and sets it aside. "Looks like we've got company. Stay back here and keep the pot stirring; can't cut yourself that way."

"I'll get better!" I insist. But Iski has already hopped down from her stool and is heading out the storeroom door.

"Welcome to the Starlight Inn!" I hear her say. "You looking for room or board?"

With a sigh, I follow the goblin's instructions and begin mindlessly stirring the stew. This is boring. I should be learning magic by now! Fighting direwolves or slimes or something. Who gets reincarnated into another world just to do housework? And I don't even get to be an elf or catgirl or anything else cool, either.

I sit on the stool Iski had been using to reach the top of the cauldron, the fire's warmth quickly stinging at my skin. At least I didn't end up as a goblin. That would probably make everything about a hundred times harder. I wonder if the heat is worse, too, when you're that small. I shift, trying to scoot away from the open flames.

Or maybe...

I eye the fireplace dubiously. Echo had said it was a low chance. But it wasn't *no* chance. And I'll heal whatever damage I take, anyway. *Echo, what's the rate of my passive healing?*

[The user regains health at a rate of one hit point per hour.]

At a total of 90 HP, that means I can heal from pretty much anything within four days. Nifty. And also probably why I'm not dead right now. Re-dead? Anyway.

I reach a hand toward the fire, then hesitate. It'll hurt, but I'll be fine. And then, maybe, I'll be able to do fire magic. That should be worth the risk, right?

Before I can psych myself out anymore, I stuff my hand in the coals. For a moment it only feels warm. Then, I scream.

[12 points of Burning damage self-inflicted.]

"What were you thinking?" Gugora demands.

I blink through the tears, trying to choke down a sob, as my hand continues to pulse with a searing heat like the fire never left it. "Magic," I croak.

Gugora looks at me like I've grown a second head.

I try again. "Don't have an Affinity. Thought maybe if I got burned…"

The orc passes a hand over his face. "You can't consciously force an affinity that way. They happen, or they don't." He frowns, checking the bandage around my hand—the slight touch wrenches a strangled cry from me. "At least it's not deep. Might scar, but won't cause lasting damage. You got lucky. I hope you treat this as the lesson it is."

I nod pathetically. I've experienced worse pain. I rationally know that. But while you're dealing with fresh second-degree burns that cover every inch of your hand, it's a little hard to internalize that.

Gugora sighs. "Stay here in your room. Rest. I need to go help Iski with the customers—assuming you haven't scared them away." He offers a small reassuring smile as he stands.

I try to summon a weak smile to meet his, but I can only grimace. Even as he leaves, though, I can't find it in myself to regret what I did. I had to try, at least.

And sure enough, as I laid in bed that afternoon, ice in hand, the pain gradually dulled. By that night, it was gone. Iski and Gugora were shocked to see my hand unbandaged and undamaged the next morning—I guess not everyone has this passive healing perk that I do. Echo tells me it's because I'm in the System, so that's good, I suppose. One mark in my favor.

Which is doubly good, considering I don't have any time to waste.

What follows, directly against Gugora and Iski's advice, is a series of magic-dowsing experiments. I stumble around blindly in the middle of the night, nearly falling off the second-floor balcony and down into the tavern. I stick my head in a bucket and inhale a lungful of water. I climb a tree in a thunderstorm and wave a metal shovel around. No luck. Or, as Gugora and Iski would have you believe, I'm *extremely* lucky. That's a matter of perspective, in my opinion.

"I'm going foraging," I announce after several days of failed experiments. "We're running out of mushrooms and swampweed, right?"

Iski squints at me suspiciously from where she's cleaning up after a couple patrons. There's been more travelers in the last few days, though only three or four ever spend the night at a time. Gugora says we're entering summer, so more people tend to be on the road.

"I suppose so," Iski says. "Awfully observant of you."

After spending the last week doing nothing but chores, attempting to force magic powers, and chopping vegetables, it's hard not to notice the few bits of detail available to me in an otherwise glaringly mundane environment. At least my Knifework has gone up to level 3. And on the plus side, all this damage I've taken has gotten me halfway to leveling up, no magic or combat grinding needed. Still, I can't afford to limp along at this pace forever. It's time to be more proactive—and that's the real motivator for my little adventure.

"Foraging," Gugora says, "or looking for trouble?"

I stick my tongue out. "I can stay out of trouble."

"You can," he grunts. "But you won't."

I turn back to Iski. "Well? Can I go?"

She exchanges a look with Gugora. He shrugs helplessly. "Alright," she agrees, even as I'm scrambling to secure my knife to my belt. "Hold up! Take a basket with you. And we're running out of blueroot, too. I'll make you a list."

I try to hide my impatience as I follow Iski back to the storeroom for her to go checking all the crates and pots for whatever items might be low. I mentally have Echo note down whatever Iski says, and after she confirms I haven't forgotten anything—well, after she confirms *Echo* hasn't forgotten anything—I'm off.

As I step out the backdoor, wrapping my scarf (well, Gugora's scarf) about my shoulders, I can hear Iski let out a labored sigh. "What agent of chaos have you unleashed upon this establishment?"

I grin, closing the door behind me. Agent of chaos. I kinda like the sound of that.

It's early afternoon still, and the trees help keep the worst of the sun off me as I trek into the forest. I run my hand over the hunting knife Gugora gave me, sheathed at my waist.

"Alright, Echo," I say. It's nice to not have to keep the conversation in my head, finally. "Keep an eye out for any monsters, will you? It's time I start training."

[There are thousands of creatures within range, if insects are to be included in this classification,] Echo says. [Display list?]

"Er, actually, no," I say. I glance around, but I don't see whatever bugs she's talking about. "I'm more looking for some low-level mobs. You know, the stuff in video games you need to grind in order to level up."

[Command unclear,] Echo says.

I chew my lip. Maybe the way this world works isn't as video game-y as I first thought. "Let me know if there's a pack of animals around," I suggest. "Excluding bugs... unless they're, like, big cat-sized bugs or something."

[Affirmative,] Echo says. [Additionally, notify user if ingredients on 'Iski's List' can be identified?]

"Sure," I say with a sigh. "Might as well."

I guess I'll have to hope she got the gist of what I want. I can't really make heads or tails of this place. Why have I got a System setup, but no one else I've met seems to? What's the purpose of these Role things except to be *really* annoying? It seems you're rewarded for working on skills that fall under the Role's jurisdiction, but only slightly; after a week of chopping food and helping around the kitchen, I still haven't earned enough experience to level up. And the punishment for *not* adhering to the Role Requirements—a gradual loss of my sanity—hardly seems worth the boons.

I have the passive healing thing, and an Echo in my head definitely helps me notice and learn things other people wouldn't, but otherwise, this System seems pretty broken to me.

I wander around the woods, trying not to go too far, so I don't lose track of where the inn is. But apart from some birds and rabbits that dart away before I'm anywhere near them, I don't find anything but the plants on Iski's list. With a grimace, I cut a handful of spotted mushrooms from a rotted log to throw in Iski's basket. Watching the animals dart away presents yet another problem; I'd just assumed I could find some slimes or whatever that would stick around and fight me. But if everything acts like a *normal* wild animal, how the hell am I gonna manage to kill anything?

And do I even *want* to? Slashing up a shadow snake or whatever sounds a whole lot more appealing than having to stab an actual deer.

(Of course, if I plan to take down the champion Maru, I'm going to need to get over that squeamishness. I try to push that thought from my mind.) Where are all the monsters? The magic? I sigh. This has got to be the lamest start to a hero's adventure ever.

[Group of creatures identified.]

Or maybe not. "Where?" I whisper, but even as I ask, a flicker of movement through the bushes in front of me catches my eye. Cautiously, I move closer to get a better look.

On the other side of the bushes is a small clearing, the surrounding air filled with a sickly-sweet smell, like rotten fruit. I wrinkle my nose and frown at the scene. The forest floor seems to be overrun with vines, among which dozens of bright pink, dinner-plate sized flowers are blooming. Those must be the source of the smell. One of the buds is closed and twitching, as if something is struggling to burst out. With mounting horror, I think I can hear a squealing sound coming from inside. After another few moments, the movement stops.

[Carnivorous Orchids, level 5,] Echo says. [Luring prey in with a sweet smell, these plants capture and devour small prey within their flowers, which snap shut as soon as any creatures crawl into their buds, seeking the source of the attractive scent.]

Smells anything but attractive to me. But it basically sounds like I'm dealing with slightly bigger Venus flytraps, which means this is the perfect opportunity for me to try hacking some things up. Given the low probability of falling into a flower that can't swallow much more than my hand, I'm not particularly worried about getting digested by one of these things. I draw my knife, and step carefully around the bush.

"Alright," I mutter to myself. "Let's start small."

I cut through the nearest vine leading into the clearing, and a thick, green goo oozes out the limb.

"Ew," I say, wiping the blade on the grass even as I'm greeted with a familiar notification.

[2 points of Slashing damage dealt.]

Hey! Look at me *dealing* damage finally. Nice.

I cut through the next vine, and the next. The vine gloop is sticky and clings to my knife like glue. Annoying, but I've got to start getting experience points somehow. The EXP bar in the corner of my vision slowly starts to fill. Time to pump those numbers up.

Ignoring the goo—I can take a bath later—I start hacking up the plant, forging a path toward the nearest blossom. This one is open, and now that I'm close, I can see a collection of small animal bones in the dirt around the flower.

"Nothing personal," I say, kneeling down beside the flower to push the petals aside so I can behead the plant at its base. "We all gotta do what we can to survive."

[10 points of Slashing damage dealt,] Echo says as I cut the flower from the plant.

More green liquid pours from the cut stem, this time gushing over my hand and forearm as I pull it away. A strange tingling sensation passes through my skin.

[Status effect sustained: Poisoned.]

[Status effect sustained: Paralysis.]

"What?!"

I drop the blossom, hurriedly flapping my hand through the air, trying to fling the droplets away. It's viscous and thick, though, and clings to my skin in a thick layer. The tingling is starting to turn into a burn.

[1 HP lost every ten seconds,] Echo reports. [Physical impairment spread at a rate of one inch every ten seconds.]

I scramble out of the nest of orchids to wipe my hand on a patch of fresh grass. My left hand is quickly feeling stuffy and numb, and the burning sensation is spreading up my arm.

"Crap," I hiss, dropping my knife to tear a piece of my shirt off and use the cloth to wipe down my arm. "Echo, did that slow the poison rate?"

[Negative,] Echo says. [The rate of Poisoning cannot be altered.]

"Can it be stopped?" I ask, fear flickering through me, buzzing like static from my head to my toes. I have 90 HP. One point every ten seconds gives me 900 seconds. How long is that? Fifteen minutes? Not enough time to get back to the inn. Not even if I ran, and given the rate of Paralysis spread, I don't think I'll be able to do that for much longer.

[Affirmative,] Echo says, and relief washes over me. Briefly. [Poisoning status effect will cease in 985 seconds. Alternatively, an antidote would stop the Poisoned status effect.]

Oh great, it'll stop just in time for me to die!

"Antidote?" I cry, still desperately trying to wipe the poison off on the nearby forest floor. "What is it? How can I get some?"

[An antidote may be brewed from carnivorous orchid root, among other ingredients and mana expenditure,] Echo says.

I can't brew anything out in the middle of a forest! "Anything else?" I ask Echo, trying not to succumb to the panic welling up inside me. "There has to be some way to stop it!"

[Affirmative,] Echo says, restoring a momentary glimmer of hope. [Removing the affected limb will reduce the spread of poison.]

My stomach drops. "Fuck."

Chapter Nine

Okay Maybe Actually Worth It

I can feel the numbing burn steadily creeping past my elbow as I hold my knife to my shoulder, wondering if I'm really capable of cutting my own arm off. I give my skin an experimental prick, then jerk my hand away.

"Holy shit," I mutter. This can't be happening. A plant. A plant?! It's ludicrously unfair! I just survived being attacked by a GOD for god's sake. Or, whoever's sake.

I don't think my passive healing will do much for me now. One point an hour is basically nothing when I'm going to die in another ten minutes.

Holy shit I'm gonna die. It doesn't shock me as much as it should. I guess because I've already done it once, and I spent a couple years getting used to the idea before that even happened. For a moment, I feel sad. Then, I'm just pissed.

"Hell no," I growl, tightening my grip on the knife. I'm going to survive, dammit! I'm going to keep fighting 'till the very end. At least this time, there's something I can do about it.

I stab the knife into my arm, and I scream even as Echo's voice rings in my ears and damage points dance over my vision. The pain ripping through my forearm dampens out everything else—sound, numbness, the heat of the poison—everything is crystalized around the searing agony in my arm. I take two gasping breaths, my whole body tenses, and then I rip the knife from my arm, screaming.

Blood runs down my hand in a quick stream. I gasp, hands shaking, as I tear a strip of cloth from my shirt. Quickly tying it around my upper arm, I grab one end in my teeth and pull it as tight as I can manage, one handed. Pseudo-tourniquet in place, I grasp my bleeding arm, squeezing around the wound, forcing as much blood out as I can manage. I growl through the pain, blink through the tears, and hope beyond hope I've slowed it enough, I've gotten enough poison out of my system, to make a difference. Stealing myself, I Check the status effects.

[Poisoned: -1 HP every 10 seconds. Duration: 753 seconds.]

[Paralysis: mobility impairment spreads 0.5 inches every 10 seconds. Duration: 753 seconds.]

I smile through a grimace. "Guess you don't know everything after all, huh, Echo?" Reduced both of those status effects. At my current 71/90 HP, though, it's still not enough to save me. I need to think of something else, and fast.

But as far as I can see it, there's only one thing left for me to do. I look at the knife. I look at my shoulder.

"Crap."

I'll need to move the tourniquet up higher. And I'll need to make it tighter if I don't want to die of blood loss. Can I do it without passing out? How do I get through the bone? I lift the knife up again, hesitating.

A whistle cuts through the forest. I jump, whipping my head in every direction, but there's no one around. Was that a bird? Something else?

"Impressive."

I snap my head in the direction of the voice—it's coming from just across the clearing from the carnivorous orchids. But I still don't see anyone. *Echo?* I ask. But she doesn't identify anyone either.

"That takes a lot of guts." The shadows in the foliage shift, and suddenly what was previously bushes and leaves turn into the shape of a boy, about the same age as myself, crouching in the brush. He's wrapped in a dark cloak which blends with the shadows, but even so, I don't know how I didn't see him before.

Echo suddenly pipes up as well. [Cyros: Level 24 Dryad Vine Rogue.]

Thanks a lot for the heads up, I think at her.

"Who are you?" I demand. "What do you want?"

The boy—Cyros—is crouched down, arms draped over his knees quite casually, head tipped to the side. Now that Echo mentioned he's a dryad, I notice his skin's not just dark, it appears to have the consistency of bark, and his hair is braids of green vines and leaves.

My gaze flickers to the beheaded flower, then back at him. I raise my knife. "If you want revenge for the orchid, you're too late anyway!"

Cyros throws his head back with a laugh. "That's a lot of spirit coming from someone who's poisoned. You don't have to worry about me—I'm no forest guardian. Tell me, were you really going to try to cut your arm off?"

I flush, somehow managing to remain indignant despite my rapidly diminishing minutes in the mortal realm. "I still can! Just you watch me."

"Okay," he says, rocking back on his heels to sit cross legged on the ground. "I'm watching."

Glaring daggers at him, and definitely not about to back down now that my ego has been challenged, I lift my hand back to my arm. Grabbing one end of the tourniquet with my teeth, I work on pulling the cloth higher up my arm to make room for where I intend to saw. Sensation floods back into my upper arm with prickly relief, which I don't take as a good sign, considering.

I finally look away from Cyros, fixing my attention on my throbbing, bloody limb. It's about to get a whole lot bloodier. I take a breath and hold it, raising the knife.

"Or you could just have the antidote," Cyros casually says.

"What?" I snap.

"That's orchid poison, right?" he asks. "They're common around these parts. Pretty rare you get enough of their juice on you for it to be a problem, though, because most people know better than to mess with one. But the antidote is commonplace." He pulls a vial out of a pouch and wiggles it in front of his face. "Or, you know, you can die of blood loss trying to cut off your own arm. Your call."

"You jerk," I hiss. "Were you just going to do nothing? I could of died!"

"Could have."

"What?" I demand.

"Nothing," he says. "As for letting you die, I *did* consider it." He flashes a smile, and I can't even tell if he's joking. "I was admittedly pretty curious to see if you'd follow through. Lancing the blood was an interesting choice. I mean, definitely not a good choice, but I'm impressed you actually worked up the guts to stab yourself."

"Are you going to give me the antidote or not?" I cry.

Cyros laughs, jumping to his feet and across the orchid patch. Each foot falls effortlessly and harmlessly between the vines, as easy as skipping over cracks in the pavement. He pauses just outside my reach, and I glare up at him.

"I won't beg for it," I tell him.

"I suspected not." He holds out the vial, and I snatch it from his hands.

The antidote shimmers in the sunlight, like little flecks of metal are suspended in the liquid. I swirl the vial, and it briefly lights up blue. Popping the cork off, I hesitate, giving the vial a Check.

[One dose of orchid poison antidote.]

No tricks then. I tip my head back and down the mouthful of liquid in one go. It's bitter, and it burns like ice.

"Ugh." I grimace, breathing through my teeth, as if that will dispel the taste.

Cyros chuckles. "You act like the taste is worse than that hole in your arm."

"I've had worse," I say.

He raises an eyebrow. "I'd love to hear that story."

I ignore him with a grunt, undoing the tourniquet on my arm to instead bind up the stab wound and stop the bleeding. A coldness spreads through me as I work, like a hand of ice has reached up from my stomach and through my arm to grab the poison and wrangle it back toward my core. I shudder at the sensation, but the burning and numbness in my limbs is already subsiding.

[Poisoned status effect negated.]

[Paralyzed status effect negated.]

[Skill obtained! Poison Resistance: Level 1]

I breathe a sigh of relief.

"That's a terrible dressing," Cyros comments, absently watching me. "How can you say you've had worse and not even know how to bandage up a stab wound?"

"And I suppose you've had a lot of practice with that?" I shoot back at him.

Instead of a denial, however, he shrugs. "Enough to know how to do it right. Want me to help?"

I shake my head, too preoccupied by the sudden roiling in my stomach to respond. A familiar queasy sensation is crawling its way up my chest. I lean forward, knowing what comes next. "Crap," I hiss. "I think I'm gonna—"

Cyros steps nimbly out of the way as I vomit, emptying my stomach into the nearby grass. It takes several heaves to get everything out of me, and I just wait for it to end, knowing that's all I can do in times like this. After a minute passes and nothing else comes up, I spit, trying to clear the acidic burn from my mouth. The taste of the antidote doesn't seem so bad in comparison.

"Watch the boots," Cyros says.

I spit again, this time intentionally in his direction. He snorts, dodging back.

I cough, clearing my throat. "You knew that was going to happen?" I finally ask.

"Of course," he says. "The poison had to go somewhere."

"Could have warned me," I growl. "Jerk."

He chuckles. "I see you're feeling better." Casually, Cyros twirls a finger through the air, and the orchid flower I'd previously cut off is suddenly buoyed from the ground, lifted to his awaiting hand by a helix of vines. He carefully takes the bud, making a pinching gesture with his free hand, and the weeping, cut stem closes itself up. He tucks the flower away beneath his cloak as I stare slack-jawed at the display of magic.

"Well, it's been fun," he says, snapping me out of my awe. "Good luck not poisoning yourself any further. I recommend trying to avoid pouring any more toxic substances onto your skin. Solid life advice right there." With a flap of his cloak, he turns to go.

"What?" I say, but he's already strolling back into the trees. His cloak shimmers, the green starting to blend in with the foliage. "Wait," I call, and to my surprise, he stops, looking back. I already know his name. I'm not even sure what I want to ask.

"What?" he asks, tipping his head. "Are you lost, too?"

I glance around, picking out familiar trees and landmarks I'd mentally tracked so I wouldn't lose track of the inn. "No. I can find my way back."

"Great," Cyros says. "Try to do that before sunset, maybe. But, hey, who am I to tell you how to live your life?" He heads back into the trees, his attire melting into the surrounding foliage as his voice grows distant. "I mean, maybe you're a masochist. Maybe you're into that."

I blink, staring after him, even as his voice and form vanish into the woods. I look down at my bandaged arm, just to convince myself this all really happened.

"What the hell?" I whisper.

Wiping off my knife before I sheath it, I eventually pick myself up, grab Iski's stupid basket of plants, and head back to the inn in utter defeat. I can't believe I almost died to a plant. The fact that I was only saved by a mysterious tree person somehow makes it worse. What a complete waste of time! I didn't even get to level up. Although—checking my progress bar—I'm now pretty close. So I guess it wasn't all for naught. Still, I'm going to need to take it easy and heal up for at least a day to avoid a repeat orchid incident. I grimace. Boy, Gugora is not going to be happy when he sees my arm.

I sigh heavily and mentally give myself a Check.

[Name: Sally]

[Species: Human]

[Class: N/A]

[Level: 10]

[Attack: 20]

[HP: 77/90]

[Mana: 10/10]

[Role: Chef]

"Echo, can you update my name?" I ask. "Sal, not Sally." Only my parents called me that.

[User name updated,] Echo says.

I tweak some other things around, too. Remove Mana—that's useless. Remove species—that's obvious. Remove Role—

[Access denied,] Echo says.

I frown. "I'm not asking you to get rid of the Role, I just want you to hide the display so I don't have to look at it all the time. It's just sitting there. Mocking me."

[Access denied,] Echo repeats.

I grumble, but there doesn't seem to be anything I can do about that. I add a couple new stats to my interface as well, then give myself another Check.

[Name: Sal]

[Class: N/A]

[Level: 10]

[Attack: 20]

[Agility: 10]

[HP: 78/90]

[Affinities: Poison]

[Role: Chef]

My heart leaps into my throat. "Affinity?" I read. "I have an affinity?"

[Affirmative,] Echo says. [Affinity obtained via traumatic exposure.]

"That means I can do magic?" I ask, excitedly.

[Affirmative,] Echo says. [Spells without an affinity requirement or within the Poison arcanum discipline will be available for the user to learn.]

I did it. I did it! I got an affinity!

"Yes!" I pump an arm into the air, then immediately wince as it pulls at my injury.

But what kind of magic can you do with an affinity for poison?

"Can I do a spell now?" I ask Echo.

[Available spells: Attunement.]

I tip my head. "What's that?"

[Attunement. Mana cost: variable. Time cost: variable. Requirement: physical contact. Attunement allows the caster to manipulate a volume of attuned arcanum at will.]

Well that sounds pretty magicy. The main problem I see in that plan is needing to touch the poison in order to Attune it. Given how well that went last time, I have some concerns about attempting the magic.

I shake my head. Even if I can't Attune any poison, the important thing is that I can do *magic* now! It might only be generic spells which don't require a specific arcana field, but hey, that's something! I'll have to ask Iski and Gugora for some spell books to start studying once I get back. I grin at the thought. I'm sure they'll love that.

The sun is setting, the forest colored with muted twilit shades of orange and yellow, when I finally make it back to the inn. I don't know if it's a side effect of the antidote, but my whole body is sore, and I'm happy to do nothing but pass out and let my arm start healing as soon as I head inside. The back door takes me into the tavern, which is by now bustling with people; half will grab a quick bite before pressing onto Fairwood while the others will spend the night here. I'm about to round the corner and dump Iski's basket of plants in the kitchen when I notice some new tenants checking in at the front with Gugora.

The first is a woman, fair skinned, sharp featured; the pointed ears tell me she's an elf even without Echo clueing me in. Her frown, sleek yet practical attire, and curt movements project a general air of "Don't mess with me," and I certainly don't intend to.

But it's the second figure my gaze is drawn to. He's standing a respectful step behind the first, eyebrows lifting in surprise as I do the same: Cyros.

Chapter Ten

Assassin

"Sal," Gugora says, catching sight of me in the doorframe. "I need to get back to the bar. Come help with the new guests. They need to be shown to room five."

Cyros's surprised expression is gone, smoothed into a neutral, bored look. He glances away from me, casually, as if he finds the inn's decor—which is to say, dust and leaves—to be more interesting.

I set Iski's basket down and slowly head over, frowning at Cyros's reaction.

"Hi," I say, stopping next to Gugora. The elf glances at me, then her gaze flicks over to Cyros. "You—"

"I'm Toshi," Cyros says, sticking out his hand. "Nice to meet you!"

I blink. *He's lying.* "Um..." I extend my hand out of instinct, then hesitate before taking his hand. He grabs me anyway, giving my hand a vigorous shake.

"We're so glad we found this inn," he says. "Mum and I never would have made it to Fairwood before dark." His squeeze tightens, almost painfully, but he lets go just as quickly with a smile.

"Sal?" Gugora says, looking down at me with a frown. "What happened to your arm?"

"Oh," I say, tearing my eyes away from Cyros. I put my hand over the bandage. "Just got scraped up in the forest. I should be fine."

He takes my injured hand anyway, and even though he's careful with it, I wince. Now that he's holding it up, the dried blood that had dripped down my arm and hand stands out stark against my skin. "Blood. Quite a bit of it. Are you sure—"

"I'm sure!" I say, pulling away from him. "What was it? Room five?" I skip away to head behind the bar counter and go rummaging for the room key tokens before Gugora can get a better look at my injury.

Gugora frowns at me for a moment longer, then turns back to the elf. "Sorry. You were asking about dinner as well?"

"Yes," the woman says, and her voice sounds just as icy as her demeanor. "We'll take our supper in the tavern. We should be back down after we've finished storing our belongings."

"Just catch Iski or I whenever you're back down and we'll grab you something," Gugora says. "Sal?" he calls.

I hurry back over, keys in hand. "This way," I say, my gaze lingering on Cyros. He smiles brightly, but it's not like the way he smiled when he was laughing at me in the forest. This smile has no humor in his eyes. A mask. But why is he pretending we didn't meet? Why's he pretending he's someone else? I decide calling him out on it probably wouldn't be in my best interest.

"Room two is bigger," I tell them as we head up the stairs. "Two full beds for the both of you, and I'm pretty sure there isn't anyone there now."

"The current room is sufficient," the elf says. "We prefer something on the end. More windows."

I shrug, leading them up to the door. "Suit yourself. And here's the key. It's magic! There's a spell in the lock, which is synched up with another spell that's in your token, so only you can get in. Pretty neat, huh?"

The woman takes the token with a raised eyebrow. "Yes... we know how keys work."

Well I still think it's cool. "Is there anything else you need, miss...?"

"Tara," she says. "And no. Everything appears to be taken care of. Except our privacy," she pointedly adds.

I Check her.

[Nieve: Level 52 Felis Shadow Assassin]

So she's also lying about her identity. Aren't felis supposed to be cat people? If so, how come she looks like an elf? Also: holy shit, a level 52 *assassin*?!

Cyros clears his throat, and I realize I've been lingering, staring at Nieve. "Sorry," I say, quickly backing off. "Okay. Yep. Privacy. Bye!"

I can feel their eyes boring into the back of my neck as I retreat down the hall. Instead of going to help Iski in the kitchen, however, I make a detour to my own bedroom. I need to clean up my arm, change the bandage, and wear something with long sleeves so it doesn't draw attention. The pain has already lessened a bit since I initially stabbed myself, but it'll still take a day for the injury to heal. Not that I want anyone here to know that. Best not to draw any attention to myself.

Well. No more than I already do.

Cyros avoids me the rest of the night. I'm not sure how he manages that, exactly, considering I'm the one going around bussing tables while he and Nieve sit in a corner of the tavern, quietly picking at their food. But he still seems to slip away from me like a fish anytime I end up in his area.

I likewise manage to dodge Iski and Gugora's suspicion, favoring my left arm with lighter mugs and cutlery whenever I have to take dishes back to the kitchen. With luck, it should be mostly healed by tomorrow.

Apart from our two suspicious guests, the only exciting thing of note that transpires that night is that some sort of noblewoman or politician buys everyone in the tavern a round of Gugora's mead—a drink I'm excited to try and doubly excited to immediately spit back into the mug.

The alcohol keeps people up late, but sends them to bed hard. I still give it another hour after the last voice finishes wafting up from the tavern before I slip from my bed, keeping my shoes off. I tiptoe across my room, mentally tracking the squeakiest floorboards to skirt around. I don't have the entire tavern mapped out, but a night or three wandering around blindly trying to unlock Shadow affinities has resulted in me figuring out the worst boards at least.

[Soft Step, level up!] Echo announces as I head into the hall. [Soft Step Level 2: instinctively find the quietest path of travel with 20% more efficiency.]

Nice. Maybe I need to keep these nightly expeditions up. But on this particular occasion, I have suspicious matters to investigate.

I make my way down to Room 5, at the other end of the hall. I pass other rooms on the way, the soft sounds of snoring or quiet discussions floating out from under the crack in the door when I'm standing next to them. It's strangely comforting to be surrounded by all these other people, all going about their lives, all with their own plans and dreams. Even if I'm the lone person on this planet from Earth, I'm not truly alone.

I stop outside Room 5. Occasional snores resonate from Room 4, so I crouch down next to five, tipping my ear toward the crack.

Nothing. No hushed voices, no heavy breathes of sleep. I hold my own breath, ears ringing, as I lean closer. But I can't make out a single sound from within. It's almost eerie. Too perfectly still. The hair raises on the back of my neck, and I suddenly glance over my shoulder, down the long, dark hall.

No one's there. At least, not that I can see. Even so, I don't feel safe. Like a rabbit caught out in an open field. I stand back up and move as quickly and quietly as I'm able back toward my room. I glance down into the tavern when I pass the stairs, but it's too dark to make anything out. The feeling of unease rises in me again, and I hurry back to my room. I fumble for my key as I get close, quickly pressing it against the lock as the runes light up. A breath of air brushes against me, and my heart rate spikes as I stumble into my room, throwing my door shut behind me. I jump as it rattles in its frame—I probably woke some patrons up with that—and then I'm left breathing hard, nerves crawling all over my skin, staring at my door as if it's about to burst open.

But nothing happens. No shadows move of their own accord. No floorboards creak out in the hall. The night continues on, and my heartbeat returns to normal, and then I'm left standing there, feeling extremely silly.

I still check the door is locked before returning to bed. Maybe I'd imagined all that. Just the dark psyching me up. I was the one out there doing all the sneaking, after all.

I let out a breath and rub my eyes. I don't know why Nieve and Cyros lied about their identities, but I'm probably blowing this all out of proportion. Sure, it's weird, but I'm not sure what I even expected to learn from eavesdropping like that. Maybe I can try to grab Cyros in the morning and ask him about it.

Restless, I rub my injured arm, roll over, and try to get some sleep.

But by morning, Cyros and Nieve are already gone.

"What?" I ask Iski as she preps the morning gruel. "When did they leave?"

"Crack of dawn," she says. "Almost wasn't awake yet myself. Turned in their keys and headed out—said they needed to get to Fairwood quickly. Why, did you know them?" She pauses stirring the meal. "Do you remember them? Are any of your memories coming back?"

"No," I say, hesitating. "It's just, I wanted to ask the boy about something."

"Oh?" Iski raises a suggestive eyebrow. "About what?"

A blush creeps up my neck. "Not like that!"

Iski cackles as I flee back into the tavern. I rub the heat out of my cheeks as I start taking orders, trying to distract myself from Iski's insinuation. She's got it all wrong. I'm not interested in boys—or girls—or anyone else! All that matters is magic. And now that I have an affinity, today's the day I'll put it to use. Then I'll level up and pick a class while I'm at it. I smile at that. No matter that I won't ever get to learn about the enigma that is Cyros. Finally, things are starting to fall into place.

The morning wanes as I rush through my chores, eager to head back out into the woods and force a level up while I play around with my Poison arcanum. Most of the guests have already checked out; as soon as the last one is gone, I can sneak away. Iski and Gugora won't need me until late afternoon, anyway, when we tend to see the most people checking in for the night.

But the last guest—that politician or lord or whatever—is still asleep at noon. Ugh, Gugora really should cut them off from alcohol at a certain point. Eventually I get impatient with waiting and head upstairs to tell her to get moving myself. Probably not the best from a hospitality standpoint, but hey, we might need that room tonight.

And, more importantly, I'm impatient.

I knock on the door of room four. "Excuse me! Ms. Rich Person! It's time to check out."

I wait a moment, but no one responds. Did they already leave? Gugora says sometimes people forget to turn in the keys. I try the knob, and it's locked. Using the master key I'd swiped from downstairs, I hold the rune up, the pad lights up blue as the latch clicks open, and I turn the knob. The door swings in.

Ms. Rich Person is not awake. She's still in her bed, blankets tossed around her in a haphazard mess. The room smells of wine and sourness. Damn, she's probably hungover. With a sigh, I head over to her bed to shake her awake. "Come on. You'll have to pay for a second day if you're going to stay any longer."

But my instincts are perking up again, telling me something isn't right. The woman in the bed still hasn't moved. Goosebumps prickle up my arms and neck as I grab the blanket and peel a corner back.

Her eyes are open, her lips are blue, and Ms. Rich Person is very much dead.

CHAPTER ELEVEN

FREAKING NINJA

I freeze, staring at the corpse. It doesn't look real, somehow. Like a prop in a Halloween store. I can't *really* be standing in front of a body. That wouldn't make any sense. Why would she be dead? How did this happen?

[Check,] Echo says, taking my questions as an invitation. [The corpse of Lord Kelwa Greenhand. It expired approximately eight hours ago via cardiac arrest.]

A heart attack? She doesn't look *that* old. It's so weird.

But reality is finally sinking in. This is a real live—well, real dead—body, and I'm just standing here staring at it. I take a step back, my boot catching on the blanket and nearly tugging Kelwa out of the bed. I jump as a mug falls from the blankets, clattering across the floor and rolling up to my boot.

"You okay?" I hear Iski distantly call from downstairs.

"Um—!" My voice catches in my throat. Am I? What do I even say? I instinctively snatch up the mug and set it down on the bedside table.

[Status Effect sustained: Poisoned,] Echo says.

My heart jolts. "What?"

[Poisoned status effect expired.]

I stand there, frozen in shock, my heart beating a mile a minute. I Check my HP: 81/90. What was that? I look down at my hand, where a few drops of wine had spilled over my fingers. Then I look at the mug.

"No way," I mutter, Checking the cup.

[Empty mug,] Echo reports. [Contains trace elements of wine and carnivorous orchid sap.]

Holy shit. She didn't just randomly die of a heart attack—she was poisoned.

And I have a very strong suspicion who did it.

"Sal?"

I whip around to find Iski standing in the doorframe.

"Is everything alright?" she asks.

"Uh." I stumble back, suddenly finding myself quivering with adrenaline. "Uh, no, I don't think so."

Her eyes go from me to the unmoving noble. Her eyes widen.

"She's dead. Poisoned," I say, finally wrangling my thoughts in order.

"What?" Iski hurried over to check Kelwa's body. "I—I don't understand. Who would do this? How do you know?"

I don't suppose explaining Echo right now would come off as believable, would it? "I don't know. Instincts."

Her look darkens into suspicion. She glances between the body, the mug, and me.

It's like a punch to the gut. "You—you don't think I did it!"

But it doesn't look great, does it? I was the one who found the body. I'm the one claiming it's poison, even though I can't explain how I know. I've only been here a week; Iski doesn't even know me.

"I think," she says slowly, "we need to go speak with Gugora. Come. Let's get out of here."

I trail her out of the room and she locks the door behind us, not meeting my eye as she leads me down the stairs. The floorboards thump with ominous finality.

I'm in the kitchen, glumly stirring the pot of stew I've been assigned to attend, but I can hear Iski and Gugora speaking in hushed tones on the other side of the wall. I might have disobeyed if I didn't have to do this to meet my daily Role Requirement anyway. So much for getting out of here to spend the day leveling up and practicing magic.

The bubbling pot hisses, obscuring Iski's and Gugora's words. I shift the cauldron over toward the edge of the fire, then using my Soft Step skill, I tiptoe over to the wall.

"...don't believe that," Gugora is saying. "Doesn't make any sense. She has no motive."

"I'm not saying she does," Iski says. "Just that it's weird. I mean, how'd she know about the poison?"

If Gugora answers, it's not with words.

"I warned you this was a bad idea," she says.

"We don't know she's involved," Gugora says. "That's for the City Guard to determine. There were plenty of other patrons here last night. Check the books—make sure they're in order. That might help the investigation. I'll send a wyvern and handle the rest."

I hurry back over to my stool by the fire and attempt to look innocent as Gugora ducks into the storeroom.

"You were listening?" he asked.

Welp. "Yeah," I admit, seeing no point in trying to lie to his face.

"Good. Then I don't have to repeat myself." He sits down on a nearby barrel, which might as well be a stepstool to him. "The guards will probably arrive this evening to investigate. Tell them everything you know. Be honest. Do that, and you'll likely be fine." He gives me a calculated look. "Unless you're planning to run away."

It might have crossed my mind. I'm not tied here, after all, and being on the run sure beats getting tossed in a cell. I'm not guilty but I'll sure *look* guilty, and that might as well be the same thing. "You really think I'll be fine?"

He shrugs. "Did you do it?"

"No!" I cry.

"Then you'll be fine." Gugora stands up. "She was a rich noble. From the way she was talking into her drink last night, sounds like she'd made several enemies, too. It won't be hard for the City Guards to put that together." He pauses. "Just don't go talking about the Maru stuff. Innocence won't protect you if you speak too much blasphemy in front of the wrong folk. You understand?"

I have to bite back how I *really* feel about that advice. "Yeah, I get it. Can I go now?" On the off chance the guards *do* declare me a likely suspect, I need to level up now before I get handcuffed and my ability to gain experience is significantly hampered.

Gugora raises an eyebrow. "Go where?"

"Gotta go stab some things."

He stares at me.

"Stab some... trees?" I add.

"I know you think that makes it sound better," Gugora says, "but it doesn't." Even so, he lets out a sigh and waves me on. "Make sure you're back before supper. Also, don't talk about stabbing things around the guards, either."

"Thanks!" I stuff the spoon in Gugora's hands then sprint for the back door.

Back in the forest, it feels like I can breathe again. Not stuck in any stuffy inns, doing chores, and having adults talk down to me like I'm a child. Out here, my destiny is in my own hands.

I check my EXP bar and note it's almost full. Took long enough! I mean, I know I spent the week doing little more than chopping vegetables and getting poisoned, but you'd think almost dying twice would go a lot further. As it stands now, all I need to do is chop a few more creatures—or behead a couple more carnivorous orchids, *carefully* this time—and then I'll get my first level up.

Tell me the base classes again, I say to Echo, even though I already combed through all the options every night while lying in bed.

[Warrior | Brawler | Ranger]

[Bruiser | Guardian | Rogue]

[Wizard | Healer | Artificer]

I don't need Echo to remind me that the top row are fighting options, the middle row are defensive options, and the bottom row are magic options. Of course, I'll be picking from the bottom row. The question is, which one? Wizard is pretty tempting, as it seems to mostly be focused on offensive damage-dealing magic. Meanwhile, Healer is of course more health and defense focused, and while that doesn't particularly call to me, the number of times I've nearly died now means it would probably come in handy. And that leaves Artificer, which as far as I can tell is the more versatile of the three, allowing you to add magic to items, like creating a badass enchanted sword. That also seemed to be the pattern with the columns as well: Offense, defense, utility.

It's a toss-up between wizard and artificer, personally. Both could be pretty sweet.

I take out my knife as I walk, which I had the foresight to stuff back into my sheath upon poisoning myself, but lacked the foresight to clean up after doing so. There's a dried streak of green smeared across the blade. I lift a finger to poke it, then pause and instead get Echo to give it a Check. See? I can be careful. When I remember to.

[A dried patch of poisonous orchid sap,] Echo says. [It is inert in the powdered form, however may become lethal again if rehydrated.]

Is that so? Interesting info. I could do something with this. I nearly stop then and there to head back to the inn and grab an empty vial to scrape the dried sap into. Then I remember the noble was killed by the exact same substance, and maybe it wouldn't look the best for me to be carrying around a container of the stuff. Reluctantly, I pause at the next giant leaf I find and use it to scrub the poison off my blade. I'll need to clean out the sheath at some point, too.

"Alright," I mumble, finally pausing once I find a suitable clearing. I'm nowhere near far enough into the woods to be near the carnivorous orchid patch—I've learned my lesson about getting too far from help—but I have another idea for trying to level up. Trying to fight or even catch up to animals is pretty much impossible with just a knife, but there's more ways to use a blade than just by cutting. "Let's see if this counts as some Knifework skills."

Holding the blade out in front of my body, arm straight, I take aim at a knot in a tree. I chamber and throw the knife. It flips lazily end over end, and falls to the ground before it even hits the trunk.

Well that's embarrassing.

I hurriedly pick it up and try again, this time putting a little more oomph into it. This time it actually manages to hit the tree, though it harmlessly bounces off the bark. I try again. And again.

My arm is starting to ache by the time Echo finally chimes in with a notification.

[Throwing Knives skill obtained.]

[EXP Threshold met. Level up! Class selection available.]

I wipe the sweat off my brow, grinning through the pain of my aching muscles. I'm going to have to work on upping my stamina, next.

"Okay, Echo," I say, excitedly bringing up the stat screen. "Let's pick a class."

The display populates over my vision.

[Warrior | Brawler | Ranger]

[Bruiser | Guardian | Rogue]

I frown. "Uh, Echo? Where's the last row? The one with all the magic options."

[The prerequisites for the arcana classes have not been met. The user's natural aptitude for the arcane and innate mana capacity are too low for such a specialization.]

"What?!" I cry. "Are you kidding me?" What kind of bullshit is this? I'm not *allowed* to pick a magic class because I don't have some inherent talent for it? Anger courses through me at the thought. Even in this world I don't have control over my own body. Even here, I'm betrayed by genetics. It's not fair.

It never has been.

"No," I snarl, shaking my head. "I don't accept it. There has to be a way around this. If I practice with my Poison magic enough, will that unlock the classes?"

[Negative,] Echo says. [The available classes at this moment cannot change. However, class evolutions will be available in the future depending on your stats at the time of level up.]

"And when will I get my first class evolution?" I ask.

[Level 20.]

I wrinkle my nose. The fact that my top picks are locked away still rankles me. In nine levels I'll still have a chance to force my path back in the magic direction. But my base class is going to be locked in now: It'll be my foundation that everything else builds from. I'll need to think this decision through carefully.

Taking in a breath, I try to sigh out all my frustration. These are the cards I've been dealt. I can't change them; all I can do now is figure out how best to play them. I sit down, twisting the knife in the ground as I think.

According to my nightly interrogations with Echo, Warrior is a straight offense/damage type class. I'd need a better weapon, like a sword, to make use of that. Guardian is the opposite, meanwhile, a pure tank build. I don't fancy myself much of a meathead, so I doubt that class would be ideal for my build and body type. Brawler and Bruiser are similar, balancing offense and defense, though Brawler leans more into attack and Bruiser leans more into defense. They can be good for attack styles that favor a sword and shield, hand to hand combat, and such—none of which I'm particularly well positioned to take advantage of. Which leaves Ranger and Rogue. Both types fall into the flexible/utility category. Ranger is more offensive, but from a distance: A whip or bow and arrow would be a good weapon choice for that class. Rogue is defensive, but only in a roundabout way: it's more about not getting hit than being able to take a lot of punches.

I tap the knife on the ground, digging its tip into the dirt. A knife wouldn't be bad for Rogue. Not terrible for Ranger, either, if I could get better at throwing them. Bruiser and Brawler are more balanced builds, but I'm worried I'm too small to engage in fights head-on. My ideal fighting style would be to avoid getting hit altogether. Deal damage from a distance, or leave traps behind as I put space between me and the enemy.

The real question, though, is what will help me kill a god?

"Hey Echo," I say. "This Poison affinity. Does it mesh well with any of these classes? Also, are any of these more or less ideal for a human?"

[A Poison affinity would naturally be more difficult to synergize with a defensive type, such as Brawler or Guardian, as Poison is an inherently offensive type of magic,] Echo says.

That doesn't come as much of a surprise to me. Sticking poison magic on your sword sounds a lot more intuitive than sticking it on your shield.

[However, the field can be utilized in more broad ways than purely damage-dealing magics,] Echo continues. [Poison magic includes debuffs and some buffs as well. Status effects might include paralysis, sleeping potions, obscured optics, and so on.]

Hey, this poison affinity isn't sounding so bad after all. Potion-making is at least a little magical. And actually, that suits my needs just fine. If I'm going to kill a demigod, I don't stand a chance at taking them head-on. Which brings me back to my top two options: Ranger or Rogue.

I unstick my knife from the soil and wipe the blade off on my pants. Given this Chef role I'm stuck with, I wonder if I'll be able to leverage my Poison affinity by leveling up through potion-making. And if I can combine poison work with Knifework, maybe I can cobble all these mismatched cards together into a winning hand.

A mundane role. A weak affinity. Little to no innate magical talent. Limited class options. And yet, I think I can start to see a path forward. It's not the path I wanted, but I'm going to make it work.

"Alright, Echo. I choose the Rogue class." I grin. "I'm going to be a freaking ninja."

Chapter Twelve

THE CAPTAIN

[Lithe Build: +10 to Athletics. Cautious Spirit: +5 to Evasiveness. Obtained skill: Toxic Intuition. Status updated.]

A warm, tingling sensation passes through me. I immediately feel refreshed. The soreness in my arms is gone, the burning in my lungs has vanished. I stand, twitching with energy, eager to put my new abilities to the test. I close one eye, taking aim at the knot in the tree I'd been trying to hit before. With a sharp flick of the wrist, I send the knife spiraling toward the tree.

It hits handle-first and bounces off. Well. I guess my level up didn't help with my knife throwing abilities.

But it *was* easier to hit the tree. It felt like it took less effort. I jog over to pick up my knife, then head back for the inn.

"Tell me about Toxic Intuition," I tell Echo as I jog back. Might as well test out this +10 to Athleticism. Did it really make me stronger, or am I imagining it?

[Toxic intuition,] Echo says. [An ability which allows the user to identify noxious ingredients that can be used in spells and potions. The skill may be leveled up for further insight into what potions and effects may be produced from the combination of ingredients.]

Could be pretty useful once I get that ability to a higher level. Might as well start practicing with it now.

I scan all the plants and wildlife I pass as I walk, though there's not much around that meets Toxic Intuition's criteria. Still, I find a bush full of red berries at one point, which Echo identifies as a mildly poisonous plant if consumed. Pulling out the sheath which still has some of the carnivorous orchid's dried sap stuck to the inside, I'm likewise provided with a brief description that the dried sap is mildly poisonous—info Echo already told me. Guess I'll need to level this skill up some more before it starts providing any real insight.

By the time I make it back to the Starlight Inn, it's still an hour or two before supper—which means it's past time I head to the kitchen and start helping with food prep. It's hard to care about cooking, though, when I have new abilities to explore. Instead of making for the storeroom, I tell Iski and Gugora I need to freshen up and change my clothes, and head upstairs.

I don't head to my room, however. Using Soft Step, I tiptoe down the other side of the hall, stopping outside rooms four and five.

My mysterious savior was staying right next to the room where the noble died. And she was killed with the same poison I saw Cyros pocketing the day before. Not to mention Cyros and his partner—whose class was an *assassin*, no less—disappeared before the noble's body was found. That's a whole string of coincidences I find hard to swallow.

I try the noble's door, but it's been locked once more, and Gugora or Iski are probably holding the master key tight. I try Cyros's door next—and it opens. That's fair; Iski and Gugora didn't have the insider knowledge I do to know something was up with these people. I quietly swing the door open and step inside.

The room is empty and clean. Iski or Gugora might have already cleaned it out in anticipation of new guests tonight. Too bad, I was hoping to find some clues. Even so, I poke around, using my Toxic Intuition to try to sus out any hints of poisonous materials. Either there wasn't any to begin with, though, or the room was thoroughly cleaned, because my ability turns up nothing. I peek under the pillows. Look in the wardrobe. Glance under the bed.

Ah. What's this? A tiny shaft of light is visible under one of the beds. It's coming from a hole in the wall—the same wall that borders room four. I shuffle my way under until I can reach the crack, although up close it seems to be a hole, perfectly and artificially round.

I poke my finger through and give it a wiggle. Just slightly larger than my pointer finger: certainly not big enough to squeeze through, but large enough for, say, a vine to sneak through. Coincidence, or a clue?

The distant sound of thumping echoes up the stairs. I scramble to get out from under the bed and hurry to the door. Voices are drifting down the hall: the familiar rumble of Gugora, along with another voice I don't recognize. They're only a few doors down, and heading this way. I hesitate, my hand on the doorknob. Too late to slip out without them seeing me now. I freeze, mind racing, as I strain to catch a hint of their words.

"...understand how this looks," the unfamiliar voice is saying.

"Completely," Gugora says. "That's why we contacted the City Guard as soon as it was discovered. You have our complete cooperation."

The door next to me rattles, and the hinges squeak as they swing open. The voices move next to me, coming through the room's wall.

"This is how you found her?" The new voice is male, gruff.

"Yes," Gugora says. "She hasn't been moved."

"I should hope not," he snorts. "Who all has been in here?"

"Only staff. Myself, Iski, Sal."

"Who's the last one?"

Gugora hesitates. "A new helper. She should be in her room now. We can speak with her after this."

"I'll be the one to decide that," the man snaps. "How new?"

Gugora pauses again. I'm pretty sure he doesn't want to answer. "A week."

The man *tuts*. "Not a lot of trust there then, eh? Now, let's have a look."

I'm not sure I like the direction this conversation is going. Since they're still in room four, and hopefully absorbed with the body therein, now's my chance to sneak past. Don't want them to go looking in my room, just for them to find that I was eavesdropping next door.

Slowly, I ease the door open, careful not to make a sound. The hall is empty. Using Soft Step, I edge out into the hall. I'll have to cross the open doorway of room four to make it back toward my room, but there's no way around it. Just going to have to make a dash for it. I take a hasty step forward—

And step on the wrong board. It lets out a loud creak, and both men inside room four whip around to look. I cringe. Guess that's why Soft Step is only 20% effective.

I force a smile. "Um, hello."

"Who's this?" the man demands.

Now that I can finally get a good look at him, I have Echo Check his stats.

[Name: Enrold]

[Species: Dhampyr]

[Class: Blood Guard]

[Level: 32]

[Attack: 75]

[Agility: 15]

[HP: 120/120]

His skin is an ashen gray, like all the pigment's been sucked out, and two fangs curl over his bottom lip as he sneers. Enrold is wearing some kind of official looking uniform striped with shades of yellow and green. He looks me over, narrowing his eyes. The feeling is mutual.

"That's Sal," Gugora says. "The helper I told you about."

"What are you doing?" Enrold demands. "Sneaking about, hm?"

"No," I object. "I was just coming to find Gugora."

"Were you now?" he says. "Coming from the dead-end side of the hall?"

Honestly, I'd hoped he hadn't noticed. "What are you saying?"

"I'm saying you're acting awfully suspicious." Enrold stalks out into the hall, and I retreat. He still towers over me. "Where was it you came from before you started working here? Why have you settled at this backwater inn?"

"Please," Gugora says, following him out. "There's no need for this. Sal is trustworthy."

"Frankly, your word means nothing to me," Enrold says. "I don't trust any of you. But you, human, are the most suspicious of the lot. Turn out your pockets."

My stomach drops. I forgot to clean out the sheath. It still has remnants of the poison in it—the same poison they'll find in the noble's cup. Something tells me this guy won't believe it's just a coincidence.

"It wasn't me," I say, edging my hand down toward the blade. "But I know who did it!"

"Do you, now?" He steps toward me even as I scramble back.

"Yes!" I cry. "It was a couple of people who stayed here last night. They poisoned the noble."

"Is that so?" Enrold says. "And how do you know that?"

My hand lands on the sheath. His gaze follows my movement. He lunges forward at the same time I twist to the side.

Echo, add the sheath to my inventory! I think.

[Item added to inventory,] Echo says, and the knife vanishes, sheath and all, from under my hand.

Enrold grabs my arm and yanks me around with a snarl. "What was that?" he demands. "What have you got?"

"Nothing!" I cry, raising my free arm, showing my empty palms. "Nothing."

A giant hand lands on Enrold's shoulder. "Enough," Gugora says. "I don't allow fights in this establishment."

Enrold smacks Gugora's hand away. "You will allow for whatever I say. This inn still falls under the jurisdiction of Fairwood law."

I try to pull away, but his grip only tightens painfully around my wrist.

[1 point of Crushing damage sustained.]

"Please stop," I say. "You're hurting me!"

He turns his attention back onto me, and his eyes are filled with cold amusement. He knows he's hurting me, and he likes it.

I feel so helpless. He's so much stronger than me. So much bigger. It's just like Maru all over again.

Bitterness stings through me like a wasp, and I'm filled with the sudden urge to pull that knife back out from my inventory and use it to stab him in the arm. I tremble with barely contained rage. How dare he treat me like this? He has no right. I haven't done anything wrong!

Enrold sneers at me. "Look at you, shaking like a leaf. I knew you were guilty. Let's go. You're coming with me."

"I'm not!" I object, digging my heels in. He effortlessly drags me across the floor. "This is a misunderstanding!"

I lurch to a stop as Enrold abruptly stops. Craning my head around, I can make out Gugora holding Enrold's wrist just as he's holding mine. Something dangerous is stirring in Gugora's eyes. His face is hard. His jaw clenched. It's only the smallest departure from his normal demeanor, but it's a look I've never seen before, and it frightens me.

"Let her go," Gugora says, his tone terse.

Enrold squirms in his grasp, but despite the dhampyr's size and physique, even he's dwarfed by the orc's stature. He might as well be trying to push through a brick wall.

"I will do no such thing," Enrold snaps. "This girl is a likely suspect in the murder of a high profile noble, which we will confirm back at the guild. Even if she's not the murderer, she claims to know who is, which at the very least makes her an important witness. She's coming with me, one way or another. And if you do not unhand me this moment, I will be forced to interpret your actions as sedition against Fairwood law." He pauses, raising a critical eyebrow at Gugora. "Unless you could offer me some *incentive* to convince me otherwise?"

I blink between the two, uncomprehending. Gugora's jaw is clenched tight, muscles standing out on his neck like cords of rope.

"All we have is in the lockbox downstairs," he says tightly.

"What?" I say, Enrold's words finally hitting me. "No way! That's not fair!" I can feel my blood boiling as a smile curls over Enrold's lips. I hate him. I hate him so much.

I angrily whip my head in Gugora's direction. "Let him go. I'll go with him," I say. "We both know I didn't do it. I'll be fine."

"Sal," he starts, but I cut him off.

"I'll be fine!" I insist. There's no way I'm going to let Enrold use me to extort money from Gugora and Iski. I'd rather be arrested. "Trust me."

Gugora stares at me for a long moment, teeth grinding slowly back and forth. Then, like releasing a scolded cat, he drops Enrold's arm.

The dhampyr snorts, straightening out his crumpled uniform. "A wise decision. But test me like that again, and I won't treat the situation with nearly so much leniency." Even so, the glare he gives both of us tells me he's none too pleased with the result. Seems he'd rather have taken the money than my cooperation. I return his look with a sneer of my own. I'll take my wins where I can get them.

I stumble forward as Enrold starts down the stairs without warning and I'm dragged along after. I glance back at Gugora, who's watching me go. That frightening look I'd seen just a minute ago is gone, replaced with a frown of worry.

"Do what they say," he says after me. "Cooperate. You'll be alright."

I sure hope so. But I don't have an abundance of faith in Enrold's sense of honor. At the bottom of the stairs, two guards in similar attire turn to face us. Iski pokes her head around them, alarmed.

"Hey! What are you doing? What's going on?" she demands.

Enrold ignores her. "Found what we need. Hatsu," he says to a dryad guard, "go do your thing with the body. Jules, take the girl. We'll be off as soon as they're done."

Enrold finally relinquishes his iron grip on my wrist as he hands me over to Jules, who steers me away by the elbow much less forcefully. I rub my wrist, kneading out the pins and needles, as I shoot daggers at Enrold. He blatantly ignores me, like I'm not even worth his attention, and heads over to Iski to talk.

"Come on," Jules says, gesturing toward the front door. "It will be easiest if you cooperate."

Yeah, I'm getting that. I cast one last glance over my shoulder, trying to get a glimpse of Gugora or Iski, but I'm unable to catch sight of either of them. Then, I'm outside.

"Your boss is an ass," I tell Jules.

The woman presses her mouth into a line. "Talk like that will not make you many allies."

I scoff. I'm not looking for allies, and I certainly wouldn't want any from this lot.

Maru, I think, scrawling her name out on a mental ledger. Then, beneath it, I write, *Enrold*.

CHAPTER THIRTEEN

TRUTHSAYER

It's a long walk to Fairwood. We didn't start until just before evening, and we're still walking hours after the sun has set. Our progress is made even slower given the wooden cart Hatsu is trailing. It's piled high with vines, but it doesn't take much imagination to wonder what's obscured underneath the human-shaped mass of plants.

As we travel, my stomach starts to growl, and I'm reminded the last time I ate was this morning—which was also the last time I fulfilled my Chef role. The meal prep I did with the stew will tide me over the rest of tonight, but what will happen if I'm not able to make anything tomorrow? That could be bad.

"How much longer?" I finally ask, limping along despite my throbbing feet. The shoes in this world have absolutely no arch support.

Jules and Hatsu glance at each other and then at Enrold, but when he doesn't answer, Jules fills the silence.

"We're less than an hour out," she says. "Can't you see? The lights of the city are just ahead."

I squint in the direction Jules is gesturing, and realize I *can* see it. I'd mistaken the lights for stars.

"But they're so high up," I say, tipping my head back to take in the wall of flickering lights. Now that I'm looking, I can make out the artificial arrangement of lights in the shapes of buildings and towers, and the murky glows where the lights reflect off their surroundings. "Is it on the side of a mountain?"

Hatsu chuckles, shaking their head. "They don't call it Fairwood for nothing."

It isn't until we approach the city gates that I understand what they mean.

Lights spiral up the trunks of four massive trees, each at least as wide as a house, before coming to a stop perhaps a hundred feet above us. I hadn't realized how tall the trees were here: apart from the four illuminated trunks in this clearing, the rest of the forest is swallowed by the dark. Above us, between the four trees, is a giant wooden gate facing toward the ground, and even as I watch, it splits open with a metallic groan, hinging down and opening toward us.

"*That's* the entrance to the city?" I cry as the gates swing open. I can make out a warm fiery glow flickering beyond them, but nothing else. "How are we supposed to get up there?"

"You either really have never been here before," Jules says, heading over to one of the glowing trunks. "Or you're a great actor." She touches a vine on the tree and it lights up with green magic, zipping up toward the city like a spark of electricity. She heads back over to us and plants her feet wide. "Hold on."

"Wh—" I lurch to the side as the ground beneath us moves. Dirt and leaves hiss away as we're lifted into the air, carried aloft by a plat-form of woven vines. It steadily climbs the four trunks, vines wrapped around each tree pulling us up the trunk like they have a mind of their own. Enrold and Hatsu don't even blink as we're soon a dozen, two dozen feet in the air, and my stomach is left back on the ground beneath us. My nerves alight with nervous tingling energy at seeing the forest floor so far away, but even so I'm grinning like mad. This is magic. *Real* magic. I have to learn how it's done.

I look up as the platform carries us in through the city gates, and suddenly, Fairwood is all around me.

The city is a forest-sized treehouse. Buildings and platforms bubble out of every tree, connected by bridges built from branches and vines. Not like rickety swinging bridges, though. These are grand things, decorated with wooden statues, glowing with purple lights, so wide they could fit a parade of elephants side by side. I crane my head up, and the bridges and buildings crisscross for several levels above me as well. The way the city exists in three dimensions puts Earth skyscrapers to shame.

Enrold shoves my shoulder, and I stumble forward. "Come on," he grumbles. "We don't have all night."

For a moment I consider making a break for it. Unlike the forest, here there are plenty of streets to run down and buildings to hide in. But a sharp look from Jules tells me she's expecting exactly this, so with a sigh I reluctantly follow the captain. Hatsu takes up the rear, still trailing the vine-covered cart concealing the noble's dead body.

There's a lot of other dryads like Hatsu and Cyros here. Their hair comes in all sorts of different flower varieties, and it's hard not to stare as we pass. There's a bunch of bird people too, covered in colorful feathers, with claws for feet and wings sprouting from their lower backs. Echo identifies these as harpies, and sometimes I stop in my tracks to watch them leap off of platforms to go sailing into the depths of the city. Jules doesn't let me watch for long, though.

Our path takes us up several staircases which spiral around the trunks of the massive trees, and over a dozen swaying bridges, thoroughly disorienting me in the process. I'm realizing now that even if I wanted to sneak away, I'd have no idea where I was going, whereas my guards undoubtedly consider the city home.

Finally, we head into a building creatively labeled City Guard. There isn't a door, just an opening that takes us into a bustling hall, filled with armored individuals and scroll-toting clerks.

A human woman rushes to meet us when we've barely set a foot in the door. "Captain Enrold!"

"Lord Greenhand," he greets. "We should speak somewhere more privately."

"Damn your privacy," she says. She's a tall human woman with light skin and blond hair pulled into a bun. The ink beneath her fingers immediately gives me the impression that her career choices are less along the adventuring sort and more along the scholarly. Her eyes are red, like she's been crying. "Is it true? Where's my sister?"

I give her a Check.

[Talia: Level 28 Human Veracity Scholar. She is a noble of house Greenhand.]

Doesn't take much imagination to guess who her sister is.

"Come, somewhere private," Enrold repeats. "I don't want to cause a scene."

"A scene?" Talia's voice goes up an octave. "My sister was supposed to be under the protection of *your* soldiers and now she's been assassinated."

"We'd first prefer for you to identify the body—" Enrold starts, but Talia is just getting started.

"The Council election was to be next week," Talia says, stepping up to Enrold and, despite her slim stature, still managing to tower over him. "She *paid* you to prevent this exact possibility! It was *your job* to ensure she was appropriately accompanied while traveling outside the city! Do you suppose the loss of such a high-profile client will reflect in your favor when we decide upon the Guard budget next rotation? Perhaps it's time for a newly appointed captain as well!"

You know, I think I like her.

Enrold has flushed, well, *red* isn't right, given his monochrome skin tone, but I guess a darker shade of gray is accurate.

"Please, Lord Greenhand," he says. "We are doing everything in our power to bring the perpetrator to justice. In fact, we have already apprehended a key suspect." He glances at me.

Talia looks at me, too, frowning. "This child?"

"Not a child," I say.

"You can't seriously think she assassinated my sister?" she continues.

I puff myself up indignantly. "I could kill someone if I wanted to."

She looks pointedly at Enrold.

"She was at the crime scene," he says. "She also knew what was used to kill Lord Kelwa. Further, she's lied to us about her past, and has no ties to anyone at the establishment."

"I didn't lie," I say, realizing belatedly I probably had. About where I came from, at least.

"She's our most likely suspect," he repeats.

"I'll be the judge of that," Talia snaps.

"Let's discuss this in the back," Enrold says with a not-quite-suppressed sigh. This time, he starts moving even as Talia lights him up with more accusations and criticisms. Enrold heads for a set of doorways further into the building, and Jules and Hatsu follow dutifully after. At the back rooms, Enrold gestures for Hatsu to follow him into one opening, while Jules points me to the room nearby.

"...and to add further insult to the tragedy, you've dragged a child into this affair," Talia is saying. "If the real culprit isn't caught within the week..."

I smile wickedly, quite enjoying listening to Enrold get reamed by the noble. I don't know if it's fair criticism or not, but it's delicious.

"Best wipe that smile off your face," Jules says as we step into the back room. "It won't help your case."

The room is fairly small, a couple chairs pushed up against the wall, and another right in the center of the room, sitting in the middle of a giant spell circle. I stop when I see the markings.

"Uh, what's that?" I ask as Jules follows me in. She touches something on the wall, and a set of vines unfurl from the ceiling, draping down past the doorway like a set of prison bars. I reach out to poke one, wondering if they're magically rigid or if they're just for show, and Jules smacks my hand away.

"That," she says, gesturing to the intricate circle carved into the floor, "is to make sure you're up to no funny business. Now, take a seat."

Hardly mollified, I instead have Echo give it a Check.

[Anti-magic spell circle,] Echo says. [When activated, users within this circle will have diminished access to their mana pool and Attunements.]

Well, I haven't learned any spells anyway, so it won't do much to me. Satisfied it's not going to tie me up or anything, I take a seat, tucking my legs up on the chair. Jules crouches down to place a hand on the circle, and the carvings light up green.

[Status Effect: Restricted Magic,] Echo says.

I drum my fingers on my knees as Jules apparently decides we've had sufficient conversation already, and stands silently at the door. Through the wall, I can hear muffled voices. I hope Talia is tearing Enrold a new one.

A few minutes later, Enrold appears at the door. "Lieutenant Jules," he says, and she turns her head. "Step out. The Lord would like a word."

Jules opens her mouth as if to say something, likely thinks better of it, then steps through the vines. The plants part for her and remain open until Talia and Enrold step through in her place. The vines return to their prison-bar pattern once more.

Talia appears more subdued now. Her eyes are puffier, her mouth set. She grabs a chair, spins it around backward, and sits down across from me, folding her arms across the backrest. Enrold remains standing by the door, taking up Jules' position. I squint and wrinkle my nose at him, but he just looks at me flatly.

"So," Talia says. "She really is dead. Enrold tells me you know how she died."

I consider lying, but since I'd already spilled the beans to Enrold, doing so now would probably only dig the hole deeper. "Yeah. Poisoned from orchid sap."

She looks to Enrold, who nods. "Hatsu confirmed that was the case."

Talia turns back to me, her look calculating. "They confirmed *after* you tipped them off, is the part he's not saying. But if you didn't kill her, how did you know?"

Telling them about Echo is probably not the right angle. I don't want to reveal anything that might tip them off that I'm not from around here. I could tell them my suspicions about Cyros and his partner, but he *had* saved my life, so snitching on him now doesn't really feel right.

"My affinity is Poison," I say. "When I found her, I touched the mug she'd drunk out of, and I could tell there were traces of orchid sap on it." All technically true!

Talia frowns. "Poison? That's a rare affinity. Especially for a non-dryad. Inherited?"

"No," I say. "I fell into a patch of carnivorous orchids and got the sap all over me." Okay so not 100% the truth but it's more believable than I was trying to level up and had no idea what I was doing.

Talia cracks a smile. "That's the dumbest thing I've heard, and I believe you. Are you satisfied, Captain?"

Enrold folds his arms. "Hardly. Any of that could be fiction. She also claimed to know *who* poisoned Lord Kelwa. If that's true, I want to know who, and how she knows."

Talia shrugs. "Fair enough. I believe you're telling the truth, for the record, but I'd also like to be sure." She lifts a hand, pointing a finger at me. "I'm going to cast a spell on you, alright?"

"Um." I lean back in my chair. "What kind of spell?"

"A truth detector spell," she says.

I raise my eyebrows. Oh, hell no. "You're going to read my mind?"

"Not exactly," Talia says. "I'll ask you some questions, and the spell will tell me if your intentions are mostly truthful or mostly deceptive. Ready?"

I look between her and Enrold. "I don't suppose I can say no?"

"Not if you want to get out of this cell tonight," Talia says.

"We won't be releasing her regardless," Enrold objects.

Talia snorts. "Please. We both know you're desperate for a scapegoat to save public face. But if I find her innocent, and you continue to detain her, then I'll be forced to be very vocal about my findings."

Enrold grits his teeth, but says nothing.

"Well?" Talia asks me.

I grip the edge of the chair. If she's just going to make sure I'm innocent, then I have nothing to hide. Still not wild about some magic doing stuff to my brain, but getting out of Enrold's clutches sounds like a bigger priority.

"Okay," I say. "Go ahead."

A pink light flashes from Talia's finger, washing over both of us.

[You have been subjected to a low-level Truth spell,] Echo says, though I don't feel any different.

"Right," Talia says, staring at me intently. "Did you kill my sister, Kelwa Greenhand?"

"No," I say. Well that was easy.

"How do you think she died?" she asks.

"Poison."

"Why?"

"I have a poison affinity. I touched the mug she drank out of and noticed there was poison on it."

"Do you know who poisoned her?"

I try not to show any reaction to the question. "I don't know, but I have suspicions."

"Who do you suspect?" she asks.

Should I sell Cyros out? What if he really is innocent, and this was all just a big coincidence? Well, I can't really dodge the question now.

"There were two people who checked into the inn the night before," I say. "They left before we found the dead noble—uh, your sister, sorry. An elf and a dryad. They checked in under the names Tara and Toshi."

Talia holds my gaze for a moment, then nods. "Is there anyone else you might suspect? The innkeeps?"

"No," I say quickly. "Iski and Gugora would never! But it's possible one of the other customers was involved. Everyone there that night were strangers. We should have all their names in the logs."

Talia gives Enrold a side-eye. "Are you taking notes, Captain?"

He merely glowers at her.

Talia asks me a handful of other questions in the similar vein, though her voice is growing strained and sweat is starting to bead on her brow. I don't notice the effects of the spell, but apparently it's a bit of a strain on her. Eventually, she sighs.

"That's enough." Talia waves her hand. "You've answered all my questions."

[Spell expired,] Echo reports.

"She answered all my questions truthfully," Talia says to Enrold. "Will you agree she's not my sister's murderer now?"

Enrold grits his teeth. "Perhaps. Such spells are not foolproof."

Talia stands. "Well until you can convince a mind mage to come work for your unit, this will have to suffice. I trust you'll be following the leads she provided?"

"Among others," Enrold says, his glare returning to me. "There were other individuals at the inn that are still under suspicion. The innkeeps, for one."

"Hey!" I stand up. "I told you already, they didn't do it!"

"So you believe." An unkind smile quirks his lips. "That will be determined after further interrogation."

"That's harassment!" I snap, anger bubbling up within me. "You're just mad you're wrong. You call me a kid, but you're the one who's acting like a child."

Irritation flickers over Enrold's expression. "We'll see if you are still willing to speak such words after a night in the Cave."

"Nonsense," Talia cuts in before I can ask or wonder about what the Cave is. "She's coming with me. And we'll both be departing immediately. If you need anything else, you know where to reach me."

"She's still a key suspect," Enrold objects.

Talia ignores him. "Come on," she tells me with a jerk of her head.

I don't need to be told twice. I don't know what this lady wants with me or why she thinks I'll be going with her, but it sure beats staying here with Captain Asshole. I jump from my chair and hurry after.

Talia holds the vines open for me, and I shoot a nervous look Enrold's way, in case he'll try to stop us. Instead, he just watches me pass, anger burning in his gaze. Yeah, the feeling is mutual.

Talia wordlessly blazes a trail through the building, and I have to jog every few feet to keep pace. When we step back outside into the city of trees, I breathe a sigh of relief.

"Look, thanks for your help," I say, slowing down when Talia begins to head off in some other direction. "But I should be—"

"Oh, no you don't." She grabs my elbow and tugs me along without breaking stride. "You're not getting away that easily."

"But I have to get back to the inn," I say.

"In the middle of the night?" She glances at me with a raised eyebrow. "Would you even know how to get back?"

Uh, good point. I could probably follow the trail during the day, but navigating it alone at night without a light was definitely going to result in me getting lost.

"Didn't think so," she said. "Don't worry, I'm not about to hold you hostage like that thug of a captain. You can stay the night at my place and head back in the morning. But first, I have a couple more questions to ask you." She fixes me with a hard look. "Like who you really are, and why you weren't telling me the whole truth."

CHAPTER FOURTEEN

MIDNIGHT SNATCH

"I didn't lie!" I object as Talia pulls me through the city, an iron grip on my arm.

"Maybe not directly," Talia says. "But it wasn't the complete truth. You're hiding something."

"If you think that's true, how come you didn't say anything in front of Enrold?" I counter.

"Because Enrold is a moron." Talia wrinkles her nose. "And he doesn't actually care about justice, only money and optics. If I called you out back at the Guards' headquarters, he would have arrested you on the spot and considered the case closed. Meanwhile, I have a vested interest in making sure the right person is caught. The killer could have been a political enemy of my sister, or they could have beef with our House, in which case, I might be next."

"I really don't think I can help with any of that," I say.

Talia looks down at me, thoughtful. "Perhaps you're right. But right now, you're the only lead I've got. Can I trust you not to run if I let go?"

"Yes," I say before I've even decided if I will or not.

She continues to stare at me.

I squirm under her look. I don't trust this woman yet, but she's been pretty transparent about her motives, and she's at least right that I need a place to stay for the evening. "I won't run," I answer honestly.

She nods, letting go of me. "Then let's get home. I'm just in the second canopy."

We head across another half a dozen bridges and climb another spiral staircase, and this time I'm able to be more appreciative of the sights I'm taking in. We pass through what seems to be some kind of merchant district, packed full of taverns and food stands whose rich smells make my mouth water. There's a lot of grilled food and gusts of smoke—despite the potential fire hazard, I guess—which cause pangs of hunger in my stomach to remind me exactly how long it's been since I'd last eaten.

Talia smiles when she hears my stomach growl particularly loud. "Hungry?

"Starving," I admit.

"Come, let's stop for something," she says. "I haven't eaten either."

She takes us around to a different tree, where a green and brown harpy is working behind a noodle stall. A dozen seats are crowded around the built-in countertops, but there's a few on the end still open.

"Hey, Bibs," Talia says as we sit down. "The regular. Two of them."

"Be up in a minute," the harpy says. They look at me, tipping their head sharp and quick to the side, very much like the movements of a bird. Their eyes are bright yellow. "Who's this? A new student? Don't worry, kid, she's this strict with all of them. Don't believe the rumor about that defenestrated understudy, it's mostly exaggerated."

I blink. "Uh..."

"Not a student," Talia says. "And stop spreading that story. It was one time."

Bibs chuckles, turning back to their steaming cauldron of broth as they prepare our meal.

"So." Talia looks at me, resting her head on her knuckles. "Tell me about yourself."

"What do you mean?" I ask. "I told you back in the Guards' building."

"You told me some things," Talia allows. "Mostly true. Partly a lie. Here are the things I do believe: Your name is Sal, you started working at the Starlight Inn a week ago, and you have a Poison affinity for magic."

"That's not much," I notice. "And the things you don't believe?"

"You don't have amnesia, you know more about the real murderer than you're telling me, and you're withholding something about your magic," Talia rattles off.

I look at her, surprised. "You could tell all that from your truth spell?"

"Partially," Talia says. "I may not be a politician like my sister, but I do have the same instincts for sniffing out bullshit like she has." Her smile falters. "Had."

Bibs sets two bowls of noodles in front of us, the steam rich and salty with a hint of lemon. It looks kind of like ramen; the noodles are accompanied by a dark broth with a variety of vegetables and a couple chicken wings. Bird wings? I eye Bibs suspiciously. I wonder if that would be considered cannibalism here. I decide it would probably be rude to ask.

Talia digs in, not waiting for me to respond to her accusations, so I happily devour the bowl as well. Warmth flows through me as I down the broth. Maybe I'm just hungry, but it might be the best thing I've ever eaten.

"Have you got any sisters?" Talia asks between bites.

This topic feels safer than the last ones, so I shake my head. "Only child."

"Lucky," she says. "Siblings are a pain. A good kind of pain, but a pain." She grimaces. "My parents always pitted us against each other. Made everything a competition. Sometimes I hated her just as much as I loved her. Have you got any parents?"

"Yeah," I say, and my heart squeezes at their memory. I didn't want to admit it to myself, but I miss them. It's only been a week, and it already feels like a year.

They're better off without you, I try to tell myself. Now, they can move on.

"Where do they live?" Talia asks.

It's then I remember I'm supposed to have amnesia. "Um..."

She snorts. "Back to playing dumb, are we?"

"You wouldn't believe me even if I told you," I say.

"Oh yeah?" She raises an eyebrow. "I've got spells to help with that. Try me."

I go silent, sipping at another spoonful of the soup. It's not that I'm not tempted by having someone to confide in, but spreading the truth is dangerous. Maru showed me that. Besides, Talia might have helped me out twice now, but that was only because she stood to gain something.

"They're not around here," I say, settling for incomplete truths. "They're far away and I can't see them again."

"Can't, or won't?" Talia asks.

"Can't."

"Interesting."

I shrug, avoiding her gaze, as I pick up the bowl and shovel more of the noodles into my mouth.

"And the magic?" Talia asks. "What were you hiding about that?"

"If you're trying to bribe me with food, it's not going to work," I say. Okay, well, it worked a little. But not anymore!

"If you insist," Talia says. "I suppose trying to pry up these mysteries was more the scholar in me than anything. If you don't want to talk about it, I won't make you." She pauses to down the rest of her bowl, emptying the last few dregs of the broth. She sets it down heavily. "What I really need you for is information on my sister's killer. That part is non-negotiable."

She sets a few coins down on the table and stands up. I hurriedly finish off the rest of my bowl as well. Talia waves goodbye to Bibs, and then we're back on the road. It isn't much longer until we reach her house—if you can call it a house.

A staircase ends in a branch-woven gate, decorated with vines and leaves and carvings of flowers. Talia touches a hand to it, then turns to me.

"Set your hand here," she says, pointing to a spot next to hers.

I hesitate. "Why?"

"I'm giving you gate access," she says. "It's harmless, I just need to authorize your magic signature so the alarm system won't go off."

Cautiously, I touch my hand to the gate.

[Your magic has been identified,] Echo says, though she doesn't elaborate on what that means.

The gate swings open, and Talia steps inside. Beyond is a network of trees connected by ornate bridges and pathways, small cabin-sized abodes mushrooming out from the trunks and hanging from thick vines as if someone had taken each room in a house and strung them up like beads on a string. There's at least a dozen different buildings all woven together in one organic network—a labyrinth of a treehouse.

"This one's the kitchen," Talia says, pointing to one of the treehouses we pass. "And that one's the library. I also have a few extra bedrooms, a living room, my study…" She goes on, pointing out and explaining each building we pass. Does she live here by herself? It's hard to gauge with everything so spread out, but this place feels massive. In the end, she takes me to one of the bedrooms.

"It locks from the inside," she says, gesturing for me to take a look around. "I'll be in the one just over there. Come get me if you need anything."

"I thought you wanted to talk," I say, suspicious of all the charity.

"We can do so in the morning," Talia says. "You'll have time before you need to get back, yes? We've both had a long day. Rest now, and I'll find you after daybreak."

Sleeping sounds pretty damn great, given all the walking I've done today. It must be after midnight by this point. Even so, I watch Talia head off to another room, enter it, and shut the door behind her. I stand there and wait for another few minutes; the lights in that room flicker out, and then all the lights around her property similarly dim until I'm left in a faint twilight. Cautiously, using my Soft Step, I creep away from my bedroom.

I go investigate the kitchen, first. The room is small, a two-chaired table taking up the center, with various utensils and pans hanging from the walls on hooks—possibly to accommodate the slight sway of the building. The room's homey, plain. It's not nearly as well stocked as Gugora and Iski's storeroom, but I go rooting around and am still able to turn up some dried meat, crusty bread, an apple, and some greens. More digging produces a dusty vegetable sack, which I fill with my spoils. Hopefully that will be enough to satisfy my role requirement tomorrow if push comes to shove.

Do I feel great about stealing? I mean, not really. But as kind as Talia has been so far, I know she has ulterior motives, and besides, my sanity is on the line. That carries a bit more weight to me than the moral offense of stealing a snack from a rich person.

Tying the sack shut and slinging it over my shoulder, I poke around a few of the other buildings as well. I move quickly past the outhouse, poke my head in a few more empty bedrooms to confirm we really are alone, and then check out the library. I nearly pop in and out of that one as quickly as I'd retreated from the lavatory, but a label on one of the shelves catches my eye. Quietly, I close the door behind me and venture inside.

It's about the same size as the other buildings: a cozy home library, nothing extravagant. Although, perhaps this *is* extravagant for this world. Two walls are covered with shelves, floor to ceiling, while the other two walls have breaks in the wallpaper of books for the door and some windows. Like the other rooms, I don't risk turning a light on, but the faint glow of dimmed lights outside is enough for me to maneuver by.

On the left side of the room is a section that says History. On the right is a shelf that says Magic. I make a beeline for the latter.

Some books look new, others look ancient. Some are bound in leather, embossed with gold print, others are simple scrolls. I squint, tipping my head sideways as I read the titles.

"This will take forever. Do you see anything here that might help me with Poison magic?" I whisper to Echo.

[Scanning titles within line of sight.]

I wait, but it only takes Echo a moment.

[On the third shelf from the bottom, seventeen books from the left, there is a book titled Uses for Common Plants of Dunmora South.]

"Uh, not exactly what I had in mind," I say. Even so, I crouch down and find the book Echo was referencing. It's fairly small and bound in cracked leather, more like a journal than a textbook. I pull it out and flip through some of the pages.

There's hand-drawn sketches of various herbs and greens, with notes beneath each one that include everything from its flavor and suggested meal pairings, to common uses, such as to make into salves for low efficacy pain relief.

"I wanted something that would help with my magic," I grumble to Echo. "Not my chef skills."

Even so, I keep flipping until I reach a section that appears to be a bunch of recipes. I stop skimming when I catch sight of one of the titles.

Potion for Enhanced Agility.

Oh ho ho ho? What is this now? The writing says it helps increase your reflexes for a short period of time.

[Agility +5,] Echo says as I read. [Duration: 2 hours.]

That sounds like magic to me! I eagerly turn to another page.

Potion of Fire Resistance. Potion for Enhanced Strength. Truth Potion. Potion of Drowsiness. Health Potion.

"Can I do all of these?" I say, excitement trilling through me. Finally, some real spells I can try! Okay, well, not in the traditional sense, but you have to start somewhere.

[The majority of the potions observed by the user require Life arcana, of which Poison affinity is a subcategory.]

Jackpot! The only limiting factor will be all the ingredients, then, and the first half of this book is all about where to find them.

Resisting the urge to sit there and read through the whole book in the room's faint light, I tuck the booklet into the sack with my confiscated lunch and go back to searching the shelves. There aren't any more that Echo points out as being relevant to my type of magic—which I'm getting the idea is pretty rare anyway—but they're all still fascinating, full of books about monsters and ancient ruins and mind magic spells. I wish I could take everything. However, by now my weariness has sunk its claws into my bones and is dragging my eyelids down, so it will have to be a mystery to investigate on another day. Reluctantly, I leave the library and close the door quietly behind me.

The premise thoroughly explored, I head to the front gate. I don't intend to leave, yet—it is the middle of the night and I'm about ready to pass out from exhaustion—but I can't be caught with the items I intend to steal, so maybe I can stash them beneath some leaves somewhere near the exit for me to pick up as I leave in the morning.

The pathway to the gate is unfortunately bare and well maintained, no leaves collected on the bridge at all. Probably magically cleaned, because on the other side of the front gate I can make out plenty of sticks and debris, and if I can find a nook in the trunk, I should be able to sufficiently hide my small bag. Placing a hand on the gate, the leaves beneath my hand light up with a faint pulse of green, and the doors swing silently out. I step out of the property.

Something slams into me, pinning my back against the tree and cracking my head on the bark. My vision spins as I struggle against the pressure holding me there. I blindly scrabble at my attacker and find purchase, raking my fingernails down an arm. They hiss in annoyance.

"Stop moving."

Steel flashes in the dark, and then I feel something cold against my neck. Alarm condenses into fear, and I freeze, afraid to even swallow. The knife prickles at my skin.

As my vision swims back into focus, I realize I know the face that's hiding beneath the hood just inches away from my own.

Cyros glares at me, his face fierce and determined in the moonlight. "What did you tell her?" he demands.

Chapter Fifteen

INTEL AND INTERROGATIONS

I grab Cyros's arm and attempt to tug the knife away. His grip tightens, his arm like steel.

"What did you tell her?" he asks again. "If you don't want to die, speak now."

I nervously swallow, and I can feel the blade scrape over my skin with the movement. I tap his hand, too afraid to speak.

He glances down at the gesture, then moves the knife back, a fraction of an inch.

I breathe out a sigh, though I hardly feel relieved. "What are you talking about?" I hiss. "Who?"

"The politician's sister," Cyros says. "I know you saw things at the inn. What did you tell the woman and the guards about me and my master?"

His master, huh. "Nothing," I say. "I only told them your fake names, I promise!"

Cyros goes still. "What do you mean, our *fake* names."

Shit. I wasn't supposed to know that. "Uh, I mean, I just assumed they were fake, right? Since you guys were trying to lay low."

He narrows his eyes at me.

"Um, I mean, you had your hood up the whole time you were at the inn," I say, stumbling through an explanation, my mind racing. "And, of course, we first met in that orchid patch, which seems pretty suspicious since the noble died from orchid venom."

"Poison," Cyros says.

I blink. "Uh, what?"

"Never mind." He nudges me with the knife to prompt me to keep talking.

"So, anyway," I say, trying to strain my neck away from the blade. "I figured, you had to have lied about your names, right?"

Cyros swears. "I should have let you die in that orchid patch."

"Well, uh, I appreciate that you didn't," I say, mind still racing. I'm the only one that saw him out there. I'm the only one that knows he's responsible. Is he going to kill me now that he got the info he needed? Crap, I should have thought of that before responding. "And, um, I'd love to repay you for saving my life."

His eye twitches. "How?"

Great question. Is there anything I can say that will convince him? What does he want? What do I have?

My inventory.

My pulse quickens, then slows. Breathe, Sal, breathe. Against all my instincts, I let go of his arm and drop a hand down by my side. "Talia—the noble's sister—she trusts me," I say. "She wants to use me to figure out who killed her sister, and why. If you want me to throw her off your trail, I could do that. Just tell me what to say."

Cyros considers my offer, frowning. Will he take it? Is the gamble that I'd play along worth letting go of a loose end? What would I do in his shoes?

I'd tie up loose ends.

Cyros seems to decide the same. His hand twitches, and I reach for my knife.

[Accessing inventory,] Echo says.

The blade appears in my hand. I rip the sheath off and I jerk the knife forward, pressing the tip against his stomach.

"Don't try it," I hiss, inching the blade forward.

Cyros jerks against the touch, eyes darting down, then leaps back with a gasp. I drop into a defensive stance, raising my knife.

"How did you do that?" he asks. "I scoped you out. You didn't have any weapons on you."

I snort. "Like I'd tell you how." Mostly because now that my inventory is empty it's a one-time trick that I won't be able to replicate.

He doesn't move, eyeing me up and down. "You don't know how to use that blade, do you?"

Guess my defensive stance isn't as convincing as I'd hope. "I don't have to be good with knives to make one appear in your stomach."

He squints at me. "You're bluffing."

"Wanna try it?" I challenge. Please don't try it.

Cyros stares at me for a moment longer. When he finally moves, I flinch, but he's only raising his hands in a gesture of stalemate. "Fine," he says, slipping his knife back into a sheath at his side. "Let's talk."

Still eyeing the blade at his hip—actually, *blades* now that I'm looking carefully—I also slip my knife back into my inventory, vanishing it from sight. His eyebrows shoot up at that, and I have to hold myself back from smiling at the reaction.

"You're really willing to lie for me?" he asks, folding his arms. "Why? What's in it for you?"

Not dying by a slit throat, I think. But it's interesting he cares so much about covering his tracks that he's willing to work with me on this. Just who is he, exactly? Why did he kill that noble? All information that would help my position in this negotiation.

Echo, can you tell me anything more about him? I ask.

[Cyros, Level 24 dryad vine rogue,] Echo says. [He is a trainee of the Blackcloaks.]

And what's the Blackcloaks? I ask.

[Local to the southern regions of Dunmora, the Blackcloaks are a small yet growing Assassin's Guild.]

I do my best not to react to that. He's an assassin? I mean, I guess that makes sense, what with his master's title and all the poison and knives and murder. But it means he *does* actually have something I want.

"There's someone I need to kill," I finally say. "If I tell Talia anything you want, you have to teach me everything I want to know about poisons."

Cyros blinks. "That's not the answer I was expecting."

"Is that a no?" I ask.

He frowns, chewing on his lip. "Who do you want to kill? I could maybe arrange that."

I shake my head. "I want to do it myself. Besides, you're not strong enough." I mean, neither am I, to be fair. But I'll get there.

He snorts. "I think I stand a better chance than you. Who is it?"

Well, if I want to kill her eventually, I'll need to start brainstorming ideas with someone sooner or later. "Maru," I say.

"Hm," he considers. "Is that Maru Climbingvine? The tailor?"

"What?" I scoff. "No! Maru the demigod! Champion of the God of War? Come on!"

Cyros laughs. When I don't join in, he stops. "What, you're serious?"

"Dead serious," I say.

His frown pinches with worry. "That's... quite the undertaking. Likely to get you..."

Killed is probably what he was going to say. He must have realized at the same time that would solve his problem for him. A faint smile pulls at his lips.

"Alright," he says. "You've got yourself a deal. You feed bad intel to the noble's sister and the City Guard, and I'll teach you some of what I know about poison."

He holds out a hand.

I nearly shake it, then hesitate. "Your skin isn't covered in, like, a thin layer of poison, or have venomous needles up your sleeve, right?"

He chuckles. "No, but good instincts."

Hesitantly, I clasp his hand. "Sal," I say, finally introducing myself.

Cyros grins. "I'm Shoti," he lies.

We hash out the details of our agreement over the next few minutes. Honestly, I probably should have taken more time to make sure I wasn't getting stiffed, but once the adrenaline of almost getting my throat cut wears off, I'm so exhausted I can barely keep standing. The Starlight Inn is so remote that it takes a 12 hour round trip to get between it and Fairwood, so the next time Cyros can afford to come visit me is a week from now. I'm not even sure I want him to; on the one hand, I *have* to get my hands on some of his assassin training. On the other, every time he comes to see me is another time he could decide our agreement has expired and kill me on the spot.

The risks we take for revenge.

Cyros tells me everything he wants relayed to Talia, I do my best to not immediately forget it all, and then he vanishes back into the night. Too tired to be relieved, I find somewhere to stash my bag, as was the original plan, then trudge back in through the gate. It swings shut behind me. I drag myself to the bedroom Talia showed me to, and without any more fanfare, I collapse into bed.

I don't wake up until the sun's shining through the windows. Back at the Starlight, Iski usually has me up before dawn to start prepping breakfast for the guests, so it's a little disorientating when I wake and the room is filled with light. Guess I needed the rest.

I consider skipping town without speaking to Talia again, but I *did* make an agreement with Cyros, no matter how sketchy it might be. With a sigh, I rake my fingers through my hair, make a half-hearted attempt to smooth the wrinkles out of my clothes, and set off to find Talia.

I don't have to look far. Smoke is curling lazily out the chimney of the kitchen and an absolutely heavenly smell is wafting from its open door. I poke my head inside.

"Finally up," Talia says from her seat at the table. She has a book in one hand and a fork in the other. A mug of something dark is steaming on the table, and she has a plate of eggs, bread, and jam. The thick slice of toast is nothing like the kind I'm used to on Earth, but it still looks hot and buttered, and therefore delicious. She snaps her book shut and stands to grab me a plate as I sit in the chair opposite.

"Sleep well?" she asks, cutting off a hunk of bread and setting it on a stone near the fireplace.

"Yeah," I say. I grab the plate of eggs as soon as she sets them on the table and start wolfing them down. "Thanks."

After returning with a second mug—tea, I think—and the now-toasted bread, she sits across from me and laces her fingers together. She may claim she's no politician, but she certainly acts like one.

"I'm sure you've plenty of things to get to today, and so have I," she says. "So let's cut to the chase, shall we?"

"Works for me," I say, slathering the steaming bread with butter and jam.

"The names you gave to Captain Enrold," Talia says. "Toshi and Tara. What can you tell me about them?"

"Toshi was a dryad," I say, repeating what Cyros had told me. I guess since others like Iski and Gugora had seen him, it would be too suspicious for me to contradict his basic physical description too much. "Tara was an elf." That part I know is a lie, but she'd certainly *looked* like an elf to me. "They didn't say much or engage with the other guests. Wore dark clothes. I think one of them had a rose design on their cloak."

"A rose?" Talia asks, perking up. "What did it look like? What color?"

I shrug, even as I try to recall exactly what Cyros had told me to report. "Yellow, I think. Or maybe white—it was pretty faded."

"Interesting." Talia taps a finger on the table. "A white rose is the symbol for the Dawnbreak family. They'd certainly have motives to get Kelwa out of the way. But why flaunt their symbol at the scene of the murder? To send a message? Or have they been set up?"

I frankly have no idea what Cyros's intent was there. Perhaps muddying the waters was all he cared about.

"What else can you tell me?" she asks.

I wrack my brain. Everything Cyros had told me to say just had to do with his and his partners appearances, and then specifically to mention the white rose. "Um, the poison that was used was carnivorous orchid sap," I say, trying to come up with anything to sound helpful.

I have to at least *appear* like I'm being honest if I don't want her to bring out her lie detector again. "And it was taken from a patch not far from the inn."

"Really?" she asks, perking up. "Now that is interesting. How do you know?"

"I sort of stumbled into that same patch myself," I admit. "Actually, that's why I have a poison affinity."

"Fascinating." She leans forward. "Now some of your earlier mistruths are beginning to make sense. I can see why you wouldn't have wanted to disclose some of this before Captain Enrold. The connection to you would be implicating. Is this why I could detect you were holding something back about your magic?"

"Yeah," I lie, thinking about Echo and my Stat system.

She raises an unconvinced eyebrow.

"Partly," I amend.

"Go on," she prods. "I'm a scholar, I can't stand to let a mystery like this pass me by."

Would she know what Echo is? In her studies, would she have heard of anyone else having something like this before?

I still don't trust her—and I still don't want to get her killed by having second-hand knowledge of my origins—but maybe I don't have to tell her everything to suss out some answers of my own. "My magic is different from most people's," I tell her. "There's... visual and sound components to what I do, that no one but me can seem to see and hear."

"Visual and auditory hallucinations?" she considers, taking a sip of her tea. "Quite interesting. There are some ocular magics that might explain such illusions. You're sure your affinity is Poison?"

Echo? I prompt.

[All user affinities: Poison.]

"Pretty sure," I say.

"Curious. Can't say I've heard of anything like that," Talia admits, sinking my hope. "There might be some references to such magical side effects recorded in tomes somewhere. I would suggest you start your investigation into your magic in the library of Miasmere, but I've heard the Athenaeum is currently under construction. Pity, it's a remarkable institution. Still, it remains an option when it reopens to the public."

"I'll keep that in mind," I say. Maybe there's more information at this library that could help with my Poison magic, too.

"Seems I've my own enigmas to start researching myself," Talia says. She frowns, chewing on a piece of toast. "House Dawnbreak, hmm? They've certainly been vying for a spot on the Council. And I can't blame them for picking Kelwa as their target given the bad blood... but would they really resort to murder?"

Despite the few times I'd seen her face puffy-eyed and tear-streaked the night before, she doesn't seem too heartbroken over her sister's death this morning. It's definitely none of my business, but if I'm going to be feeding her information on Cyros's behalf, I might as well figure out more about what information she's digging for.

"How come you want to find her killer?" I ask. "Not that I don't think you're just in it for the justice, but..."

She chuckles coldly. "Aptly observed. I certainly never wanted my sister dead, but it would be equally accurate to say we were never close, loving siblings. She and I were both driven, which engendered a certain competitiveness in us, only fanned by our parents. It's lucky our career paths diverged so sharply or we certainly would have been at each other's throats in our professions as well. No, it's not justice I seek—not entirely."

Talia finishes off her toast and takes another sip of tea before continuing. "Unrelated to my sister's demise, there's a power vacuum in Fairwood. One of the eldest seats on the Council died earlier this year—right after the election cycle, resulting in the seat remaining open until the next term. That of itself has been enough to tip the scales, upsetting a previous balance among the council, but now with my sister murdered, two of five seats are up for grabs. Any of the three houses remaining on the council would love to use this to secure their positions more permanently."

"This sounds like politics," I say, growing bored. "And why do you care, anyway? I thought you're a scholar."

"Indeed." She smiles wryly. "And if I want to keep the Academic Guild well-funded, I'll need to make sure the Council's still keeping my best interests at heart. However, I can't help but feel some bigger play is in the works. Enrold admitted the guards he assigned to Kelwa left the day before her murder, and even *he* didn't seem to know why. Someone's pulling strings. And the timing of this with the Gods' Tournament can't be a coincidence."

"What?" I say, sitting up. "What about the gods?"

"Ah yes, I suppose you wouldn't have heard out in such a remote side of the country," she says. "It's the reason Kelwa was passing through your inn, actually. She was off in a nearby town when the announcement was made, and she came hurrying back as soon as she heard. About a week ago, nearly a dozen gods simultaneously announced they would be holding events to elect new champions. Widengra selected the location of his Gods' Tournament to be here in Fairwood."

Goosebumps prickle my skin, running over my body in a wave of prickly static. "Widengra? God of War?"

"Absurd, isn't it?" Talia says. "Our city should have been claimed by Lorata if anyone."

"When is it?" I lean across the table. "Will Maru be there?"

Talia arcs an eyebrow. "Maru, his champion? I suppose she would be; she'd need to approve of any potential new champion ascending to her rank. Why do you ask?"

"When?" I stress, excitement and fear lighting up my body like a shock of electricity. Maru was going to be back. I'd know exactly where and when to find her. "When's the tournament?"

"A little less than a month," Talia replies, perplexed. "Please tell me you don't intend to enter. You hardly seem a devout worshiper of Widengra."

"Never," I hiss, clutching the edge of the table. "I'd never worship him."

Talia leans back, giving me an appraising look as she sips at her tea once more. "You've some disagreement with the gods?"

I grind my teeth, thinking about Gugora's words. *Just don't say it out loud.*

Talia can read between the lines anyway. "That's a dangerous path to walk. While many of the gods may be deserving of our ire, it's best first to have earned another's blessings before making such frustrations known."

I don't want *any* of their blessings. If Widengra is the kind of god that lets his champion go around murdering people, and if the other gods do nothing to put a stop to that, then none of them have my respect.

Talia just shakes her head. "Whatever your history may be, I will only say that it remains in your best interest to avoid drawing their attention. They will have plenty of potential champion candidates to focus on in the coming weeks; it should not be difficult for you to remain beyond their sight. Pray keep it that way."

I finish off the rest of my cold breakfast in silence, stewing in the knowledge that Maru would return in one month: and that was when I'd have my chance to kill her.

Just one month to grow stronger. One month to learn about my magic and absorb everything I can from Cyros. One month to find a way to kill a demigod.

The food churns uncomfortably in my stomach.

"Thanks for the meal," I mumble when I finish, standing up to finally leave. I have a lot to think about and plan.

"I appreciate the company," Talia says. "And I'd like to hope you'll visit me again soon, should any new information regarding my sister's case arise?"

I think about it for a moment; returning here would be another excuse to meet up with Cyros for assassin training, and he'd definitely want me meeting up with Talia more to keep drip feeding misinformation. Plus, I'll need to get familiar with the city's layout before Maru arrives—and there might be more resources around town to help me learn magic.

"Definitely," I agree. "I'll come back again soon."

"Great," Talia says as I head out the door. She follows me to the doorway, leaning against the frame. "I look forward to it. And when you do, perhaps you can return that book you've borrowed," she adds with a wink.

Chapter Sixteen

Holiday Effects

Gugora crushes me in a hug before I've even finished setting foot back in the Starlight Inn.

"You're alright?" he asks. "You're not hurt?"

"Well, I think my ribs are about to crack," I gasp.

He lets go, and I rub my arm; pretty sure there will be bruises there later.

"I shouldn't have let those thugs take you," he says, worry in his eyes.

Behind him, in the inn, I can make out Iski serving lunch to a handful of customers. She squints toward the open door, then her eyebrows shoot up in surprise. "Sal!"

I wave around Gugora's side. "It's fine," I assure them. "They didn't hurt me, and I didn't even have to spend the night in one of their cells."

He frowns. "Where did you sleep, then?"

"Can I at least come inside first?" I tease. "I've been walking all morning."

Gugora abashedly ushers me in, and soon I've got a bowl of steaming stew and a hunk of crusty bread. Over a familiar, warm lunch, I recap everything I went through.

Well, not *everything*. I don't tell them about Cyros. Or the book I stole. Or the Gods' Tournament. Just, you know, the *pertinent* details.

"So you'll have to go back?" Iski asks.

"Probably," I say. "I promised Talia I would help, even though I told her everything I know already. And it's likely those guard bullies will be back here to ask you guys more questions, too."

"We can handle them," Gugora says with a rumble that almost sounds like a growl.

Iski nods in agreement. "Next time they show, just make yourself scarce. They might have decided you're innocent for now, but there's no sense in reminding them of you if we can help it."

"Sounds great to me," I say. Besides, I need to be focusing on my poison magic anyway. "Well, I guess that's the end of that. Need help in the kitchen?"

Gugora looks at me, surprised. "You hate working in the kitchen."

Iski narrows her eyes. "You sure you aren't sick?"

"I'd just rather be busy after all this," I say, fully aware of how flimsy my lie is. "And after walking most of yesterday and today, it sure would be great to do something that doesn't involve standing."

That seems to be convincing enough. Iski shrugs. "If that's what you want, she's all yours, then. The stew needs tending. There's some greens out on the counter that need to be prepped for tonight."

I hop up. "Got it. Well, I'll see you guys later, then!"

Gugora and Iski exchange a perplexed look, but I truly am excited to get back into the kitchen for once. The whole walk back from Fairwood I spent reading through Talia's book on herbs, memorizing as much as I could. I'm pretty sure I recognized a bunch of names from the storeroom. Now it's time to make a complete catalog.

Okay, Echo, I say. *Remember all those potion recipes I read through before? Help me identify any relevant plants in here. Ready?*

[Affirmative,] Echo says.

I rub my hands together. "Alright. Let's go."

I spend the next hour going through every jar, every shelf, every crate I can get my hands on. I only pause to go stir the stew, which I could smell I'd very nearly burned in my negligence. The vegetables are also still sitting there, waiting to be chopped, but they can wait another hour longer. It's hard to remember to cook when there's potions to make. (Well, it's hard when Echo's not hammering my Role Requirements home.)

By the time I'm done, I have a list of 43 ingredients to various potions, out of a list of, apparently, 235 unique ingredients mentioned throughout the book. Not a great start, but not bad either. I bet I can find another couple dozen in the forest if I go foraging for them. And maybe, back in Fairwood, I could find some more to buy or trade for.

But I'm too impatient to wait on ingredients I don't have yet.

Echo, given the ingredients in here, are there any potions I could make?

[Affirmative,] Echo says. [Two potions have all required components to produce: General Poultice, and Smoking Cauldron.]

I have Echo display both sets of instructions over my vision, then quickly scan the recipes.

The General Poultice sounds only vaguely useful. Seems like it makes a sludgy mixture that you can slap on an injury to help heal wounds, infections, and various toxins. However, it's less potent than my passive healing. I look at the Smoking Cauldron recipe next.

This one's more promising. It seems to rapidly produce a huge quantity of smoke—for "holiday effects" according to the instructions. But it sounds like the perfect recipe for a smoke bomb to me.

I decide to give that one a shot first and flip open the book to go through the full set of instructions. Echo compiles a list of "Spell Requirements" I'll need to fulfill as I do so.

[Ingredients:

1 small cauldron of boiling water

2 strands of wormroot

3 rasptoad warts

5 pinches of sage

Life arcana]

[Instructions: Add wormroot and sage to the cauldron, mixing until dissolved. Add warts once color is a faint yellow. Infuse with magic to activate ingredients.]

Pretty sparse instructions. Which should make it easy, except I don't know how to do the final step.

Infuse with magic? I ask Echo. *How do I do that?*

[Mana cost: 30] Echo says.

Not exactly what I asked, but that presents another problem. *How much mana do I have?*

[Mana: 10/10]

Crap, that's what I thought. Well, I guess I'll just have to reduce the rest of the ingredients accordingly. Fill up the cauldron a third the way, only use one rasptoad wart, and, uh… one or two pinches of sage? One and a half should be fine. And I guess one strand of wormroot? That should probably be close enough. It's not like 'a small cauldron' is very exact anyway.

I add a second pot to the fireplace, shifting the stew over a bit to make room, then fill the pot and grab the other ingredients as I wait for it to start boiling.

I still don't know how to add my magic, I tell Echo. I'd go ask Iski or Gugora, but they'd surely be suspicious. And anyway, it can't be *that* hard, right? The book just says "infuse with magic" like anyone can do it. I rub my fingers together, squinting at them like just staring long enough would make them light up purple or blue.

[As the magic is an ingredient rather than a spell cost, the user will need to summon the appropriate amount of Life arcana to physically add to the potion. Given the user's affinity for Poison magic, a volume of elemental Poison magic can be summoned at the user's will.]

You mean I could have just been summoning magic all this time? I ask.

[Affirmative,] Echo says. [However, without Attuning the substance—or immediately infusing it into a spell or potion—the raw magic would rapidly disperse.]

So magic is kind of like… electricity? I say, thinking through this. *You have to plug a computer or something into the outlet, or it'll just be useless sparks?*

[Comparison unrecognized,] Echo says.

It'd make sense if you were from Earth.

Echo is probably too confused to respond.

Can I try it now? I wonder, cupping my hands in front of me. *Wait. How long would it take to recover the 10 mana if I used it all up?*

[The user recovers mana at a rate of 1 per 10 minutes.]

"Ugh, that's so looooong," I groan. I guess I'll just have to wait until I'm going to finish the potion.

Speaking of which. The water's finally come to a boil, so I add the first two ingredients as directed and start stirring. Eventually, the water begins to yellow. Once the discoloration hits the right shade, I excitedly add the last ingredients.

"Okay," I whisper to myself, almost shaking from excitement. "All that's left is the magic."

I'm really about to do this. My first bit of magic. Like a real witch or something!

Cupping my hands over the pot—well, a couple feet over the pot to avoid the steam—I start focusing hard on my magic. *Poison*, I think, willing it into existence. Picturing it pooling into my hands. *Magic. Come on, work. Please work.*

And it does.

Green light spills from my fingertips, flooding my hands with liquid light. I don't feel anything—there's no weight, no real liquid, yet the glowing emerald light ripples in my palms like I'd caught a handful of sunshine.

I marvel at the sight. That's *my* magic. I did that. I'm magical!

[Mana extinguished,] Echo abruptly says. [0/10]

Afraid it will disperse like Echo warned, I part my hands, spilling the arcana into the potion. The pot immediately lights up like I'd dropped a flashlight into it. Now what? Do I need to stir it? The instructions just said the magic needed to be "infused."

Echo? I ask. *What do I...*

I don't need to finish that thought, though, because smoke starts wisping across the top of the cauldron the next instant.

"Yes!" I say, leaning in. It worked! I can feel my heart swelling with pride. I found a potion, followed the instructions (mostly), did what it said, and it worked!

Green smoke swirls across the top of the pot, quickly obscuring the water underneath. Green is a little weird for a smoke color. I thought it would be black. I guess I had no reason to assume that, but I'd been hoping for a smoke bomb sort of use for this, and black seems like more of a ninja-y color. I can work with green, though. It's a start.

The pot fills with smoke until it reaches the brim, then whisps begin to pour over, drifting silently into the fire.

"Um." Hmmm. I probably need it to stop now.

Echo? How do I turn it off?

[If the magic is removed from the spell, the potion will become inactive,] Echo says. [Otherwise, the reaction will last until the added mana is extinguished.]

And how can I remove the magic? I ask.

[As the magic was not Attuned, it cannot readily be unmixed from the solution,] Echo says.

Uh-huh, uh-huh. *And how long will the reaction last before the magic is all used up?*

[15 minutes.]

I chew my lip, watching as the smoke continues to drift out of the pot and onto the floor in front of the fireplace. Not great. I mean, maybe I can stick some rags under the door to the tavern and keep it from drifting out into where all the customers are. I can probably just open a window and let it all air out, right? Fifteen minutes isn't *that* long.

The green smoke starts spreading across the floor. Dang, this stuff is persistent! Good for my ninja smoke bomb idea, but maybe I didn't completely think this whole thing through. Does it leave a residue? Will it ruin the food? I don't think I can afford to wait the fifteen minutes for it to run out.

I jog over to the window and throw open the shutter, glancing around. This side of the tavern is only trees. Good. No one to witness my embarrassment. I should be able to dump the potion outside and Gugora and Iski will be none the wiser.

But wasting my first ever batch of smoke juice pains me, so first I snatch up a couple of glass bottles and corks from Iski's stores. Carefully, I ladle a few spoons of my potion into the bottles, wincing as the boiling liquid quickly heats the glass and starts to burn my fingers.

I lurch over to the counter, setting the potions down and stopping them up. There! Some saved for posterity's sake. Wiping my hands on my shirt, I hurry back to the fireplace.

Using two leather pot holders to seize my beautiful, perfect potion, I quickly lift it from the hearth. Unfortunately, in my haste, my right hand slips.

The pot's weight falls entirely on my left, then gravity tears it from my grasp. The bubbling, smoking pot of water crashes to the ground.

I don't even have time to finish thinking, "Iski's going to kill me," before the room explodes in an impenetrable cloud of green.

CHAPTER SEVENTEEN

PLAYING WITH POISON

Everything is green. The crates are green. The walls and floor and ceiling are green. I am green.

Despite Iski and Gugora both typically being green, I think they're about to turn red in anger.

"The food is ruined!" Iski cries. "We're going to have to make a new batch from scratch. And not to mention all the dried herbs and meat that were exposed to that—that explosion! We need to clear everything out."

"That was dangerous," Gugora says, glaring down at me. I have to actively stop myself from cringing like a scolded puppy. "You can't go mixing potions next to food. What if you poisoned someone? Even if you hadn't dropped it, that smoke was brewing right next to the stew. Do you know what the side effects would be of consuming that? Did you stop to think you might hurt people?"

"I'm sorry," I mumble. I can't even argue; I *wasn't* thinking of others. I was just excited to finally be able to do some magic. To make some headway on getting stronger. And to be fair, I *do* have a skill that can tell me what the side effects of a potion are. But he's right that I could have hurt someone on accident. If I take innocent lives in the process, I'll be no different from Maru.

"Do you know how much this will cost us?" Iski cries.

"The food can be replaced," Gugora says with a sigh. "We were lucky that's all the damage that was done."

Iski snorts. "Easy for you to say. What're we supposed to do for dinner? Or breakfast tomorrow?"

"I'm sorry," I say again. "I'll make it up to you guys. I promise."

"Just promise not to do it again," Gugora says.

I hesitate.

"See?" Iski scoffs. "Empty apologies."

"I *will* make it up to you," I say, looking up. "Starting now. I'll go get some food so you can still eat tonight and tomorrow morning."

"How?" Iski asks, suspicious. "You don't even know how to hunt."

"No, but I do," Gugora says. "I'll go grab us some meat. I've already got some things stored out at the butcher shed. But I'll have to go hunting again tomorrow to make up for the lost product."

"Then I'll get the herbs and vegetables," I say, jumping at the opportunity. "Mushrooms, spices—I'm really good at foraging. Trust me!"

Iski's look says everything she thinks about my trustworthiness. Gugora, however, dips his head in a nod. "Fine. You can start earning back that trust and paying off your debt now."

I leap to my feet. "Thank you! I'll try to do better—I promise!" I snatch up a basket and dash to the backdoor before I can be subjected to any more admonishments.

"Really?" Iski asks Gugora in disbelief.

I hear a rumbling chuckle. "Idle hands wield Shirasil's hammer."

Iski snorts as I'm left wondering who exactly Shirasil is and why I feel vaguely offended.

Relief fills me once I step outside, basking in the late afternoon sun. I do feel bad about disappointing those two. But I also have a deadline to meet. I'll definitely make it up to them—*and* use this as an opportunity to forage for some ingredients of my own.

"Alright Echo, help me out here," I say. "Bring up the list of plants and herbs from Iski and Gugora's storeroom. And also bring up the list of ingredients from my potion book."

[Affirmative,] she says, displaying a scrolling list of both requests along the side of my vision.

"I'm going to start searching for anything on either of these lists," I say. "If you see anything, let me know. We're going to speedrun this."

[Herb detected,] Echo says almost immediately. The word *Swampgrass* appears over a familiar looking weed. I dart over to the herb and pluck the plant, tossing it in my basket, already looking for the next plant before I've even stood. [Herb detected. Foraging Skill Level Up!]

Almost a single clearing doesn't go by without me finding something. I start recognizing the plants on sight, identifying them almost as fast as Echo does. I grab roots, mushrooms, herbs and spices, grass and weeds and flowers and seeds; more plants than I'd ever cared about in my life on Earth. But here they're not just things to spice up a meal: each one is a piece of a puzzle that unlocks another kind of magic I can learn. While I'm at it, I have Echo start tracking which potions the ingredients can be used for.

An hour in and I'm panting like I've just run a marathon. I'm crouching down, hopping up, and darting between plants like my life depends on it. And I suppose, in a manner of speaking, it does. If Maru or one of the other demigods finds out about me, I'm dead. The faster I get stronger, the more likely I am to survive. I wipe a sheen of sweat off my forehead and keep going. Can't stop now. Have to keep moving forward.

[Experience Threshold Reached,] Echo says when I'm in the midst of picking chokeberries, startling me. [Level up!]

[Name: Sal]

[Class: Rogue]

[Level: 12]

[Attack: 22]

[Agility: 12]

[HP: 90/90]

[Affinities: Poison]

[Role: Chef]

Another level already? Nice! I forgot that doing things that fulfill my Chef role also count as experience toward leveling up. It's too bad that making potions doesn't count—but some of my chef skills will help me with potion making, so I guess I can't complain. Grinning, I dive back into the thicket.

Two hours later I limp back to the Starlight Inn, covered in dirt and about to collapse from exhaustion. Iski is waiting for me, arms crossed, a frown creasing her brows.

"Back so soon?" she asks. "Still an hour before it gets dark. No sense in burning daylight, hm?"

"Sorry," I pant, sinking down beside her to rest against the side of the building. "The basket was full."

"The basket...?" She pauses as she sees what I've placed beside her.

The basket I grabbed is not a gardening sized basket. It's a laundry sized basket, three feet deep and half as wide, fitted with straps so you can carry it on your back. I filled it up—all of it.

"Hmph." Iski chews her lip, looking at me with narrowed eyes. "Alright, I'll admit it. Not bad. I'll get this thing unloaded in a bit and see what all you found. But first, get your ass inside and start helping me clean the walls. That smoke left residue everywhere and I can't reach some of it."

I groan, pushing myself to my feet, but I do what she says. It's the least I can do after ruining all their food.

Besides, I'll need a clean workspace to practice my next potion.

Okay so I don't *immediately* brew another potion in the kitchen. I wouldn't betray Gugora's trust like that. But I do go through the list of potions that don't require boiling water and stash some ingredients away in my bedroom to experiment with later.

Gugora is able to bring some meat in from the butchering shed, Iski picks a bunch of vegetables from the garden, and all is well. Well, Iski is still pretty peeved at me. But we're all able to eat, at least, and things go back to the normal routine.

Only now, I'm mixing potions every chance I get. I swipe a pot from the kitchen and stay up all night making general salves and poultices. I pick every toxic berry, ivy, and mushroom I can find, and then I make their antidote. And if the antidote isn't in the book, I use the potion recipes for the other ones as a template to try to mix my own recipe. I'd love to get my hands on some venom next and try to brew an antivenom, but I'm not terribly equipped to go snake hunting. Not yet, anyway.

That week, I level up a second time, hitting thirteen. I'm finally working this chef role to my advantage; spending every free moment running around the forest grabbing ingredients and then mixing them in my room means I can work on leveling up skills and gaining experience almost all day long. But that's when I notice: my HP and Attack stayed the same, but my Agility increased by three points.

"What gives?" I ask Echo as I work on another antidote in my bedroom.

By now I've got a small collection of jars and bottles lining the wall, each one packed with ingredients or successful potions. So far, my spoils include: Potion of Acid Resistance, Burn Salve, Greater Poultice, Healing Potion, Carnivorous Orchid Antidote, and Smoke Potion. Not really sure how I'm supposed to test the acid resistance, but I was doing it for practice more than anything. And actually, it's not even a completed Acid Resistance potion. Right now, it's mostly just green tinted water. I discovered that I could brew the potion's ingredients, cool the water down, and then add the magic at a later point to activate the potion for a slightly less potent effect. I've experimented doing that with a lot of these, actually. It seems like you can prep most potions in advance and wait to add the magic until you want to activate the spell. I get a longer shelf life that way, and I can save my precious supply of mana for when I really need it, but the tradeoff is that the potion's effects are lessened. I wonder what other effects I can discover through experimenting that aren't mentioned in the book?

[Question not specific,] Echo says.

"I mean, how come some of my stats went up, but not others?" I clarify.

[Like Skills, Stats increase with the degree to which the user utilizes them,] Echo says. [While Skills are a direct reflection of practiced abilities, however, Stats may be boosted by the System as a reward for engaging with relevant user attributes.]

"Relevant?" I murmur, partially distracted by my potion. I scrape some chopped up swampweed into a bowl and add a dusting of sage. My Knifework skill is up to level 4, now, too.

[Stats as relevant to the user's Role, Species, and Class.]

I frown. "Is that why my HP and Mana haven't increased? Even though I've been hurt a lot and have been using magic every day."

[Affirmative,] Echo says.

"Weak," I grumble. I wish I could boost my Mana up more, at least. "But Agility can go up?"

[Affirmative.]

"And Attack? Why didn't that increase?"

[The user has not utilized offensive abilities since their last level up.]

Aha. The last time I used offensive abilities was probably when I'd fended off Cyros, which is why I got a boost to my attack after that level up, but not since then. And I'd spent the last several days running around grabbing herbs and plants, so that's why my Agility went up. Which means, if I know which of my Stats stand to change between level ups, I can decide what I want to spend my time on and min-max the shit out of this system.

"What other Stats have gone up the last few levels?" I ask Echo.

[The top ten stats which have been granted point boosts since Level 10 include Constitution, Stealth, Speed, Agility, Obstinance, Curiosity, Wisdom, Attack, Antipathy, and Perseverance.]

I tip my head. "Okay, Attack and Constitution and stuff I get, but Curiosity? Perseverance? That doesn't sound like a stat."

[Stats include physical, mental, and emotional qualities.]

"Hm. I guess that makes sense." I grab my knife and start chopping up the last ingredient, brownskull mushrooms. "Wait, what does *obstinance* mean?"

My knife slips and it nicks my finger.

[2 points of Slashing damage self-inflicted.]

"Crap!" I cry, sticking my finger in my mouth as a bead of blood begins to well up. A metallic taste floods my mouth—along with the earthy taste of mushrooms.

Uh-oh.

[Status Effect sustained: Poisoned,] Echo says.

"Shit!"

I lunge for my potions, grabbing the healing potion and the greater poultice.

"What are the effects, Echo?"

[Poisoned,] Echo recites. [1 HP lost every minute until the status effect expires. Time remaining: 2 hours.]

Whew. Okay, a lot less potent than that handful of orchid sap I'd poured over myself. I don't have to worry about dying anytime soon. At least now that I'm at the inn, I can get help from Iski or Gugora if I need it. Not that I like the idea of admitting to either of them what I'm doing up here in my room.

I pop open the poultice first and stick my finger into the brown sludge.

[Status effect reduced,] Echo reports. [Time remaining: 30 minutes.]

I guess that tells me how effective my poultice is: it reduces the effects of a poison by a quarter. To a quarter? It... quarters it. Whatever. And 30 minutes means this poisoning officially won't kill me. I can wait it out without having to worry about my 90 HP hitting zero. Even so, this seems like a good opportunity to test out my health potion.

I set the poultice back and pop the cork off the potion. A faint green light shines out of the bottle—actually, much fainter than it was yesterday. Hmmm. "Echo, Check my potion."

[Simple Health Potion. Healing capacity: 10 HP. Efficacy: 49%.]

"Efficacy?" I ask. "That wasn't there yesterday."

[The shelf life of magical brews gradually decreases with time,] Echo says. [How long the efficacy remains high depends on the user's school of magic within umbrella arcana. For health potions, healing magic produces the highest efficacy of Life arcana, whereas necromancy produces the lowest.]

"Where does Poison fall under that umbrella?" I ask.

[Poison is a subcategory of Nature magic,] Echo says. [It produces medium-to-low tiers of efficacy for health potions.]

Figures. Well, at least I'm able to make health potions at all, even if they are subpar. I stick my finger in the glowing green bottle and the throbbing in my finger immediately vanishes.

[2 points HP regained.]

I go back to finishing up the brownskull mushroom antidote I was ironically in the process of making as the poison works its way through my system and my HP creeps steadily downward. I start to feel a little weak and hot, but don't notice any other side effects.

I wait until I've lost about 20 HP before finally trying the health potion again. I don't have any physical injuries this time, so I'm curious to see how effective the health potion is.

I sniff suspiciously at the bottle. It was made with swamproot and ratwarts, so I'm not terribly enthralled by the idea of drinking it. Without any injuries to pour it over, however, I see little alternative. I pinch my nose, throw back my head, and take a gulp.

"Ugh!" I cough and splutter, fighting the urge to spit the vile mixture all back out onto my floor. It's like I licked the floor of a barn. After I finish coughing, I go back to plugging my nose, desperate to dilute the flavor.

[5 HP regained,] Echo says.

Better than I was hoping, really. And good to know for future use.

Finally, eventually, the Status Effect timer runs out.

[Poisoned status effect expired,] Echo reports. Then, [Poison Resistance Level up! Poison Resistance skill is now Level 2. When the user is inflicted by poison, venom, or a toxin, their HP decay rate and status effect timer is decreased by 10%. Note: this percentage is 20% for carnivorous orchid poison and brownskull mushroom poison due to prior exposures.]

"Oh really now?" A smile creeps over my face. This just gave me an idea. A reckless, stupid, dangerous idea. But I'm not about to let those details stop me.

"Hey Echo, if I cut up some mushrooms and Checked it, would the dose be able to indicate how bad the status effect should be?"

[Affirmative,] Echo says. [Toxic Intuition would identify the potency of a poison the user is familiar with.]

I grin wickedly. "Well then. Time to grind my Poison Resistance skill up a few levels."

Chapter Eighteen
Maybe One Day

I hold in a groan as I chop up a board of carrots, wondering if there's anything more mind-numbingly boring in the whole world than food prep. If it weren't for the fact that I still need to do this every day in order to meet the Role Requirement, I'd have already shirked the chore through malicious compliance and used mushroom-hunting as an excuse to sneak off to practice my knife-throwing skills and find more ingredients for my potions.

But instead, here I am. Chopping vegetables when I could be training to be a ninja.

[Daily Role Requirement met.]

I stand back and stretch my arms above my head. There's tomatoes, mushrooms, and a pile of blue root-like vegetables called nereid fingers left to dice, but I think I'm due a break. I flip the knife around in my grip, then add it into my inventory.

[Kitchen Knife added to inventory.]

I take it back out again, mentally rotating the position so it appears back in my grasp in the reverse orientation: and it works.

[Kitchen Knife removed from inventory.]

These inventory rules are so strange. And so far, no matter how much I've used it, it hasn't leveled up or gained any more slots. Why just one?! So unfair.

It was interesting, though. When Cyros had confronted me, I'd tried to pull just my knife out of my inventory, but the sheath had come, too. For that matter, when I'd tried to only put the sheath in my inventory to hide it from Enrold, both the sheath and the knife had vanished together. Like they're a package deal. Setting the kitchen knife aside, I grab my hunting knife next, adding it, sheath-and-all, to my inventory.

[Sheathed Knife added to inventory.]

Testing my previous theory, I try to remove just the knife, leaving the sheath in my inventory, but both reappear.

[Sheathed Knife removed from inventory.]

So it is all or nothing. But does this rule just apply to my knife, or is the same true for other things? I grab a jar of seasoning, full of thousands of dried, ground up flecks of herbs.

[Jar of Winter Spice added to inventory.]

Hah! It worked. I take it back out.

[Jar of Winter Spice removed from inventory.]

"That play by play is getting really annoying," I mutter to Echo. But if tons of things can count as one thing by Inventory rules, then what's the limit? I uncap the jar and stick my finger in the herbs. *Echo, add these spices to my inventory, I think.*

[1 grain of Winter Spice added to inventory.]

One?! But I just put a thousand grains of spice in there just a moment ago. What's different? Does it have to be contained for it to count? Well, that's certainly interesting.

I grab a potato sack next, and put a bunch of jars into the bag. Then I try to add the entire sack of potions to my inventory.

[Sack added to inventory,] Echo reports.

And *only* the sack. A dozen jars drop to the floor the moment the sack vanishes, several of them popping open and spilling their contents out onto the floor.

"Oh, crap!" I scramble to pick everything up. "What the hell, Echo?!"

She doesn't acknowledge my exclamation with a reply.

How come a jar of herbs worked, but a sack of jars didn't? Was it because the jar was sealed, while the sack was just held shut? Or is it something else? Size? How secure the contents are? I'll need to do more experiments to—

"Sal, what in the heavens happened to my herbs?" Iski demands.

I jump, midway through trying to sweep a handful of spices back into a jar. "Um. Scientific curiosity?"

The goblin snorts, then lets the back door swing shut behind her as she drags a basket of herbs and vegetables into the room. "Why am I not surprised."

I quickly set the salvageable jars of spices back on the counter, and sweep the rest into a hopeless pile to deal with later. Hurrying over to Iski, I grab the basket she's struggling with and hoist it off the ground to waddle over to the crates where other dried food is magically preserved.

"Thanks," Iski grunts. "So have you spent all your time wasting my spices, or are we actually going to have dinner to feed to the patrons tonight?"

I nod to the cutting board. "Finished the carrots. Was about to start on the others before I, er, got distracted."

Iski hops on a box to check the veggies. She purses her lips, looks back to me, and gives a curt nod. "Good start. Maybe we'll make a cook out of you, yet."

"Ugh," I groan. "*Cooks.*"

Iski hops down from the crate to check the fire. After testing the temperature of the cauldron, she snaps her fingers and a small, orange will-o'-the-wisp appears in a flash of light. She points to the fireplace, and the creature zips down to the flames like an obedient dog, nestling into the coals. The fire flares a little higher.

"You know, you don't have to work the kitchen," Iski says. "We've got plenty to do around the Inn that doesn't involve meal prep."

"No!" I object. Doing the laundry and scrubbing the grimy floor boards on a nightly basis would be even worse than stirring the stew pot. Besides, I still need this job for my daily Role Requirement. "No, I want to keep working here."

Iski shakes her head as I return to the cutting board, starting in on the tomatoes next. "You're the only person I know who desperately begs to do a job they spend all day complaining about."

"Cooking and I have a complicated relationship," I say.

Iski chuckles. "Clearly." She climbs up to the counter between me and the cauldron and begins to sort through the seasonings, adding a few here and there to the brewing stew. After a minute, she pauses. "Here. Your hand's too far back on the handle. Move your thumb over here, on the side of the blade." She repositions my hand. "Try cutting like that. It's safer; you have more control."

"Feels awkward," I say as I try a couple more slices. "I thought the point of the handle was so you *don't* have to touch the blade."

Iski shrugs. "Give it a try and see if it helps."

I shrug and continue to cut up the veggies. After a few minutes of quiet work, Echo abruptly chimes in.

[Knifework skill level up! Level 5: cut with more precision. +10% to speed when using a knife to cut or dice food products.]

"Oh hey!" I say. "That worked pretty well, actually. What other tips have you got for me?"

Iski raises a surprised eyebrow. "You want my advice?"

I shrug, embarrassedly glancing away. "I mean, you don't have to."

She chuckles, her perpetual frown softening the smallest amount. "I don't mind. What do you want to know about?"

I pause, considering. I've unlocked a couple level 1 cooking-related skills that I've found double-dip with my potion-making. Stuff like Boiling Intuition, proficiency with a Mortar and Pestle, and gaining a Discerning Palette (when the draught I'm making isn't deadly to take a sip of). Working on those skills will help me get better with potions and will also help me level up overall.

"How about tending to the fire?" I suggest. "How do you know when it's too hot or too cold?" They don't seem to have thermometers here.

"Oh, well that's easy," Iski says, gesturing me over to the fireplace. "I've got an enchantment on this cauldron. See the runes here around the lip? How far around the rim they're lit indicates how hot or cold the contents are."

"Oh," I say. "I'd always figured those were for keeping the food fresh or something."

"There's enchantments for that, too," Iski says, "but those are too rich for my blood. If you don't have a temperature enchantment, though, there's other ways you can tell..."

She starts doling out more tips and tricks than I was prepared for. Check the size of the bubbles. Look to the edge of the pot first. The color and sheen of the cauldron will change subtly, depending on the material. Keeping track of timing and the size of the fire can point you in the right direction, too.

"Speaking of fire," I say, "how can I get one of those will-o'-the-wisps of my own?"

"Can you do summoning magic?" Iski asks.

"Um, I'm not sure," I admit. "No?"

"Well ask me again when you can," she says.

The kitchen warms pleasantly and begins to fill with a mouth-watering aroma as I continue to prep the stew and Iski starts in on a massive bowl of bread dough. Her arms plunge shoulder-deep into the dough as she kneads it, and I'm a little scared she'll fall in, never to be seen again.

Gugora arrives when Iski's showing me how to place the buns on the hearth and when to rotate them to keep them from burning.

"Nice to see you two getting along," he rumbles, ducking through the doorframe.

"We get along," I object.

"Yeah," Iski agrees. "I mean, sometimes she's fairly tolerable."

I turn to her, offended.

Gugora chuckles. "Coming from her, that's a compliment." He slings a couple of dead jackelopes from over his shoulder onto the counter.

"Shouldn't those go in the butcher shed?" I ask. I've never seen him take dead animals directly into the inn before. He usually retrieves meat from the butcher shed as needed.

"Checked the traps on the way back from hunting," Gugora says. "Figured some fresh meat in the stew tonight wouldn't hurt. You want to help clean them?"

My stomach does a nervous tap dance. "By clean, you don't mean scrub them with soap and water, do you?"

"If you're working in the kitchen, you'll have to learn how to prep meat at some point."

He's right, even though it's sending nervous tingles all through my fingers and toes. I've never cut up raw meat before, let alone skinned the animal and yanked out all its organs, first. The idea fills me with disgust.

But if I'm going to kill a demigod, I'm going to have to get used to the idea of death sooner or later. Swallowing down my jitters, I follow Gugora over to the tabletop where he's laying out the animals.

"I'll work on this one," he says, gesturing to the jackalope before him, "while you repeat what I do on that one. Let me know if you don't follow anything. Alright?"

I grimace, but take up my place beside him. "Alright."

"Good." He selects two curved blades from the knife block, and hands one to me. "First thing you do is make a cut from here to here. Shallow, so you don't damage the intestines..."

My face is scrunched up in disgust as I repeat every step, following each of Gugora's slow and measured instructions. Once the skin is off, though, it becomes a lot easier. It doesn't look so much like an animal anymore. And when it comes to taking the meat from the bone, that isn't so bad at all. By the end, I no longer feel sick and nervous—in fact, I think I could do it again!

[Skill obtained,] Echo says. [Butchery, Level 1.]

"Well that wasn't so bad," I say, allowing my taut shoulders to relax. Not to mention, I got a new skill out of it! A cooking skill, but there's no surprise there.

"You did well," Gugora says. "Especially for your first time. You might be a natural."

I beam as his praise fills me with a comforting warmth. "What should we do with the meat now? Throw it in the pot?"

"No!" Iski cries. "Don't be boorish! Come here, I'll show you how to braise it with some of the leftover bacon fat from breakfast."

I didn't think it was possible for the room to smell even better, but as soon as the jackalope meat hits the grease, the room becomes dense with the rich, salty smell of popping fat. Gugora leans over and watches as Iski shows me how to brown the meat before adding it to the stew. I follow her instructions, flinching at each spark of fat that flies off and burns my skin, but the specks are so small and inconsequential, they heal almost instantly. And weirdly, I'm kind of having fun.

This isn't ninja training. This isn't time spent funneling mana into potions, or learning new recipes. But spending time with Gugora and Iski brings me a kind of relaxed peace I haven't felt since... Well, I guess I can't think of the last time I felt this way. Even before I came to this world, it had been years and years since I was able to help my mom and dad with anything so simple.

The reminder sends a sting of pain through my heart. I've been trying not to think about them too much. I probably will never see them again, anyway. But it sure would be nice to let them know I'm alright, at least. To give them peace, like the kind I have now living with Iski and Gugora.

I shake my head. No. This is just the illusion of peace. A reprieve from my true mission. As much as this simple life fills me with comfort and happiness, it's still a distraction from what I really need to do.

Layf. Rena. Terimus. I won't let their deaths be in vain. I'll avenge them. I'll get them the justice they deserve.

I tighten my grip on the pan as I tip it to the side and scrape all the sizzling rabbit meat into the boiling broth.

Maybe one day I can return to this life. But first, Maru must pay.

CHAPTER NINETEEN

FAILED OBSERVATION SKILLS

By the day Cyros is supposed to meet back up with me, I've leveled up again.

[Name: Sal]

[Class: Rogue]

[Level: 14]

[Attack: 26]

[Agility: 15]

[HP: 90/90]

[Affinities: Poison]

[Role: Chef]

[Skills: Level 7 Knifework. Level 5 Poison Resistance. Level 4 Soft Step. Level 4 Throwing Knives.]

Not too shabby, if I do say so myself. I've started to notice some of my higher-level skills, like Knifework, are harder to level up even though I'm using them way more than any of my other skills. The growth curve is probably exponential or something: easier to level up at low levels, hard to level up at high levels. Considering I've been able to Level Up from 10 to 14 in two weeks, I'll probably see that growth starting to slow down before long, too. Unless I can find some actual monsters to fight and level up faster that way.

Although I'm starting to wonder if the only monsters this world has are the gods.

Four weeks. The reminder comes to me unbidden. Only four more weeks until the Gods' Tournament and I'll have my chance to face Maru once more. Suddenly, my scant handful of level ups doesn't feel like nearly enough. At this rate, I'll barely be over level 20 when I plan to face down a level 92 demigod. How the hell am I supposed to pull that off?

Faster. I need to get stronger fast.

I pace around the carnivorous orchid patch once more. Where is Cyros? He said he'd meet me here. I don't have the wrong day, do I? Unless he got everything he needed from me and isn't planning on coming back.

I shake my head. No. He still wants me to work with Talia. He'll come. He has to.

Still, as the minutes pass, he doesn't show. I practice my Throwing Knives skill at a knot in a tree for a while, the blade sticking in the bark almost every time, and usually close to the knot. Then I get bored with that and switch to working on my Soft Step, picking my way around sticks and leaves. Leveling up my skills is always time well spent, but I'd rather be spending it learning new skills.

I come back to the orchid patch, glaring at the carnivorous flowers. Tiny animal bones litter the forest floor between the plant's vines. The buds are still: I guess they're not digesting anything today. I can still pick out the plant I'd beheaded the week before, its cut stalk now scabbed over with sap. I mentally replay the scene in my head of when I first met Cyros. I pick out the spot on the other side of the clearing where he'd been watching me, half melted into the foliage. His clothes and skin had seemed to blend right in with the thicket. What kind of magic had that been? Nature? Shadow? Something else? I squint at the bush, imagining the boy's silhouette. And strangely, like focusing on one of those 3D eye puzzles, the leaf pattern seems to resolve into his shape.

"Took you long enough to notice," Cyros says, and I nearly jump out of my skin. The Cyros-shaped patch of leaves ripples as he stands, though when he stops moving, I can once again hardly tell he's there. "I see you're getting better with that knife, but you need to work on your perception skills."

"How long have you been there?" I demand.

"Before you got here," he says, stepping around the orchid patch.

He's not dropping the camouflage shtick, and I'm not taking my eyes off him again. Even so, I struggle to track him as his outline moves around the clearing. I take a hesitant step back.

"What are you doing?" I ask.

"Testing where you're at," he says. "So far, you've failed observation. How's your combat?"

"What?" I scoff. "I can't fight you like—"

Something flings through the air and strikes me in the forehead.

[1 points of Bludgeoning damage sustained.]

"Ow!" I clutch my head as I glance down at the pebble that's clattered to the ground at my feet. "What was that for?"

"Combat training wasn't a request," Cyros says.

I look up in time to see another pebble flying my way. I flinch away, and it deflects off my arm. "You jerk!"

"If you want to stop me, then stop me," he says. "Feel free to use that blade of yours. I doubt you'll be able to land a blow anyway."

Still rubbing my forehead, I back away as he steps behind a tree and doesn't come out the other side. I raise my knife, gaze darting around the forest. "Cheater!"

"You're a human," he says, the voice coming from my right. I slash in that direction, but my blade only cuts air. "And you're small. You won't win a fair fight against most other species. If you're serious about trying to take down a demigod, the odds will be overwhelmingly stacked against you."

I focus on his voice as he speaks, trying to gauge how far away he is. "So what are you saying? I should just give up?" I lunge forward, stabbing toward his voice. A blade flashes out of the air, deflecting my own and jarring it from my grip. My knife goes spinning away, and I jump back before Cyros's parry can turn into an attack of his own.

"Not at all," he says. "What I'm saying is that you need to evaluate your opponents' abilities and manufacture a way to level the playing field. That's what being an assassin is about, you see. Some people are seen as untouchable. But everyone has a blind spot. It's our job to figure out that opening and exploit it."

I circle away as his rippling form moves to the side. He ducks behind a bush, and I lose track of him once again. I swear under my breath.

"Yeah, real noble," I say, trying to draw a reaction out of him. I glance at my knife, only a few feet away. I'll be exposed when I duck down to grab it. "And I bet you guys go around killing random Lords out of the goodness of your own heart."

"That criticism is a bit hypocritical, don't you think?" he asks.

I track his voice to my left, and I continue to circle around the clearing. It takes every atom of self-control to wait.

"You want someone dead, too," Cyros continues. "Don't you think the world would be a better place without the suffering that some people cause?"

There. "I guess we'll find out."

I dash for the knife. A blur of movement follows. But instead of bending down for my weapon, I pivot and draw my arm back like I'm about to lob a baseball.

[Removing item from inventory.]

The clay jar appears in my hand just as I'm swinging it forward with all my might. Cyros is only a few feet away; he doesn't even stand a chance. The jar strikes him right in the head, exploding apart on impact.

[7 points of Bludgeoning damage dealt.]

Then, the smoke potion goes off.

The liquid that had been contained in the jar explodes in a cloud of green. Cyros cries out, stumbling backward and clutching his face, his outline suddenly clear as day amidst the swirling smoke. Before he can recover, I run forward and tackle him.

We both hit the ground hard, but I have the advantage of landing on a somewhat soft body where he gets to slam into a bunch of grass and rocks. Oh, yeah, and orchids.

[Status Effect inflicted: Poisoned,] Echo chimes in.

Cyros flails at me as I try to disentangle myself, hurriedly backing away while giving him another good kick into the orchid patch. All that struggling sure is squishing the plants and splattering their poisonous sap everywhere. I back away, panting, as I watch in satisfaction as the plant goop slowly outlines his transparent form.

"What the fuck!" The invisible act drops as Cyros looks up at me in horror, scrambling out of the patch of poisonous flowers. "You're crazy!"

"No, I won," I say, smiling devilishly. "What was that about manufacturing a way to level the playing field?"

"We're both poisoned," he says, fumbling with a pouch at his side. "You're suicidal!"

"Hey, I'm not the one that started throwing stones while invisible," I say, reaching for my pocket as well. I take out the orchid poison antidote I'd made and down it.

[Poison status effect reduced,] Echo says.

This stuff isn't as potent as the antidote Cyros gave me that first time, but it slows the damage way down. Between that and my Level 5 Poison Resistance, I'm in no danger.

Cyros pops something in his mouth as well as I Check him.

[Name: Cyros]

[Class: Vine Rogue]

[Level: 24]

[Attack: 54]

[Agility: 43]

[HP: 92/100]

[Cyros is suffering from the status effect Poisoned.]

His HP ticks down two more points as he swallows the draught he'd been carrying, then stops.

[Status effect negated.]

"See?" I say. "You're fine."

"What if I hadn't had that antidote on me?" he asks.

I pull a spare out of my other pocket.

He grunts, looking at me with an odd expression. I can't tell if he's impressed or annoyed. "You had this planned from the start."

Well, not exactly. I knew we were meeting at the orchid patch and I wasn't about to take any chances. I'd put the smoke potion in my inventory on a whim, just in case he could show me how to practice any smoke-bomb-ninja-vanishing-tactics. But I'm not about to let him know it was all desperate improv.

"Is that enough combat practice?" I ask, putting the spare antidote away and offering him my hand.

He takes it, pulling himself to his feet. "Not hardly. You still don't know how to use that knife properly—I'd be embarrassed you caught me with it last week if I still didn't understand how you're doing that sleight of hand. Seriously, where did that smoke bomb come from?"

I shrug with a grin.

"All right then." He glowers. "Don't tell me. But I'll figure it out one of these days."

Somehow, I doubt that.

"So, what next?" I ask.

"Well, that smoke potion was pretty impressive, actually," he says. "Have you got more like that?"

"Not with me," I say. "But I've got a couple back at the Inn. Actually, I'm thinking of making a belt or something so I can carry more around with me at a time. Figured the smoke bombs could be good to use to cover up my tracks if I need to escape anything in a hurry."

"Hm, it's more likely to draw attention than anything," Cyros says. "But a distraction can be equally useful for an escape. The belt idea is good. Strapping it across your chest, like a bandolier, might make the potions easier to reach. What else are you working on?"

I tell him all the potions I made over the last week: the health pots, the general salve, and various antidotes. He seems mildly impressed, although with that wooden dryad face of his, it's a bit hard to gauge.

"I saw you practicing walking intentionally, too," he notes.

"Walking intentionally?" I ask.

"Before I showed up, when you were stepping around the leaves," he explains.

"Oh yeah. Soft Step."

He blinks. "You named it?"

"I didn't—uh." Well, Echo named it, but I can't exactly tell him that. "I mean, I guess."

"Right," he says, skeptical. "Well, at any rate, that's good practice, and it'll pair well with your other abilities. Like I said before, you're at a disadvantage. Getting around without being noticed or drawing attention will help. Those potions are a great start, too. If you can brew something that would work like my camouflage, you might really get somewhere."

"How are you doing that, anyway? Can I learn?" I ask, excited.

"It's a Plant type of magic specific to dryads," he says, "so I doubt it."

I deflate, disappointed.

"You'll want to figure out your own style, anyway," he continues. "What kind of magic have you got?"

"Poison," I say.

He hums thoughtfully. "Interesting. That's a subset of nature magic, which is what I have. Of course, my focus is plant manipulation. There's some overlap between that and fostering poisonous plants, but I've not delved much into potionry. You're already more versed in that subject than me. You should be able to pair it well with knife skills. So that's where we should focus next."

He steps back, clasping his hands behind his back. "Let's see what you've got. Stab me."

I blink. "Um. That doesn't sound safe."

"Come on." He grins, egging me on. "You were taking swipes at me earlier, weren't you? Don't be such a pans—"

I stab my arm forward, aiming for his arm.

He blocks the attempt with his forearm, then wraps his hand around my wrist. He gives it a twist, and the knife slips from my grasp.

"You're too obvious," he says. "You recoil before you stab forward. Try to remove tells so your opponents don't have a warning before you strike." He picks up the knife and hands it back to me. "Now let me see your grip."

Apparently, I've been holding the knife wrong. He moves my thumb, then shows me another couple of ways to grip the knife. Cyros has me try a couple other attacks on him, all of which he blocks or disarms, and soon my arm is sore and throbbing from all the abuse. Then he turns it around, makes slow stabs and swipes toward me, and has me replicate his defenses. It's not nearly as easy as he makes it look, and I can feel my attempts to disarm him are all wrong. As we practice, however, it starts to get a little easier.

[New Skill Obtained,] Echo says. [Self Defense, Level 1.]

Definitely a valuable skill to level up—although I'm not sure how I'll do that on my own.

After hours of practice, Cyros finally calls for a break, glancing toward the sky. The sun is filtering in through the trees but tracking steadily toward the horizon.

"It's late afternoon; I'll need to be heading back soon if I want to make it to Fairwood before my watch starts this evening."

"Your watch?" I ask, sitting down heavily as I catch my breath. It's absolutely annoying that Cyros doesn't even seem to have broken a sweat. I mean, assuming wood people can sweat.

"We mostly work at night," Cyros says. "Technically, I'm supposed to be sleeping now."

"Oh," I say. "Sorry, I didn't mean to interrupt your sleep schedule. I'm sure it's hard enough to get good sleep, what with the weight of everyone you've killed on your conscience."

He looks at me, unimpressed. "You're the one who begged me for classes. And you know, you'd make a good assassin, too. You've got the motives for it."

"That's different," I scoff, offended. "I'm going to kill someone who deserves to die. It's justice."

"Justice is subjective," Cyros says. "And the only person you know I've killed was that politician. Did you know she was tied up with a local gang?"

I snort. "I could care less about her."

"Couldn't care less," Cyros says.

"Huh?"

He shakes his head. "She'd pay them to beat up and threaten the families of political opponents. Never did any of the dirty work herself, of course—plausible deniability and all that. But she funded their operations, and there's plenty of blood on their hands. Killing her dissolved the gang she was keeping propped up and prevented the deaths of more innocents. So you tell me. Was that justice?"

I'm silent for a moment. "I don't know. Depends on the details."

"See? Subjective." He quirks a smile. "If you ever have a change of heart, come find me. You could be a valuable member of my guild. But you don't have to answer now. Just think about it."

I frown, not sure how I feel about being lumped in with a bunch of murderers, even if they claim to be the Robin Hood sort. "When will you be back next?"

"Not for another week or two," he says.

"What?" I cry. "That's not nearly soon enough!"

"I can't just drop everything to spar with you," Cyros says. "I've got obligations too, you know. Besides, you made a lot of progress today."

"Not enough progress," I say. "And not nearly fast enough to get stronger by the Gods' Tournament."

"The Tournament?" Cyros repeats, incredulous. "You can't intend to compete?"

"No!" I object, aghast. The winner of the tournament would become a champion—Widengra's champion. My stomach roils with disgust. "Never!"

"Then why... ah." He shakes his head. "You want to use that as an opportunity to get close to Maru, don't you?"

"Maybe," I admit, glaring.

"You should give that idea up now," Cyros says. "Wanting to challenge Maru is foolish enough as it is, but theoretically not impossible—if you trained all your life and became an expert in your field of magic. Champions might have been given incredible powers by the gods, but they're still mortal."

I open my mouth, but he puts up a hand.

"But trying to achieve that level of power in a few short weeks is highly improbable. If you challenge her now, you'll die. There's no other likely outcome."

"I can't afford to wait my whole life," I say. Especially not when the gods want me dead *now*. What happens if Maru stumbles upon me at some point and realizes she didn't finish me off like she was supposed to? No, I can't leave it up to chance. I have to get her before she gets me. "I need to get stronger as fast as possible."

He lets out a long sigh. "Alright, I'll tell you what. If you can get to Fairwood the night after tomorrow, I should have a couple hours to work with you. That's the best I can offer."

"I'll be there," I say, pouncing on the opportunity. "Anything helps."

Cyros just shakes his head. "Your funeral."

Already had one, I think. And I don't intend to have another.

CHAPTER TWENTY

THE ARENA

"You sure you'll be alright?" Gugora asks. "Fairwood is a big city."

"I got back fine last time," I say. "Don't worry! Talia will let me stay at her place again." Probably, if I ask her. She'll want to hear more about the new 'clues' I found, anyway.

"Just don't forget the ingredients," Iski says. "You sure you won't forget?"

"I won't forget," I promise, shaking the bag she's lending me. It jingles with coins. "Not that you'd let me. That list was very thorough."

"Can't waste a trip to the city," Iski says with a shrug. "Don't go getting arrested again this time."

I grin. "No promises on that one."

Gugora lightly pats me on the shoulder, though with his giant hands it still about knocks me over. "Stay safe."

"Okay, *Dad*." I immediately regret it. Loss twists in my gut, and my own dad comes unbidden to my mind. Gugora's eyes also flicker with some emotion at the word, but I awkwardly turn away before I can identify it.

"Be back tomorrow," I say, trying to throw a nonchalant wave over my shoulder as I start away from the inn, even as my stomach is still doing summersaults. I shove the feelings down, way down, as I make for Fairwood. No time to dwell on the family I'll never see again. No time to think about Gugora or Iski. I've got the mission to focus on. *It's kill or be killed,* I remind myself.

Since I left early, I make it to Fairwood a little after noon. Touching the bark of one of the four giant trees that mark the entry to the city, the magic lights up just like before, and the vines carry me up into the canopy.

The city is an absolute maze of bridges, platforms, and treehouses bubbling out of the trunks like mushrooms on a log. No matter where I look, I can't see an end to it. Does the city extend as far as the rest of the forest? I wouldn't be surprised.

Through a good amount of trial and error, I manage to backtrack my way to Talia's property. When I try to open the gate, however, nothing happens. Maybe Talia took me off the "approved users" list after I left.

Seeing little other options, I head over to the trunk that the path is wound around. The bark looks rough enough that I think I can climb it to get over the fence. I stuff my hand between a gap in the rough surface and push myself upward. Sure enough, it's pretty easy to scale. These fences aren't very secure, are they? Once I'm fence-level, I start to shimmy my way over.

A blur of movement is the only warning I get before a branch swings down out of the tree and smacks right into me. It rips my grip from the bark, and then I'm airborne. I have the briefest moment to feel surprised before the ground rushes up to meet me.

I slam into the path and go rolling.

[8 points of Bludgeoning damage sustained.]

I groan, rolling over and pushing myself up to my knees. Vines are hanging down over the gate, slowly undulating back and forth like a watchdog looking for an intruder. Okay, then. I won't be sneaking in that way. Guess that also explains why Cyros was out here waiting for me when he ambushed me.

Limping back down the trail, my pride bruised almost as bad as my tailbone, I glance around for anyone who might have seen my failed attempt at a break in. Luckily, it seems no one was present to notice my embarrassment.

"Hey," I say, stopping at the first person I see. The dryad looks up at me. "Do you know where Talia is? Er, Talia Greenhand."

"I suspect she's at the arena," the dryad says. "That's where everyone is these days."

"Right, the arena." I pause. "And where is that exactly?"

They lift an eyebrow. "New to town?"

"You could say that. So, the arena?"

The dryad points me in the right direction and I head off. Too bad—I'd wanted another chance to snoop around her library before meeting up with Cyros tonight. Maybe I can convince Talia to swing by after she's done working. What does an academic do for a day job, anyway? Surely she can read books from her house.

As I follow the dryad's directions, there's more and more people about. I mean, that shouldn't be surprising, given I'm in a city, but the bridges are clogged with people, the air filled with harpies. Man, that guy wasn't kidding when they said everyone's here these days.

Stuck in the foot traffic, I shuffle up a spiraling set of stairs, taking me into the treetops. When I reach the top, I have to shield my eyes from the sun suddenly bearing down on me. I squint at my surroundings through the bright light, then stop in my tracks.

"Whoa."

Arena is an understatement. An enormous wooden field has been built into the treetops, benches ringing the perimeter like a sports stadium, the tallest trees of which loom over the field like viewing towers. The arena itself doesn't look new, but the seating is under construction, with dozens of dryads raising further wooden benches and branch scaffolding with plant magic.

Someone jostles me from behind, and I stumble forward, realizing I've been holding up traffic.

"Is this where the Gods' Tournament will be?" I ask the nearest passerby.

The harpy nods. "Where else?"

"Seems like it's still being fixed up," I say. "Is that why there's so many people here?"

He gives me a funny look. "Not hardly. They're here to sign up—or watch others sign up out of curiosity."

"That's today?" I ask, surprised.

"Every day this week," the harpy says. He heads off—rather purposefully, I'd note—before I can ask him anything else.

Well, might as well snoop around while I'm here. This is where Maru will be the day of the tournament, after all. I'll need to familiarize myself with the ins and outs of this place.

I start to circle around the path I'm on, near the top of the seats, looking down into the stadium. There's a small crowd down there, though I can't make out the details of what they're doing.

I wander the grounds, making half a loop around the arena before heading down the benches. They're almost like bleachers, in that there's hollow space beneath the wooden seats where I can see more foliage below. Possibly a good place to hide, assuming it doesn't just drop straight through the forest. Something to investigate later when I have some rope.

As I wander the stadium, approaching the field at its base, I gradually get the feeling I'm being watched. I glance around as goosebumps prickle my arms, unsure if it's just my imagination. The group of people on the field are closer now, and one seems to be looking my way: a human girl, maybe in her late teens or early twenties, wearing round black glasses.

Echo, Check, I think, focusing on the girl. I can't even say why, she just gives me the willies. Uneasily, I continue my approach toward the bottom, circling around the stadium seats.

Check? I say again, realizing Echo hadn't replied.

[—]

[Lisari: Level 21 human alchemist,] Echo replies. [She is a visiting academic from Hearthstone studying under Talia Greenhand.]

As I reach the field, the girl remains facing the direction I'd been, however, rather than following me around. And as I get closer, I can see why. Embarrassment floods through me at the realization: she's blind.

"Sal?"

I turn to find Talia stalking over in my direction.

"What are you doing here?" she asks.

"I came to visit you," I say. "Went to your house but you weren't there. What are *you* doing here?"

"The council hired me as a consultant for the architecture," she says, gesturing around the stadium. "Apparently they need a historian to get the decorations right. Don't want to offend a god." Her tone is dismissive, almost sarcastic: I guess she's just as impressed with the gods' bullshit as I am. "You should have given me notice you were coming."

"How?" I ask. "If I wanted to send a letter, I'd have to walk it to the city anyway."

"Fair point." She's looking anywhere but at me, clearly distracted. "We should move this discussion somewhere private."

I suppose rumors around her sister's murder are probably not best discussed in public.

"Lisari?" Talia calls.

The girl turns in our direction, a breeze accompanying the motion. Leaves swirl around her as she heads over to us, brushing against the ground and clothes of those she passes.

"Professor?" Lisari asks. The wind dies down and the leaves come to a rest around her: I'm not sure what she's doing, but it's clearly some kind of magic.

"I'm heading inside if you care to join," Talia says. "Sal, this is Lisari, a visiting research associate from a sister academy come to help with the tournament preparations."

"I couldn't help but jump at the opportunity," Lisari says. "It isn't every day you meet a god, is it?"

"Yeah," I say flatly.

Lisari tips her head at my tone.

"You two might have something in common to chat about," Talia quickly cuts in, perhaps suspecting I was about to go on an anti-god tirade in public. "Lisari might be able to help you with your magic, Sal. Her area of study is Alchemy, which has a good bit of overlap with your Poison affinity."

"Poison? How interesting!" Lisari says. "I could definitely offer some reading suggestions."

"Yeah?" I say.

"Of course." She smiles. "Always happy to have an excuse to talk about my passion. Oh, but where are my manners? It's a pleasure to meet you!" She holds out a hand.

I almost don't shake it—I'm not looking to make friends with any god fangirls—but she can't be all bad if she's willing to teach me some

Poison magic. I clasp her hand and she grins, shaking it much firmer than I was expecting.

"Come on," Talia says, gesturing for us to follow. "You two can chat on the way."

I hesitate for a moment, unsure if I should help Lisari, but a breeze picks up once more and she strides confidently after Talia. For a moment, I wonder if I was wrong about her being blind. I catch up with them both, glancing at Lisari and trying to get a good look at her glasses. They're thick and black, completely obscuring her eyes.

"You're wondering about these?" she asks, tapping the lenses.

I startle at being caught staring and quickly glance away. "Um, yeah... Sorry. Wait, how did you see that?"

"I didn't," she says with a chuckle. She raises a hand, and a leaf swirls around her fingers. "Well, not with my eyes, anyway. Wind magic helps me sense my surroundings. I can 'see' pretty much everything around me within a small range as long as I have my wind moving. Where people are, which way they're facing, the expressions they're making. The only real downside is I can't read books. But I've other ways to work around that."

"And the glasses?" I ask.

"I've been told my eyes can be a bit unnerving," Lisari says. "I wear them for the benefit of others."

I'm quickly reevaluating my previous judgments of Lisari. She might be a fan of the gods, but frankly, that seems true for most people here. I'm a little impressed with her, actually. She started with less than what most people have and was able to overcome it. Maybe I can do the same.

Talia takes us to a passage at the base of the arena that leads beneath the stands. Under the stadium is a whole new labyrinth of buildings, strung about the trees in the standard Fairwood style.

"You should stay down here," Talia tells me once we're out of the crowd. She leads the way over a network of swinging bridges toward a nondescript building labeled 'Storage.' "Probably not a good idea to be visiting this place regardless."

"Someone told me people are registering to compete in the tournament," I say. "Is that why you don't want me here?"

"Indirectly, yes," she says. "It would be wise to wait until this week is over before returning. Also, I'd prefer if you didn't come see me while I'm at work. Our matters should be discussed at my home." She glances toward Lisari significantly.

Message received: no talking about dead sister in front of the work colleagues. Not that I have real information to tell Talia anyway; it would just be more made-up crap from Cyros.

"So, Poison," Lisari says as we step into the Storage building. "That's such a unique affinity. I'm sure there's some story there. Not inherited, was it?"

"I got poisoned," I say flatly.

She chuckles as she wanders off into the room. "That's one way to do it."

Storage is a one-room building, like most the others I've been in, and it reminds me vaguely of Talia's home library, except this one is four times the size and packed with all manner of junk. Flags, trophies, track equipment, cleaning supplies—no wonder Talia seems less than thrilled to be working here. They stuck her in the supply closet.

She and Lisari move toward a corner of the room that has been cleared away, mountains of junk stacked in makeshift walls around their workspace. This area looks a bit more scholarly, with tables covered in stacks of books.

"Poison," Lisari muses, raising a hand. A breeze stirs in the room, fluttering papers. "Hmm, tricky. Perhaps it's personal bias, but I think you could start with something closer to my field of expertise."

She heads over to a cluster of books next to the table and crouches down next to them. Pulling a red stone on a chain from around her neck, she runs the necklace down the spine of a book. A quiet voice emitting from the stone begins reading the titles Lisari scans.

"Alchemic Theory. Advanced Circle Applications. History of Widengra. Of Alchemy and the Gods."

I Check the device, curious.

[Amulet of Translation,] Echo says. [Enchanted to convert Common text into Common speech.]

Pretty handy. It's interesting to see how magic has supplemented certain technologies we have on Earth. I wonder if they have anything that can help someone like me who has little-to-no mana pool to work with.

"Aha!" Lisari runs her hand down the spine of a thick, cracked leather book and pulls it from the stacks. Compared to the flimsy herb book I'd nicked from Talia's place, this one is so heavy and dense it could probably be classified as a weapon.

"Try this," Lisari says, coming back over to me. "It can be a bit advanced in places, but it starts with the basics and works up from there. I've found the content invaluable."

"Thank you," I say, taking the textbook from Lisari—and nearly dropping it. Damn, this thing is heavy. I flip to the front page and check the title: *An Exploration of Alchemy*, it says. "You really think it will work with my kind of magic?"

"Not every spell, but many of them." She quirks a smile to one side. "Of course, there's only one way to find out."

I return the grin. That's my kind of learning. "Can we try here? Now?"

"Well, I don't have all my equipment with me," Lisari says. "But we could at least go over some of the simple spells together. It's a little bit of potion making, a little bit of spell circles, and a lot of ingredients and ritual. You know, some people see alchemy as a science but I think there's a certain artistry to it. From this chaotic mix of materials and practices comes some effect that's entirely new. That's beautiful, don't you think?"

"That's enough philosophy, Lisari," Talia grumbles from her desk. "If you two are done, then I could use some help with—"

A crack of thunder shakes the air, and the shelves in the room quiver, shaking off a layer of dust.

"What was that?" Talia says.

An icy fear lances through my chest. I grab the side of the desk, my legs suddenly weak, my head swimming as hot and cold flash through me in alarmed waves. It's a sound I'll never forget. A sound that still snaps through my nightmares right when I've convinced myself I'm no longer scared. The sound that precedes death.

"Maru," I try to say, but it comes out as a whisper.

Chapter Twenty-One

Maru

"What?" Lisari says. "Maru? How do you know?"

Talia swears under her breath. "Come on." She beckons to me. "We have to get you out of here."

"Why?" Lisari asks, her eyebrows knit together in confusion. "We were expecting her to appear sometime today. Shouldn't we be heading out to greet her?"

Images of Maru flash through my mind. Those emotionless, liquid silver eyes. Her stabbing Terimus in his gut. Kicking Rena across the ground. The cruel laughter as they died and bled out at her hand. My shoulder throbs with the memory of her spear lodging into my back.

I jump as a hand touches my shoulder.

"Hey," Lisari says. "Are you okay?"

I shake my head, trying to clear my thoughts. My body is trembling. I thought I'd boxed all this terror away; I thought I'd drowned it with anger and revenge. But I'm still just a frightened kid after all.

"Come on," Talia says, heading for the door. "There's an emergency staircase that should lead us back to Fairwood without having to pass back through the arena. Quickly now."

I stuff Lisari's book in my bag and force my legs into motion, adrenaline spiking through me with each footfall. I can hear my heart beating in my ears. I can feel my body pulse with each beat.

Your funeral, Cyros had said.

He's right. I'd die if she found me now. I'm not ready. All I can do is run.

I swallow down the fear that's threatening to drown me and hurry after Talia. Lisari tips her head in confusion but follows with a gust of wind.

"Why?" I ask Talia as we head out of the Archives, in the underbelly of the stadium once more. She's helping me get away from Maru, but all I'd told her last time was that I didn't like her or Widengra. She's acting like she knows I'm in danger, though. "How did you know?"

"Having a sister on the Council gets you access to certain communications not everyone has access to," Talia says. "After your last visit I did some digging. I remembered my sister mentioning some murdered adventurers on the outskirts of town a few weeks back—not far from your inn, in fact. From there it wasn't hard to track down the healer who had been called to help with that event. After speaking with her, your comments about Maru suddenly made sense." She glances back at me. "For what it's worth, I'm sorry. Were the ones who died your friends?"

My throat tightens. "We'd just met. Maybe we could have been. But I'll never know. She killed them." I squeeze the strap of the bag. *And someday, I'll pay her back in kind.*

"What?" Lisari demands. The anger and disbelief in her voice surprises me. "Maru tried to kill you?"

I don't have the emotional bandwidth to argue over the morality of demigods, so I just nod sharply.

"That was a mistake," Lisari murmurs.

Above us, the arena rumbles and thumps, like boulders are being knocked around the field. The bridge we're on sways and all three of us stop, waiting for the path to stabilize. Unlike the rest of the city, the bridges down here are less permanent streets and more catwalks and wooden plank bridges suspended by vines.

"What's going on up there?" I ask.

"Tryouts," Talia says, moving once more. "Maru informed us she would be inspecting the candidates throughout the week and endorsing the finalists who met her acceptance criteria." She grimaces. "She didn't say *how* she was gauging worthiness. Of course it's probably making them fight each other or something. I don't know what else I expected from the Champion of War."

Her derision surprises me. I thought everyone here worshiped the gods. Or maybe they do, but the gods' champions aren't given the same reverence.

"Here." Talia stops next to a tree where a rickety staircase spirals down the thin trunk.

My stomach does a flip when I look down and can see the streets of Fairwood several stories below me.

"This should get you back in the crowds," Talia says. "And as I said before, I strongly suggest you stay away from the stadium for the next week. In fact, you should probably stay away from Fairwood altogether. I doubt she intends to wander our streets, but it would be best not to risk it."

"Thank you," I say, shame filling me with the knowledge that I'm really about to run away like a kicked dog. All that bravado, all that practice and training, just for me to show my real colors when I'm finally given what I want. *It's too soon,* I try to tell myself. *I wouldn't be running if I had more time.* But even I don't know if I believe it.

"Just tell me one thing," Talia says as I linger at the top of the staircase. "Do you know why she did it?"

"Yes," I say. Because I'm from another world. Because she sees me as some kind of abomination, or something.

"Can you tell me why?"

I hesitate, glancing at Lisari. It's not that I think Talia would turn me over to Maru. If she put this much together before now, it shows she's able to keep my secret. But I'm not sure about Lisari. As much as she's willing to help me with my magic, would her loyalty to the gods prove stronger?

Talia follows my gaze. "Right. We'll talk about it later. For now, I have to get back up there—I was supposed to greet Maru when she arrived and my absence has likely gone noticed. Lisari, let's go."

Lisari rests a hand on my shoulder and gives it a reassuring squeeze. "I don't know what you did to draw this champion's ire, but I wish you luck. It is not cowardice to choose to live another day."

Indignation instinctively swells within me at those words. I didn't do anything to deserve this. I know Lisari doesn't mean it like that, but it still stings. I'm not a coward, either! I'm just... retreating for now. That's the smart thing to do.

[—]

Lisari drops her hand and hurries after Talia, a breeze accompanying her departure. I take a step down the stairs and stop.

This might be the tactical thing to do, but thinking of Terimus and Rena and Layf, it doesn't feel like the *brave* thing to do. It's not right. They deserve vengeance, not for people to assume they did something wrong to have drawn judgment from the gods. They protected me, while I'm standing here ready to abandon a chance at avenging them.

I close my eyes and scrunch my face up, fingernails digging into the palms of my hands. I can still leave. I can still walk away. Taking Maru on now is suicide.

But if I give up this chance, will I be sure to have another? Sure, there's always the tournament, but there will be thousands of more people here then. Too many unknowns.

I open my eyes and blow everything out in one breath, weight falling from my shoulders now that I've made up my mind.

I have to at least take a look.

I wait until Lisari and Talia vanish back into the maze of bridges, then head back down the bridge as well, leaving the staircase behind. Above me is a network of catwalks and vines, all hanging from beneath the floor of the stadium, and above that are the rows of branches-turned seats, slanting up toward the canopy. I don't have to make a move just yet. But if I could get up there, I could at least scope out the scene in secret. Maybe, like Cyros said, I could learn something that might clue me in to any of her weaknesses.

I keep my eyes on the stadium seats, trying to chart a path as high as I can climb. The stairs and platforms and wood plank bridges only take me up about level with the stadium floor. Beyond that is all support branches and vines, but no paths with guardrails or handholds. I glance down and immediately regret it.

"Okay," I mumble to myself, setting my sights on some stadium seats where sunlight is slanting through the slats. They're about twenty feet overhead and the same distance away. A tangle of plants between me and the bleachers provide a way for me to get there—as long as I don't slip.

First things first. I take off my scarf and wrap it around my forehead and mouth, leaving room for my eyes and nose. Suspicious? Yes, but at least if she does see me, she won't recognize me at first glance.

Checking that my knife is on my belt, I next remove the one item from my inventory: well, items, really.

[Removing bandolier from inventory,] Echo says.

A belt of potions appears in my hands. After further experiments, I discovered that as long as two things were securely attached to each other, they counted as one object. That was why the bag of spices hadn't worked before. But if I sewed a pot onto the mesh of a bag, then it all vanished and reappeared together.

It took some trial and error to get the belt of potions idea to work, as anything that wasn't strapped down tight enough didn't "count" and would get left behind in reality. But that wasn't anything some leather and thread couldn't fix.

I strap the potions on now, secured like a bandolier, as Cyros had suggested, running from my left shoulder to right hip. The seven potions I'd made are arrayed across my chest, all sealed with a cork and wax. It's not a lot, but it's what I've got to work with. I add Iski's bag back into my inventory so I won't have to carry it.

[Bag added to inventory.]

The book *thumps* to the ground and the coins that had been in the bag go scattering across the walk.

"Shit!" I pounce after them, snatching up half the coins and for-lornly watching the other half slip through the cracks and fall down into the city. Well. I guess it will be someone's lucky day.

I angrily take the bag back out of the inventory and put the re-maining coins back inside it. I guess Echo didn't deem them secure enough. I add Lisari's book to the inventory instead, as it's the heaviest and most unwieldy of my belongings, and then put the bag over my opposite shoulder, crossing the bandolier. That will have to do, I guess.

Potions out, book secured, face covered, hands free—I grab two support vines and pull myself up onto the guardrail of my bridge. I really, really wish I'd been training some sort of balance Skill before now.

My grip tightens on the vines as I keep my gaze glued on my target and refuse to look down. I step away from the bridge and out onto the nearest branch. It's thin and bends beneath my weight, but holds. I scoot my hands along the vine, and begin to tightrope-walk my way through the underbelly of the stadium.

The path isn't actually that difficult. It's kind of like playing on a jungle gym, climbing between beams and ropes; the only difference is certain death if I slip and fall. Yeah, just like a jungle gym.

By the time I reach the seats, I'm covered in cold sweat. My arms are shaking with adrenaline, and every limb aches from tension. When I finally grab onto one of the benches, pulling my face up to the gap between seat and floor, I'm ready to fall over with relief. Instead, I loop my arms around some nearby vines for extra security, then lean forward, blinking against the light.

The arena looks like a battlefield. There's scorch marks on the ground where there hadn't been before, and scratches and dents cover the field, including some of the seats. Even as I watch, a woman summons a fireball and launches it toward me. No, toward the woman standing in front of me.

My stomach turns to ice the moment I see her. Even from behind, over fifty feet away, her form is unmistakable.

Like before, her armor is red, swirled with silver designs that seem to weave seamlessly into her braided hair. Her skin is radiant like the clouds, and the giant spear she wields is decorated with dozens of colorful tassels.

In my mind, I watch as the spear pierces Terimus's stomach once again. I feel it slam into my back, pinning me to the ground. I scream as Maru gleefully wrenches it out of me.

The hatred kindling in my core bursts into a flame, its heat comforting and empowering.

Maru dismissively slashes her spear through the air, cutting through the fireball and sending a wave of flame to either side. Both dissipate before they can reach my hiding place.

"Pathetic," Maru says. "Someone show me some real power!"

They're showing off their magic, is it? Figures a show of force is all she'd care about. Strength is the only metric that matters to the gods, it seems.

Her back is to me. She's distracted by all the champion wannabees, each pathetically begging for the opportunity to join her ranks. If I wanted a chance, this is it.

I run a hand down my bandolier, lingering at the bottom one: orchid poison. Would it be enough to kill a demigod? She might be level 92, but she's not immortal. Maybe it would be enough to weaken her. Enough that other poisons could finish the job.

I pop the cork off the orchid poison and unsheathe my knife, carefully dipping the blade into the sap. I point the blade up, letting the poison slowly drip down its length to cover the knife as much as possible, then I use the lip of the bottle to wipe off the excess and replace the cork. Carefully holding the knife to the side, I use my free hand to touch each of the other six bottles in turn, mentally cataloging their contents. My knife hand trembles.

Maru moves, and my attention snaps back to the arena. Am I too late? Did I hesitate too long? Miraculously, though, I realize she's not heading away from me, but *toward* me. Maru leisurely wanders backwards until she reaches the bottom seat of the stadium, then sits down, one ankle kicked up on her other knee, elbow planted on her leg, chin resting in her hand. I stare in awe. She's only six rows down from where I'm hiding.

"Boring!" she calls to the candidates in the field before her. "And you think you're worthy of the gods' time and attention? Don't make me laugh. Give me a real show!"

You want a real show? I think. *Alright. You got it.*

I quickly cut through the vines that serve as a guard beneath the seats, then quietly set my knife down, grabbing the lip of the bench and getting ready to pull myself through. My legs are crouched on the branch just beneath me. My arms are shaking with anticipation. Electricity jolts through my limbs, taut and ready to leap into action.

I gauge the distance between us. It'll take a few seconds to shimmy between the seats. I can probably jump down to Maru in two leaps. It will all be over in ten seconds. All that's left now is to pick the moment to strike.

I wait another minute, maybe two. The candidates all show off their pathetic excuses for magic and combat abilities. Then, a shadow passes over the arena. Someone on the field is waving their arms as a giant cloud is conjured into existence overhead. Everyone's looking up as electricity flashes from inside it. It's the perfect distraction. Now. I have to go now!

Chapter Twenty-Two

CANDIDATE'S MARK

I throw myself forward, scraping and squeezing myself beneath the bench. A knot catches on my side, scratching along my ribs, but I hardly feel it. I wiggle forward, desperate, clawing—grab my knife—and then I'm through.

Maru tilts her head as if she's going to look back. She must have heard something, but it's too late, I'm already jumping down the seats toward her, knife raised. I slam down on the first bench, still four rows away from Maru. I stumble, my leg giving out. Now, she does turn.

Terror, desperation, exhilaration all crash through me. I grab the second bottle on my bandolier, already springing to my feet as I yank it from its strap and throw it at Maru. Her eyes land on me, halfway twisted around, as the bottle strikes her shoulder, exploding as if it hit a brick wall.

I jump toward her, my last jump, probably to my death, as the smoke bomb in that bottle erupts into a geyser of green. The smoke engulfs both of us, and there's nothing more I can do now as I fly blindly through the air, knife swinging for her neck.

My knife strikes against something hard. I crash into her next, and then everything is a blur of pain. I scramble to latch on, to gain leverage so I can plunge my knife deeper, but I only feel it scrape over something unyielding, like trying to pierce a rock, and then white flashes through my vision and I'm pinwheeling through the air. I only register the pain in my head from where I'd been struck when I crash into the ground and go rolling.

[14 points Bludgeoning damage sustained.]

[3 points Bludgeoning damage sustained.]

[6 points Bludgeoning damage sustained.]

[3 points Bludgeoning damage sustained.]

[2 points Bludgeoning damage sustained.]

The sky is spinning above me. My arm and head and knee are all screaming in pain. Someone nearby is coughing. A hint of green drifts into my vision, and my thoughts finally stop rattling around enough for me to gather my wits—my knife isn't in my hand anymore. Where's my knife?

I struggle to roll onto my side and stand, but the blow to my head knocked loose my sense of balance, and I tip back over onto the ground once more, landing hard on an already injured shoulder. Pain lances through me, and I gasp in a breath.

People are yelling. There's a thunder of approaching footsteps. The coughing turns gradually into laughter—unhinged laughter. A laugh I'd know anywhere.

No. The fear creeps back in. *No, no, no!*

I struggle upright, only making it to my hands and knees, still swaying from Maru's blow. A crowd of contestants gather around me, weapons drawn, but I pay them no mind. Where's Maru? Where's my knife? I can't give up now. I can't!

"No!" Maru shouts, her voice booming across the field. "Leave them for me."

The competitors back away, and finally my swimming vision slows enough for my gaze to land on Maru.

She waves a wisp of my smoke away, crossing the ground with a feral smile on her face. My insides seize up, a cold so intense it burns, and I'm not sure if my fear or hate for her is stronger.

"You tried to kill me," she says with a chuckle, causing many of the onlookers to gasp and whisper.

I push myself to my feet, but the world tips and I crash to the ground once more. No, not now. Work with me, body. You can't betray me now!

Maru laughs at my pathetic attempt at defiance. I try to get up, but the butt of her spear cracks into my chest, flipping me onto my back.

[3 points Bludgeoning damage sustained.]

She plants the end on my chest, its pressure pushing down on me like a promise. "I recommend you stay down," she says.

I grind my teeth, grab the butt of the spear anyway, but I might as well be trying to push a piece of rebar out of the way.

She holds up my knife with her other hand. "Is this yours?"

If I'm going to die, I won't do it begging for my life. "Yes."

"You landed a blow," she tells me. "You never could have done any damage, but you at least connected. You know where you hit me?"

I stiffly shake my head, mentally seething. She's mocking me. Belittling my attempt. I hate her all the more because I know she's right: I never had a hope of doing any real damage.

She taps her temple. "Any mortal would be dead. Not to mention..." She runs her finger down the length of the blade, then rubs her fingers together.

Echo chimes in. [Status effect inflicted: Poisoned]

And then the very next moment: [Status effect expired.]

My last flicker of hope snuffs out.

Maru throws her head back and laughs once more. "Delightful." She excitedly holds it up for others to see. "Can you believe that? She poisoned it!"

She tosses it to the ground next to me, and I immediately grab for it, but the blade is just out of reach.

Maru leans in, grinning. "See? Even now she hasn't given up. She's still trying!"

My ears grow hot at the mockery, and I stop scrabbling for the knife. *Pathetic.* I must look like a child. Instead, I turn my glare back on her, narrowing my eyes.

"Oh, I love that look," Maru says. "That's the look I've been waiting for. No fear. No reservation. That *passion.* I could eat it up." She turns back to the crowd who's by now giving us a wide berth. "You all should be ashamed. This kid is making you look bad. I demanded no hesitation. I demanded that you show me everything you've got. And the only one who's piqued my interest today is this runt. Now." She leans down, reaching for my scarf. "Let's see what we're working with."

Fear edges out my anger and humiliation as I realize she's about to see my face. She'll recognize me for sure. She'll know she failed to kill me the first time. "No!" I cry, grabbing her outstretched hand. She brushes past my grip like I'm not even there, then tugs the scarf away.

I freeze as Maru's eyes trace over me. I stop breathing, pinned to the moment like I'm frozen in time, knowing this is it: the last thing I'll ever see is Maru's mirthless smile bearing down on me.

"Well what do we have here?" she says. Then she touches a finger to my forehead, and time restarts with a searing pain.

I gasp, arching under her grip, as it feels like a hot iron is driven through my skull. My mouth opens, but no scream comes out. I want to thrash, but every muscle has seized up. I want to curse Maru, to tell her how I feel, but all I can think about is the lance of heat through my mind.

Then, the sensation vanishes. The pain dulls to a faint ache. My sight returns as Maru releases me, and the pressure of her spear against my chest vanishes.

"Congratulations," Maru says. "We have our first contestant for the Gods' Tournament."

What? I touch my forehead, where the ghost of her touch still burns on my skin. No, she can't mean that. That has to be a mistake. "Wait," I croak.

Maru strolls away, surveying the rest of the applicants. "I'm done with you all for today. Come back tomorrow and show me a real fight."

And with a crack of thunder, she's gone.

I lay there, stunned, thoughts buzzing through my brain like a hive of bees. She didn't recognize me. She didn't kill me. And not only did I fail to kill her, she didn't even consider me a nuisance. She was *amused* by my attempt. Frustration stings my eyes, burning alongside the brand on my head.

I touch it again, as if I'd merely imagined it the first time, numb with shock. She couldn't have. She *can't*.

"Sal!"

Talia's voice breaks through the murmurs of the other contestants, all still milling about and talking amongst each other in hushed tones.

I groan, rolling over onto my side. Everything hurts. *Echo. Health Check.*

[HP: 59/90]

"Are you alright?" Talia drops down to my side. Before I can even answer, she sucks in a startled breath. "Lorata's Grace. What did you do?"

"What is it?" Lisari jogs up behind Talia, her head cocked curiously to the side. "Sal, how did you get up here?"

"I fucked up," I mumble as Talia helps me sit up. "I should have just left. Why? Why didn't she recognize me?" I blink rapidly, trying to banish the tears before they can fall. "Did we really mean so little to her? It would have been better if she recognized me."

"Gods Above," Lisari says, likely putting things together. "You didn't come up here to confront Maru, did you? How did you survive?"

I don't say anything, but Talia answers for me. "She's been marked. Widengra's insignia. You've been entered in the tournament, haven't you?"

My throat seizes, frustrated, angry, desperate. "I didn't want to. She just did it. She—she thought I was *competing*. She didn't even take me seriously." I look up at Talia. "I don't have to do it, do I? I can just not show up."

But the apologetic look in Talia's eyes doesn't lend me any hope.

Lisari grimaces. "When the gods expect something from us mortals, it's never an ask," she says. "It's a promise."

CHAPTER TWENTY-THREE

CONGRATS, YOUR APPLICATION HAS BEEN APPROVED

"What do you mean I don't have a choice?" I demand.

Talia had refused to answer anything else until we made it back to her place and I got patched up. I slipped my knife back into my Inventory, just so it wouldn't accidentally poison any present company, which meant I had to carry my bandolier and Lisari's alchemy book all the way there. Whatever Talia thinks of my new accessories, she's kept it to herself.

Lisari sips at her lemon mint tea, appearing quite content to listen to Talia and I go back and forth, as I throttle my own mug between my hands.

Talia grimaces. "The spell circle she marked you with. There's a summoning component. I suspect you'll be pulled into the arena the day of the tournament no matter where you are."

I glance down at the hand mirror Talia had lent me, once again catching sight of the mark. It's an intricate circle about an inch across, shapes and runes making a complex network of lines, and at its center is the likeness of a spear. I clap a hand to my forehead, as if hiding the brand would make it go away. It throbs faintly beneath the warmth of my hand. "It's not fair. They can't just make me compete against my will!"

"They can, and technically, you tried out for it," Talia points out. "You just had to go sneaking back in after I took you to the exit. I *told* you to avoid the arena!"

"I didn't know attacking her was the tryout!" I exclaim. "I thought they were just showing off their magic or something."

"So what outcome were you expecting, exactly?" Lisari pipes up. "You thought you could kill a demigod?"

"I thought this was my best shot at it," I say.

"That doesn't sound very confident," Lisari points out. "You were expecting you might fail, then?"

I shrug. "I was hoping to win, but... yeah. I knew losing was an option."

"And then what?" she presses. "Did you really think she would be forgiving of a failed assassination attempt?"

"I'm not stupid," I grumble.

"Just suicidal then," Lisari says. She takes another sip of tea. "Why would an attempt on Maru's life be worth dying for?"

"Because it's me or her," I say before I can think any better of it.

Lisari and Talia are silent for a moment.

"You're referring to the others Maru killed a few weeks ago," Talia says. "Can you tell me why? You seem to believe she wanted you all dead, but you haven't explained."

I shake my head, stuffing down the sorrow almost as soon as it starts to well up. "Not all of them. Just me."

"Why?" Talia presses.

I hesitate, glancing between Talia and Lisari. "I... don't think it'd be safe for you if I said why. But I guess it doesn't matter. She didn't even recognize me." Like I was nothing to her. Inconsequential. I could have just continued on with my life and she would have been none the wiser.

Perhaps. Why do the gods want to kill people from another world in the first place? What if they find out Maru didn't finish the job? Can I avoid them forever?

Well, one thing's for sure: I won't be able to avoid Widengra at the end of this month.

I groan, sinking into my chair and knocking my head against the table. "What am I going to do?"

"It doesn't seem you've much choice in the matter," Talia says. "Show up to the tournament. Intentionally lose in the first round before you can be hurt by anyone far more experienced. And pray their tournament is not a fight to the death."

"Who am I going to pray to?" I scoff. "The gods?"

"Not all the champions are like Maru, you know," Lisari says. "And not all of the gods are like Widengra. If you've got gods working against you, you best find some to work with you."

I roll my eyes. Of course she'd say that. She doesn't have any gods trying to kill her. And how could I trust a god not to act the same way Maru did? They have to know people like Maru are champions. If none of the other gods have objected to Widengra's choice in champions, then they're all equally complicit.

"She's right," Talia adds. "If you really do believe Widengra is against you, you won't stand a chance without some other Patron God to protect you. We have many temples in the city. Perhaps if you made an offering and prayed for their assistance—"

"No," I cut in, disgusted. "I'm not going to go begging for their help. As far as I'm concerned, they're all the same. I'll find my own way."

"What can you expect to do in just a few weeks?" Talia asks.

I rub my forehead. "There's really no way to remove it?"

"No," Talia says, at the same time Lisari says, "Yes."

We both look at her.

"I mean, it's technically not impossible," Lisari says. "Maru could choose to dismiss the mark any time."

I snort at that.

"Or, her magic would vanish if she were to die," Lisari adds.

I sit up. "Really?"

Talia sighs. "Please, Lisari, she doesn't need encouragement."

"So it *is* possible," I say, my mind racing. A way to get out of the tournament. A way to avoid Widengra. And I'd get my revenge on Maru, too.

Sure. Easy. But... "I have to try."

Talia rubs her temples. "What exactly do you intend to do?"

The only thing I can do, I suppose.

"Study," I say, putting a hand on the alchemy book Lisari lent me. "Practice." If I want to survive this, I need to expedite my magic and fighting progress tenfold.

"I can't say that sounds wise," Lisari says, smiling faintly, "but that's some resolve. Here, let me mark some of the passages in that book before you go. It's as much as I can help."

"Thank you," I say.

Talia just shakes her head. "If I'd known you were this much of a fool, I doubt I would have conscripted your help with my sister's murder."

Oh, yeah. With everything else going on, I'd forgotten about that. "That reminds me," I tell her. "I talked with Iski and Gugora—ah, the inn's owners—and I might have some more information for you."

Talia just sighs, not appearing nearly as interested as I'd expected. "All right, then. Let's have it."

While I dole out some more lies Cyros gave me, Lisari flips through the Alchemy book, her translator quietly reading out excerpts of chapter titles as she skims through the tome, dog-earing important passages. Although I'm more interested in what spells Lisari is gathering for me, I try to stay focused on Cyros's mistruths. This time, repeating them to Talia makes me feel a little guilty. *She wasn't even close to her sister*, I tell myself, hoping that makes the betrayal feel less, somehow. *The lies don't hurt anyone.*

Talia listens intently, nodding along to my "report." It's some bullshit about timelines, when Cyros had supposedly come and gone, and something else that had supposedly been "overheard" in the Starlight.

"The Architect's Guild," Talia repeats, skeptical. "But what would they stand from making a move on the Council? Their position's already secure."

I shrug. "I don't know. Doesn't mean anything to me." Probably the first truthful thing I've told her since the talk about the tournament.

"Very well," she says, idly spinning her cup around on the table. "Thank you for the additional information. I will put out some feelers and see what progress I can make on investigating these claims."

I mentally grimace. Good luck with that.

"In the meantime," Talia says, "you should be more focused on how you're going to survive the tournament. Especially if they won't let you forfeit in the first round."

"I've got some ideas," I say, touching a hand to my bandolier. "First, I need to get stronger."

I do, in fact, buy the ingredients Iski asked for. Probably not as much as she wanted, given I lost half her money sneaking into the arena, but at least I'll have something to show for my trip to Fairwood when I return.

You know, besides a mark from the gods burned into my forehead.

Talia seemed a bit sad when I left, and Lisari was a bit disappointed as well, though I think for her it was more morbid curiosity. But I couldn't stick around all day. After completing Iski's grocery run, I still have one more stop on my list.

I spend the last two coins on dinner at Babs' noodle stall, the harpy Talia had taken me to the first time I'd been in Fairwood. The broth is salty and hot, and it warms my whole body as I slam the meal down. It's almost enough to forget about Maru for a moment.

Almost.

"That's new," Cyros says, sliding into the seat beside me.

I give him a sideways glance and see he's looking at the strip of cloth I have tied around my forehead.

"Helps keep my hair out of my eyes," I say shortly.

It irritates me that he wanted to meet here. That means he'd been following me and Talia the whole time she'd been taking me through the city. I guess I should have expected that, given how he was waiting for me outside Talia's home, but I still don't like the idea of being followed. Worse, I don't like the idea that I had no idea I was being followed.

He shrugs, gaze dropping from my new accessory. "Hope you didn't eat too much. Eating a bunch of food isn't a good idea right before training. Would be a waste to throw it up."

"Shouldn't have asked to meet here then," I say, polishing off the last of my bowl. I set it down with a content sigh. "Let's go."

Cyros slips off his stool and back into the flow of people, and I hurry to catch up.

"What am I learning next?" I ask, knocking shoulders with some of the passersby as Cyros forges a path against the flow of traffic. "Running up a wall? Backflips? Swords? Shadow magic?"

"Do you have shadow magic?" Cyros asks me.

Echo?

[Negative.]

"Uh, no."

"Then we'll stick with the basics," Cyros says. "All the fanciest weapons and magic won't mean much if you're dead at the end of a job. Living to fight another day should always be your number one priority."

If only he knew how appropriate that advice has become.

"One of the most important skills you can learn," Cyros continues, "is slipping away."

And just like that, he ducks around a stranger, and I lose him.

Crap! I jump after, pushing around the stranger. The flow of people passes me on both sides, and I snap my head around, trying to catch a hint of Cyros's black cloak. I pick up my pace, knocking into people as I press ahead, but he's gone. All it had taken was an instant.

A hand taps my shoulder.

"That was pathetic," Cyros says from behind me.

I whip around. "How did you do that? Did you go invisible again?"

"I can't go invisible," Cyros says. "And no, I didn't use my camouflage. That spell only works around plants, anyway. I just did what you're not doing."

"Which is?"

Cyros steps around me and begins ducking through the crowd once more. He sidesteps a passerby, then slips past the next. "Displaying bodily awareness," he says.

"Bodily—I'm aware of my body," I object, shouldering after him.

"If you are, then stop knocking into every other person you pass," Cyros says. "Don't fight the crowd, slip through it. Watch three people ahead. Plan your route, angle your body, and flow through them."

"That sounds like more than just bodily awareness," I grumble.

"It's awareness of your own, and others," he admits. "Like a game of stones, you can't just make each move independently of the next; you need to be planning ahead, predicting your opponent's moves. Let's try again. Keep up."

Once more he glides ahead, and once more I struggle to follow. I try to do what he suggested, watching the other people around me, trying to predict their movements and step around them accordingly. And I do, for a moment—until I realize I've lost sight of Cyros again.

He taps me on the opposite shoulder, and I sigh.

The game of cat and mouse continues for nearly an hour as we weave through the city. I get better—a lot better—but he still manages to slip away from me each time.

Finally, he stops at the edge of an alley, and I pause for a breather, leaning heavily against the wall.

[Stat Level Up: Agility,] Echo announces.

I smile faintly. Good. This combined with Soft Step has the potential to develop my stealth abilities. And if I could work in smoke potions...

"What are you smiling about?" Cyros asks. "You didn't improve *that* much."

"Every bit helps," I say. "But I'd really like something more proactive. Less fleeing and chasing, more hands-on. I've been working on my knifework, but I've barely even held any other kind of weapon. Not to mention tools—lockpicks, tripwire, you know, ninja stuff."

Cyros raises an eyebrow. "What's a ninja?"

Uh. "I just mean, I want to learn more than the basics," I insist. "As much as I can. As fast as I can."

I steady my breathing, uncertainty bobbing to the surface for only a moment. No. I can't falter now. If I want to kill a demigod, if I want to avoid being killed by an actual god, this is the best path forward. The *only* path forward.

"Take me to the Blackcloak Guild," I tell him. "I want to join."

Chapter Twenty-Four

THE BLACKCLOAKS

Cyros narrows his eyes. "Blackcloak?"

Oops. Right. He never really told me the name of the organization he worked for. That was insider knowledge from Echo. I gotta get better at tracking what I am and am not supposed to know.

"That's the group you're a part of, right?" I ask, scrambling to make something up. "I heard people talking about them in Fairwood. Unless you're gonna tell me you're part of some *other* super-secret assassin guild."

"You shouldn't have heard about us at all," Cyros says, frowning.

"So that means you are part of the Blackcloaks?" I ask brightly.

Cyros winces. He knows I got him. "I thought you said assassins were immoral."

I fold my arms. "So?" He can't dodge my questions forever.

"So why the change of heart?" he asks. "You only told me that two days ago, but now you're singing a very different tune."

I grimace, wondering if I should tell him about Maru's mark. "Things just got a whole lot more pressing, alright? I need to train my body *and* magic as fast as I can, and the best way to do that is through your guild."

"We don't just let anyone in, you know," he says. "It's invite only."

"And you invited me," I point out. "So let me have that chance! Look, if I don't figure out a way to kill a demigod in the next three weeks, I'm dead."

"You shouldn't say that aloud," Cyros warns with a frown. "But what you want to do..."

"I know." I roll my eyes. "It's impossible."

"Technically, only highly improbable," he says. "The chances of success are exceptionally low."

"So help me increase them!" I say. "You're not the one who'll be in danger here—I will be. Cyros, please."

He freezes. "What did you say?"

"Please," I sigh, hating that I have to resort to begging, but I'm out of options. "I'll do anything."

"No," he says, eyes narrowing. "What did you call me?"

Crap, I did it again! I'm not supposed to know his name. "Uhhh, I said Toshi. No, I mean, Shoti. No wait..."

He's not buying it at all. "Say it again. What you actually said."

I sigh. The jig is up. "Cyros."

"How do you know my name?" A knife is suddenly in his hand, his stance defensive and tense. "First the Blackcloaks, now this. Who are you really?"

"I'm Sal!" I object, raising my hands. "Just Sal, I promise! And it's, uh, it's this kind of magic I have. It tells me information about people."

"What kind of information?" he demands.

"Just basic stuff," I say. "Name, species, level."

He frowns. "Level?"

Gah! "I mean, how strong you are. It quantifies it."

"What kind of magic is that?" he asks. "I thought you had a Poison affinity."

"I do," I say. "This is different."

"Two affinities?"

Echo had said that was less common, but not unheard of. "I guess so. Look, I don't know much about it myself. That's why I need your help."

Somehow, none of what I've said appears to mollify him. "How can I trust you?"

I snort. "Dude, *you're* the assassin here."

The shadows in the alley move.

"An excellent point," the figure says, appearing to stride right out of the wall of the building. I jump back, but Cyros doesn't appear fazed. If anything, the person's presence only makes him grimace. "After all, she had the opportunity to expose both of our identities to the city guards but didn't. Isn't that right?"

I take a hesitant step back, giving the figure a Check.

[Nieve,] Echo says. [Level 52 Felis Shadow Assassin]

Last time I'd seen them they appeared to be a female elf. The person standing before me is anything but.

In the place of pointy elf ears are two black cat ears, and likewise a tail swishes impatiently behind them. Their face and attire are androgynous, though it's their bright blue eyes, slitted like a cat's, that I can't look away from. They stare at me, not with a frown, but intense and unsettling nevertheless.

"Tell me," the felis says. "What's my name?"

I swallow. "Nieve."

"There." They turn to Cyros, gesturing back toward me. "You see? She's kept our secret this long. Most interesting."

I straighten up, trying to appear more confident than I look. "You're Cyros's mentor?"

"In a manner of speaking," Nieve says.

It doesn't escape me that Cyros has gone totally silent, letting Nieve take over the conversation.

"Will you let me join your guild?" I ask. "Cyros invited me."

Nieve smiles mildly, and Cyros seems to shrink into himself. "Cyros knows we don't accept just anyone into our fold. Nor is he, himself, ready to be training new recruits."

"I'm sorry," he blurts. "I was just trying to help her out."

"You were just hoping I wouldn't notice your unexplained absences," Nieve corrects him. They don't seem particularly bothered by it, however. The felis turns back to me. "The timing of your ask is conspicuous. I don't suppose your desire to join our ranks has anything to do with the commotion that happened at the arena today?"

My gut sours, but I try not to react. "What do you mean?"

They've closed the space between us before I even have a chance to blink. Their hand reaches out and I flinch back—there's a tug at my temple, and then my headband is in their hands.

I slap a hand to my forehead, covering up the mark. "Hey!"

"What was that?" Cyros asks.

"The mark of a tournament contestant," Nieve says passively.

"Give that back," I growl, still covering my forehead.

They shrug, handing it over. "Covering it won't make it go away."

"I know," I spit, slipping it back on. I can still feel it there, as if it will burn its way through the headband. "But that's why I need your help."

"We don't dabble in the matters of the gods," Nieve says. "That would be sure to draw unwanted attention."

I open my mouth to object, but they hold up a hand. "However, you are lucky that you interest me in other ways. This identification magic of yours, for instance, has many practical uses in our line of work. Not to mention, given you already know our secret, it would be unwise to let you simply wander off. If Captain Enrold didn't wield the competence of an exceptionally intelligent toad, we might have actually been in some trouble."

Hope flutters in me. "Then you'll let me in? You'll train me?"

"You will be given an opportunity to prove your commitment," Nieve says. "The rest is in your hands."

"Thank you!" I cry. "Thank—hey, wait up!"

Nieve hadn't even let me finish talking before they started to stroll away—into the alley instead of out of it. Cyros hurries after them, and it's all I can do to dash after both and try to keep up. My legs and arms are already screaming at me, both from Cyros's "bodily awareness" training session, and the earlier abuse I'd experienced at the hands of Maru this morning. I Check my health as I catch up: [71/90]. I groan. The passive healing is helping me, but it'll still be another day before I'm fully recovered, and only another 20 days beyond that until the tournament.

Not fast enough, I think. I need to move faster.

As I catch up, Nieve casts a glance over their shoulder, then flicks a finger at me and Cyros.

[The spell Shadow Walk has been cast on you,] Echo says.

"What?" I ask. "Hey, what did you just do?"

"You noticed?" Nieve asks, raising an eyebrow.

Well, no, but Echo did, so close enough.

"You cast a spell on us," I say.

"It's nothing to worry about," Nieve says. "If you're serious about joining the Guild, don't stop now."

Wow, super enlightening, thanks. *Echo?* I ask, still walking quickly to keep pace with Nieve's long strides. *What does the spell do?*

[Shadow Walk,] Echo recites. [So long as the user continues to move, the spell persists. While in effect, the user is difficult to perceive, appearing like a disembodied shadow to those unaffected by the spell.]

Guess that's why she told me not to stop. Seems like a great ninja spell though. *Echo, can I learn this spell?*

[Negative,] Echo says. [Shadow Walk requires ocular arcana to cast.]

I pout. Figures. I don't get access to any of the cool magic.

Now mostly invisible to the outside world, Nieve leads us on a winding route through the city that thoroughly rids me of any sense of direction. We cross a couple bridges, but the path more closely keeps to clustered buildings lashed together with vines; sometimes we walk over the top of them, where impromptu footpaths spread across the rooftops like a path along rolling hills, and sometimes we cut through the buildings, themselves often opening directly into each other, creating large indoor spaces which feel more underground than amidst the trees. Once, Nieve even has us jump a gap between two bridges. They don't look back to make sure I don't slip and plunge to my death. I jump across anyway. I'm not going to let them leave me behind. Not after coming this far.

Finally, they slow at the trunk of an enormous tree, one similar to the four that mark the entrance to the city itself. The bridge we're currently on dead-ends at the tree trunk, although we're hardly remote; plenty of businesses are strung about us, and the people who walk (or fly) these parts all seem to be dressed rather respectably. If I had to guess, I'd say we were in some kind of financial district.

"Here we are," Nieve says, taking us around the side of the tree. The gnarled trunk bulges out and in, causing the path to weave around the uneven face of the tree. In one such alcove, Nieve steps forward and disappears.

I stop. "What?"

But as soon as I hesitate, I realize my mistake: Cyros vanishes as Echo says, [Shadow Step spell expired.]

An invisible hand grabs my wrist.

"Come on," Cyros's voice says as he tugs me forward. "They told you not to stop: you can't just stand around out here. You'll give away the entrance."

I'm not sure what entrance he's talking about, because there's just more tree in front of me—which the invisible grip is pulling me directly toward. I raise my free hand before my face, flinching back and squeezing my eyes shut. But a moment later my ears pop, the air around me feels warmer and stuffy, and suddenly there's voices all around me. I crack an eye back open.

My first impression is the City Guard's hall. My second impression is an occultist thrift shop.

Dozens of people are lounging around, chatting, and bartering inside a room that must be larger than the tree itself. Several tables and chairs fill the middle of the room, and nearly half of the circular space is taken up by shelves of bottles, lining the wall from the ceiling to the floor. There's jars full of eyeballs, vials filled with salt and herbs, baskets of dried plants—hundreds, maybe thousands more ingredients than I've had a chance to work with.

"Is that bone thistle?" I ask, stepping toward the wall. Belatedly, I realize all the bottles are tucked behind a curved counter that similarly runs around half the room. There's a hooded dryad behind the counter, and even as I watch he raises a hand, vines sprouting from about his wrist to pluck four items from the upper shelves to hand over to someone at the counter.

"I need some," I say, turning to Cyros, whom I can now see. Nieve is also standing nearby. "How much do they cost? Can anyone buy some? Can I take out a loan?"

"Any member of the guild can purchase from or sell to our stock," Nieve says. "However, you are still a guest. If you desire full membership, then you'll need to earn it, first. Come, this way."

"They really let anyone in here?" I ask Cyros as Nieve leads us across the room. Stairs wind up the wall to another floor above, and I suspect there's likely a staircase that disappeared somewhere through the floor as well. Just how big is this place?

"Not exactly," he says. "As I said before, it's invite only."

"Doesn't seem terribly secure," I note, still turning my head every which way in awe. "I mean, what if a guest doesn't become a member? Now your secret's out." I pause. "Wait, you don't mind-wipe people, do you?"

"No," Cyros repeats, hesitating. "But we don't have guests, either. If the invited individual fails to commit to membership, they're taken care of in a different way."

"Different how?" I ask.

Cyros shrugs helplessly.

"Cyros, different, how?" I ask again, this time a little alarmed.

"Just don't fail the test," Cyros says.

"Test?!"

"Yes," Nieve says, coming to a stop. "The first step of which is right here." They gesture to the wall we've stopped before—or, more specifically, the board that's mounted to the wall.

My alarm quickly melts into awe as I gawk at the hundreds of notes stuck to the wall. "Is this a quest board? A real quest board?!"

"Uh, they're jobs," Cyros says.

"That's close enough." Hell yeah! Now we're talking. *This* is the kind of stuff I signed up for.

I mean, not that I really signed up to die and get isekaied to a fantasy land with crap magic powers, homicidal gods, and a system that wants to drive me insane. But hey, at least there are quests!

"Once you're a member of the guild, you may choose to complete any of these jobs at your leisure and be compensated as the post indicates," Nieve says. "Or, if you'd rather, you can simply make use of the trading hub or various training rooms. There's equipment for potion making that may be rented out as well."

Potion making? I mean, that's exactly what I need, but how much exactly does Nieve know about me and my magic? Maybe they were hanging around eavesdropping on Cyros and I longer than I'd thought.

"Pick one," Nieve says, sweeping a hand to the job posts. "To demonstrate your commitment to the Guild, you must first complete one job—without claiming its reward. Instead, entrance into our ranks will be your payment."

"No problem," I say, stepping up to get a closer look. "This'll be a cinch."

"Take your time," Nieve says. "There's no rush."

I start reading through some of the jobs. There's the low-level stuff you might expect, like harvesting some herbs or hunting some creatures and bringing back various materials that would be sold to the guild directly. Those all have decent payment—some of them offering a lot better payment than the couple of coins I'd managed to scrape together working at the Starlight Inn—but the big money is with the more dangerous jobs. Stealing something from a noble, gathering intel on individuals. A couple of these don't even offer money as the reward, but rather valuable and magical items.

And then, of course, there's the hits. People who someone wants dead for some reason or another. The idea still leaves a somewhat sour taste in my mouth, but I try to ignore it. That's why I'm here, isn't it? It's kill or be killed. And I'll have to get practice at some point.

But which to choose for my guild entrance? Something easy would probably be best to guarantee I won't fail. I've already identified a couple herb quests I could complete in a day or two; I know where I can find those ingredients back in the woods near the Starlight.

But something Cyros had said gives me pause. He told me not to fail the test. I initially assumed he was referring to completing one of these jobs. But Nieve had said the *first step* was here. Maybe the kind of job I pick is just as important as completing it.

I can't risk going with one of the easy ones then. Intel might not be too bad with Echo's insight. And I could maybe steal something—my inventory would sure help with that. I'm leaning toward one of the cat burglar type quests when a different note catches my eye.

I grab the paper and rip it from the wall. "This one," I say. "This is the job I'll do."

Cyros's eyebrows shoot up. "Are you sure? That won't be easy—not even for me."

But Nieve is smiling faintly, so I think I picked right. "Interesting choice. But Cyros is right. There is a significant likelihood you'll fail. I won't hold it against you if you want to switch to an easier job."

I shake my head, anger burning in my gut, my mind already made up. "No. This is what I want."

"Very well, then," Nieve says, holding out their hand for the paper. "I will mark this job as claimed. You have two weeks to complete the job before it will be returned to the general pool, at which point your application to join the Blackcloaks will be considered expired. In the meantime, you may access our facilities with the accompaniment of Cyros or myself. Do you accept these terms?"

"Yes," I say, nerves, excitement, and revenge all warring within me. "I accept."

[Quest Obtained,] Echo says, summarizing the information on the note.

Hah! I knew it was a quest.

[Reward: 1000 Gold Crescents]

[Scope: The night before the last Council session of the month, the target is to be drugged with a poison of the user's choosing and put out of commission for a minimum of three days.]

[Report: Anonymous. Report completion through The Guild.]

[Target: Captain Enrold]

Chapter Twenty-Five
THE BUTCHER SHED

[20 Days until the Gods' Tournament]

[13 Days until Blackcloak membership is due]

I idly stir the cauldron with my right hand as I keep the alchemy book propped up on my knees, left hand scrolling down the page as I read through the book Lisari had lent me. She's right: this is dense stuff. A lot of the theory it's going through might as well be written in another language. But I don't give up. I can't. I get Echo to explain whatever she can elaborate on, and I try to infer whatever she can't.

The first big difference between potions and alchemy is that alchemy uses spell circles where my potions had been made from pure ingredients. The first step is largely the same as potion making: first I have to mix ingredients and meet certain conditions, like heating things up or cooling them down. But instead of adding a bit of magic to complete the process, this is where things turn a little more occult. Some alchemy spells require candles or crystals, and nearly all of them require the user to draw an alchemic circle, within which the potion mixture (or other materials) must be placed. The magic is then added to the spell circle instead of directly mixed into the draught, which will, theoretically, create the desired effect.

Looks like I'll be needing some chalk.

It's different from what I've been practicing, but being able to do alchemy would open up a whole other field of magic to me. It seems a lot of other fields of the arcane also use spell circles, but generally speaking those spells require a good amount of mana, whereas my natural quantity of mana is about the level of a magically stunted toddler. It seems, at least, this won't *stop* me from being able to do alchemy, anymore than it's stopped me from making potions: it'll just limit the potency and quantity of whatever I'm working with. I wonder if the Blackcloak Guild might have something that can help me overcome my pathetic excuse for a mana pool.

I flip through the handful of alchemic spells Lisari marked for me.

Potion for enhanced strength: increases the user's fortitude and power.

Potion of augmentation: boosts the potency of any potion it's added to.

Swift Step: increases the user's speed.

I'm excited to try all of them out, but I lack the ingredients and equipment for most, so I'll need to head back to Fairwood first. Maybe I can talk Talia and Lisari into lending me the stuff. Talia would probably frown on the idea, but I suspect Lisari would be excited to further my foray into alchemic experimentations.

"You're going to burn the stew," Iski says.

I jump, not having noticed Iski sneak up on me. She makes a habit of doing that. "You startled me."

"The stew." Iski gestures. "You stopped stirring. Honestly, if you're not even going to be paying attention to the food you're supposed to be watching, what's the point of working in here?"

"Sorry," I say, reluctantly closing the book and setting it aside. "I was distracted."

"You've been distracted the last two days, ever since you got back from Fairwood." Iski catches sight of the cover. "Alchemy, huh? I hope you're not planning on practicing that in here."

"No!" I object, hurriedly turning my attention back to the cauldron and dragging the giant ladle around the pot. "I promised I wouldn't do anything in here again." Which is why I've been doing everything in my bedroom.

"No practicing anywhere near customers," Iski clarifies as if reading my mind.

I hesitate.

"Aha!" she points a finger at me. "I knew it."

"I'm sorry," I say. "But I can't stop practicing altogether! This is too important."

"Why?" Iski demands. "I've never seen someone become so obsessive with magic before. You've no natural inclination for it, either. Why not pick up something that better suits your talents?"

The words sting, even though I know she isn't wrong. "I can't," I tell her. "I just have to get stronger." Because the gods want me dead for being from another planet. Because if I can't kill Maru first, I'll almost certainly die in the tournament. Because in the next two weeks, I'll need to poison a man, or the Blackcloaks will kill me.

Iski's frown softens. "You can talk to me, you know. Or Gugora. I can tell how fond he is of you. We might not be family, but we're here to help."

A ball of emotions threatens to rise up my chest, and I swallow it down. "I know. Thank you."

Iski purses her lips like she has more to say about that response, but in the end all she does is shake her head. "Just think about it," she says, turning to head back out of the kitchen. "And don't burn dinner!"

I'm not given much of an opportunity to practice any alchemy that day or the next, not least because I'm lacking on equipment and access to a fireplace. Gugora and Iski keep me busy cleaning the tavern, prepping meals, and tending to the garden—maybe to make up for the day I spent in Fairwood. I don't mind terribly, as I use the opportunity to work on my Knifework and Soft Step skills and my Agility stat. By the time I find five minutes of free time, I'm beat.

Heading up to my room to develop some of my in-work potions, I freeze when I find the door open. The floor is clean. My potions are gone. First disbelief, then anger flashes through me.

"Iski!" I call, dashing down the stairs. "Gugora! Where's my stuff?!"

"Calm down," Iski snaps. She's at the front desk, checking in a traveler. "You'll scare all our clients away."

"My room!" I object, darting a glance at the newcomer. He glances between Iski and I, clearly uncomfortable. I take a steadying breath. "*Please* where's my stuff?"

She waves me on, still writing on the ledger and sorting through the coins. "Go talk to Gugora. He's the one who's been up there. I think he's out in the—"

I don't even let Iski finish, turning and sprinting for the garden. He wouldn't have dumped all my stuff outside, would he? Not without talking to me first? I mean, I did promise I wouldn't do any more potion making in the kitchen, but they said nothing about my bedroom!

Given how long my mana takes to recover, and how little of it I have to begin with, losing all my potions and ingredients now would set me back over a week, and I don't have a week to lose.

I burst outside, skidding to a stop before the garden. He isn't here. "Gugora!" I call, rounding the side of the inn. "Where—"

I nearly crash into his side, managing to pivot away at the last moment before I do any real damage to myself.

"Ah, there you are," he says, turning to me. His arms are filled with bottles and pouches.

"My potions!" I cry. "Give them back!"

He grumbles and frowns. "Yours, hm? I seem to recognize these bottles from my storeroom. And where did you get the ingredients?"

"From the forest," I say. Well, that's true for most of them.

Gugora seems to know this as well. "The pebbleback crystals, too? The jackalope horn?"

"Please," I say. "I'll pay you back for the materials. Just don't throw them away!"

"Payment is not the issue," Gugora says. "Keeping these in our inn, is. The room next to yours is public. What happens if you spill something dangerous?"

"I haven't," I say. "I've been careful!"

"Everyone makes a mistake eventually," Gugora says. Even so, he shuffles the armful of bottles, leaning down toward me. "Well, you're here now, so you might as well carry them."

"Thank you," I start to say, snatching my potions from his grasp. "I promise I'll be—"

"Not so fast," Gugora says. "You're not taking those back to the inn. Follow me."

Gugora turns and strikes out from Starlight, and I hesitate, considering making a break for it. I can't take them back to my room, though, and I'm not sure where else to stash them. Reluctantly, potions in hand, I follow after him.

It only takes me a minute to recognize the path we're taking. "The butcher shed?" I ask.

He nods with a grunt, but doesn't elaborate.

At least this time I'm pretty sure he won't be murdering me in a remote location, but I can't guarantee the same safety for my precious potions. When we approach the small cabin, all the sun-dried meats are gone from the racks outside. The area still smells strongly of tanning hides and death, but not as overpowering as it had before.

Gugora pushes the door open, gesturing me inside.

Weapons still adorn the wall. The room is still dark and stained with the smell of offal. But there's changes as well, namely, a table where several of my potions are already placed, and a fresh stack of wood by the fireplace, where a large, shiny cauldron has been placed.

"If you're going to be doing such magic," Gugora says, "I'd rather it not be a risk to the guests."

I look up at him dumbly. "You mean it? I can really work here?"

"Don't make me regret it," he says, though beneath all the tusks and grumbling, I think I can make out a smile.

I begin to set my potions down on the workbench, already imagining how I could use this place. A cauldron of my very own would do wonders! I can go back to recipes that require boiling. And if I can get some chalk, there's plenty of floorspace to work on some alchemic circles. Not to mention, this room is four times the size of my bedroom. I can stash way more herbs and materials in here! Now if I can just borrow some more alchemy equipment and potion ingredients from the Blackcloak Guild...

"Sal?" Gugora repeats. "Did you hear me?"

"What?" I say, jerking up from the table. "Sorry."

He sighs. "I said, the weapons are still off limits." He taps a bow mounted to the wall. "I didn't have time to move them, but I also don't have a better place for them to be stored. Understand? This is a requirement for using this space: you are not allowed to use or borrow any weapons without prior consent. I am trusting you on this."

"Understood," I say. I don't intend to mess with them, anyway. I'm just barely starting to be competent with a knife after three weeks of practice; I don't have time to learn a new weapon. Plus, knives are way more covert. "I won't touch any of them. Promise!"

Gugora doesn't seem particularly convinced, but I guess he's equally unwilling to press the point. "Good. Then one final piece of advice: be careful."

I can't help but snort at that. "Do you even know who you're talking to?"

He chuckles. "It does seem futile. But I can try." He rests a massive hand on my shoulder. "Sal... You've had a rough start here. But you can still find peace. What you do with the tiles you've been dealt rests in your hands."

I purse my lips, biting back a retort. A rough start sure is a laughable understatement. And *peace* isn't exactly what I'm looking for. "Thanks," I say anyway, not wanting to disappoint Gugora. "I'll think about that."

His hand slips from my shoulder. "That's all I ask."

He removes a key from his pocket and offers it to me. I reverently take it from him, clasping it with both hands.

"Don't lose it," he says.

"I won't."

"If there's anything else you need, let me know."

"I will!"

His gaze shifts up from my eyes, and he nods toward my headband. "And if you ever want to talk about that, I'm here to listen."

My throat tightens. Beneath the cloth, I can feel Maru's mark burn.

CHAPTER TWENTY-SIX

SPIRIT EXPERIMENTS

[18 Days until the Gods' Tournament]

[11 Days until Blackcloak membership is due]

[Frost Seed: A condensed pellet of mana infused with freezing properties. Once activated, the tablet has various effects: if swallowed, it will inflict a slowing de-buff onto the consumer. If cast upon a surface, it will create a creeping spread of ice that grows at a rate of ten inches per second until the seed mana expires. Affinity Requirements: any subfields of Life or Water arcana.]

There's more that goes into the spell: various ingredients, an alchemic circle, and of course magic. I doubt my 10 mana will go very far, but it will at least be a good practice spell to start with. I mean, not just because it happens to be the only alchemy spell I have all the ingredients for, but I'm sure I can find *some* use for it. Probably.

First, I bring the water to a boil, adding in redwood bark, brownskull mushroom caps, and rootwarts. As that steeps, I head back to the middle of the room, where I'd begun to sketch out a spell circle. I have the alchemy book opened next to it, which I use to double check the lines and runes I currently have sketched out. I have absolutely no idea what any of the runes mean—the book does have a whole section dedicated to the meaning and use of each one, but I don't have time to screw around with learning a whole new alphabet. I'm not about to design my own spell circle here—I just need to learn what I can use as fast as I can.

Satisfied the circles are correct, I go over it with some charcoal, which Gugora assured me would work in place of chalk until I next have time to go into the city, then set a copper bowl (okay, a copper measuring cup) at its center. I use Echo to keep track of the time for me, and after ten minutes are up, I go back over to the cauldron and ladle out some of the brew. Belatedly realizing I should have made the circle way closer to the fireplace, I slowly waddle my way across the room, carefully not to spill any of the potion, and then spoon the liquid into the bowl at the center of the circle. I repeat the process three times until it's full.

"Okay," I say, sitting down at the side of the circle. "Let's do this."

Carefully, I set my hands inside two circles specifically designed for such purposes, then focus on activating the spell circle.

[Circle recognized,] Echo pipes up. [Mana Requirement: variable.]

"We're using all of it," I say. All whopping ten points of it. "Let's go. Activate."

My hands bloom with green light, and a moment later the lines in the spell circle similarly illuminate. Like water on a track, the lights flow from the outside in, converging at the bowl at its center. The magic bleeds from the circle into the bowl, causing the water to glow. Instead of growing more dim, however, the light only grows brighter. At the same time, the water level decreases. Like a hole has been drilled in the bottom, the water spirals down, growing brighter and brighter, until eventually there's only a white-hot seed sitting at the bottom of the cup. I lean my head over, watching.

"Is it done?" I ask. "Did I do it?"

The glow slowly fades from the pebble at the bottom of the cup until all that's left is a little white stone. Only when all traces of the magic are gone does Echo speak up.

[Spell complete.]

"Hah!" I snatch up the cup from the center of the circle. "I made this! *I* made this. I'm a freaking alchemist." I roll the stone around a few times, considering it.

"Echo, is it okay to touch it? It won't activate if I do, right?"

[Negative,] Echo says. [The tablet's spell will activate when the user reawakens the dormant mana with a triggering imbuement.]

"A triggering what now?" I ask.

[When the user introduces a new external quantity of mana to the frost seed, the magic will act as a catalyst that will result in activation of the spell.]

I frown. "So it'll take more magic to make this thing start working?"

[Affirmative.]

Well that's extremely annoying. That means I'll need to wait another hour before I can use it. On the other hand, at least it means these things are stable and can be carried around with me. I roll the seed out into my hand, still plenty happy with my invention. I could create a whole pouch of these guys to keep on hand.

Too bad each one will take 10 hours to make.

Ugh, I really need to figure out a way to up my Mana stat.

But there's no rest for the wicked. I can't just sit around, twiddling my thumbs, as I wait for my mana to recover. I've got more spell circles to prepare, more ingredients to go scavenging for, more alchemic spells to read.

"Alright," I say, dropping the frost seed in a pouch and setting it back on my ingredients table. I turn back to the alchemy book, flipping to another spell Lisari had earmarked for me. "What next?"

[17 Days until the Gods' Tournament]

[10 Days until Blackcloak membership is due]

Health potions are actually pretty simple. As long as you have access to Life arcana—which, luckily, Poison is a subcategory of—anyone can make them. The big drawback is the shelf-life, which gradually decays from the moment of creation, and the fact that the potency is limited by the amount of mana used to create it. It's an annoying trend I'm starting to notice in potion making.

"Ingredient List," I tell Echo. Now that I've made it a few times and officially "learned" the potion, I don't need to consult the herb book and can get Echo to pull up the instructions for me.

[Ingredients,] Echo recites. [A simmering liquid of choice. Life arcana.]

And that's it.

"What happens if other magical ingredients are added to this liquid of choice?" I ask Echo, checking the temperature of the cauldron. Almost there.

[Unknown,] Echo says. [The effects would vary depending on the ingredients added. It is possible the user would inadvertently create a different potion.]

"So what you're saying is, I can learn new potions by experimenting." I grin wickedly.

Echo neither confirms nor denies this.

I go over my store of ingredients, all spread across the table. Rasptoad warts? Those show up in my smoke bomb potions. Brownskull mushroom? Those are fairly poisonous and the resulting potions can be volatile. How about swampweed? No, too stinky...

Eventually I settle on wormroot, which is frequently used in debuff potions but otherwise pretty harmless. Heading over to the fire next, I spoon a bowl of water from the cauldron, which I've been trying to keep at a simmer for the last couple of days. If this works, I might be a genius.

I add the wormroot into the steaming bowl of water, mixing until it's fully dissolved. Then I set it down and cup my hands over the bowl, summoning a little bit of magic to drip into the potion.

I watch my mana as the points tick down: it was only up to 5/10 when I started this most recent experiment, as I'm too impatient to wait the full ten hours to completely refill my tanks. But I don't need to use up all my mana on one of these experiments, anyway.

[Mana: 5/10]

[Mana: 4/10]

[Mana: 3/10]

"That should do it," I mumble, mentally cutting off the flow of magic as the liquid light pools in my palm. I tip my hand and spill the magic into the potion. The water swirls, the steam evaporating away as the color changes from green, to blue, to purple. The light dims, but doesn't completely go out. Well that's new.

"Is it done?" I ask Echo. "Is the potion complete?"

[As the user was not intending to create a specific potion as followed by a known recipe, this unit cannot identify the theoretical stage of completion.]

Well, guess I'll just have to test it out then.

Since a healing potion is intended to spread over a wound to make it better, and this potion was a healing potion infused with ingredients used in debuff potions, that means it should theoretically be able to reduce the rate at which a person heals instead. Maybe I could use this to weaken Maru.

"Only one way to find out," I mutter.

Setting an *actual* healing potion nearby—look, I *can* be taught—I pull out my knife and nick my pointer finger on my left hand. I wince at the cut, but it'll be healed up in a minute or two anyway with that healing potion sitting nearby. Instead, however, I pick up the new purple potion.

"We'll call you Potion X," I say. "Please don't let me down."

I stick my finger into Potion X. The blood on my finger clouds out into the surrounding liquid, which suddenly turns a dark garnet red. My finger begins to sting—then it burns.

[Status Effect sustained: Debuff,] Echo says.

Yes! Just as planned. I've made an opposite healing potion. Now, my rate of healing should be reduced.

[Lose mana at a rate of 1 mana per second for the duration of the potion's effect,] Echo says.

"Hey, wait!" I say. "That's not what I wanted!"

[Mana: 2/10]

"Crap!" I whip my hand from Potion X and stab it into the real healing potion.

[Mana: 1/10]

[HP: 90/90. You are fully recovered.]

[Mana: 0/10. Mana extinguished.]

"Dammit," I grumble. Well that's annoying. Now I'll have to wait hours again before I can try another potion or alchemy spell.

[New potion learned,] Echo says. [Mana Drain.]

"Yeah, I figured that," I grumble. Not exactly what I was intending. But at least I'll be able to make it again now, if I ever have the need.

And if nothing else, it did prove one thing: I can discover potion recipes on my own through experimentation. The only drawback is that I won't know what they do until I try them out.

What could possibly go wrong?

Chapter Twenty-Seven

Fewer Suicidal Guessing Games

[15 Days until the Gods' Tournament]

[8 Days until Blackcloak membership is due]

"So what do you think?" I ask, seated across from Cyros inside the Blackcloak Guild Hall. A handful of others are checking the job board or speaking with the vendor behind the supplies counter, but otherwise it's much emptier than it had been the previous week. I guess assassins don't hang around at the secret base in the middle of the day.

Cyros takes the Mana Drain potion from me, eying it dubiously. "I think that was extremely rash of you. What if it actually created something toxic that you didn't have the cure to?"

"I had the cure to wormroot," I say. "And I wasn't too worried. They're not that venomous, anyway."

"Poisonous," Cyros corrects with a sigh. "But just because you have the cure to individual components doesn't mean they'll combine into a new effect you *do* have the cure to. Next time you mix a mystery potion, take it back here so we can get it appraised before you start poisoning yourself."

The last time I poisoned myself it actually turned out pretty great, but I doubt he'll agree with me on that point.

He sets the bottle down and slides it back across the table. "So this is your plan for dealing with Enrold, then? Mess around with spell circles and ingredients until you stumble upon something useful?"

"Well, I mean, I'm *also* following the instructions on some potions," I say. "Most of the time."

Cyros sighs, shaking his head. "That's not going to cut it for getting into the Blackcloaks. You need to be going about this more methodically."

"What's there to be methodical about?" I ask. "I break in, dump some drugs on his food, and break back out."

"Oh yeah?" Cyros says. "What food?"

"I dunno." I shrug. "Whatever's in his kitchen?"

"He's a dhampyr," Cyros says flatly.

I blink. "Okay, explain what that means to me as if I might have no idea why that's significant."

"How do you not know what a—never mind. Dhampyrs are carnivores. They subsist off of blood and rare meat."

"Oh!" I say. "Like vampires! Ohhhhh." I think about his ashen skin and fangs. "Now it all makes sense."

"Vampires?" Cyros repeats, confused. "No, *dhampyrs*. What are you even talking about?"

"Doesn't matter," I say. "So you're saying he only eats fresh meat?"

"Very likely," Cyros replies, massaging a temple. "He probably keeps some frozen meat on-hand, too, in case he needs something in a pinch. But he might only eat it if he's short on getting something more fresh, which means your plan to drug whatever's in his house hinges on information you don't yet know."

I open my mouth, then shut it. "Fair point. So what's the plan, then? Scope out his house to figure out where and when he's eating?"

Cyros points a finger at me. "Now you're getting it. And as far as what you'll use to drug him..."

"I don't suppose there's some dhampyr-specific drug that knocks them out for a few days?" I venture.

"No," Cyros says. "But any of the generic ones should do. You'll just need to make sure he consumes a higher dose; dhampyrs are tough to take down. Triple the amount needed for a human of his size should do it."

"Which means I need to get an estimate of his weight, too," I realize. "Wow, thanks! This is great info. What would I do without you?"

"I'm beginning to wonder the same," Cyros says with a sigh.

"Don't worry about me," I say. "I've still got eight days before membership is due—and six days before the council meetings I'm supposed to drug him for. Plenty of time to stalk him and figure out his weight and eating habits. After that, all I'll have to do is brew the right potion to send him to Dreamland."

I riffle through my pockets, pulling the pouch of Frost Seeds (now up to three) off my bandolier to show Cyros. "I made these from the potion book I stole from Talia. See? I can follow instructions."

"Okay." He smiles slightly. "These won't take down Enrold, but this isn't bad, either. Good progress."

I grin at the compliment. "The biggest thing holding me back is my mana. I've got like *no* magic in my tanks at all. I use it all up with one spell and then I need to wait hours before I can make a new potion. I could have done ten times this amount if I didn't have to worry about refilling my tanks."

"Hmm." Cyros rubs his chin thoughtfully. "Well there's some mana potions that could help with that."

I sit upright. "Really? Do you have the recipe?"

He waves a hand at me to temper my enthusiasm. "Yes, but it wouldn't make any sense for you to make them. The mana that goes into the spell is the same that comes out—well, the amount of magic it can restore will actually be *less* than the magic that was put into it, since potions tend to degrade in effectiveness over time. So if you're looking for a cheat on how to gain more magic than you'd naturally recover, your best bet is to buy them."

I lean forward across the table. "Do you guys sell them here?"

"Yes, and the price varies by how much you need restored," Cyros says. "Since it sounds like you don't have much natural ability to begin with—"

"Watch it."

"—you can probably try one of the cheaper ones."

"Oh, well that sounds good, actually. How much?"

"For a low-grade mana potion, probably something like 10 silvers," he says.

I wince. I only make a few coppers from Iski and Gugora each day—that adds up to a little over two silvers per week. I've only got seven silvers to my name so far.

I must be making a face of some kind, because Cyros chuckles. "Once you're a full member, that's nothing. Most of the easy quests up there will give out a few silvers."

"Well that's great for you, but doesn't help me at all," I grumble.

Cyros drums his fingers on the table. "Tell you what. If you find some jobs up there you could complete—just the herb stuff—if you hand the ingredients over to me, I'll use the funds to buy a mana potion for you."

"Deal," I say, jumping at the opportunity. "I saw like five last time I could already do. Some of these aren't very hard to find in the woods."

I tip my head. "How come they pay so much for just a bunch of plants and animal parts?"

He shrugs. "Most of the ingredient jobs are posted by our traders." He thumbs a hand over his shoulder to the hooded individual working behind the counter. "Time is money. It's half a day's travel just to get somewhere remote enough, like your inn, that everything isn't already picked over. Most people who purchase materials here are willing to spend the extra coin for the convenience and privacy."

"You mentioned the Guild has other stuff besides just potion ingredients and alchemy materials," I say, eying the three stairwells spaced around the walls. Each one has a symbol carved above the stairs, though they don't mean anything to me. "Like tools and weapons."

"We do," Cyros says with a nod.

"If you've got some leftover money from the quests—er, jobs—could you buy me some of those supplies, too?"

Cyros looks a little uneasy. "I suppose so. I'm not *really* supposed to buy anything for people outside the guild, but I guess since you're trying out, it should be fine."

"Great." I grin. "Then how do you feel about lending me some coins now? You buy me the mana potion, maybe that drug I need for Enrold, and I'll get you the herbs to cover the cost next time I see you."

He wrinkles his nose. "I suppose..."

Got him. "And while we're at it, there's some supplies I'd like to borrow."

"Um..."

"And a couple weapons I want to use."

Cyros squirms in his chair. "I'm not sure they'll let me do that."

"Just the supplies then," I say, having known the weapons would be a bust.

He's still hesitating, but doesn't say no, so I jump in before he can make up his mind. "Great! Thanks for the help. Let's go check out what alchemic equipment they've got."

I grab Cyros's arm and drag him from the seat. Reluctantly, he leads me to one of the sets of stairs. Cyros pulls back the hem of his cloak. A yellow symbol glows from within the fabric, matching the mark carved into the stairwell. Both fade out, then Cyros starts up the steps.

"What was that?" I ask.

"Permission to access this floor," he says. "You have to earn it from someone higher up. Same way you get into the Guild Hall itself. Nieve or one of the other masters will grant you a mark once you pass the acceptance test."

"Neat," I say. "So I'll get a cloak like that, too?"

"Ah, no," Cyros says. "They just give you the enchantment: the cloak was already mine. You'll need to pick your own badge, weapon, or article of clothing to imbue your access enchantments in once you're a member. Ah, actually probably don't go with a cloak; it's seen as a bit of a cliche these days." He grimaces. "They didn't tell me that until after I'd joined."

Unlike below, where the walls were stocked with jars of perishables, up here are things like paper, chalk, twine, crystals, and candlesticks. There's also different types of cauldrons and even stone tablets spelled to preserve the ingredients placed on them. I'm itching to get my hands on everything, but if I'm going to get Cyros to eventually buy me bigger and better things, I'll need to start small and work my way up.

"Just some chalk for now," I say. "I've heard you can get some infused with different kinds of arcana. I need Ocular."

He looks a bit relieved at my request. "Sure, chalk should be cheaper than most other stuff. Let's go see."

My stomach flutters with anticipation as I mentally start going through all the spells in the Alchemy book that hadn't previously been accessible to me. With a mana potion or two, things are about to start getting really interesting.

[13 Days until the Gods' Tournament]

[7 Days until Blackcloak membership is due]

I finish tracing the circle on the floor of the butcher hut, the now-familiar sound of crackling wood and water bubbling away in the fireplace. The windows are cracked open to let in some light and keep the room from getting too hot and stuffy; the spell requires that the draught be cooled back down to room temperature before the magic is added. I'm all topped off, 10/10 mana, though I haven't used the Mana Potion Cyros got for me yet. I want to save that until I absolutely need it. In my downtime between spells and reading, I've been practicing my other skills, mostly Soft Step, Knifework, Poison Resistance, and Toxic Intuition. The last especially has come in handy with potion experimentation. Although Echo doesn't seem to know what I'm making when I throw random ingredients together, when I activate Toxic Intuition I'm able to glean some surface level information about the use of a potion. No more "suicidal guessing games," as Cyros calls it.

Well. Fewer suicidal guessing games.

Cracking my neck and stretching my back, I tuck the chalk away and head back over to my workbench, where the book is open to the page of one of the spells Lisari had suggested I check out. And to be fair, it's pretty freaking useful.

[Lesser Potion of Invisibility.]

"Alright," I mutter, going over the instructions for the thousandth time. "Blackroot, camouflaged spiked lizard skin, and ground jackalope horn boiled. Circle drawn. Mana tanks full. Wormwood chopped. I think we're ready to do this."

I'd already measured out a large bowl from the simmering brew in the fireplace, which has been sitting at the middle of the alchemic circle for the last half hour.

"Temperature?" I ask Echo.

[41 degrees centigrade.]

That's about right I think. No time like the present.

I sit down next to the transmutation circle, placing my hands in the correct slots. Reaching for my mana, I hold my breath and start to pour my magic in. This spell can only be activated by ocular arcana, which I don't have. However, the circle was drawn in ocular-infused chalk, so, according to the book, it should be a work-around. I wait for a moment, my stomach churning, as nothing happens. Then the circle illuminates as the spell begins to take effect. I let out my breath. Yes!

[Mana: 9/10]

[Mana: 8/10]

I cut it off at 5/10. If it's not potent enough, I can take the mana potion and try again: I still have more of the potion brewing over the fire. In the meantime, I lean forward, watching the magic swirl.

As always, the lines glow with the green of my magic. This time, however, there's also threads of purple woven into the light. The colors climb up the sides of the cup and spill into the water, where they swirl into a brown, brackish color. I wrinkle my nose at the sight, but a moment later, the colors vanish. In fact, all the water in the bowl vanishes.

[Spell complete,] Echo says.

Cautiously, I pluck the bowl from the spell circle. The sides are still hot, and I can feel a liquid sloshing around in its center, even though I can't see it.

"Looks promising so far, Echo," I say. Setting the bowl before me, I dip a tentative finger into the potion. My finger vanishes. Laughter bursts out of me in disbelief.

"I did it. I made an invisibility potion!" I push the rest of my hand into the bowl, and it all vanishes as well. Cackling with glee, I pull my hand back out of the bowl, waving my seemingly severed arm in front of my face. As I do, however, I can feel the liquid streaking down my arm and dripping off. In a few moments, I can see bits of my hand, a hint of movement where my skin is drying. Flexing my fingers and waving my arm around, it only takes another ten seconds or so for the form of my hand to fade back into sight.

"Echo, what's the efficacy of this potion?" I ask her.

[Efficacy: 70%]

That's pretty good, all things considered. Must be the ocular chalk that's helping.

"But how come it wears off so fast?" I ask. "Is it due to the small amount of mana in it?"

[Affirmative,] Echo says. [Half Life: 5 seconds.]

"That's not much time to do much of anything," I say. But if I use twice as much mana, hopefully I can also double the effectiveness. Of course, most other people could probably make this potion, like, ten times as effective. I'll just have to make do with mana potions.

"Application is also going to be a problem," I note, dipping both hands into the invisible brew and then lathering the potion over both arms. They disappear in invisible streaks, but if I miss any spots, I end up with visible patches of skin floating around. And by the time I move to my legs, my arms are starting to fade back in again.

"Hmm. Tricky. Think drinking it will be more effective?"

Echo doesn't reply.

I shrug. "It can't hurt to try."

I sniff the liquid: it doesn't smell like anything. Cautiously, I stick out my tongue, and tip the cup forward until the smallest amount spills over it.

I wait for Echo to say I'm fatally poisoned, or something, but no status effect window pops up.

"Whew."

Which leaves one last step in the experiment: I take a generous gulp of the invisibility potion, and...

Nothing happens.

"Booo," I say, setting the bowl down as I check myself over and determine I'm very much still visible. Maybe my stomach is invisible, for all the good that will do. "Rip off invisibility potion."

I'll need to try some other way to make this potion effective, then. I go back to my work station and start sorting through my completed potions and ingredients.

"Aha," I say, stopping at one. I uncap the mana potion and take a small sip. It tastes like dew and sunlight, sparkling over my tongue and down my throat, filling me with warmth.

[Mana restored.]

I re-cork the mana potion and set it aside. "Alright. I think it's time for another experiment."

Chapter Twenty-Eight
The Hit

[9 Days until the Gods' Tournament]

[2 Days until Blackcloak membership is due]

[Name: Sal]

[Class: Rogue]

[Level: 16]

[Attack: 35]

[Agility: 18]

[HP: 90/90]

[Affinities: Poison]

[Role: Chef]

[Skills: Knifework lvl 10, Poison Resistance lvl 9, Soft Step lvl 8, Throwing Knives lvl 7, Toxic Intuition lvl 3.]

[Potions and Alchemic Store: Smoke Potion (2), Mana Potion (1), Frost Seed (5), Mana Drain (1), Invisibility Potion (1) (modified), Health Potion (3), Orchid Poison (2), Sleeping Potion (1) (concentrated).]

Despite all that, I can only comfortably fit six bottles on my bandolier. I keep that in my Inventory for now, because I'll need to be covert, and a bunch of potions strapped to my chest are decidedly not that. My knife goes at my hip on my belt, my scarf at my neck, and of course my headband, now a standard part of my attire, is kept snuggly over Maru's mark on my forehead. Over all of this I wear a black cloak, borrowed from Cyros.

All that in place, I'm ready.

My chest feels tight. There's still two days until the due date for the Blackcloaks, but tomorrow is the council meeting, which means tonight's the night I need to act to fulfill the quest's requirements. That's just fine by me. After I get through tonight, I'll be a real member of the Guild, and I'll need to leverage every advantage they can offer to prepare for the Gods' Tournament.

Right now, though, I need to stay focused on my mission.

My stomach flutters nervously as I allow myself to consider what that means. Captain Enrold. I'll have to drug him. I hate him, and so it's not like that breaks my heart or anything. But knowing how close I'll have to get to him in order to do it... Well, I try not to let myself feel how scared I really am.

I take a breath in, then let it out, carefully boxing my feelings away. It's not like I can go back now, even if I wanted to.

I step out of my room and head down into the tavern. It's still late afternoon, the sun up but coloring the horizon, and there are half a dozen people at tables eating the standard stew. Guilt faintly stings my conscience. I'd been so busy getting ready for tonight that I hadn't even helped Iski with meal prep today. I'll have to make it up to her tomorrow, when I can breathe again.

"Sal?" Gugora asks as I head for the front door.

I bite down on my tongue, willing myself to sink into the floor. Reluctantly, I turn around to face him.

His eyes narrow at my suspiciously dark attire. "Where are you going?"

"Out," I say.

"Don't stay out too late. It will be night soon."

"I'm going to Fairwood. I won't be back until tomorrow."

Gugora stares at me. He doesn't ask for elaboration, and I'm relieved, because I don't know if I could lie to him at this moment.

"I think you should stay," he says instead.

I swallow. "I can't."

"Then will you at least be careful?"

The emotions are threatening to leak out, and I rein them back in. "I'll try."

He nods slowly. "Be back here tomorrow."

"That's the plan."

Gugora sighs. He looks like he's got more to say, but Iski calls him then.

"Gora! We've got some orders at the bar."

Gugora looks from me to her and then back to me again. He lingers, and so do I. Like I'm waiting for him to say something that could fix everything. Like words will prevent the Blackcloaks from killing me if I fail their mission, or prevent the gods from killing me once they realize I'm alive. *I just want to live,* I want to tell him. And I'll do anything it takes to keep from dying again. Anything.

"Coming," Gugora says, leaving me.

I leave then, too.

The air outside is tinged with the cool breath of the coming night, and I suck it in like I'd been drowning. No doubts. No hesitations. I can only keep moving forward. Tonight, every move I make will need to be decisive.

The night has settled quiet and cool like a blanket over the woods by the time I make the familiar trek back to Fairwood. It's only been two weeks since I was first taken here by Enrold's crew, falsely accused of murder. I smile wryly at how that's turned out.

Once up in the city, I trace a path to the Guard's Hall. Plenty of streetlights have bloomed to life, bioluminescent bugs rattling around globes strung up through the streets, but there's more than enough patches of dark to hide and wait in.

According to Echo, I wait one hour and twenty-three minutes.

People head in and out of the Hall all night long, mostly guard rotations, chatting and laughing with one another. If they take their position seriously, they sure aren't showing it. Finally, however, I see the hulking figure of a familiar form step out into the night. He turns and strikes out into the streets, and I follow, using Soft Step to quietly trail him.

It must be close to midnight when we finally arrive at his home. Unlike Talia's house which requires access to be granted to anyone allowed on the grounds, Enrold's abode is more humble, a cluster of hanging rooms which might fit inside the Starlight Inn twice over, and no security gates in sight. I don't know if it's that Talia has more money to spend on security as a noble, or if it's just that Enrold is cocky enough that he would never expect anyone to make a move against him. I suppose both might play some part.

He disappears inside as I settle into a hiding spot I'd previously picked out among the trees. Cyros and I had scoped the place out earlier this week. The bridges that surround Enrold's property are made from wood planks and vines, swaying slowly in the breeze, and creaking beneath any misplaced step. While the rickety footpath poses a noisy threat, one upside is that his house is so remote, there's no street lights nearby. I wait in the shadows, counting the minutes as they pass.

The light that had been on when Enrold first entered goes out a few minutes later. Now everything is quiet, dark, and still, yet my pulse is beating rapidly in my ears like a set of drums. This is it.

I remove my bandolier of potions from my inventory and strap it in place. The lowest bottles clink against my knife when I move, so I pull my knife from its sheath and add it to my inventory instead. Giving it another few minutes, just to be safe, I decide I need to move. It's now or never.

I climb up a lattice of vines that are suspending the wooden path, then climb over to Captain Enrold's house, bypassing the creaky planks. I slide down another vine, softly landing on the roof of one of the rooms. It's the furthest away from where I last saw the light on, so hopefully any sound I make will be muffled. Letting the instincts from Soft Step guide me, I pad my way over to the open chimney. From my previous investigation, this should lead into his living room, and aside from his front door, it's the only way into or out of the house.

All light is consumed by the hole leading down into the room. It's a pit of black, a yawning mouth, waiting to swallow me up. There's a tremor in my hands, and I try to still them. *Keep moving forward.*

I swing my legs over the lip and into the abyss. Pressing my feet against one wall, I brace my back against the opposite, and push. Slowly, quietly, I inch my way down. Images of Enrold's face appearing beneath me or a light flickering on to expose me keep flashing through my mind no matter how hard I try to dislodge them. My heart flutters with nervous energy.

It feels like an eternity passes until I reach the bottom. When my foot finally touches the floor, I want to let out a sigh of relief. Instead, I breathe out slowly and silently, lowering myself into a crouch. There's pieces of wood in the hearth around me, and I take care not to disturb them. I sit there, unmoving, for several minutes. The silence rings in my ears.

As my vision adjusts to the dark, I can start to make out my surroundings. In addition to the fireplace there's a seating area and table; a dining or living room of sorts. The kitchen is on the other side of the house, two rooms down.

Slowly creeping out of the fireplace, I straighten up. Two doors on two different walls. The one to my right leads outside. The one to my left should take me where I want to go.

I step softly over to the door and grab the handle. My heartbeat picks up, and my skin tingles. Enrold should be asleep. I confirmed his schedule with Cyros already. I'll be fine. This will all be over in a matter of minutes.

I push, and the door creeps open. The gentle scrape of wood on wood sounds like a buzzsaw in the quiet house. I freeze, holding my breath. Nothing moves. The silence continues to press in. After a minute or two, I continue to push the door open, and it swings softly inward. I slip through.

Another not-kitchen. This room has some sort of tools in it—weapons, I think. I can make out large shadowy forms along the walls, glinting where the filtered moonlight strikes them. Two more doors face me. This time I'm not sure which one to pick. This room doesn't have windows, so I wasn't able to get a solid understanding of its layout in advance. Both doors should lead further into the house, but which one leads to the kitchen?

I pick the door to my right. Once again I try the handle, quietly press the latch, and then inch it open.

This room is black. No windows, no light of any kind. And I think I can hear breathing.

Echo. Check.

[Enrold: Level 32 Dhampyr Blood Guard]

Fear electrifies me. I struggle against my lungs which want to gasp, against my limbs that want to shake. Enrold's in here, sleeping, just feet away. He could spring to his feet in an instant, grab me before I could even react, slam me into the ground—

I fight against the intrusive thoughts, despite the adrenaline spiking through my body and, glacially, I pull the door back closed.

As I release the doorknob, I let out a slow, shaky breath. I stand there for another minute, listening for any sounds that he might have stirred. Nothing happens, however. Heart still hammering in my chest, I step away from the door.

The last one I try is the kitchen.

Relief floods through me. Finally. I can just lace his food with the drug and then get out of here. I take a moment to look around.

A small stove with a single slim smokestack sits in one corner of the room, just large enough to warm some bread—not even wide enough to fit a cauldron. There's a few jars of herbs on some shelves, but nothing like Iski's kitchen. That's technically food stuff, but not the steak I know he chomps down on each morning. I keep looking.

A basin is set into the counter. Some empty dishes sit nearby, a few with stains, others clean. I check the cabinets, and it's mostly mugs and dishes. All that's left is a chest against the wall, which I initially avoid due to the spell circle carved in its top. I still haven't learned to read runes or lines, so I'm not sure what it does, and I don't want to screw with magic that might be a trap. However, after turning up very little meat and creeping closer for a proper inspection, the faint blue glow from the circle is illuminating a crust of ice that's flecking the chest's seam. I cautiously lift the lid, peering inside.

Bingo.

There's stacks upon stacks of frozen meat. Keeping the lid propped open, I pop the cork off the concentrated Sleeping Potion Cyros bought for me, and begin dribbling the liquid all over the food. I'd tasted a drop of it myself this last week: it has a faintly bitter taste, but no smell. He'll probably notice as soon as he takes a bite, but hopefully by then it'll be so potent it won't even matter. Just in case, though, I plan to stick around till morning and make sure to finish the job if the potion doesn't take full effect. I've got the mana drain potion and some orchid poison I could use as well; in moderation it won't kill him, just make him violently ill. Not as subtle as sleeping through the Council Session, but hey, whatever I have to do to get the job done.

I empty the entire bottle over the top row of the meat. I keep the lid open for a few minutes longer, ensuring the liquid doesn't freeze on top before it has a chance to sink into the food, then slowly shut the lid and step away.

It's done.

My pulse is finally slowing down to non-lethal levels again. The hard part is over. Now I just need to sneak back out, hole up in a hiding spot somewhere, and watch how things unfold in the morning.

And that's when Echo says, [Role Requirement.]

CHAPTER TWENTY-NINE

ROLE REQUIREMENT REPRISED

[Role Requirement.]

Ice chills through me. *What? What do you mean?*

[The day ends in 56 seconds and the user has not fulfilled their Role Requirement. The Chef role requires the user to engage in cooking, baking, or food preparation on a daily basis.]

Crap. Shit! How did this happen? I always make sure to help in the kitchen with meal prep!

Except today. I was so busy preparing for tonight, so laser focused on making sure I didn't forget anything, that I forgot the one important thing I've come to take for granted.

[Sanity Level: 99%]

I glance rapidly around the kitchen for any kind of food I could prep—but of course, I'd just drugged everything available.

I mentally groan. Maybe I can run, make it out of here and find a market somewhere I could grab some food.

In the middle of the night? Not likely.

[Sanity Level: 98%]

What do I do, what do I do? No time to run. Nothing here to slap together. Couldn't he have at least had a hunk of bread?!

There's only two options: run and try to find something out in Fairwood, or make do with the meat here. I don't have to eat it, after all. I just need to do some meal prep.

[Sanity Level: 97%]

I can start to feel it now, like TV static in my brain. It's prickling at my conscience, building an unwilling sense of urgency, digging its claws into my mind. I shake my head as if I could dislodge it, already knowing the gesture is futile.

[Sanity Level: 96%]

I silently throttle the air in front of me. Ugh! No other choice.

I cross quickly to the ice chest, grinding my teeth as I do. I grab one of the pieces of meat, then lift it up to take something underneath. I need to leave as little trace as possible. Maybe I'll be able to bury the cut pieces back at the bottom of the icebox once I'm done. I'll just need to do this quickly and, most importantly, quietly.

[Sanity Level: 95%]

Pulling the steak out, I head over to the counter and grab a knife. I don't bother with a plate. I don't even pay attention to if the knife's clean or dirty. I just want to get this over with.

I begin sawing at the frozen meat, trying to chop it up into pieces—that should satisfy the role requirement. But it's frozen solid. I can't even cut a corner off.

Mentally growling, I throw my gaze around the kitchen. I could add some wood to the stove and heat it that way, but there's no way I could covertly start a fire. What else, what else? The mind static is spreading.

[Sanity Level: 93%]

I catch sight of the jars of seasoning again and pounce on them. One looks like it might be salt, so I sprinkle that over the still-frozen slab of meat. I pause, watching my sanity counter. It lingers at 93%, not heading up, but not heading down either. I grab the next jar of spice and throw it onto the meat too. So much for leaving no trace.

It could just be my slipping sanity, but a part of me wants to laugh. The absurdity of the situation is too much. Here I am, breaking into the house of someone I'm supposed to drug, and I'm in their kitchen silently trying to throw a meal together like my life depends on it—and it probably does.

A floorboard creaks.

I pause, hand still halfway toward putting the lid back on the salt jar. What was that? Had I imagined it? I don't move a muscle.

The house is quiet.

[Sanity Level: 92%]

I can't stand around all night. I need to figure this out now and run. In fact, maybe I'll just grab the piece of meat, take it with me, and then find somewhere safe to doctor it up and throw it away. That would be taking implicating evidence with me, but staying in here is creeping me out, and so long as I'll still be a functional human at 50% sanity, it's worth the risk.

I hastily grab the piece of meat, swipe the grains of salt and herbs off the counter, and then make for the door.

My hand is outstretched, reaching for the handle, when a thump sounds on the other side of the door.

I didn't imagine that one, I'm certain of it. I step away from the door even as I hear footsteps thud across the floor, in the next room over, heading toward the kitchen. I leap back, ice crystalizing in my veins. Ducking into the furthest, darkest corner of the room, I squeeze between the stove and the wall and wait for my nightmare to become reality.

[Sanity Level: 91%]

The kitchen door swings slowly and silently inward, a living shadow in the dark. My stomach sinks into the floor as my heart catches in my throat. I feel like I'm being pulled apart at the seams. This can't be happening. No, please, not now!

I Check the open door frame, that solid rectangle of black.

[Enrold, level 32 dhampyr blood guard,] Echo says.

He's here.

The dhampyr steps into the room, needing to duck under the frame. The world's black and white, all abstract shapes and impressions, but nothing has ever felt more real, the moment terrifyingly brittle and present.

"I know you're here," he says. His voice is barely a murmur, but in the close, quiet room, it might as well have been spoken right next to my ear. "I thought I heard a mouse sneaking around."

[Sanity Level: 90%]

I'm keeping so still, holding my breath so tight, I nearly jump at Echo's update. An irrational part of me briefly worries that he can hear her. He can't. I know he can't. But even though I can't see which way his head is turned, it still feels like he's looking right at me.

"Come out, little mouse," Enrold says. "There's no point in hiding."

Not fucking likely! I'll just have to wait him out. If he moves away from the door, maybe I can make a break for it.

[Sanity Level: 89%]

Except waiting this out is the one thing I can't do right now.

Enrold chuckles darkly. "Clearly you don't know whose house you trespassed in. It was a bad move to try to rob the *captain* of the City Guard. An even worse move to sneak into a dhampyr's house at night."

Despite the tense situation, I make a face. This guy is such an arrogant ass. Even now he's bringing up his title.

"I suppose as a human, this might not occur to you," Enrold says, and I go cold. How does he know I'm human? "But it's a relatively well-known fact that dhampyrs can see in the dark."

Oh, shit.

I leap from my hiding place as Enrold surges forward. He grabs for me, and I fling the frozen slab of meat at him like a frisbee, which cracks against the bridge of his nose.

[5 points of Bludgeoning damage dealt.]

[Sanity Level: 88%]

I scramble away as Enrold swears, clapping a hand to his nose. I dash past him and toward the door, grabbing the handle.

"Bastard," Enrold growls, coming after me.

Throwing open the door, I dive through—but not fast enough. A hand snags my cloak, yanking back. For a moment it pulls across my neck and shoulders, then the slipknot comes free and the cloak goes flying back into Enrold's hands as I race forward, unhindered.

I'm in the armory room. The front door is just one room away. I slam into the living room door next, throwing it open in a panic, and rush inside. The door outside, the door to freedom, is just to my left—

[15 points of Bludgeoning damage sustained.]

[Sanity Level: 87%]

The force strikes me so hard I'm facedown on the floor before I even know what hit me. The terror doesn't let me stay stunned for long, though. I try to roll over, but Enrold has a hand on one of my legs. A strangled cry rising up my throat, I kick viciously at his arm and face. He grabs my free leg and quickly slams it down next to the first. I desperately try to struggle from his grasp, but his grip is like iron. I can't shake him.

Enrold chuckles darkly. "It's been a while since I've had some fun like this. Making me thirsty." Even in the half light I can make out his smile, his fangs glinting white and stark against their surroundings.

[Sanity Level: 86%]

Fear threatens to choke me. It squeezes my heart, my lungs, my mind. And that static from my Role Requirement is making it all worse, making it hard to think, ratcheting up my anxiety, narrowing my focus to the sole need to escape, survive, and fulfill my role. Restlessness tingles through my fingers like ants under my skin.

"Let go of me!"

Enrold snorts. "Not likely." He pulls my ankles back, dragging me toward him as I struggle against his grip. "You broke into my house. Assaulted me. You've no right to be making demands. In fact, I think you owe me something as compensation. A bit of your blood, perhaps."

[Sanity Level: 85%]

"No, you can't!" My fingernails scratch uselessly against the ground as I'm dragged across the floor. My stomach is in frozen knots. My legs, where he's squeezing them, have gone numb. "The guards—"

"I *am* the Guard," he sneers. "My word is law. And your continued existence is more trouble than I need. But we can take care of that now, hm?"

He's so much stronger than I am. Faster. He can see everything in the room while I'm half blind. I look up at Enrold's face, largely dissolved into the dark, and the wicked grin that looks down at me sends me back to Maru, to her laughter, to that overwhelming feeling of helplessness. *Never again.*

[Sanity Level: 84%]

I fumble with my bandolier as he lets go of one of my legs, reaching for an arm instead. I rip a bottle from its strap, but he grabs my wrist and slams it into the floor. He looms over me, victorious.

With my free hand I grab the bottle and smash it across his face. Shards of glass cut into my skin as it shatters, and the liquid sprays everywhere, coating half his head and splashing back onto me.

[4 points of Slashing damage dealt.]

[2 points of Slashing damage sustained.]

[Status Effect Inflicted: Poisoned (major)]

[Status Effect Sustained: Poisoned (minor, reduced due to Poison Resistance)]

[Sanity Level: 83%]

"Fuck," Enrold snarls, turns his head away from the blow. "What did you do?"

He grabs for the arm I struck him with, but with half his vision obscured I'm able to pull it away. At the same time, I kicked my legs up between his legs, hard.

[9 points of Bludgeoning damage dealt.]

Enrold howls, yanking me out from underneath him. My arm feels like it's nearly pulled from its socket as he throws me across the room. I go flying like a rag doll, my arms and legs and head striking the ground before I slam into the wall and crumple to the floor. Another one of my bottles breaks in the confusion, and smoke begins to vomit into the room.

[Sanity Level: 82%]

"Bitch," he growls. I can no longer see him—I can no longer see anything—but I can hear his footsteps thumping across the floor. Inevitable, like lightning before the thunder. "You'll pay for that."

Chapter Thirty

[IN]SANITY

I fumble blindly for a pouch, my fingers stuffy and numb as I pull the drawstring open and dig my hand into the sack. My fingers close around several frost seeds, and I push mana into them as I pull them back out and throw them across the floor.

Enrold's footsteps stop. I hold my breath. My pulse is a jackhammer. All my nerves are alight with heightened sensation. The rough grit of wood pressing into my hip and elbow. The throbbing pain from where Enrold's hand had been around my wrist. Spotting burns where the poison had splashed against my skin. I blink rapidly, willing my sight to return, but the smoke won't clear for several minutes at least.

[Sanity Level: 81%]

His footsteps rapidly stomp a few feet to my left.

"Cheap tricks," he growls. "But it's only buying you a few seconds."

He's blinded by the smoke, too. The thought gives me a brief burst of hope, but Enrold's right that it's only bought me a little time. I'll have to take it—every second counts.

I throw another seed, this time so it strikes several feet away. Wind gusts against me as Enrold moves, racing toward the sound. And then, finally, I hear what I've been waiting for. His boot scrapes across the ground like he's slipped.

Thud.

The force of the fall shakes the whole room, sending the house swaying. I don't give him an opportunity to recover. I leap to my feet and feel my way across the wall, reaching for the doorknob I can see in my mind's eye, only another two paces away.

"What did you do?" Enrold demands, his words slurred.

The poison must finally be taking effect. I Check him even as my hand finally closes around the doorknob.

[HP: 45/120]

Meanwhile, I'm down to 68/90. It was close, but I'm going to make it out. In the end, that's all that matters. I turn the knob, and the door *clicks* as it begins to swing open.

Enrold roars, throwing himself at me. I slam into the doorframe as he smashes into my side, and we both tumble to the ground as the front door swings open. I reach for the hearth, for freedom, but he yanks my arm away with a violent twist. I feel something *pop*, and I cry out as pain lances through my shoulder.

[19 points of Sundering damage sustained.]

[Sanity Level: 80%]

I struggle to twist around, all rational thoughts fleeing me. I'm no longer thinking, no longer planning—I exist only as a desperate thrashing of pain and emotions. Every last one of my instincts is screaming at me: you won't die here. You won't die here!

Enrold slams me onto my back, and my vision flashes white with a stab of agony as my arm catches under my hip, now limp and useless. Bile threatens to surge up my throat as the pain overwhelms me. I desperately and repeatedly strike his temple with my free hand, but I might as well be punching a wall. My fist stings, and Enrold ignores the blows, closing a hand around my neck.

[Sanity Level: 75%]

[Status Effect: Suffocation. You will lose 1 HP per second while the condition is in effect.]

I thrash against his grip, kicking and punching and jerking to get free as his hand tightens and I gargle in half a breath. My body flashes hot and cold, every frantic move fueled by terror and hate. *I won't die, I won't die, I won't die!* I reach for everything, anything I have left.

[Knife removed from inventory.]

The handle manifests in my grip as I draw my arm back to punch him again. This time, when I slam my fist toward his head, I finally feel the blow connect. Enrold jerks to the side with a grunt, his hand loosening from around my neck. I gasp in a lungful of air, then I jerk my arm back—feeling the knife come un-stuck from the hard surface it had been embedded in. I stab at him again. And again.

[Sanity Level: 71%]

Enrold raises a defensive hand as he slumps to the side, tumbling off of me, and I surge upright to continue my onslaught.

[Sanity Level: 68%]

I am rage. I am revenge. I am euphoric with triumph, with an earned victory, hard-fought and deserved. He won't be a threat to me or anyone I care about ever again.

I bat Enrold's arm away as he weakly tries to protect himself, plunging my blade up and down like a machine. In the dark, in the thinning smoke, I can't even see where I strike, and the *thump* of each blow feels surreal and distant. Like I'm not even here, it isn't really me doing this. I watch, detached, as Enrold's HP ticks away to 0.

[EXP threshold met. Level up!]

[EXP threshold met. Level up!]

[Sanity Level: 63%]

A healing warmth washes over me, but the pain in my mind only continues to grow. I growl, clutching my skull as the static swirls through my brain. I *need* to do something. What is it? It's important.

Cut. Chop. Dice.

I shudder, my knife still embedded in the body before me. This time, instead of yanking it out, I drag the blade down, cutting through the flesh.

[Sanity Level: 64%]

A shiver of elation passes through me. That was it. That was the right thing to do. So I do it again.

Instincts take over. After all the practice working in the Starlight's kitchen these past few weeks, my hand practically moves all on its own. I only catch flashes of what I'm working on in the dark: a distant streetlight casts just enough light to trickle in the door, reflecting off the steel of my knife, and the wet along my arm. An overpowering odor of copper and death rises to engulf me.

[Daily Role Requirement satisfied.]

Gradually, my self awareness returns. The Sanity bar is filled back up. Sluggishly, my mind begins to process the graphic scene around me. What I've done. What it is I'm cutting to bits.

A horrified laugh burst from my mouth. This isn't real, is it? This is some nightmare. Some other person is sitting here, not me. My hand quivers, and I drop the blade. It clatters to the floor, the sudden noise like a gunshot. I jump at the sound, and then I begin to shake. Even my throat quakes as I take in a shaky breath, and when I let it out it's more laughter. More horrified, shocked laughter of denial. This isn't me. I didn't do this!

I try to stop laughing, but it keeps pouring uncontrollably out of me. I've lost my mind. I'm going crazy. I just butchered a person like they were stew meat, and all I felt was relief.

"Sal?"

Cyros's voice comes from outside. I twist around to look and try to bite down my laughter. I manage to hold it in for a second, but my breath bursts out of me once more—this time as a sob.

Cyros's face is pinched in concern, but as his gaze trails down to my arms and hands, to the gore-soaked floor beyond me, his expression turns into one of shock.

"Gods' grace," he says, taking a half step closer. "What happened?"

"I—I messed up," I say, my voice breaking. The trembling in my limbs turn every breath into a nervous laugh or sob, and I can't seem to stay consistent between the two. It's not funny. It's repulsive. It's surreal. "What have I done?" I croak. "What have I done?"

Cyros hesitates a moment longer, glancing around the bridge, then hurries to the door. "Come on," he says, putting a hand on my shoulder. "We need to get you out of here before anyone sees. If the City Guard realizes you're involved..."

"They'll what?" Manic laughter bursts from my lips. "I killed their captain. Oh, god." I sob, my chest tightening as tears sting my eyes and blur my vision. "I killed him."

"Come on," Cyros says. "This is a mess. We'll figure it out later. Now, we need to get out of here."

He grabs me under each of my armpits and hoists me upright. I wasn't sure I'd be able to stand, but my feet stumble into position beneath me, and I sway, numb.

Cyros stops to bend back down and snatch up my knife, which he presses into my hand. "If you leave this behind, someone determined enough will be able to track it back to you. Is there anything else in there that could be traced to you that we need to grab before we leave?"

The knife swims in and out of focus in my blurred vision. Its handle feels cold and unwelcome in my grasp. I don't want to be touching it anymore. I add it back into my inventory, and the blade vanishes from existence.

Cyros shakes my arm. "Sal, hurry! Did you leave anything behind?"

The edge in his voice rattles me out of my stupor. Cyros is putting himself at risk trying to help me. I have to focus—I need to pull myself together.

"Glass," I mumble.

"What?" Cyros asks.

"And pottery," I add, forcing myself to speak, even as I'm unable to still the uncontrollable shakes that continue to wrack my body. "Some of my bottles and jars broke. They're in pieces. In... in there." My eyes wander over the gore-soaked floor: Bits of broken potion bottles would be impossible to pick out amidst the mess.

"Great Abyss," Cyros swears. "That might be a problem. I'll tell Nieve when we get back and see if they can send someone to clean up. For now, there's nothing we can do about it. Let's go."

Cyros tugs on my arm, and I let him lead me away.

He takes me on a route I haven't been, across dark, deserted bridges I hadn't noticed before. His hand remains tight around my elbow, steering me on, as if he expects me to collapse or drift aimlessly away without his guidance. And maybe I might. My mind keeps circling between numbness and horror and revulsion, settling on neither long enough for me to fully process what I'm feeling. I don't think I want to.

"Why are you here?" I finally croak, focusing on Cyros instead of everything else that's fighting for attention in my head.

"I followed you, of course," he says. "It's your first mission. Someone needs to report the status back to the Guild."

"You were watching?" I ask. That whole time I was fighting for my life—all that time after I started carving up the body—he only watched?

"From a distance," he admitted. "I was waiting for you to slip back out the way you went in. As time passed, I realized something was wrong. I didn't realize you'd opened the front door until I circled around the house."

I sag, relieved. He didn't just leave me to die. He didn't just watch as I committed an atrocity. Even though he's an assassin himself, even though he didn't really do anything to help, somehow, that makes me feel better than anything else he's said so far.

"I want to go home," I say, tears spilling over and running in tickling rivers down my cheeks. I brush one hand across my face to rub the streaks away, but instead I feel something sticky smear across my face. I look down at my hands. The world is only black and white to me right now in the moonlight, and my hands are as dark as the shadows, glistening and wet.

"We'll get you back to the Guild to get you cleaned up," Cyros promises.

"The Guild," I repeat.

The Guild doesn't feel like home. But even as I think that, I'm not sure what home even means to me anymore: not Talia's house, not Cyros's presence, not the Starlight Inn. Before that—in my last life—what was home even then, either? Hospital beds? My childhood bedroom slowly cannibalized by machines and pill bottles? My parents?

My heart about bursts when I think of their faces. The faces I'll never see again. They're gone forever, left back on Earth, and now I'm starting to think a big part of me got left behind there, too.

I'm not really Sal anymore. Not the same Sal, at least. This Sal has less of her mind. Less of her heart. Less of her soul. This Sal is hollow from all the missing pieces.

Home? No. There is no home anymore.

Chapter Thirty-One
Augmentation

The rest of the night passes in a sleep-deprived haze. As the adrenaline wears off, my body crashes hard. My insides feel hollow and cold, and every pain I hadn't been feeling before, I feel now. I shouldn't, because my level up healed all my injuries. But maybe this kind of hurt isn't entirely physical.

I numbly obey Cyros's instructions when we make it back to the Guild. Others stop to stare when I step through the door, and I don't blame them—I'm dyed crimson from head to toe. Cyros quickly ushers me down a set of stairs where there's water basins with heating spell circles carved into the metal bins, and I climb into one, clothes and all, as the blood begins to stain the waters red.

I lay there, floating in warm nothingness, as Cyros hurries off to speak with Nieve. Halfheartedly, I run my hands through my hair and over my skin. Gore drips from my scalp. Not mine, though. My skin is perfectly smooth, not a scratch on it. I touch my neck, where the bruises should be, but there's nothing there. Like I didn't almost die. Like the trauma never happened.

I drift—never asleep, not entirely. But my mind goes blank. I stop registering my surroundings. Then, without warning, I snap back into the moment, and reality crashes down on me.

I sob.

I sit silently.

Finally, I mechanically clean myself with soap and a sponge.

At some point the night turns into morning, and by then I've nothing left to feel. I've cried and scrubbed it all out.

I sit in the guild hall wearing a borrowed tunic and trousers, my other clothes going through a magical blood-stain-removal cleaning session. Cyros sets some spiced oats with nuts and fruit in front of me; I take one bite without registering the taste, then leave the rest to go cold.

Nieve sits down across from me. "We were able to attend to the scene before anyone else discovered the target's death. We recovered the pieces Cyros mentioned. There was also a cloak that we took with us that we believe must belong to you."

Oh yeah. I had lost my cloak in the confusion. I'd forgotten about that. Another mistake.

Nieve waits, but when I remain silent, they continue. "By now the City Guard is aware and investigating. I would suggest you lay low for a time."

"I'll leave," I say. "If the Starlight isn't a good idea, then I'll go to another city."

"Is that so?" They touch a hand to their temple. "With such a mark, I doubt any distance would make much difference for long."

I touch my own forehead, reminded again of the brand there. Crap, they're right. It doesn't matter where I go; the Gods' Tournament will pull me back here in eight days regardless.

"However," Nieve says, a faint smile gracing their lips. "I don't believe such extremes are necessary. You are free to stay here, or leave—wherever you believe you'd draw the least attention in the interim."

It takes a moment for their words to sink in. "I'm free to leave," I say slowly. "So does that mean... I passed the test?"

Nieve snorts. "*Pass* is a strong word. I can at least allow that you didn't fail. If this were a typical job, you would be collecting no coin for the hit that you butchered—literally."

I think of the blood, of my knife, of the impact of each strike, and my stomach roils. I swallow, pulling my thoughts away.

"That said, I truly didn't expect you to go through with it at all," Nieve says. "And for that, I was proven wrong, and you've surprised me—a rarity, which deserves some praise. I am still unsure if the way you chose to prove yourself was out of ardent loyalty, or madness."

I open my mouth to respond, but they cut me off.

"Please don't respond to that," they say, chuckling. "I fear I wouldn't like the answer. Either way, you have earned access to the Guild and our resources, and so long as you follow our code, you will be accepted here as an apprentice. Congratulations." They pass my scarf—Gugora's scarf—back over to me. As the silk shifts beneath the light, I can make out the glow of a spell circle: the same symbol that's on Cyros's cloak.

The spell circle that grants admittance into the Guild Hall.

"A bit of advice," Nieve says. "Choose your next job more wisely if you wish to keep that."

I marvel at the mark. The gold shape of a gnarled tree fades from view, melting back into the black of my scarf. I actually made it. I'm in.

Despite everything, despite this pervasive hollowness, I feel a spark of hope ignite within me once more.

"So then... do I have access to the next floor?" I ask. "If I want to survive the tournament, there's some potions I'll need to prepare."

"Hm." Nieve appraises me with a smile. "Driven. I appreciate that. But no matter your need, exceptions cannot be made for Guild members. You currently have access to the base floor, which includes the job board and the general store. No more, no less. If this isn't sufficient to your needs, you'll need to earn your access to further areas of the Guild."

"I think it will be enough," I say, a little disappointed. There are plenty more interesting and useful things locked out of my reach, still. But if I can afford some of those rare herbs in the general store, then I'll at least have a few new potions up my sleeve to try.

Slowly but surely, my resolve returns to me once more. I still feel fragile—hollow—like a jack o' lantern with all its guts scraped out. But that flickering flame of defiance remains in me. A possible road to survival. A path back to my revenge. I'm one step closer, even if I had to throw everything on the line to make it this far. I'll just have to be willing to do this again, and again, and again, until I've crawled and scraped my way to the top, bruised and bleeding.

It doesn't matter if I only survive by a hair's width margin. All that matters is that I keep surviving.

I turn to Cyros. "You had to borrow stuff for me from the Alchemist Lounge before. Do I have access to it now?"

Cyros looks to Nieve, and they wave him on. "I'm done with her," they say. "So long as you're staying in the guild hall, you're laying low, so whatever you explore is fine with me. And, Sal."

I pause, already halfway standing up from the table.

"Anyone admitted to the Guild is to be mentored by the individual who invited them. Officially, you are now Cyros's responsibility. However, he is not yet qualified to apprentice a pupil of his own. If you should wish to speak about anything, you know where to find me."

A lump forms in my throat, so instead of replying, I just nod. Their sharp eyes follow as I step toward Cyros, then I turn away so I don't have to see them anymore. Speak about what? Killing a man? Cutting him up into stew meat?

That nervous instinct to laugh takes hold of my chest again, but I fight it down.

I needed to gain experience taking a life, anyway. Now, there will be no hesitation when I confront Maru. I'm one step closer to being able to protect myself—one step closer to revenge.

"Come on," Cyros says, pulling me out of the dark fog of my thoughts. "The Alchemist general store is this way."

"Right," I say. Even if I won't be able to explore more of the interesting sounding areas, like the magical armory Cyros had let slip before, I should still be able to make some headway on a few of the spells in Lisari's book. "There's a few new ingredients I need to pick up."

He leads me down the stairs to the lower floors, including the washroom I'd been in before. Beyond that are more staircases heading down, and though they're all unlabeled, so far as I can tell, Cyros seems to know exactly which one to take.

He steps down the stairs, vanishing into the shadows, and I follow. The mark on my scarf seems to flash as my foot hits the bottom step, but nothing stops me from moving forward. We step into a new room.

This one is full of vials and tubes that look like the chemistry equipment in a mad scientist's lair. Rather than herbs and dry ingredients, all the items behind the sales counter in this room are liquids of varying colors and opacities. I start having Echo Check them all, trying to gauge what I'm working with.

[Potion for enhanced strength. Draught of firebane. Necrotic bonefang poison. Potion of wind walking. Shadow elixir.]

So many things I want to try, so little time.

And money. Mostly money.

I lean against the counter, scanning all the other bottles. I can't risk missing the one thing that might save my life.

The vendor, a dryad with aspen-patterned skin and yellow leaves for hair, wanders over to me. "Can I help you? If you need me to explain anything..."

Cyros shrugs. "Probably everything. She's new to potions so she probably won't even know what she's looking at."

"That one," I say, pointing to a red liquid in a small bottle on the last shelf. "The augment. How much?"

Cyros gives me an incredulous look. "Seriously?"

The vendor grabs the bottle and sets it before me on the counter. It's the size of a grapefruit.

[Potion Augment,] Echo says. [Efficacy: 98%. When incorporated in the brewing stage, the effects of the completed potion will be magnified.]

It's exactly what I need to defeat Maru. I've won!

"The entire bottle is fifty gold pieces," the vendor says.

Or maybe I spoke too soon.

"I only have a handful of silvers," I groan. I glance hopefully over at Cyros.

He shakes his head. "No way. I don't know why you'd think I have that kind of money, but I'm almost as poor as you."

"I could sell you a smaller portion," the vendor suggests. "A thimble is the smallest size we go. That would be one gold piece."

I groan. "That wouldn't be nearly enough. And I don't even have any gold, anyway."

The vendor shrugs, taking it back over to the wall.

I sigh, disappointed. "Well, can I get some of that underwater potion instead?" I ask.

The vendor takes a different bottle off the wall, this one a swirling blue-green, and sets it down before me. "This one is forty silvers for the bottle, one silver for a thimble."

That, at least, I can afford. I've got seven silvers to my name from working in Iski and Gugora's shop. "I'll take five silver's worth."

The vendor grabs a smaller vial and takes both potion and container back to some measuring equipment on the back wall, beginning to prepare my order.

"A water breathing potion?" Cyros asks, perplexed. "You planning on going swimming?"

"Nope," I say. "Did you know that potion actually transforms the water you breathe into air? And that it can do that no matter what kind of water it is—freshwater, saltwater, water filled with dirt. I read about it in my alchemy book. Isn't that wild?"

Cyros frowned. "I suppose. I mean, that's the purpose of the spell, so it's not particularly surprising. But if you're not planning to go underwater, why do you need it?"

"Experiments," I say, grinning wickedly. "Trust me, I know what I'm doing."

The look Cyros gives me indicates that he doesn't, and I don't.

The vendor returns with my water potion and I tuck it into a pocket. Before we leave, I look wistfully back at the augment potion with a sigh.

"Sorry," Cyros says. "I know how much you wanted to check out the advanced draughts down here. You'll just have to go on jobs and save up enough money the old-fashioned way."

"I don't have time for that," I say. "There's only eight days until the tournament, and I need to spend them practicing more and making new potions." I used up basically my whole store during the fight with Enrold. Not to mention, nothing I currently have would be effective against a demigod—not without that augment.

Cyros shrugs helplessly. "Unless you've got some rich benefactor I don't know about, I'm afraid I can't help."

"Someone rich?" I perk up. "I do know someone rich!"

Cyros frowns in confusion. "What? You do?" But he seems to understand who I mean even as he asks, and his eyebrows shoot up. "Wait, no. That's a terrible idea. We're *using* Talia to cover up my hit. And she's a truth-sayer! If you start asking for enormous lumps of cash, she'll definitely get suspicious. In fact," Cyros says, "I forbid you from continuing to see her. We planted all the misdirections we needed to, *and* now you're a member of the Blackcloaks. She's dangerous to be around."

"You forbid me?" I snort. "I don't think you have any say. Besides, she trusts me. And I don't need a *huge* lump of cash. Just enough for some of this potion."

Cyros grimaces. "She'll catch on. This is a bad idea."

I shake my head. "Yee of little faith. Just watch me. I'll be as subtle as a mouse."

"Alright," Cyros says, dubious. "But don't forget; you're supposed to be laying low. And you're *my* responsibility now. If you do end up risking the Guild, that will fall back on me—and affording that potion will be the least of your worries."

"Stop nagging. It'll be fine," I promise.

CHAPTER THIRTY-TWO
OF GODS AND GOLD

I slam open the Storage building's door. "Talia, I need a shit-ton of money!"

Talia sets down her teacup as the City Guards turn to face me.

"Hello, Sal," Talia says. "Thank you for joining us so… unexpectedly. Would you give me a moment to finish my business with the guards here?"

"Um," I say, trying not to stare at the guards. "Sure. Sorry. I thought you were alone."

I shuffle off to the side and stand awkwardly by a cluster of training dummies which have been shoved aside in the storeroom to make room for Talia's equipment. As I wait, I catch sight of Lisari in the back, bent over some books. A faint breeze wisps through the room, and she waves over her shoulder at me. I awkwardly return the wave. Even though I know she can "see" me with her wind, it still feels strange waving at someone's back.

The guards turn back to Talia and I strain to listen in. Are they questioning her about Enrold? She and him didn't seem to be on good terms when she busted me out of the guard hall. I scan the group of guards, and my heart skips when I recognize one of them.

Check, I tell Echo.

[Jules: Level 28 Human Spellsword,] Echo says. [A lieutenant in the city guard.]

Crap. She's one of the guards who originally picked me up from the Starlight Inn. She'll definitely recognize me. Enrold had already been super suspicious of me when Talia intervened. Does Jules harbor that same suspicion? Ironically, I was innocent of murder then, but would be completely guilty if they thought to question me now. I sink in on myself, trying to appear as small and unassuming as possible.

I definitely need to work on my laying low abilities.

"You have our assurance," Jules says to Talia. "The entire stadium will be patrolled by every available guard. Each entry point will be staffed. There will be no surprises."

"So you say." Talia takes another long sip of tea, and the guards stand there awkwardly, waiting for her to finish. Finally she sets it down on her desk. "Alright, I'll take your word. But if indeed the event does not transpire smoothly, you can expect the guards' funding will reflect that next cycle. Just because I no longer have a sister on the Council doesn't mean I no longer have any sway."

Jules presses her lips into a displeased line, but dips her head in acknowledgement. Then the group turns to leave, a few giving me curious looks as they pass by. My stomach flips, and I shrink back as Jules heads my way. She glances at me, and I think I see a flicker of recognition in her eyes. She doesn't stop, however. A moment later, they're gone.

I let out a relieved breath as the door shuts behind them. She has no reason to suspect me. I was worrying over nothing.

"What was that about?" I ask, turning to Talia.

Talia scrunches up her face in distaste. "Preparations for the tournament. The Council should be handling such details, but given their gradual descent into chaos in the wake of my sister's death, I've had to pick up some of their slack. With two seats open, the city's power structure is tenuous, and I wouldn't put it past a councilmember to use the distraction of the tournament to try something rash. The guards have promised to station themselves around the stadium during the event, but I'd feel a lot better about things if I could get the Captain to promise the support himself. Apparently I'm so beneath him that I only receive assurances from his second in command."

I try not to squirm at the mention of Enrold. "Oh?" I ask, innocently.

Talia fixes me with a sharp look. "What's that tone?"

"Nothing," I say. Before she can press the topic, I hurriedly add, "So can I borrow some money?"

Talia snorts. "I seem to recall you were asking for more than just some."

"A shit-ton, to be exact," Lisari says, still bent over her books. "What do you need it for?"

"Precisely what I was going to ask," Talia says. She looks at me expectantly.

"Important things," I say. "Potions."

"Of course," Talia says dryly. "Potions. The most important thing."

"Well I'm rather partial to potions," Lisari says. She finally peels herself away from her books. "What are you looking for? Maybe I could help."

I perk up at the offer. "That would be great. I need an Augment potion."

"Ah," Lisari says, a little disappointed. "Then I won't be able to help. Wind magic, you know."

I look at Talia hopefully, but she shakes her head as well. "I'm more a scholar than a mage. But I *could* potentially purchase this potion you're looking for. An augment, hmm? I've heard of them. What spell are you looking to boost?"

"One that will keep me alive in the tournament," I say, which is, strictly speaking, the truth. Of course, it's Maru rather than the other contestants I'm worried about.

"How much?" Talia asks, suspicious.

I force a smile through my grimace. "Only about fifty gold?"

Talia scoffs, and Lisari whistles.

"I mean, I suppose I could also work with forty," I add.

"You can't possibly need that strong of an augment," Talia says. "I doubt anyone in the city even works with potions at such a price."

Well, not normal merchants, anyway. "Let me worry about buying it," I say. "I just need the capital. I'll pay you back?"

"How?" Talia demands. "You'll be working that debt off the rest of your life."

Depending on how soon my life gets cut short, she might be on the money there. But with the Blackcloak Guild, I'll be able to pay it off with maybe a year's worth of safer jobs—jobs that *don't* involve murdering the head of the city guard.

"Look, I promise I can pay it back, no matter how long it takes," I say. "Please? My life *literally* depends on this."

Talia frowns, drumming her fingers on the desk. "Oh, alright. It's not as though I was planning on using the money for anything else anyway."

"Thank you!" I cry, throwing my arms around her in a hug. "Thank you so much. When can you get it to me?"

Lisari giggles. "Yes, she's truly appreciative."

Oh, shut up, Lisari, you don't have gods trying to kill you.

Talia extracts herself from my hug. "Tomorrow, perhaps, if you meet me at my house in the evening. Will that do?"

I was supposed to head back to the inn tonight. It wouldn't make much sense to head back there today just to turn back around and return to Fairwood the very next morning. Guess Iski and Gugora will have to go another day without me. Even though I'd promised Gugora I'd be back soon. My gut sours at the thought.

"If you don't mind me spending the night at your house again," I say. "I don't have anywhere else in Fairwood to stay."

"That will be fine," Talia allows. "So long as you promise not to steal any more books."

An embarrassed heat climbs up my neck. "I'm just borrowing it."

Talia laughs. "And I'm only teasing you. Honestly, I never touch that library anyway. While you're here, however, I could use your help. Well, Lisari could. You don't mind, do you, Lisari?"

"Not at all," the young woman says.

"I was going to work with her on some of the cultural research for the tournament—the city wants appropriate decorations—however my time is better spent overseeing the workings of the Council and making sure one of the snobs aren't about to gut my department," Talia says, rather bitter. "Sal, if you want to start earning back your keep, here's your first task."

I can think of other things I'd rather be doing than researching culturally significant decorations for a god who I'd love to see dead—like making potions that will keep me from dying by his champion's hand—but at least I'll be working with Lisari, and maybe I can use that opportunity to get some more Alchemy info out of her.

"Sounds good to me," I say.

"Great." Talia gathers up her things and departs as Lisari beckons me over. I suppress a groan as I see the stack of books Lisari has set aside to work through.

"Don't you love research?" she asks. "I can lose myself in a good book for hours."

"I was more into fiction," I say, pulling up a chair next to her table. "Escape from reality and all that."

"Was?" Lisari asks, tipping her head. "What did you have to escape from?"

I grab a giant book off her pile and thump it down in front of me. *Widengra's Conquests*, the title reads. I wrinkle my nose at it.

"Cancer," I say.

"Ah," she says. "I'm sorry. I would never have guessed. You seem quite healthy now. It was curable, then?"

No. It ate me up until I was more cancer than me. Every moment spent loathing my own body, feeling intimately betrayed by myself. If you don't even have control over your own limbs and organs, what *can* you be in control of? Memories of despair and helplessness wash over me, bringing tears to my eyes. I blink them back.

"Yeah, I'm not dealing with it anymore," I say. "Can't you guys just fix it with healing magic?"

"That's a strange way to word it." Lisari smiles softly. "But no, we can't. Healing magic doesn't work that way."

"How does it work?" I ask.

"Well, I'm no Life arcana expert myself," Lisari says. "But I also had plenty of healer consultations back... well, a long time ago."

She taps the side of her glasses, the dark glass completely obscuring her eyes, but not her frown. "My parents wanted to fix it, but you can't heal what isn't wounded. I was born without fully formed eyes, and healing magic is really just a way to accelerate the natural process your body would go through, anyway. It might be able to assist with reattaching a limb, if you're quick enough, but it can't regrow one any more than it can shrink cancer or cause underdeveloped organs to finish developing."

"Oh," I say. "I'm sorry."

She shakes her head. "Don't be! I am very happy to be who I am, as I am. Other people seem to find it more bothersome than I do. People are funny like that, aren't they?"

I grimace. "*Funny*'s a nice way to put it."

She chuckles. "I try to give them the benefit of the doubt. Now, enough about me. We're supposed to be doing research."

I groan, looking at the stack. "Why do you even care about the gods so much? What have they ever done for you?"

"Quite a bit, actually." Lisari puts a finger against her lips. "But that's between me and them. You could try speaking to one yourself. Attend any of their shrines and who knows—they might be listening."

"I don't think they're interested in talking," I say. "Maru wasn't, anyway."

Lisari frowns slightly. "Yes, so you've said. Well, the God of War has always had a one-track mind. Incapable of examining matters complexly."

I raise an eyebrow. "Isn't that blasphemy? Everyone tells me I shouldn't go around saying stuff like that."

Lisari chuckles. "You've got me there. Words like those would certainly cause a stir in more polite society. However, in practice, it is perfectly safe to say such things, unless at a shrine or in the presence of a god yourself. They can't be everywhere at once."

"Good," I say. "Then screw the gods."

Lisari laughs, shaking her head. "You know, they're not all like Widengra—or his champion."

I snort. "Somehow, I doubt that."

"Well, allow me to enlighten you," Lisari says, running her translator stone over the spines of a few books. She pulls one out from the middle of the stack. "Please stop me if any of this seems to break through your, ah, *amnesia*."

Oh yeah. I need to be better at remembering that I'm not supposed to remember anything. Lisari certainly seems to doubt it, and after talking about my cancer diagnosis—which I probably wasn't supposed to remember either—I don't blame her.

"There's dozens of gods, each with their own domains," Lisari says, opening the book. She runs her interpreter stone over the pages, and it quietly reads off words as she flips to a chapter toward the beginning of the book. An illustration fills the page, depicting a white marbled temple adorned with gold and jade. The people in the temple might be dressed in extravagant clothes, but otherwise appear surprisingly mundane. Humans, orcs, harpies, dryads, and plenty more species I haven't encountered before.

The one in the center is labeled Lorata, and her skin appears to be glowing with some internal light. In contrast, the man standing to her right, Shirasil, is dressed in black, accentuated with equally dark hair and smoking pits of darkness in place of eyes. But it's the next god I can't peel my gaze away from. *Widengra*, the text reads. The orc stands at least a head taller than Shirasil and Lorata, and twice as wide. Red tattoos swirl over his green skin. I burn his visage into my mind.

"They might reign over a concept, like war, or a kind of magic, like water," Lisari continues. "Some are more powerful than others. Some are more proactive in their blessings. Most of these gods have several champions, usually between one and three, who carry out their will in the mortal realm. Like mortals, some are violent, some are indifferent, and some are kind."

"I find that hard to believe," I say. "If any of them cared, why would they allow gods like Widengra to go around murdering people?"

"Or rather, his champion," Lisari corrects me. She shrugs. "It is rare to witness infighting among the gods, but every time it has happened throughout history, mortals were always the collateral. Perhaps it's better for the gods to avoid conflict with one other if doing so means more mortals would die in the process." She turns the page, displaying depictions of two beings fighting in the distance as a volcano erupts beneath them, lava raining down on the city below. Another page depicts a typhoon tearing through a town. Another one cratered by some impact.

"Those seem more like natural disasters than a result of some divine punishment," I point out.

"Sometimes, the two are not so different," Lisari says.

I cross my arms. "They still don't sound very benevolent to me."

"Not all are," Lisari says with a shrug. "But I doubt anyone would speak ill of gentle Yua Tin, god of starlight, guide to all sailors searching for home. And Rinviu, god of the winds, has served me well. Meanwhile, I've never found Lorata and I see eye to eye." She smiles at some inside joke. "Perhaps her insight is only apparent to those who can see as she does."

"Does it actually help?" I ask, skeptical. "Praying to a god who is the patron of one of your arcana affinities?"

"It certainly can't hurt," Lisari says, which sounds like a no to me. "But yes, there have been times when the gods have bestowed advice, gifts, or powers onto a mortal when one catches their attention. That's where their champions come from, after all."

"Don't suppose any of them are the god of Poison?" I ask, mostly joking.

"Hm." Lisari taps her chin. "Not directly, no. Not every niche field of magic has a corresponding god, though every major field of magic does. Poison's umbrella field would be Life arcana, and the god of that is Kero. However, he has been known to favor the healing fields over the necrotic ones; poison might not be to his taste. I think you'd be better off following a god who represents values you aspire to embody. For instance, Widengra is often prayed to by hunters and warriors."

And probably people in the Blackcloak guild, but I'm not about to pay any respect to that god.

"How about alchemy?" I ask.

"Perhaps Lorata, god of light," Lisari suggests. "She's most often associated with knowledge and study."

"I thought you didn't like her," I point out.

Lisari chuckles. "I just said she hasn't particularly been beneficial to me. But you're right; I find her too... by the books, I suppose you could say. For Alchemy, it's less about order, and more about change. Turbulence. Sometimes, experiments." She smiles. "For that you might be better off with Shirasil, god of chaos."

"Chaos?" I repeat. "Praying to a god of chaos while mixing potions doesn't sound terribly safe."

Lisari laughs. "No, I suppose not. But it does sound terribly fun, doesn't it?"

I smile. Maybe I pegged her wrong and she's not the celestial fangirl I originally thought she was.

"Well, thanks for the tip," I say, "but I think I'll leave the worship to more devout followers. I'm perfectly happy to figure all this magic out on my own."

"Speaking of." Lisari pulls another book out from the stack, this one much smaller than the others. "I've another book you can borrow if you have time. This one's just potions that use Life arcana, so you should be able to create most of them, I think."

"Thank you," I say, excitedly taking the book. "I can't wait to look through this. If only I had more time and mana to try everything out! This stupid mana constraint is slowing everything down."

Lisari tips her head. "Oh, I didn't realize you were dealing with something like that. Unfortunate."

"Is it common?" I ask. "Are some people just unlucky when it comes to mana reserves?" It wouldn't be the first time I was born without luck.

"Unfortunately, yes," Lisari says. "Some species are predisposed to be naturally inclined toward magic—for others, the opposite. Humans tend to be the least magical; arachnoids, elves, and halflings tend to have the most."

"Oh." It just figures. Why would anything be easy for me, after all?

"However, as long as you have access to even a drop of magic, you can train yourself to increase that pool," Lisari says.

I lean forward. "Really? How?" I've leveled up several times now, and my mana hasn't gone up even a single point. I've been able to train up other skills and stats simply through repetition, but no matter how many potions I've made, nothing seems to move the dial for my magic.

"Various ways," Lisari says. "There's potions you can take that will temporarily expand your mana well. Items that will provide you with a larger pool of magic to pull from. Blessings from a god. As for permanent improvement, I've heard that casting spells and practicing attunements can also help exercise that muscle—though I do realize that attunements might be a bit difficult with Poison as your affinity."

"Maybe," I say, thoughtfully. Attunements are one thing I haven't tried yet, because it requires you to be touching the element you are trying to Attune. If I'd tried it before, the poison would have killed me. Now that I've built up a bit of an immunity though, I wonder if I could try again and be able to Attune at least a drop.

What could one do with Attuned poison, though?

I think I'd like to find out.

"Now," Lisari says, clapping her hands together. "That's enough talk. Talia promised you'd help me with the tournament prep today. Let's get started."

Chapter Thirty-Three

MAD MAGICS

[7 Days until the Gods' Tournament]

"Chaos and potions, huh?" I stir the pot as steam hisses up from the bubbling brew. "I guess it's not the worst idea."

I haven't added any magic to the potion yet; I'm just preparing the solvent. Once it cools and I activate it with my mana, it will be another standard smoke potion, which I've practically memorized by now. But what happens if different components are added first? Like, say, a frost seed? Could I use this smoke bomb to freeze a roomful of people? One way to find out.

I wrap my scarf around my nose as I drop a frost seed into the brew. The potion hisses, turning white-blue, and then the steam vanishes. A moment later, the bubbles stop, and then ice starts to crackle across the surface.

"Hm," I grunt in disappointment. I attempt to ladle out a serving of the potion before it freezes over, and I'm rewarded with a bowl full of slush. I add a couple drops of magic to it anyway, but nothing happens.

I set the failed potion aside. Maybe I should add the components of a frost seed rather than the finished product itself. According to

Lisari's books, such combinations should be possible—trial and error was how potions were discovered in the first place, after all. I just need to uncover the right conditions.

[5 Days until the Gods' Tournament]

[Skills: Knifework lvl 13, Poison Resistance lvl 9, Soft Step lvl 8, Throwing Knives lvl 7, Toxic Intuition lvl 4.]

The bowl of poison sits on the floor in front of me. It's been diluted with water 10:1. If it does poison me at all, it won't be enough to overcome my Poison Resistance. I lean forward, sitting cross-legged, and push both hands into the bowl. The water level rises to just under the brim.

[Status Effect sustained: Poisoned]

[Status Effect nullified. The rate of poisoning is negated by Poison Resistance.]

Perfect. "Alright then. Echo, can I Attune the poison that's in here?"

[Affirmative.]

My heart flutters with excitement. Finally!

"How much mana will it take to Attune all the poison in this bowl?" I ask.

[Mana requirement: 3]

I grin. That's not bad at all. "Time requirement?"

[2 hours.]

"Really?" I wrinkle my nose. "I have to sit here for two hours with my hands in a bowlful of water just to Attune a few drops of poison?"

[Affirmative.]

I groan. Well that's annoying as hell. But at least it's a one-time thing. According to Echo, once I Attune something, that little volume of Poison will be mine to control forever. Or at least until I lose it. I'll just be careful not to lose it.

"No time like the present," I say with a sigh, focusing on the water. I press my mind out, feeling for the Poison. Leaking mana into the water, magic bubbles up through my fingers, and I feel something in my mind *click*. The magic dissipates into the bowl, but I can still sense something *else*. Something in the water, just outside of reach. I mentally grasp at it, and it seems to move closer.

My mind turning inward, I relax, closing my eyes. The sensation is peaceful, meditative, almost. Like a mental ocean, I reach for the element and it pulls away, the tides ebbing and flowing. I fall into sync with the instinct, trying to bring my mind into lockstep with the magic, trying to become one.

Time slips away from me. I'm not asleep, but I'm not entirely conscious. My mind wanders in the way only a dreaming mind can, drawing connections, examining ideas in impossible ways. Like turning a cube over in my hands, only to find it has more than six sides. In my mind's eyes, something connects into place.

[Attunement complete.]

I open my eyes, and it feels like waking up from the most restful nap I've ever had. My mind is clear. Serene. And in the bowl...

I lift my hands from the bowl, letting the water drip back into it. But there's something else in the bowl I can feel. Faintly, ever so faintly, yet it's there. An extension of my magic.

I mentally swirl the sensation around, and the water ripples. I laugh, mentally condensing the sensation into something more physical, more concrete. A tiny dot of green coalesces from the water, no bigger than a grain of rice. I crook my finger in a beckoning motion, and it lifts from the water, coming to hover over my hand.

"Hah!" I laugh giddily, pointing my finger around the air in front of me. The dot of poison moves with my will, flying around the air. "I did it!"

Now *this* is magic. No chemistry, no instruction books or ingredient lists. Just waving your hands around and making shit fly through the air.

Too bad it's such a pathetically tiny amount.

"What's the potency of this thing?" I ask Echo.

[Check: Attuned Poison. If consumed, the poison would inflict 1 point of damage per 10 seconds for a duration of 5 minutes.]

I frown. "Why that duration?"

[Within 5 minutes, the quantity of poison would be processed by the body and rendered inert.]

"You're saying it will get used up? I can't reuse it?"

[Affirmative.]

I groan. "Well what's the point of that? I just spent two hours attuning a speck of poison that will only do... Echo, how much damage would that do?"

[30 points of Poison damage.]

I groan even louder. "That's stupid. I might as well just use some orchid sap and be ten times as lethal."

Echo does not respond.

I sigh, wiggling my finger and causing the poison to do a happy dance. I smile faintly. "Ah well. I guess I better do *something* with it. What's the efficacy?"

[Efficacy: 100%]

Oh, now that *is* interesting. "So the potency won't decrease over time?"

[Negative,] Echo confirms.

Well, at least there's that. Infinite shelf life. I might find some use for this thing yet. I grab a finger-sized vial from my stash and direct the speck of poison inside of it, stuffing the cork back on. The tiny drop of poison at the bottom of the vial looks fairly pathetic. But at least I won't lose it this way. And over time, I should at least be able to build up the volume, Attuning more poison little by little.

Assuming I don't die next week and actually have time to work on that.

I set the vial of Attuned poison down on the counter and turn to my potion and alchemy books.

"Okay," I say to the table of toxins. "What's next?"

[3 Days until the Gods' Tournament]

The smoke potion is coming along. It's my fourth try at the combination experiment. Last time it nearly worked. I mean, it exploded in a ball of sticky black smoke that left a residue on every surface, but I can *feel* it almost worked. This time, I'll get it.

I sprinkle some ground up redwood bark in first. It looks like cinnamon, floating on top of the bubbling pot. Once it finally vanishes into the brew, I add the crushed rootwart next. I don't touch the pot as it boils, I just wait. Eventually, the water takes on a blue tinge. That's when I know it's ready for the last ingredient: the mushroom caps. Carefully prepared, I add the bowl of diced brownskulls in as well. The potion hisses as the mushrooms hit, and I lean back as it belches forth a cloud of green. I hold my breath—both due to the noxious gas, and because this is the pivotal moment. Will it take?

The potion continues to boil. Nothing explodes. I grin, ladling out a sample bowl of the brew to activate with my magic. I hold my finger over the bowl and summon a single, 1 mana drop of magic into the potion. It strikes with a hiss, turning the draught green.

[Modified smoke potion complete.]

"Yes!" I pump a hand in the air, causing the bowl to rock. As a few drops of the potion spill on the floor, they immediately evaporate into a cloud of dense green-black smoke. I scramble back, pressing my scarf against my face as I take care not to breathe any of the smoke in. As eager as I am to increase my Poison Resistance, I need to be careful I don't brew anything potent enough to accidentally kill myself. I've got a small set of health potions and poison antidotes on me for emergencies now, but even with my Poison Resistance they won't save me from a toxin with a long-duration status effect.

I carefully transfer the sample potion to a vial and stop it shut, then return to the pot boiling on the hearth. Before I activate it with my mana, I've one last ingredient.

Reverently, I take the Potion Augment from a box on my workbench. This bottle is worth more than all the money I'd make at the Starlight in a decade.

"Echo, proportionally, how much Potion Augment would I need to add to this cauldron to double its potency?"

[1.4 scruples.]

"Yeah, can you, um, convert that to, like spoonfuls?"

[Approximately 1/8th of a standardized spoon.]

"Thanks," I say. "Stick with spoons from now on."

[Scruples are more precise.]

I raise an eyebrow. "Are you arguing with me?"

Echo doesn't respond.

"An eighth of a spoonful," I say to myself. Hot damn, that's not much at all! Then again, the bottle isn't that big, and it did cost a fortune. I'll need to ration it.

Except... I need something potent enough to down a demigod. If an eighth of a spoonful would double the potency of my potion, what would a whole spoonful do?

I grin. "I guess we'll find out."

Carefully, I unclasp the Augment, and a pleasant citrus smell, like lemons and summer, wafts from the cap. Not daring to waste a drop, I pour out a spoonful over the cauldron, then carefully, *carefully*, drip the Augment in. The potion doesn't seem to react to the new addition—which is great, because if this thing is powerful enough to take down a demigod, it's definitely powerful enough to kill me. I pull my scarf up again, carefully tapping the last drip of Augment off the spoon, then stop the bottle back up once more. Once it's safely tucked away, I hold my hands over the potion.

"Not sure I really buy into this praying crap," I say to the room. "But if there is a god out there who hates Widengra as much as I do, now's your time to pull through."

My mana pools in my hand like liquid emeralds, and I pour it into the draught.

Chapter Thirty-Four
MY TERMS

[1 Day until the Gods' Tournament]

I plunge my scarf into the wash bucket, then pull it out, holding it up to the sun.

Water drips off the cloth, and I flip it over, watching the water run down the side of the fabric. I wring it out, then uncap the water breathing potion, sprinkling a bit over the scarf. I knead the potion into the material, then try again, plunging the scarf back into the water. Once more I lift the scarf from the water, a puddle forming on top of the material and slowly trickling over the side. I hold it up over my head, watching the bottom.

"Doing some laundry?" Iski asks. "You've been here a month and a half, I suppose it's about time."

I wring out the scarf, flicking the ends against the side of the basin to beat out any excess water. "Hah, hah."

Iski sets her basket of picked vegetables aside and leans against the side of the inn, watching me. "So what is it you're actually doing?"

"Waterproofing," I say, draping the scarf over the drying rack. Given it's my key into the Blackcloak Guild, I hate the idea of letting it out of reach, even for a minute. But I guess letting it dry for an hour out back is better than wrapping a wet rag around my face.

"Planning on going for a swim, are you?" Iski asks.

I shake my head, putting the cap back on the water breathing potion. My bandolier of potions is on the ground next to me from where I'd removed it from my inventory. I try not to wear it around the inn typically, but the only running water is out here at the pump, and I needed a basin to test my theory.

"That really is some kind of water-proofing potion?" Iski asks, curious. "Sounds pretty useful, actually. Could use some of that around the inn."

"Well, it's not made for water proofing," I say. "I'm... adapting its original purpose." I wish she'd stop asking questions about my potions. I can't answer most of them without lies.

"Mhm." Iski watches me as I strap the potion back on my bandolier. Now the bandolier includes the water breathing potion, two mana drain potions, a bottle of orchid sap, three smoke bombs (two of them modified), a mana potion, a healing potion, an invisibility potion, my Attuned poison, and a pouch of frost seeds. I left the Augment locked in the cabin because I don't want to risk breaking the bottle and losing the whole store. Not to mention, there's no point in me carrying it around. It has to be added to a potion as it's brewing to affect the potency, and I doubt I'll have a chance to brew potions on the fly in the middle of the tournament.

"I don't suppose all those other potions are for housework, too?" Iski asks.

I frown, avoiding her gaze as I quickly vanish the bandolier back into my inventory. Iski doesn't react to the sleight of hand. By now she's witnessed me do it plenty of times in the kitchen when trying to grab stuff off the top shelf. Not that I *intended* for her to see the first time. Goblins are surprisingly stealthy.

"I'm heading back to Fairwood tomorrow," I tell her, dodging the question. "Thought maybe I could sell some."

She snorts. "And my mom's a harpy. Please, Sal, you don't need to insult my intelligence. You want me to believe this has nothing to do with the Gods' Tournament?"

I glare at her. "And what if it does?"

Iski doesn't look irritated by my challenge though. There's no sign of anger or disappointment on her face. She just looks... sad?

"What happened to you was wrong," Iski says. "No one would deny that. But look... You don't have to be so set on revenge. You can always walk away. Live a full life. Stay working at our inn—or don't! The world's your nut to crack. Just don't waste it all on a single gamble. Death can't be solved with more death."

Her words might have meant something if I actually had any choice in the matter. But she can't really expect me to throw everything I've worked for away, right when it's within reach, can she?

"I can't just walk away," I say. "Someone has to do something. The gods can't just kill people and get away with it."

"And what exactly do you think you can do about that?" Iski shoots back. "The title isn't just for show! Gods are immortal—and their champions might as well be. You really want to end your life making a statement?"

"No!" I say, voice raised. I try to lower it, despite the anger warming my stomach, threatening to grow into a flame. "No. I don't want to die. I've always, *always* just wanted to live. A normal mundane life. But that choice was taken from me." Again, and again, and again. "So I'm going to fight back, with everything I have. And if it kills me, at least I'll go out on my terms. At least I'll go out on my feet, fighting."

"You do have a choice," Iski says. "Just stay here. Don't leave for Fairwood."

Like a branch crackling in a fire, I feel something in me snap, and anger burns through me. "You're not listening. I don't have a choice!" I grab the band tied around my forehead and yank it down.

Iski frowns at the mark on my head, confused. "Is that Widengra's symbol? I don't understand. How did—"

"Maru put it there." I spit out her name. "It's a summoning spell. To pull me back to Fairwood to compete in the Gods' Tournament."

Her look turns into surprise—and finally, a dawning, dismayed understanding.

"Oh, child," she says, and for a moment, I hear my mom's voice in hers. "What happened?"

And just as abruptly as the anger swept through me, a great sorrow descends, drowning out the rage. "I didn't want you and Gugora to know," I say, slumping as my voice cracks. "I didn't want you to be there to see."

"Child." She pushes off the wall to come over and take my hand, kneeling by my side. "If you'd told us, maybe we could have done something. Perhaps we could have appealed..."

I shake my head, squeezing her hand back. It's smaller than mine, the size of a child's, but it's coarse from years of labor, and its firmness and warmth fills me with a sense of stability. Like a boulder in the sun.

"Maru put the mark there," I tell her. "There's no removing it. And tomorrow, it will summon me to the tournament, whether I want to go or not."

"Abyss take the gods," Iski swears, startling me. I'd never heard her say a word against them before. "We'll figure it out. Come on, we need to tell Gugora about this. He'll help figure something out. He's good at that kind of stuff."

I hesitate, torn between two wants. On the one hand, I know there's nothing they can do. I still ache for revenge. I want to see Maru fall more than anything.

But another part of me is scared, grasping for any form of comfort, and here Iski is, offering it. Telling me it will be okay. They will take care of me. With them, I'm safe.

"You really think anything can be done?" I ask, not daring to let myself hope yet. Hope, once broken, isn't easily mended. I'm not sure it can ever be fully mended at all. Like pottery glued back together, the scars will always be there.

"We can try, can't we?" Iski says, standing. Even then, she's only about eye level. "At the very least, we can try to prepare."

I don't get up yet. "What do you mean?"

"Well, that's what you're doing with all those potions, right?" Iski asks. "They're a way to fight back. But even with magic, you can't underestimate a good blade. I think it's time you've upgraded from that little hunting knife." Iski gestures to the sheathed blade propped against the drying rack, where I'd removed and placed it so as not to damage the leather while experimenting with my scarf.

"You mean it?" I ask, a different kind of warmth kindling in me. "You would really help me? I can have a real weapon?"

Iski snorts. "Why are you acting so surprised? We've been helping you since we first dragged you out of the woods."

Tears sting the back of my eyes. She's right. She and Gugora have been so kind to me, so understanding, so patient every step of the way. And I'd been keeping them at arm's reach. Was I afraid if I let them in, I'd have to deal with losing them one day, too? Like how I lost my parents? Or had I never truly seen this world as my new home, my new future?

Future. An idea I haven't thought of as real in years.

I let go of Iski to rub my eyes and swallow down the tightness in my throat. "Thank you. You're right. You two—you two mean a lot to me. I appreciate everything you've done. I just—I don't want to be a burden on you, like I was for... I just don't want to be a burden. You guys have been like second parents to me."

"Aw, gods," Iski says, blinking rapidly herself. "Now you're going to make me tear up. Well, I never had kids of my own, but I'm sure Gugora sees you as a second daughter. It's been... some time since he had a family."

I frown, looking up at Iski. "He has kids?"

"Had," Iski says shortly. She pats me on the shoulder. "He'll tell you about them someday, when he's ready, I suppose. In the meantime, let's get you on your feet. Come on, we don't have much time now, do we? And we've a lot to prepare for!"

She steps back as I stiffly climb to my feet. I allow myself a small smile. "You were mentioning an upgrade for my knife?"

"Well, we've got quite a few hunting weapons lying around," Iski says, planting her hands on her hips. She frowns in thought, and suddenly she's the everyday business woman I'm used to, always focused on the next problem that needs solving. "Not enough time to teach you a bow. There's some short swords that might work, but still not much time to learn the basics." She jabs an accusing finger at me. "You should have told us about this weeks ago!"

I can't help but sadly laugh. "You're right. That was a mistake. How much training do you think we can make up in the next twenty-four hours?"

Iski grins. "That depends. Are you faster at learning weapons than you are at learning to cook?"

"Ouch," I say, but I'm smiling. Iski's enthusiasm is infectious. I know there's less than a day until the tournament. I know the deck is stacked against me. I know I'm just a kid trying to face the gods. But somehow, it all seems a little more possible with Iski and Gugora there to help.

"What's all this now?" a familiar rumble greets us.

Gugora pokes his head out from the backdoor of the inn. "Been waiting on the tomatoes for ten minutes. Heard a bunch of talking instead. We going to eat dinner, or our words?"

"No time for dinner," Iski says. "We've got a crisis on our hands! Sal?"

He turns to look at me, raising a questioning brow. Even though she's put me on the spot, it doesn't feel like an interrogation. It feels like a war room. Like I'm about to lay out all the intel so we can make the battle plan—together, as a team.

"Okay," I breathe, gathering my thoughts. Where to even begin? With the tournament? With Maru? With why she wants me dead?

"Well," I say. "I guess I should probably start with the fact that I'm from another world."

Iski and Gugora stare at me. Then Gugora turns to Iski. "Am I the butt of a joke?"

"Hey, don't look at me!" she objects. "That's not what I was expecting Sal to reveal, to say the least."

I can't help but grin. It feels good to tell other people. *This time it will be different.* "It's not a joke," I say. "It's why Maru attacked me in the first place. I arrived here from my world, and she appeared shortly after. She asked which one of us was from another planet, and then she started killing. The others died but I... I guess I just got lucky."

They're both staring at me with wide eyes. I don't know if they're shocked, or think I've gone insane—maybe they haven't decided yet, either.

I touch the mark on my forehead. "When I ran into her again in Fairwood, she didn't even remember me. At first I was mad about that, but I guess I lucked out. It doesn't matter, though, because when this pulls me back to Fairwood to compete in the tournament—"

"When the mark does *what?*" Gugora interrupts.

"—I'll have to survive all the other candidates," I continue. "But even if I manage that, I might have to face Widengra. And if he figures out what I am, then it's over." I lift my chin. "But this time I'll be prepared. I have my potions, I have a plan, and I have you guys. Now all I need to do is upgrade to a better weapon, and—*ahh!*"

I slap my hands to my head as fire lances through my skull. My skin is burning, a radiating pulse wrapping around my head, starting from—

From my forehead.

"No!" I look in panic at Iski and Gugora, who are staring back in shock.

"Your mark—" Iski starts.

Not yet. Not now! I still need more time!

I can feel the magic activating, pulling me away like I'm a fish on a hook. I look around, mind racing. My scarf! I lunge for it, and my hand wraps around the cloth. What else? My gaze falls to my knife, leaning against the base of the stand. I dart my hand toward it, fingers closing around the handle. Only when they squeeze shut, there's nothing in my grasp but air.

My surroundings blur into streaks of color. It feels like my brain is about to be ripped from my skull. Then the pain abruptly stops, and the world snaps into focus. I stagger, the ground under my feet not where it's supposed to be. My left hand holds my scarf, still damp from the washtub, but my right hand is empty.

"Welcome, rats," a familiar voice says.

Hatred stirs within me as I look up. Maru folds her arms, staring back down at me, mouth wide in a spiteful grin. "Ready to have some fun?"

Chapter Thirty-Five

PRACTICE MATCH

Nearby, a couple people groan, and my own head still pulses faintly from the summoning spell, but my eyes are glued to Maru.

I can kill her now. Leap forward and attack. Pull out all my potions, throw everything I have at her—

Except I don't have my knife. I'm weaponless. And without a blade, nothing I have prepared will mean anything.

Shit!

"Pull yourselves together," Maru snaps. "You think you're champion material? Pathetic. I hand-picked each and every one of you—don't make me regret it."

A few mumble apologies. Reluctantly, knowing there's nothing else I can do, I tear my gaze away from Maru and quickly take in my surroundings. Judging by the wooden surroundings, we're somewhere in Fairwood. I crane my head around and finally catch sight of something familiar: the latticed structure of the underside of the stadium's seats. We're somewhere beneath the tournament field. The room we're in—if you can call it that—has three walls which reach up to the underside of the bleachers. The fourth angled side is taken up by the seats themselves. There's circles drawn across the floor, for training rings perhaps, and against two of the walls—my heart leaps. There! Rows of spears, swords, shields, and all sorts of weapons I've never seen before. At least I'll have some way to arm myself.

But even as I'm looking at them, I realize there's not enough. There's perhaps a hundred other people in the room, and only six racks of weapons, each with less than ten weapons a piece. In fact, if I had to place a bet, I'd guess there's *exactly* half as many weapons as there are people.

Slowly, I begin edging back.

"Welcome," Maru says, her voice booming through the room. The people in the back are moving up, trying to get closer to the demigod, which isn't helping me slip away in the opposite direction. I bump lightly into a few shoulders, then mentally switch tracks, focusing instead on my Agility. Bodily awareness, as Cyros called it. Predict where others will move, and slide around them.

"If you're standing in this room," Maru continues, "then congratulations—one of you might become a demigod. I say *might*, because Widengra will only choose someone who truly embodies his spirit. If all of you fail to meet his expectations, there will be no qualms over establishing a new tournament and starting again. Here's a tip free of charge: it will be in your best interest not to disappoint him."

A few other people are looking around in confusion now, sizing up our surroundings, not entirely paying attention to the demigod. More than a few are coming to the same conclusion I did, slowly drifting toward one of the weapons racks.

"Why are we here early?" a man grumbles to a woman he's standing next to. "I was planning to get some extra training in tonight."

"An excellent question," Maru says, her head snapping in his direction, despite the fact that she shouldn't have been able to hear from so far away. Well, no *mortal* would have been able to.

I pick up the pace, dropping all attempts at subtlety as I make it to the nearest rack. This one has a longsword, a spear, a shield, a whip, and a small bladed weapon that looks like a one-handed scythe. I grab that, since everything else is too big for me. Next to me, a woman grabs the whip and hurries away.

"You're right," Maru says. "Your summoning is a day early, after all. Regretfully, Widengra informed me that I was too generous with my initial selection. Apparently, he would rather the pool of candidates who are given the opportunity to display their skills tomorrow be of a more...impressive stock. As such, I've been instructed to pare down the crops." She smiles as a stir goes through the room. "Whomever remains standing when I return will be allowed to participate in to-morrow's tournament. I'll be back in... Oh, whenever I feel like it, I suppose. Good luck."

With a flash of light and a thundering boom, the demigod vanishes.

For a moment, the room remains stunned. The contestants look around at each other with wide, shocked eyes. Some of them finally notice the weapons racks. Those ones are too late.

The room erupts into chaos. People are yelling, swearing, diving for the weapons. A lucky few already had their own with them. The rest, well. Something tells me this was no mistake on Maru's part, and the violence that is about to take place is exactly what Widengra had in mind.

I run away from the weapon stands even as the crowd presses to-ward them. Luckily, with a sharp pointy object already in hand, most people dodge out of my way as soon as they see what I've got. I make for a corner near the underside of the bleachers, where there are no weapons and therefore less people.

Briefly, I consider trying to squeeze my way out. Maybe Maru won't notice. I reach for the nearest gap in the slats, intending to grab the vine cross-bars and tear them away, but an invisible force stops my reach.

[Access Denied,] Echo says. [Zonal barrier in effect. Minimum required level to penetrate: 20.]

Of course it is.

I put my back to the wall, eyes darting around for anyone who might wander too close. I use the moment to drape my scarf around my shoulders, then I grasp the sickle with both hands, my grip so tight it burns.

The dash for the weapons is over in a matter of seconds. Fighting breaks out near the racks, people scrabbling over the weapons. Someone screams. Red splashes the floor.

It's like the ebb and flow of a tide. One minute it's a rush toward the racks, the next it's a rush away. Several unarmed candidates race for a door on the opposite wall, probably hoping to flee the carnage, but the door won't open, and many are slain from behind then and there.

The brief moment of people avoiding me due to my weapon is over; now I notice a few who are eying my weapon and sizing me up. They probably think they can take me; they'd probably be right.

I need to get my bandolier out of my inventory. If I summon it now, it'd fall to the floor and probably break several of my bottles. I need just twenty seconds in a corner somewhere to pull it out and strap it on. But at this moment, twenty seconds might as well be an hour.

A man dashes toward me. I raise my weapon with a yell, startling both of us. He reaches a hand out toward me, and I swing the weapon around. The blade slices through his arm, spraying a crescent of blood, and now he's the one screaming. Echo recites the damage dealt, but I try to brush the notification aside. I need my head clear.

I sidestep the man as he stumbles to the floor, cradling his arm to his stomach.

"Stay down," I shout at him, looking around wildly for the next attacker. Luckily, a couple of the individuals who had been eyeing my scythe are now backing off. "You won't win a fight like that. Keep out of the way." Good advice for myself, in fact. Maybe if I can find somewhere to hunker down and not appear as a threat—

Before I'm given a chance to find one such hide away, a woman runs at me with a spear. I raise my scythe, fully aware of how pathetic my weapon looks against hers. It's enough of a deterrent, though, as her gaze slides off me, and she runs past. With an arc of the weapon, she slashes the man I had previously downed across his back. Only a single, shocked breath escapes him as he collapses to the floor.

"Why?" I cry, but the woman is already gone, swallowed up by the chaos of the crowd. And I *know* why—easy targets will be the first to go. It's kill or be killed.

It always has been.

I jump over the man, still bleeding out, and crouch down behind him. I quickly drop the scythe and summon my bandolier, which falls into my waiting hands. I sling the belt over one shoulder, snatching up my weapon once more. The bandolier is hanging loose, but I don't have time to get it strapped down tight.

Echo, Check anyone who gets within twenty feet of me, I tell her. *But only level and class: nothing else.*

[Affirmative.]

Level numbers and class names start appearing above the heads of anyone who gets too close. The man I'd downed is a Level 21 Hunter. I guess that means he's not dead yet. Maybe if Maru returns in time, he can get healing before he bleeds out.

I touch the health potion on my bandolier. Then I push myself to my feet and leave him behind. I don't feel as much regret as I think I probably should.

Another person comes at me, this one unarmed. I sink into a defensive stance, tightening my grip on my sickle. They raise a bare fist, and I prepare to cut through their hand. I register their stats only a moment before they strike: Level 25 Wind Mage.

Their punch blasts forward with a gust of air. My weapon is ripped from my hands before I can react. Their fist strikes me in my chest, and then the world spins around me.

[5 points of Bludgeoning damage sustained.]

[3 points of Bludgeoning damage sustained.]

I land on my back and go skidding across the floor. My brains are jumbled and my vision swirls. Even so I scramble upright, trying to shake the disorientation away. I'd been so focused on the weapons, I'd forgotten about magic. Talia had said most of the population wasn't trained in magic that could be used offensively—but I'm willing to bet the people in this crowd aren't representative of *most of the population*. Crap. Yet another thing to worry about.

The wind mage is coming at me again. I plunge my hand into the bag of frost seeds, already activating my magic, and withdraw a handful to throw across the floor between us. Shards of ice explode across the ground at contact—thanks to my Augment potion—and crystalize up one of the wind mage's feet. They stumble, their boot stuck in the ice, and fall forward with a cry, hand falling on one of the icy stalagmites. I leave them there, bleeding and screaming, as I scramble over to my scythe, snatch it up, and run once more.

The room's become a bloodbath. The wooden floors are slick with red, and the air stinks like death. Everywhere I look is the flash of weapons, a belch of flame, screams and pleading. My stomach roils at the horror of it, but I keep moving, just focused on staying on my feet and out of everyone's way. As more people fall, I order Echo to expand her range, and I pay particularly close attention to anyone at level 30 or higher. Circling around the highest level individuals, I manage to avoid most of the fights. A few more people still target me, and I take one giant man down before he can close the gap by throwing my scythe into his chest—I guess working on my Knife Throwing skill came in handy after all. I pull it out, trying not to think about the way it stuck in his flesh, trying not to remember the way it felt to stab Enrold again, and again, and again—and I keep running. I never finish any of the kills. If they're down, they're out of the way, and my number one priority is to survive. I watch more than one person caught blindsided by a different opponent as they move in for the final blow. Perhaps putting them out of their misery would be kinder, but I won't make the same mistake.

Time stretches insensibly. Surely, it's been hours? A day? My arms ache, and my mouth tastes of blood. My chest hurts from where the wind mage struck me, and somewhere in the chaos I've earned a cut down the length of my left arm, burning and pulsing as blood saturates my sleeve. My breathing is labored. I can feel myself moving slower. More and more of the high levels are left. Once it's just them and me, it's over.

One maniac is running blindly through the room with a giant shield, knocking people over like bowling pins. He turns my way, and I leap out of his path, watching him go by. There's red veins glowing on his skin, and I briefly catch a glimpse of Level 28 Berserker over his head. I turn back to—

Agony lances through my shoulder, fire ripping through my arm and chest. I scream out in pain as I look down, the head of a spear protruding from my shoulder. Shock and numbness wash over me in electric waves, and some detached part of me thinks, *That probably severed an artery.*

A boot plants itself on my back and shoves forward. I scream again as the weapon is ripped through my arm and I go stumbling forward. Blood gushes from the wound, from the *hole* in my body. I stumble forward, but force myself to remain standing. If I go down here, I'll never stand up again.

I stagger around to face my opponent, trying not to fall or scream or be sick. My left arm is dead, a numbness spreading through me as I fumble for the health potion with my right hand. My fingers are slippery with blood. I can't undo the latch. My knees tremble.

The spearman sneers, raising his weapon again. "Good," he says. "There's honor in dying on your feet, looking your killer in their eyes."

There's no honor in dying, I think. *You're just dead.*

The clasp on my potion snaps open. The man stabs forward.

"Time!" Maru's voice booms through the room.

CHAPTER THIRTY-SIX

TAKING OUT THE TRASH

I collapse to my knees as the spear flies overhead, the breeze kissing my face. I pull the healing potion from my bandolier and bite the cork with my teeth, ripping the topper out. Some of the liquid splashes away in my trembling hands, and more of it dripples useless onto the floor and my clothes as I try to pour it over the wound in my shoulder. It feels like splashing myself with acid, and I clamp my teeth shut around a strangled yell.

I squeeze my eyes shut, head spinning, as I lean forward to pour the rest of the potion over the back of my shoulder as well. It's all I can do to hold onto my consciousness, fighting against the pain as I feel muscle and bone knitting itself back together again.

"I said, TIME."

The word is like a thunderclap, suddenly silencing all sounds of combat that had still been ringing throughout the room. I force my eyes open, staring at three bright spots of blood on the ground before me, waiting for them to stop swirling.

"Excellent work," Maru says, and the words summon a new wave of hatred and defiance within me. "That should be enough. Let's clear the room."

I hear a snap of her fingers, and feel a gust of displaced air. When I look up, the room is empty. Or, nearly empty. All the bodies that had been on the floor—dead and alive—are gone. All that's left is their blood.

"My brother," someone cries. "What did you do with him?"

Maru shrugs. "I took out the trash. All the disqualified candidates have been un-summoned. Back to wherever you rats were before I called you here." She grins. "Hopefully somewhere near a healer, but let's be honest, if they couldn't survive this little spat, they probably weren't long for the world anyway."

[Healing potion depleted.]

I groan, attempting to roll my shoulder, then stop with a hiss of pain. It might have stopped me from dying of blood loss, but the wound is far from healed.

Maru glances my way with a frown, and I immediately regret drawing her attention. What if she recognizes me? What if she remembers?

Instead, she spins away, making for the door at the end of the room.

"Rest up," she says. "It would probably be in your best interests to find a healer. The tournament begins at noon tomorrow, and ends by dusk. May the most glorious warrior win."

Then the champion strolls out, and she's gone.

I glance around the room at the other candidates—no, *survivors*. There's about thirty of us. Maybe only a third of what we started with. Some are bent over, nursing wounds, like me, but a handful have their heads held high, barely a scratch on them. I focus on these individuals.

A dryad woman with a long, flowered braid and skin like an aspen tree is a level 38 thorn mercenary. A harpy man with red feathers is a level 36 blood warrior. An androgynous human with spiked black hair and brown skin is a level 39 fire blade. All of them are unscathed, and all of them are several levels higher than the next highest contestants. Even though they're all around Enrold's level, and I'd still managed to survive a fight with him, I'm pretty sure if I went up against any of these competitors in the daylight, face-to-face and expecting a fight, I'd be fucked.

In fact, as I scan the room, I confirm what I'd already suspected: I'm the lowest level here.

Some voices and movement draw my attention back to the end of the room, where a handful of people are hurrying in the door. They pause at the nearest contenders. From the blooms of light and accompanying increase in HP for the people they're tending to, they seem to be healers.

I relax, letting myself go slack. At least I won't have to be in pain for much longer. That's one problem solved, as I don't know any healers in Fairwood, and my coin purse got left behind at the Starlight. Which is doubly bad, considering I'd already used up some of my brews that I'd needed for the tournament—and Maru.

I won't make it through the whole tournament, I realize. If she has us fight to the death tomorrow like she did today—and let's be honest, she probably will—my potions won't last more than one or two fights, and once I'm out, I'll be dead.

My only option is to find Maru and kill her before someone in the tournament kills me. I could go looking for her tonight, but given her ability to teleport, she could be literally anywhere by now. I'll have to wait until tomorrow morning. She should be around before the match begins. That will be my only window.

I suck in a breath, steadying my nerves. For better or worse, it all ends now.

A breeze brushes up against me.

"Sal?" a familiar voice asks. "Gods' grace, you're alive."

I look up to find Lisari standing over to me. She beckons to a nearby healer, wind ruffling their clothes with the gesture. "Over here! This one needs help."

"What are you doing here?" I ask, wincing as she touches a hand to my wounded shoulder. "Careful."

"Sorry," she says, crouching down next to me. "I'm supposed to be taking names and titles of all the competitors. She never gave us an opportunity to talk to any of the candidates, and now I suppose we know why." She grimaces. "But you're alive, at least."

Is that surprise I hear in her tone? I snort. "Glad to hear you had so much faith in me."

She chuckles. "I wasn't placing any bets against you, at least."

The healer makes it over to me, and I gesture to my shoulder and forearm. The rest should be fine on its own. A warmth washes over my arm, leaching the pain away. I sigh in relief as Echo reports, [HP restored. 90/90]

"Thanks," I say, but the healer is already hurrying off to the next person. I wonder how all the "disqualified" candidates are faring. The ones that weren't dead yet, at least. I hope there's more healers out there in the city helping them.

Then again, they signed up for this. They worship the god of war. What's one less fanatic in the world?

"Shouldn't you be running off to someone else, too?" I ask Lisari.

"Probably," she admits, taking out a scroll and a stub of charcoal. "But I still need to get your details, and as long as you're dragging things out, I have an excuse to stick around."

"Happy to distract," I grunt, rolling my now healed shoulder. It still feels a little stiff, even though my HP is back up to max. I know even healing magic has its limits—maybe some things, when broken too far, can never be fixed exactly as they were before.

"Name?" Lisari asks as I stretch out my limbs.

"Sal," I say, cracking my neck. "Do you know anything about what the tournament tomorrow will entail?"

A flash of light in Lisari's hands wraps itself around the piece of charcoal. She lets go, and the nib stays suspended over the scroll. It writes down, "Contestant Name: Sal."

"I don't know much," Lisari admits. "We didn't even know this preliminary... *match*... would be happening until right before you all were summoned. We all scrambled to get here in time. Some are probably still heading over. Anyway, it's to be set up like a bracket tournament. The winner of each round progresses to the next, until there's only one victor. Family name?"

I hesitate. My family is gone. Is my last name even mine anymore? Does it mean anything? It doesn't *feel* like me. The me I am today is a different person from the me I was on Earth.

This me is a murderer.

"Blight," I lie.

Lisari raises an eyebrow, but the charcoal writes down the name anyway. Sal Blight.

[Updating Status,] Echo also pipes up, surprising me. [Name change complete.]

Huh. That was easy.

"Expertise?" Lisari asks.

I blink. "Uh, what do you mean?"

"Fighting style," Lisari says. "If you've studied at any school or have any specialty or... You haven't had any combat training, have you?"

"None," I admit. "Um, does poison count as an expertise?" Though I hardly feel like an expert with only a month and a half of study.

"Not... really," Lisari says, giving a pained smile. "I can put the scythe down?" she suggests, nodding at the nearby weapon.

"Actually, put down knife," I say. At least I've practiced with those a lot. The charcoal begins scribbling once more. "Anything else you can tell me about tomorrow?"

"I'm afraid not," Lisari says with an apologetic look. "Just that Widengra is expected to show up sometime during the tournament. I mean, of course—he'll have to be present if he chooses to ascend a champion. Will you... will you be okay?"

I shake my head. "I don't know. I guess that depends on if he'll know who I am."

"He's a god," Lisari says, as if that says everything. And I guess it kind of does. "In your shoes, I'd try to drop out of the tournament as soon as possible. The first round will have at least a dozen consecutive fights. Easier to blend in. If you can find a way to lose without dying..."

I snort. "Oh, is that all?"

She smiles sadly. "Anything else you'd like to add?" She gestures to the paper. "Other candidates are giving a small bio or intro."

"No," I say. Grabbing the scythe, I finally push myself to my feet. "There's nothing I want to say."

Lisari stands too, plucking the charcoal from the page and rolling the scroll back up. She takes my hand and gives it a squeeze. "Well. Good luck."

[—]

"Thanks," I say. I'll definitely need it.

As Lisari heads off to speak to other candidates, I make for the door. I look down at the scythe, wondering how far it might get me tomorrow. *Not very,* I think. But at least I have my scarf—that will get me into the Blackcloak guild. There I might be able to trade the scythe for a better weapon. Not to mention, I need to make some new potions to cover the ones I used up today—at least enough to survive a couple rounds of combat tomorrow *and* fight Maru. I chuckle darkly to myself. Yeah. No sweat.

I yawn, then stop myself. I can't be tired now. There's less than twenty-four hours until the tournament, and I'll need every second of it.

CHAPTER THIRTY-SEVEN
NOT GOODBYE

"Hurry up with that potion, Cyros!" I quickly count over the bottles on my bandolier, spread out over the table before me. The water breathing potion, half empty. Two mana drain potions. A bottle of orchid sap. One classic smoke bomb, two modified smoke bombs. A mana potion. An invisibility potion. My Attuned poison. A pouch of frost seeds, only four left.

It's what remains of what I brought with me to Fairwood; honestly not bad, considering the preliminary elimination only cost me a healing potion and most of my frost seeds. I move the bandolier over, then stretch out the impromptu belt I'd slapped together with Cyros in the last few hours. Like my bandolier, it has straps for fixing each potion into place, so hopefully everything can get stowed in my inventory together as one object (a belt of potions). Unfortunately, I haven't had time to test how tight the straps are, yet. I'll just have to hope for the best.

"Working on it," Cyros says, bent over a sink at the potion station. He's holding a bottle with tongs, pouring a newly brewed potion into the flask.

"It's just a mana drain potion; it's not going to bite you," I say as I start fixing the rest of my potions to the belt. One newly purchased health potion (well, Cyros purchased it), one mana potion, and some orchid sap antidote. I swap the water breathing potion and a modified smoke bomb over to the belt, and move the orchid antidote to my primary bandolier while I'm at it. I've swapped everything around five times, but I still keep changing my mind and nervously moving things back. What if I won't have what I need when I need it?

"Yeah, and not wanting my magic sucked away is exactly why I'm being careful," Cyros says.

"I'm the one that's got to worry about my mana stores today, not you," I shoot back. I take out my knife next. I'd traded the scythe for it at the Guild's general store. The grip feels foreign in my grasp, but it will have to do. It's better than the scythe, at least; my Knifework skill is up to level 13, and finally I can *feel* it. Carefully, I coat the blade in orchid sap, then hold the knife over a candle to dry the residue.

"There," Cyros says, setting the corked bottle down next to me. "What's next?"

I glance at the sand timer we'd set sometime last night. At the most, we only have another hour until Maru will summon me. I hate the idea of just *waiting* to be summoned, but I have no idea where she is right now, and I couldn't risk wasting the whole night looking for her when she might not even be in this physical realm. There's still so much to do. *Too* much to do.

Where had the night gone? Getting back to the Blackcloak Guild and finding Cyros had burned the first hour after Maru's "preliminary" match, and then I'd spent my time exchanging weapons, gathering ingredients for my potions, making a second bandolier—not to mention my Role Requirement came knocking, which forced me to pause and do some meal prep. I mean, I *did* need to eat something. But it was still a distraction I didn't need.

"More frost seeds if we have time," I tell Cyros. "But I'm going to suit up now, in case I get pulled away again before I'm ready."

Cyros nods solemnly as I strap my main bandolier on, helping me tighten it across my shoulders and secure it to my belt at my waist. Maybe someday I can find a better way to carry all these around. I could even create a whole giant storage system in my inventory—although I'd have to take everything out just to grab one potion, so it wouldn't be as convenient as a bandolier. Someday—

I stop that train of thought. There won't be a someday if I can't survive today.

I grab the last potion Cyros made and secure it on the backup bandolier. I double check the straps holding each potion in place, tightening them as far as they'll go, then hold my breath.

[Bandolier added to inventory.]

The entire bandolier vanishes, potions and all. *Whew*. No broken bottles. Good.

"I guess that's it," I say, sheathing my new blade and securing it to my waist.

The adrenaline that's been keeping me going this long is starting to fade, replaced with a hollow weariness that sits heavy in my chest. Despite the fact I'm about to walk into a death battle, I stifle a yawn.

"Not quite," Cyros says, heading back over to the potion table. "Here. I made one last potion."

"You should have told me before I put everything away," I say, tilting my head at the glowing purple mug Cyros retrieves.

"It's to drink, not to take with you," he says.

"What is it?" I give it a Check.

[Check: Potion of Vitality,] Echo says. [This potion restores wakefulness and reduces fatigue. Effect: 5 hours.]

Cyros holds it out. "It will help you—"

"Oh my god, it's an energy drink." I grab the mug from his hands and chug it down. The potion fizzles on my tongue like soda, but tastes bitter and sour like cold coffee someone squeezed a whole lemon into. I gag, nearly spitting it back out.

"Uh, yeah, it does give you energy. It also tastes like crap." Cyros grins. "I was going to warn you."

I grimace, pinch my nose, and down the rest of the potion.

[You have been buffed,] Echo says. [Effects: the user will experience reduced fatigue and heightened alertness for the next 5 hours.]

Energy floods through my body. A lethargy in my limbs I hadn't even noticed before vanishes, and it feels like I just woke up from a full-night's sleep. My eyelids are no longer heavy, my chest no longer feels like there's an anchor pulling it down. My fingers are itching to move, and my mind is sharp.

"Thank you," I wheeze, setting the empty mug down. "You're a life-saver. Literally, I hope."

His smile vanishes. "Good luck."

"Don't suppose there's a potion for that?" I ask.

"If there were, I'm not sure it'd be enough for what you have planned." Cyros clasps his hands behind his head as he blows out a sigh. "You really should just focus on surviving the tournament."

"I *am* focused on surviving the tournament," I say. "And also, killing Maru. It's a two step plan."

"Three step," Cyros says flatly. "Widengra kills you as soon as you so much as look at Maru the wrong way. I've heard the gods can read minds."

Talia and Lisari didn't seem to think so, but Cyros is right that Widengra's presence will definitely throw a wrench into things. "You think he'll be there the whole time?"

Cyros shakes his head. "The gods don't like to spend much time in the mortal realm. That's what they have champions for. He could be there already, but I doubt it. At the very least, he'll have to be there for the finale, when a new champion is selected."

I nod, squeezing my fist tight as if I could squash the tingling feeling of anxiety trying to spread through my bones. I'll just have to kill Maru before he arrives. Then, with the mark removed, I should be able to flee before I'm forced into a death match with anyone else.

Or, before Widengra shows up and smites me.

I check over my bandolier, my knife, my inventory. Everything is in place. My hands are trembling slightly, and I don't think it's just from the vitality potion. I take in a deep breath, then let it out.

"Ignore Maru," Cyros says again. "Just focus on the candidates. With this whole arsenal you put together, and with surprise on your side, you can beat them. I'm sure you can."

And then what? Become Widengra's champion? Hell no. I'm not winning this thing—but I sure as hell won't die in it either.

"Thanks, Cyros," I say instead. "For... everything."

He grimaces. "I'll come find you at the tournament field. Help however I can. This isn't goodbye."

"I'll make sure it isn't."

At that point, I think we're both waiting for the inevitable. We go back to the potions anyway, working on one last batch of frost seeds, but it isn't another fifteen minutes before I feel the pull of Maru's mark.

I appear in the stadium to the roar of a crowd. After the dim of the Blackcloak Guild, the sunlight lances through my eyes. I squint against the glare, turning in a circle as I take in my surroundings.

"Welcome, candidates," Maru's voice booms over the field.

I can't pinpoint where the sound is coming from. Around me, the other candidates are likewise gathering their bearings and sizing each other up. So few of us now.

"Today, a demigod will ascend," Maru continues. "Just as I rose from mortality three centuries ago."

There, near the top of the stadium. An ornate overlook appears to house several key figures. I recognize Maru—but I also notice Lisari and Talia standing among a small crowd of individuals. I give the strangers a Check, and Echo identifies them as members of the Fairwood council. They're flanked by guards, including the lieutenant, Jules—although I suppose she's probably Captain, now, given Enrold's death.

Given I killed him.

I shake the thoughts away. Focus on surviving the now. Widengra doesn't appear to be present. Maru is out of reach. But maybe I can get up there between the first and second match.

"Several rings have been designated for matches throughout the arena," Maru says, gesturing out over the field.

Looking around, I find myself already standing in one. A raised ridge of wood an inch tall and twenty feet across. There's over a dozen more like it spread across the tournament grounds.

"The fights will be randomized," Maru says. "Once all matches in the first round conclude, the winners will be paired off and the next round will begin. I have been informed there are healers on standby to tend to individuals between matches; it is in your best interest, then, to win your match quickly. The winner of each match is decided when their opponent is incapacitated."

Even though I can't see it from this distance, I can hear the sneer in her voice. *Incapacitated*. How many of the candidates here, how many who are willing to murder in the name of the god of war, will stop at merely knocking their opponent unconscious?

Crap. If I lose, I will either be killed, or I'll be injured enough I won't be able to make a move on Maru. But if I win, I stay in the tournament, and I won't have an opportunity to slip away. What do I do? What do I do?

I take a steadying breath. Survive. I just need to survive.

"I think that's enough rules," Maru says. "We're here for battle, aren't we?"

The crowd roars in excitement, and like an old friend, anger returns to me once more. They're all just as bad as Maru. Just as morally corrupt as Widengra. I hate them all.

With a snap of Maru's fingers, the Gods' Tournament begins.

I stumble as the ground shifts under my feet. The wood moves, ferrying me along, spinning me around the circle like the wooden floor is made of giant interlocking gears and puzzle pieces. Once it stops, I find another competitor on the other side of the ring. Around me, I catch a glimpse of other competitors who have been paired off. I can't afford to spare them any thoughts, however. My world narrows to this twenty-foot circle.

My match is a lanky, human man with a black braid and blue draped clothing. His skin appears stretched over his skeletal frame like he's malnourished—hardly the kind of person I would have expected to make it through Maru's first elimination round. But that's what worries me. He looks me up and down, and his mouth quirks with amusement. I give him a Check.

[Minji. Level 29 human osteomancer.]

Osteomancer? What the hell does that mean? *Echo, what school of magic is that?*

[Osteomancy falls within the school of Life arcana.]

I draw my knife with my right hand, and run my left down my string of potions. Without knowing what he can do, I'm not sure which potion would be the most effective, and I can't afford to waste a single one. Then again, orchid poison should work no matter what kind of magic he's got.

"Ready!" Maru's voice booms over the stadium.

Can you be more specific? I ask Echo. *What kind of Life arcana? What does it do?*

[Osteomancy falls within the school of necrotic magic,] Echo says.

I get a sinking feeling as Minji unclips a large sack from his belt and holds it up before him.

"Set!" Maru calls.

[Specifically, it relates to the control of bones.]

Minji turns the sack upside down and a waterfall of white clatters onto the field before his feet, clicking and clacking like macabre wind-chimes.

"Begin!" Maru booms.

The bones glow with green magic, shuddering to life.

I drop into a defensive stance. "Shit."

Chapter Thirty-Eight

OSTEOMANCER

The bones rattle together like pieces of a toy set, rising from the ground and clicking into place. It's half formed into some sort of creature—a dog, maybe. I don't let it keep forming.

I dash up to the bone creature and smash the pommel of my knife through it. The skull pops from the neck and crashes into the ground, shattering on impact. The creature stumbles to the side, but doesn't fall.

Of course it doesn't. It's just a cluster of bones. Why would it need the skull?

The headless animal springs at me, claws extended. I stumble back, slashing at the limbs, and my knife skips over the bones. One paw deflects to the side, but the other finds its mark, stabbing into my shoulder.

[6 points of Slashing damage sustained.]

I bite down a cry and crash my knife through the arm, popping the leg off at the elbow. The creature falls to the ground, staggering on uneven limbs, but its claws stay embedded in my flesh. I aim a kick at the rib cage and the creature crashes to its side, bones scattering across the floor.

The claws in my shoulder wiggle in my flesh like maggots trying to dig themselves deeper. I growl, grabbing the paw and ripping it from my skin. I throw it back at my competitor, but Minji doesn't even flinch as the bone slows to a stop, hovering in the air before him.

"Nice try," he says. "But you can't hurt me with my own weapons. Not while I can sense the presence and control the movement of every one."

I grimace, holding a hand to my bleeding and throbbing shoulder. That's damn convenient. Why couldn't I have gotten a useful type of magic like that?

"Done already?" Minji asks. He smiles, raising a hand. "My turn."

Abandoning the shape of an animal, the bones shoot toward me like a cloud of shrapnel. I stumble away, slashing haphazardly at the flurry of bones. I strike some, deflecting them, but there's too many to block. They nick my arms and legs, cutting through my clothes and slashing my skin, as a flurry of damage notifications pass over my vision. I hear the sound of breaking glass with one of the impacts—one of my potions. I glance down and grab the health potion as the bone pulls back: precious drops of the liquid splash to the ground. I yank it from its clasp and splash the rest over myself before it can go to waste. My health begins to creep back up, relief flowing through me as dozens of small cuts and slashes begin to close.

It won't be enough to weather this fight, though.

The bones swirl back toward Minji like feathers on a breeze. They're not retreating, however—merely readying for a second attack.

I can't give him the chance to follow through.

I gauge the space between us. How many paces apart? One, two, three—

Minji raises a hand, and I snatch my smoke bomb from its clasp, throwing it at the ground. The glass shatters on impact, and green fog erupts from the bottle, covering our circle. I can't see anymore, but I count my steps as I race forward, swinging my blade.

Something hard blocks my blow. The bones resist for a moment, then I throw all my weight into the attack and they go clattering to the side. One, two, steps past them, I swing for Minji, bracing for impact—

My blade cuts through air. I swipe to the left, right, but he's gone. With a growl I spin in a circle, but there's nothing within arm's reach. Which way am I facing now? Shit.

The strike hits me on my right. I stumble away, swiping at the bones, but they've retreated into the smoke once more. I race after them, slashing the air, but again I'm left stabbing at phantoms.

Minji chuckles to my left. I slash and strike bone.

"Perhaps not the best move," he says.

I blindly kick forward, my blade still pressed against bone, and my foot makes contact. More bones scatter away.

"If you could see through the smoke, now, that might have been clever," the man continues.

I growl and stab toward his voice. I must be getting close, because bones rise up to block my attack. They clatter around my blade, wrapping around my wrist like a skeletal hand. I backpedal, ripping my hand away.

"However, the bones give me an advantage," he says. "I can use them to scope out my surroundings. Every one you stab or kick tells me where you are."

Like Lisari's wind.

Which gives me an idea. I grab another vial and pop it open.

"You've stacked the match against yourself," he continues.

A bone flies at me from the side, striking me in the arm. I cry out as I feel the skin break—a shard of bone stabbed into my flesh—but I don't drop the bottle. Without another health potion, I'll just have to bear it until the end of the match.

"If that's true," I say, swiping a hand over my blade, "then why haven't you won already?"

"That wouldn't be much of a show, would it?" Minji asks. "We are here for the god of war, after all. He deserves a real fight. And blood."

I yank the bone out of my arm with a snarl, then throw it back in the direction of Minji's voice.

He chuckles. "You don't really think you can strike me with my own weapons, do you?"

"Nope," I say, narrowing in on the voice. "But how about mine?"

I snap the knife forward. I hear a muted *thud*. Not the thud of knife through a flesh, but of another blocked attack—metal through bones. I close my eyes, listening, feeling, and waiting.

Minji laughs. "Was that the best you had? Throw a knife at me from inside the smoke?"

My knife is moving through the air, re-orienting itself. The sensation is dizzying. I've never tried using my magic this way. But If Minji and Lisari can sense their surroundings through their magic, then why can't I?

The Attuned poison I'd smeared over the blade rights itself, moving less smoothly than before. He's grabbed the handle, I think.

"Well," he says, and I can feel my knife being aimed back at me. "I guess two can play at that game."

I mentally yank back on my Attuned poison, and I feel the blade jerk in his grasp. Minji doesn't let go, the blade isn't pulled from his grip, but that wasn't my intent. My poison pulls from the blade and strikes something soft and giving, then burrows down into the flesh.

Minji yelps. "What—"

I throw my next potion. He notices in time to block it with his bones, and the glass bursts open on impact. The potion sprays forward along its original trajectory. Minji cries out, showered with bits of glass and, more importantly, a healthy dose of mana-drain potion.

[Mana debuff inflicted.]

Now, I open my eyes and run.

"What did you do?" he cries.

The smoke bomb is clearing out, a light breeze gradually sweeping it from our ring. When Minji can see me again, I won't have a way to defend myself from his bones. I move with the smoke, trying to buy a few more seconds of cover, as I let my Attuned poison disperse into his body.

[Attunement lost,] Echo reports.

[Poison status effect inflicted.]

Regrettable, but I can make more. Right now, I just need it to do what poison does best.

Echo bring up his HP, I say.

[HP: 78/100]

It ticks down another point, but it's not falling fast enough. *Mana?*

[Mana: 140/200]

That one is at least draining away as I watch: 135, then 130, then 125. Still, plenty of magic left to kill me.

The smoke parts, and our eyes lock. No longer the picture of collected control, there's anger in Minji's eyes. I dive out of the way as he throws my knife back at me—followed by a wall of bones.

I hit the ground and go rolling, and a staccato of impacts shakes the wood behind me. Pulling out of the roll, I stumble to my feet, hand running down my dwindling line of potions. Without stopping, I grab the invisibility potion and fumble with the pouch of frost seeds.

"Stop running!" Minji shouts, his bones still flying after. But they're slower now. It's taking more effort for Minji to yank them from where they're lodged in the floor. The mana drain potion—or my poison—is taking effect.

Stumbling, I spill a handful of the invisibility potion onto the pouch, which immediately vanishes, along with streaks of my hand. I better not freaking drop these, or I'll never find them again. Going on feel alone, I pull the seeds from my bag and throw them Minji's way—one to his left, one to his right, and one right at his head.

"What—"

He flinches back from the invisible blow, then shrieks and begins clawing at the air in front of his face as, presumably, the ice begins to creep over him. It probably won't be enough to suffocate him or do any real damage, but I imagine the mental toll of having something cold and invisible growing over your face is distraction enough.

His bones shudder and clatter on the ground with aimless direction as I loop around my circle, making it back to my knife. I spill more of the invisibility potion over it as I yank it from the ground; it's not completely gone from view, like someone took an eraser and scribbled over most of its surface, but it's enough to confuse, and with Minji still wrestling with the living ice, now is my moment to end this.

Despite his panic, Minji notices as I come barreling his way. He raises his bones as he retreats—and steps right on the patch of invisible ice I'd planted for him. He goes down, and I crash through the floundering bones and leap on top of him.

There's a flash of fear in his eyes. He struggles to throw me off, and the blows wrench me back in time. I'm in the dark, in Enrold's house, the smell of blood, and offal, and desperation—

My knife sinks into Minji's chest, and we both gasp. I let go as blood begins to bubble out of him like oil, and then I roll away, revulsion and horror swelling within me.

The bones rattle on the ground like fish flopping on dry land.

"Someone help!" I call. "Healer!"

I glance around wildly. My surroundings suddenly return to me in a rush, as if the whole world had vanished while I was fighting, and now sound and my surroundings are crashing back in. The other matches are still taking place. The crowd roars as people fight and stab and die. Where are the healers? Maru had said there were healers!

I look around for my health potion and find it: the broken glass shattered nearby on the ground, only scant droplets collected on the remaining curved shards of glass.

I stumble to my feet, hovering over Minji. His eyes are still open and flickering, but he's stopped moving. What do I do? I can't leave the blade in, but I can't pull it out either.

"A health potion!" I call, spinning around. "Anyone!"

But no one answers.

[Level Up!] Echo announces, and begins reading off my Level 19 stats.

My heart sinks as the numbers scroll past me. I don't look back at Minji. My stomach roils, and I brace my hands on my knees, waiting to be sick.

"Winner: Sal Blight!" a voice booms over the stadium.

Finally, someone comes jogging over. I don't look up when they go to Minji, first. I scrunch the fabric of my pants beneath my hands, forcing myself to breathe slowly and ground myself. I'm alive. That's all that matters.

The healer appears next to me.

"Can I go?" I croak. "Please."

The man shakes his head, instead holding something out to me. My knife, dripping with blood.

I almost don't take it from him. I don't want to touch it. But if I leave it behind, I might as well be dead the second the next match starts. Hand shaking, I reach out and gingerly pluck the weapon from the healer's grasp. As soon as I do, he raises a glowing hand to my shoulder, then hesitates.

"Are you injured?" he asks.

"Yes, I—" But when I check my health, it's completely restored. Right. The level up. "No. I'm fine."

The healer turns to leave.

"Wait," I call. "Can I leave? Please, I just want to sit down somewhere."

"Sorry." His gaze meets mine with apologetic eyes. "The next fights will be starting soon. You have to stay here." He hesitates, like there's more he wants to say, then he shakes his head. "Good luck."

I watch him leave as the fights continue on across the arena floor. Could I follow him? Would anyone stop me? Even as I consider this, more names boom out across the stadium. The candidates drop in rapid succession. What was once innumerable, then many, has now become countable. Even if I tried to sprint off the field at this moment, I probably wouldn't make it to the stadium walls before the round concluded. As I impassively watch the last fight, a large, muscular woman with a shield against a lightning mage, I do the mental math.

There's sixteen of us left. Eight will be walking out of the next fight. Then four, then two, then one. I don't have enough potions for four more fights. I might not even have enough potions for one more. Not to mention, I've already burned my only healing potion. And if I don't survive the future matches, the healers on standby won't mean anything.

I turn to look up at the spectator box. Maru is standing at the front, leaning over the railing as if she can't get close enough to all the bloodshed, gore, and death that's come to litter the field.

And yet, she's so far away she might as well be untouchable.

A horn blares through the stadium, and I look back to the last two fighters: the woman with the shield is down.

"Winner: Zathar Han. The first round of combat is complete."

The ground shifts without warning, and I stagger to the side. The wooden floor comes alive under my feet and the circle I'm in pulls apart, carrying across the field like driftwood on a wave. I watch each of the competitors as they flow around me, trying to track which ones are the high levels and where they're headed. When I finally come to a stop, I'm already facing my next opponent.

My heart sinks into my gut as I recognize them. The human Fire Blade I'd noted in Maru's preliminary elimination round. Level 39.

The highest level on the field.

Fuck.

CHAPTER THIRTY-NINE
'TIS BUT A SCRATCH

[Name: Kelle]

[Class: Fire Blade]

[Level: 39]

[Attack: 186]

[Agility: 24]

[HP: 100/100]

[Affinities: Metal]

They've got me beat on every stat across the board. That's a great start.

I grab a bottle from my bandolier. "So how do you feel about, like, just trying to knock each other out?" I call across our circle. "No blood. No death. Just spar until someone's unconscious, and we both live to fight another day?"

Kelle frowns. "This would not honor the god of war."

I gesture up to the spectator box. "Well, I don't see him yet. Do you?"

Kelle crosses their very toned arms across their very wide chest. Fire blade, huh? It looks like they're more used to lifting weights than daggers.

"Blood must be spilled," they say. "This is a good offering."

Figured as much. Is everyone in this tournament a psychopath?

I mean, yeah, probably. Everyone but me knew what they were signing up for when they became a candidate.

"Well," I say, crouching in a ready position. "It was worth a shot."

Kelle doesn't move to draw any weapons. In fact, I can't actually see any weapons on them. I don't know what their deal is, but with an affinity like "metal" and class name like "fire blade" I'm not excited to find out. There's one thing I do know: if I give them a chance to use their full power, I'll be dead.

"The second round of the tournament will begin with the horn's signal," Maru's voice again booms over the stadium.

There's delight in her tone. She's loving this. I struggle not to turn around and glare at her. For the next few minutes, the only person who exists in the world is Kelle.

Their gaze flickers to the potion in my hand, no doubt wondering what it's for. It's one of my modified smoke bombs. This time, I won't wait for my opponent to get the upper hand. Once the smoke bomb goes off, I should have time to—

The horn blares.

Kelle blurs into action.

Unlike Minji, who had waited for me to make the first move, Kelle has no such reservations. They dart forward, already closing half the distance before I manage to smash the smoke bomb into the ground.

A plume of white erupts around me, and Kelle cautiously skids to a stop and skips back. I yank out the orchid poison next, spilling it over my blade. Plenty splashes to the ground around my feet, but I don't have time to be cautious: I only have seconds.

I send the bottle rolling to my left at the same time I use Soft Step and dash right. Kelle cocks their head, squinting at my bottle which is clattering over the bumpy wooden floor. Or I should say, *in the direction* of my bottle. After being coated in the particles from my invisibility-potion-infused smoke bomb, my bottle is invisible.

And so am I.

[Invisibility Timer: 9 seconds]

Given my pathetic excuse for mana, that's the best effect I can get from my invisibility potion, so I need to make use of every second.

I silently race away from Kelle, circling around so I can come at them from behind. Meanwhile, they've withdrawn two tiny throwing knives from their belt, both resting in their open palms. A moment later, they levitate above Kelle's hands and begin to rapidly spin in place.

[Invisibility Timer: 6 seconds]

If it wasn't for the timer on my potion, I'd be skidding to a stop right now. The knives glow red hot, and in a matter of seconds they're no longer holding throwing blades, but spinning plates of molten metal. One of them zips from Kelle's hand, smashing into the ground a few feet away. I hear glass shatter. The wooden floor catches fire where the red-hot metal sits embedded and sizzling in its surface.

[Invisibility Timer: 2 seconds.]

I'm behind them. When the potion wears off, at least I won't be in their line of sight. Of course, they didn't need to see the empty bottle to tear through that, and I doubt I will fare any better against a red-hot razor-sharp spinning hunk of metal launched through my spine.

[Invisibility Timer: Expired.]

I'm right behind them. Knife raised. One more step—

A piece of glass crunches under my foot. Kelle turns.

My blade sinks into the back of their shoulder as fire flashes from their hand. White-hot pain stabs through my fingers as their metal flashes by. Kelle screams, twisting to the side and falling to the ground.

[Status Effect inflicted: Poisoned]

[25 points of Piercing damage dealt.]

[6 points of Fire damage sustained.]

[17 points of Sundering damage sustained.]

Blood pools out beneath them as they shudder and cry, and I stand there, panting, unable to believe that my plan worked. My left hand burns from where they nicked me, but I don't dare tear my eyes away from Kelle. I can't risk letting them out of my sight for a moment—this fight isn't over until it's over.

I step around their body and grab my knife, pulling it from their back. My stomach turns at the way I can feel the blade scrape out, and the river of blood that follows, but I can't leave my only weapon behind. Kelle doesn't try to fight back. I watch their HP as it ticks rapidly down; this time, I had enough orchid poison on my blade to do the job.

The horn blares over the stadium. "Winner: Sal Blight!"

I reach for my scarf to wipe the blood and poison from my blade, but the moment my fingers brush against the cloth, pain seers through me. I suck in a startled breath, looking down at my hand.

For a moment, I can't understand what I'm seeing. There's so much blood and charred skin, it's like looking at something that's not even real. Definitely not something that's attached to me. Like a movie prop: a grizzly, burned, fake hand.

A hand that's missing three fingers.

I guess that's when the shock wears off.

Fire shoots through my bones, from my fingers all the way up to my shoulder. I drop my knife, grabbing my wrist as I scream in agony. Something touches my shoulder, and I jerk away, tears blurring my vision and streaming down my face.

I've felt pain before, but this is different. This is so much worse. It feels like my whole hand is on fire, burning and clawing its way into bones, raking needles through my marrow.

"Stop," the person says. "Hold still! I'm a healer."

I clamp my mouth shut, screaming through closed teeth as I try to hold my shaking hand out to the healer. I squeeze around my wrist tighter and tighter, as if I could cut the sensation off.

A light glows through the watery vision in front of me, and the pain begins to lessen as relief washes up my arm.

[Health restored.]

"Thank you," I stammer, my breath coming in shaky gasps. I squeeze my eyes shut to clear away most of the tears. When I open them again, the charred skin is replaced by pink scar tissue. The bones are hidden beneath skin once more.

But my fingers are gone. From my pointer to ring finger, there's just a scarred stub of flesh. I try to flex my thumb and pinky finger, but the motion pulls at the skin and sends a new wave of pain through my arm.

"That's as good as I can get it for now," the healer says, stepping back. "You should go see a doctor after the tournament."

A spiteful laugh bubbles out of me. After the tournament? I'm dead. I might have survived the first two rounds, but I've only got a scattering of potions left, and now I won't even be able to open them. Not with this hand, anyway. With my knife needed for the other, this might as well be a death sentence.

The healer bows their head and backs away as I'm left standing there, reeling in the knowledge that my fingers are really, actually gone.

The ground shakes beneath me, and a great crack slams through the stadium.

Widengra, I think, my heart sinking. Will he know what I am? Will he smite me on the spot? The thought only makes me feel hollow. I'm so tired of fighting.

But instead of cheers, the crowd is roaring with fear. Screams. I turn to find what's going on, but I don't need to look far.

There's a great crater in the center of the stadium. A hole through the wooden floor, levels of the forest showing beneath. Cracks in the stadium have speared away from the crater and are heading for the audience. One of the candidates stands at the edge of the hole, looking down, hands raised as if to finish the job.

One of the officiants pulls the candidate away from the hole as dozen of dryads spread out over the field, summoning vines and twisting tree branches up in an attempt to patch the crater in the stadium floor.

A voice booms over the stadium. "There will be a brief intermission as the arena is repaired. Candidates, please make your way out the designated exit points and await further instructions."

The borders around a series of tunnels at the base of the stadium flare with color: the blooms of flowers, I realize, twisting and turning like flashing lights. Numb, I pick up my knife, sheathe it, and cradle my injured arm to my chest as I make for the exit.

The shadows falling over me feel like a cool blanket as I step beneath the stadium. I blink against the dimmer light, eyes adjusting, looking around the quiet mumble of workers on the platform I now find myself on. It's almost scaffolding rather than an actual room. Healers, city guards, and other employees of the stadium shuffle about their bridges and catwalks, all intent on some important mission or another—like keeping the stadium from breaking apart from overeager candidates, apparently.

"Sal? Sal!"

I glance around until I catch sight of Talia hurrying down a spiral-ing tree trunk, flanked by a grinning Lisari. Further behind them are a couple city guards, crying out for Talia to wait as they ineffectively try to flag her down.

The woman rushes over to me and wraps me in a hug before I can react. She's warm and boney, but the gesture cracks something inside me. I lean into the hug.

"Thank the gods," she says. "You're alive."

"Well done," Lisari adds. "You actually took those two down. I'm impressed."

I think of Kelle's body in a pool of blood. The surprise on Minji's face when I plunged my knife in his chest.

"Yeah," I say.

The guards finish rushing down the stairs, puffing as they jog over. One of them I don't recognize, but the other is Jules.

"Lord Talia," she says. "You need to stay close to us. It's not safe down here."

Talia waves her off with an irritated sigh, which turns into a hiss of breath as she catches sight of my fingers. "Your hand."

I wearily hold it up. "Yeah."

"It doesn't matter," Talia says. "You're alive. That's what counts."

"Plus, it wasn't your primary hand," Lisari cheerfully adds.

Talia gives her a withering look.

I just shake my head. "Doesn't matter." I'm too tired to feel upset. Besides, everything will be over soon enough—one way or another. I look up toward the top of the stadium, imagining Maru through the latticework. Now's my chance, but do I even stand to have one? Killing her was already a longshot, and that was when I was at full health and had two fully functioning hands to work with. I try to summon that fire I've felt before, that anger that's fueled me, but the warmth feels like it's behind a pane of glass.

I'm just so tired.

"Lord Talia," Jules tries again. "Really, we must get back upstairs."

Talia grimaces, but beckons for me to follow. "Come on, then. You can come, too. Let's get out of here."

"They'll just summon me back to the field when the next match starts," I say.

"All the more reason to spend our time elsewhere," Talia says. "No point in sticking around, hm?"

"And what, you'd rather just stay here and wait for that to happen?" Lisari asks. "Have you given up?"

I glare at her, irritation cutting through some of my mental fatigue.

"Lisari," Talia warns her.

"No," I say, turning to Talia. "She's right. I'll come. Lead the way."

The city guards look relieved when Talia makes for the stairs. Lisari falls into lockstep next to me, smiling.

"You're rather clever," she says. "By all accounts, you shouldn't have won either of those fights."

"Thanks," I say flatly.

"Sorry," she says. "I just get so excited when I see creative uses of alchemy like that. What all have you got left? Although, I understand if you don't want to talk about it."

I take in a breath, and let it back out. I frankly don't want to talk about it, and I'm rather annoyed with Lisari at the moment, but her words have shaken me from my stupor. I'm not ready to give up. I don't want to die. And no matter how slim the chance I have at beating Maru, the moment to act is now, and I have to take it.

"All I've got left on this belt is one mana drain potion and some orchid poison antidote," I tell Lisari. "Actually, would you hold them for me for a moment?"

"No problem," Lisari says.

I take my primary bandolier off and pass it to her, then I summon my backup from my inventory. Lisari tips her head as I do that, but doesn't comment on the newly appeared belt of potions. Perhaps with her wind magic, she couldn't really tell where I removed it from.

I strap the second one on as we climb, fumbling for a minute with the clasp as I struggle to tighten it down one-handed. The injury throbs as the movement pulls at my tight, recently healed skin.

"On this one, I have a mana potion, some orchid sap, the rest of my water breathing potion, and a modified smoke bomb," I explain.

"Modified?" Lisari asks.

I just nod. "Yeah."

She raises a curious eyebrow, but doesn't push it.

Sunlight breaks through as the stairs stop at a landing, and the platform leads out to a ledge of the stadium, looking down over the arena. I breathe a sigh of relief, stretching in the sun and fresh air, and lean on the railings, taking in the sights. The floor is about a quarter of the way patched already, and despite the enormity of the crater, the tournament grounds look so small and insignificant from up here. No wonder it's so easy to cheer for so much death, being so removed from any of its horror.

From this vantage point, Maru's spectator box is beneath us, lavishly decorated and crawling with guards, so it's not hard to pick out.

It's not far away, either.

"Please, my lord," Jules again urges. "We should return to the other honored guests. It is easier to protect you all when you don't scatter about like leaves on a wind."

"You couldn't even solve my sister's murder," Talia says, bitter. "Why should I trust you all with protecting us in this giant crowd?"

Even so, she turns to me with a grimace. "I shouldn't keep the Captain from the others for much longer."

"That's fine," I say. "I'll come with."

Talia frowns, eye flickering to Maru's spectator box. "I don't think that would be wise."

I press my mouth into a line. "This is my only chance. If I don't get rid of this mark now, I'll die in the next match." I tap Maru's spell circle, burned into my forehead.

Talia squeezes my hand. "We'll figure something out."

"With what time?" I ask, irritation rising within me. "Figure *what* out? What other options do I have?"

"Hush," Talia says as my voice raises. "All I know is that we can only solve this with level heads, not more violence and aggression. Perhaps given your injury, she'll allow you to withdraw."

"It's the Champion of War, Talia," I snap, that familiar hatred finally stirring in me once more. "She can't be reasoned with."

"Just let me try," Talia says. "That's all I ask. Let me try to speak to her, first."

Vitriol churns in my gut like one of my potions, boiling and toxic. It won't work. And more than that, I don't *want* Maru to just suddenly act all congenial and agree. I want revenge. For Terimus. For Rena. For Layf. For myself.

"Please," Talia says again. "What's the harm in trying the peaceful way, first?"

There's harm in losing my window of opportunity. Harm in the betrayal of having an olive branch met with violence. Harm in giving the enemy an opportunity to strike first.

But Talia's gaze is silently pleading with me.

I glance back out onto the field; they're still only about a third the way through repairing the crater, tree branches stretching up from the forest below to slowly grow and fill the gap. I have ten minutes, tops.

"Fine," I say, sighing out my frustration. "You can try to talk to her. But we don't have much time."

Talia smiles, squeezing my hand again. "I'll fix this," she promises.

I grab the railing and squeeze as she and the guards depart, hoping I haven't made a lethal mistake. I want to believe her. I want to have someone I can trust. But I'm not sure I think Talia's persuasiveness can trump Maru's bloodlust.

At least the spectator box is close. I can wait until the crater is three quarters patched, then make my move if I haven't heard anything by then.

As Talia and the guards depart down a set of steps leading toward the spectator box, Lisari starts to follow after them, then pauses.

Without turning around, she jerks her head to the side in a beckoning gesture. Then she keeps walking, but not toward the stairs.

I hesitate for a moment, then hurry after.

"Lisari—"

"Shh," she breathes, ducking around a patrol of guards as she weaves toward the back of the platform. "You want to see Maru, don't you?"

I nod.

"Then follow me," she says, pausing at the railing that marks the back of the stadium. Beyond it is open forest, and stories below us is the city of Fairwood. "And stay quiet," she adds.

And with that, she jumps over the ledge.

Chapter Forty

CHANGING OF THE GUARD

I rush to the edge of the stadium and lean over the railing, trying to catch sight of where Lisari vanished. She's only a few feet below me, however, standing on a catwalk fixed to the back of the stadium. There's a whole series of precarious paths and bridges built into the struts beneath the stadium. I glance back to make sure no one is watching, then swing myself over as well.

I slip as I go to grab the rail. My left hand slides right off, pain jolting up my arm as my injury strikes the railing.

I drop down beside Lisari with a hiss of pain and stagger to the side before I find my footing. Pressing my hand to my chest for a moment, I wait for the waves of pain to finish washing over me. That's going to take some getting used to. Maybe my fingers will grow back with my next level up, but that won't make a difference at this moment. Right now, only the next ten minutes matter.

Lisari raises an eyebrow as if to say, "Okay?"

I nod, beckoning her forward. "Let's go."

She takes me into the underworkings of the stadium, navigating a narrow passage of catwalks and beams. I wonder when she's had time to explore all of this. I know she's been working at the stadium for the last month, but I'm still a little unclear on what her job *is*, aside from assisting Talia. Regardless, it appears she's got a more adventurous side than I'd given her credit for.

Lisari slows down as she comes to the end of a walk, a wooden wall in front of us, then carefully, quietly, begins to climb up a series of crossbeams. It's awkward to follow with one hand, but I manage without too much difficulty. When Lisari reaches the top of the wall, she swings herself up onto a crossbeam and lays down on it, squirming along another foot until her head pokes out over the top of the wall. I follow on a beam next to her. Beneath us are a series of red and white cloths hung from our rafters which sway in the breeze. Between their flaps, I can make out the contents of the room. Voices waft up to us from below.

"...must be a way?" Talia is saying.

A handful of guards line the back of the spectator box. At the front is a row of chairs, all positioned to overlook the stadium, most filled with people in fancy attire—the council members Talia has mentioned, presumably. They flank two large, ornate chairs at the center, practically thrones. Both are empty, but a giant, subtly glowing woman is leaning casually against one of them: Maru.

Just her sight causes anger to rise in me like a tide. She's using a knife to pick at her nails, and I'm not even sure she's listening as Talia speaks.

"This girl was entered by mistake," Talia continues. "She didn't want to compete. Can't she forfeit the next round?"

"I made no mistakes in who I selected for this tournament," Maru says. "If she was chosen, it was because she demonstrated herself worthy of my attention. Quite unlike you." She groans, craning her head back to look out over the stadium. "Aren't they done yet?"

"Please," Talia tries again. "All I'm asking—"

One of the guards steps forward. "The champion has made herself clear. Please return to your seat, Lord Talia."

"Yes, come on," one of the council members says, beckoning her over. "It looks like it will only be another minute or two before the match can resume."

"I'm afraid I must insist," Talia says, but gasps in surprise when one of the guards roughly grabs her by the arm. "Let go of me!"

"Take a *seat*, Lord Talia," Jules says, dragging her away from Maru. "You may be as forward as your sister was, but you do not hold her authority. You are lucky to have been permitted such attendance in the first place."

Talia rips her arm from Jules's grasp. "Careful, Captain. I oft had to remind your predecessor where the City Guards' funds came from. I should hope I won't have to do the same for you."

Jules's lips curl in distaste. "You do not."

"Let it be, Talia," one of the council members speaks up again. "Politics can wait. Enjoy the entertainment for now, won't you?"

Talia looks to Maru, but her back is turned, now leaning over her own chair, chin resting on her fist in a bored posture as she looks down on the stadium below. Talia's shoulders sag in defeat. She glances toward the exit.

I sigh out a quiet breath. That's it, then. She failed. I hadn't expected it to end any other way, but at least she kept her word. At least she tried.

Now, it's time to do things my way.

Silently, I wiggle around until I can grab the water breathing potion at my waist. I cringe at the quiet *snap* of a clasp coming undone, then I grab the cork with my teeth and pop it out. Using my legs to hold onto my beam, I slowly pour the potion out onto my scarf. A couple drops soak through the cloth and fall below: most are caught by the swaying curtains. A few fall all the way through, tapping quietly on the wooden floor. I stop and hold my breath, but no one notices. I go back to pouring out the potion. It takes an agonizing minute to empty the bottle.

Once I'm done, I struggle to one-handedly get the empty bottle clasped back on my bandolier. After a moment, Lisari offers her hand, and I pass it to her. I pull the scarf up over my nose. I rest my hand on my modified smoke potion, ready to pull it free. I can feel my heartbeat pulsing quickly in my fingertips. This is it.

I sit up, getting into position so I can jump down onto Maru, but Lisari puts out a hand. She frowns, tipping her head.

"Wait."

I tense. Why did she stop me? Does she not want me to go through with this, even now? I don't have time to wait. The next match could begin any moment, and I'll be wrenched from my perch and lose my one chance at escape. At life.

At revenge.

"What?" I hiss.

She puts a finger to her lips, then nods below. I grind my teeth, but glance between the swaying cloth, trying to make out whatever Lisari noticed.

I don't have to look far.

Beneath us, in the center of the room, a pool of blood is bubbling up from the floor. The surface ripples, spreading out across the wood, then rises from the floor in a pillar of red. Someone gives an alarmed shout.

"Ahhh." Maru drops to a knee, bowing her head. "Lord Widengra. We are graced with your presence."

Ice shoots through my veins as the living blood shapes itself into a person. Blood runs from their form in rivulets, splashing back down to the floor to reveal green skin and black hair. The man is an orc, like Gugora, but leaner, sharper, and red tattoos swirl over his arms and face in ever changing patterns. No, not red markings: living blood. His head nearly brushes against the fabric hanging beneath us.

"Praise Widengra," Captain Jules says, sweeping into a bow.

The guards and council members stumble over themselves to hurry around their chairs and throw themselves at the god's feet, all mumbling similar praise.

Apart from his height and gory tattoos, he wouldn't appear much different from any other orc. But I can feel the god's presence like a radiating heat. Only it's more of an aching numbness. A prickling against my skin, a fear tingling in the back of my mind. Like the first time I encountered Maru, every one of my instincts scream *danger*.

"What's this?" Widengra speaks, and his voice is low and rumbling. "I thought we'd have a finalist by now."

Maru stirs, but it's Captain Jules who straightens from her bow, first. "I wish to offer you my deepest apologies, your holiness. A few of the candidates were... *overeager* to prove their devotion and delayed the process. I wish to make an offering in recompense." She nods curtly to her guards. "My lord, this blood is in your name."

The guards all stand, stepping around the prostrate council members. Then, without any pretense, the guards grab the hair of their council member, yank back their head, and slit their neck.

Static horror washes over me. I gasp, flinching back, but Lisari grabs my wrist, squeezing. Neither of us move. *If I jump down there now, I'll die,* I realize.

Talia cries out in horror, twisting away as Jules reaches for her.

"Traitor!" Talia yells, backing away. Rivers of blood splash beneath her shoes. "Treason!"

The god rumbles with laughter. "And to think I was worried I would be bored. What a show you've arranged for me, Maru."

His champion stands. "It's no doing of mine, Lord. It seems the mortals had schemes of their own."

Jules flicks a hand toward Talia and two guards seize her, grabbing either arm. I tense, and Lisari's hand squeezes tighter. No. I can't stand by and do nothing. I have to help her!

But I don't want to die.

Self-loathing washes over me as I hesitate, fear holding me back.

Talia struggles for a moment, but she's clearly no match for the guards in strength or magic. "Why are you doing this?"

"Power, obviously," Jules says. "The way you always acted as if you were better than the Guard, as if your station gave you any power over us. Maybe if Enrold hadn't pathetically caved to the Council's every demand, he wouldn't have needed to be disposed of, too." Then she pauses. "Really, now, Talia, a truth spell? Seems a bit pointless at this stage, don't you think?"

"You don't have to do this," Talia says, glancing around wildly. As if any of the guards will realize what they're doing. As if the god preceding over this whole scene would intervene.

But no one moves to save her.

I don't move to save her.

Move, I tell myself, but my limbs only tremble. *Help her!*

Jules draws her sword. "Truthsayers are terribly inconvenient. That's why your sister was the first I had to dispose of. It was embarrassingly easy to get her guards to leave her unprotected at the right moment. Poetic you'll be the last to go, hm?" She raises her blade. "My lord, this blood is in your name."

"*No!*"

I shatter through my fear in an explosion of movement, leaping from the rafters as I draw my blade. I slash through the cloth overhangs and dive into the room, striking the wood hard and turning it into a roll. Streaks of red splash around as I leap to my feet, diving for Jules.

Her sword is in Talia's chest.

I scream in fury and fear, slashing at Jules's arm. She cries out, surprised, and goes stumbling back, her sword pulling free from Talia. Talia collapses to the ground. I fall to her side.

"Talia!" I shout. "Talia!"

She's alive, but her eyes are darting around wild and unfocussed. Blood bubbles up with each gurgling breath. Red spreads across her torso. I desperately press my hand over the wound, but the blood continues to pour out.

I fumble with my potions, wet fingers slipping over glass, as fear grips me and wrings tears from my eyes. Don't I have anything that can help? Not a single extra healing potion? No, no I have to be able to do *something*. What's the point if I can't do anything? What's the point of only brewing things that can kill?

Is this really all I'm good for? Just a cancer that breeds more death? I grab Talia's hand and squeeze, rocking back and forth. Helpless. The moment she dies, I can feel it, all tension leaving her grip.

"Where did you come from?" Jules demands. She narrows her eyes, pausing to take me in. "It's you. That kid from the inn. What are you doing here?"

I dig my fingernails into the wooden floor and clench my teeth. I want to scream. I want to cry. I want my blade buried in Jules's chest, in the exact same spot she stabbed Talia. I pick up my knife.

Laughter booms through the room, raising the hair on the back of my neck.

"You did promise the day would be entertaining," Widengra says.

From this vantage point I can see his eyes: they're a solid, glossy red. Streams of blood trail down from them, forming the living tattoos that swirl over his skin.

"However, I do not intend to linger here long," the god continues. "As amusing as this distraction is, we are in need of our new candidate."

"Apologies, my lord," Jules says, stepping toward me. "We will resume the tournament just as soon as I tie up this loose end." She raises her sword.

I scream, feral, angry, and launch myself at her. I don't want to die. I'm not ready. But neither was Talia. Neither were Terimus and Rena and Layf. And if now is my time, at least I'll do it on my feet with a weapon in my hand.

"No. Wait," Widengra says.

There's a blur of movement. I stab toward Jules, and her swing veers off course. She falls against me as my knife finds her chest. But there's no cry of pain or shock from her; I stagger out of her way as she slumps to the side, collapsing to the ground. The only part of her that moves is her head as it rolls away across the floor. I stare, stunned.

Maru withdraws her spear, flicking blood from its tip. "My lord?" she asks.

As Jules goes down, the other guards in the room scatter, retreating from the gods. Neither of them seem to notice. We're nothing more than ants.

My instincts are screaming at me to run, too, but I can feel Widengra's gaze on me like a physical force trying to crush me into the ground.

[Your interface has been identified,] Echo says.

I take a step back, forcing myself to face him. He's watching me with a peculiar look. Curiosity, then a frown.

"Ah," he says. "You're disguising yourself, hm?" He raises a finger and casually swipes it through the air. "Clever."

[Permissions changed.]

"What?" I ask. *Echo, what do you mean?*

[Per—]

Echo stops talking.

"What did you do?" I demand.

Widengra ignores me. "Maru, I thought you'd killed the aberration. You wouldn't lie to me, would you?"

"No, my lord!" Maru objects, aghast. "I swear on my blade, I eradicated the anomaly."

He frowns at her next, and she bows her head reverently before him. "Ah. Now I see. No, it was not your fault, Maru. Someone is interfering." He makes another motion, this time toward Maru, but I don't notice any change, and Echo says nothing.

"Troubling," Widengra says. "But that should fix it. Now you may have your chance to fulfill your mission."

Maru looks up, blinking. When her gaze lands on me, it turns hard. "You!" she says, and my stomach drops. "I remember, now. I thought I killed you in the forest with the others."

Oh, crap.

I don't understand everything that's happening, but one thing is as clear as ice: Whatever was keeping her from recognizing me before is gone.

Maru steps forward. "My apologies, Widengra. It seems I *did* fail my initial task." She levels her spear at me. "I will not fail you again."

CHAPTER FORTY-ONE

THE CHAMPION OF WAR

Maru draws back her spear.

I have just enough time to gasp in a breath, then I smash the hilt of my blade into the smoke bomb on my bandolier. The glass shatters, and the potion explodes into the room.

Literally. The blast is so intense it knocks me off my feet. I don't even realize I'm flying through the air until my back strikes a wall and the air is knocked from my lungs. I fall to my hands and knees, gasping involuntarily.

[Status Effect sustained: Poisoned.]

[Status Effect sustained: Mana drain.]

[Mana extinguished: 0/10]

I fumble with my scarf, pulling it up around my mouth and nose from where it had fallen back to my neck. With one hand it's hard to tighten it back up, so I hold it there, breathing through the fabric.

I knew the Augment would strengthen the effects of my potion, but even I hadn't expected it to strengthen the explosive force of the smoke. I'd also been planning on not breathing any of it in, but I guess it's too late for that now. I take another breath through my scarf, the water potion transmuting the smoke into breathable air as I'd planned. I eye my health points, rapidly ticking away from my own poison. I'll have to hope my Poison Resistance will prevent the one breath I did take in from being a lethal dose, before I have a chance to drink an antidote.

And if it is lethal, I'll just have to work fast.

Maru is coughing somewhere nearby.

I've been waiting for this moment ever since I hit her with that first smoke bomb a month ago. As soon as she'd started coughing, I'd known she had a weakness. Her skin might be as tough as metal, but even she needs air to breathe. Her insides are more vulnerable than the rest of her. And vulnerabilities can be exploited.

I infused the smoke bomb both with orchid poison and my mana drain potion, and the Augment magnified their effects a thousand-fold. Given Maru's only five times my level, that has to be enough.

I hope it's enough.

Echo, Check, I think, eyes stinging as I blink against the smoke in Maru's direction. Carefully keeping my scarf pressed to my mouth, I silently climb to my feet.

There's a pause, and for one gut-wrenching moment I fear the interface is still locked away from me. Then, Echo responds.

[Name: Maru]

[Debuff: Mana loss at a rate of 9/second]

[Debuff: Health loss at a rate of 5/second]

[Debuff: -8 Speed/second]

[Debuff: -10 Dexterity/second]

[Debuff: -6 Strength/second]

[HP: 476/500]

Even as I watch, her HP continues to quickly tick away. At this rate, it will take another two minutes to hit zero.

It's not enough.

Sure, it will get there eventually if I wait, if she stays in the cloud and keeps breathing it in, but it'll only take seconds for her to clear the smoke away, and less time than that to snap my neck. I only have one option left: move fast, and get more poison in her system.

Using my Soft Step, I silently run in her direction, holding up my scarf with my injured hand as I raise my knife with the other. Blood squelches beneath my fingers as I squeeze it tighter. I can't lose my grip on it now.

I live or die by this moment.

I jump for Maru, and my silence is broken as my foot splashes in a puddle of blood. A flash of metal cuts through the smoke. I stab my knife forward.

Contact.

Maru screams. My knife sticks in place as something strikes me in my side. I crash backward, skipping across the floor like a stone on water.

[12 points of Piercing damage dealt.]

[Debuff inflicted: Greater Poisoning effect]

[18 points of bludgeoning damage sustained.]

My ribs burn, which turns into a stab of pain when I gasp in a breath.

A breath I shouldn't have taken in. I watch my HP tick away as my vision blurs and my chest burns and my limbs become leaden with the poison.

[HP: 8/90]

[HP: 7/90]

[HP: 6/90]

I failed.

I gave it everything I had, and it wasn't enough. What should I have done differently?

Gugora and Iski. I never should have left their inn. Never should have sought revenge. I should have just become a chef, like my Role wanted me to. Lived a quiet, simple life.

[HP: 5/90]

[HP: 4/90]

Something thuds against the floor. Numb static crawls through my limbs. I feel... regret.

[HP: 3/90]

Warmth floods across my body. The pain vanishes beneath a blanket of bliss, like I've been wrapped in sunshine.

[EXP threshold met,] Echo says. [Level Up! EXP threshold met. Level cap implemented. Select class evolution!]

[Name: Sal]

[Class: Rogue (pending evolution)]

[Level: 20]

[Attack: 41]

[Agility: 27]

[HP: 90/90]

[Affinities: Poison]

[Role: Chef]

My debuff is gone. I'm healed—alive. But how?

"Enough!"

A gust of wind blows through the room, and the smoke vanishes. Widengra scowls about the scene, his gaze landing on me, crumpled against a wall, before shifting over to Maru. She's lying on the ground, motionless. My dagger lodged in her eye.

I Check her, unable to believe it.

One word appears over her head: [Deceased.]

The tattoos on Widengra's skin peel away from him, becoming living lines of red, floating in the air like streamers. One of the lines jabs toward Maru, wrapping around the hilt of my knife in her eye. It yanks the weapon from her corpse, then levitates the knife back over to the god. He runs a finger along the blade.

"Poison," he spits, and the blood tattoos writhe with the word. "No, this isn't right. Blades are made to draw blood. To paint the fields red. Where is the gore? The violence?" He's almost mumbling to himself, the bloody tattoos twitching with each suggestion. "This poisoned dagger and your toxic smoke were enough to take my champion down? Pathetic."

The living blood tosses the blade to the ground in disgust, which spins across the wood and out of reach. Crossing the room in two quick strides, he crouches down before me. The lines of blood grab my jaw like skeletal hands, wrenching my head up to look at him. I try to jerk away, but my face might as well be in a vice.

"You were one of the candidates she chose? She was foolish then. Poison is weak. Underhanded. To be killed by you, when you were supposed to be killed by her—disgusting. She deserves her fate."

The grip of his blood tightens, and pressure squeezes through my head. I whimper, unable to speak or fight back.

"Do you realize what you've done, Aberration?" the god hisses. "How you threaten the peace?"

He curls his lip in revulsion, then releases me, shoving me back. Something *cracks* as my head strikes the wall, and I'm not sure if it's my skull or the wood.

[17 points of Bludgeoning damage sustained.]

He growls, pacing over to the edge of the spectator box, and looks down over the field. "At least there are a handful of candidates, still."

I struggle to pull myself upright, pain lancing up my arm as I put weight on my injured hand—the fingers of which didn't grow back with the level up. Maybe I can still crawl away. Maybe I have time to take that class evolution. Maybe it will save me.

But at least Maru's dead. At least I killed her. At least I avenged Terimus and Rena and Layf.

I try to embrace that knowledge, that victory, but it feels like trying to wring warmth from a shadow. My victory sits hollow and empty in my chest.

Widengra lets out an angry, hissing sigh. "I suppose I should finish your extermination first."

A glass bottle drops from the ceiling, shattering against the floor to Widengra's side. He spins toward the noise, and I look too. What—

Something grabs the back of my shirt and pulls me down. I fall backward, but instead of striking the floor, I continue to fall. Like the ground has vanished. Darkness closes over my vision and vertigo spins through me. I flail against nothingness, against a horrific impression of falling through a void—

And then crash back into sensation. My back slams into the ground, stirring a layer of dust, as every one of my senses briefly fritzes out from my abrupt change in surroundings. The smell of blood is gone, replaced with a familiar scent of dust and dried sweat. The roar of the crowd still rings in my ears, only now it's distant, somewhere muted and above me. Overhead are the beams of a ceiling. One I think I've seen before, even if I don't immediately recognize it.

Laughter peels through the room. Young. Feminine.

"I can't believe it," Lisari manages to say between gasps and cackles. "You did it. You actually did it!"

I roll onto my side, and my surroundings slowly slide into clarity, like a kaleidoscope slotting into focus. I'm in the storage room beneath the stadium, the one Talia and Lisari had been working in.

Talia. An image of her body flashes through my mind, her eyes staring up at me, unseeing. My heart squeezes. But I don't have time to dwell on her.

"Lisari?" I ask, wincing as I push myself up. "What's happening? How did we get here?"

The girl is bent over laughing, and the sound sends chills up my spine. "I have to say, I was beginning to think I was wasting my time. I've never seen someone so set on trying to get themself killed. But what's the harm, I figured. Perhaps it'll pay off. And my, has it!"

She removes her glasses to wipe a tear from her eye, and I freeze. I'm not sure what I'd thought her eyes would look like, but I hadn't been expecting two pits of darkness. They're not hollow, as if her eyes are merely missing. These are truly voids: an infinite, lightless abyss.

She pauses as she notices my look. "I did say they tend to bother people." With a shrug, she casually tosses the glasses away, and they shatter as they strike the floor. "But I'd expected you to be a bit more open minded. We're friends, aren't we, Sal?"

There's an odd distortion in her tone, like two voices are speaking at once.

I Check Lisari.

[—]

There's a moment where I can nearly feel Echo's reply before she stops, as if the signal is cut off.

I take a nervous step back. "Who are you?" I run my hand over my bandolier, but every slot is left empty or shattered. "*What* are you?"

Lisari snaps a finger and points at me. "See, you catch on quick. That's what I've come to like about you." The distortion in her voice is growing worse, but it's not the only thing that's changing. There's a black mist that's leaking from her eyes and wisping about her form. Her clothes are slowly shifting into something ornate. She's taller. Only her hair remains unchanged, long and black. And her eyes: Those unnatural voids continue to bore through me.

"Maybe you've just made it this far on luck," Lisari says, now with a deep rich voice. "Maybe it's something to do with your Aberrant nature."

She—he?—has taken on the form of a man. His skin appears to faintly glow in the dim light of the study. It's a form I now recognize. One of the gods in the history books Lisari had shown me.

"Maybe this endeavor is doomed to end in tragedy." Shirasil smiles. "But I do love a good gamble."

Chapter Forty-Two

LISARIHS

My mind races, fear coursing through me, as I take a step back and raise a fist. Even if it'd be useless, I wish I had my knife right now.

Shirasil arcs an amused eyebrow. "Come, now, Sal, I'm not some philistine like Widengra. I'm on your side! I've been helping you since we first met."

"You're a god," I say, taking another step back. "You're all the same."

"You still believe that, after all the time we've spent together? I'm wounded," Shirasil says, but his lips are still curled in a smile. "Every time you faltered, I was there to helpfully nudge you back in the direction of the justice you sought. It was me who gave you those alchemy books so you could develop your abilities. I was the one who guided you toward the right spells needed to kill Maru. Without my interference, she would have recognized you a month ago and killed you on the spot. Isn't all that deserving of *some* gratitude?"

"Screw you," I snarl, continuing to back up.

Shirasil barks out a laugh. "That's the spirit. That's the fire I want to see! Harness that. Hone it. Turn in against everyone who has wronged you in this world—like Widengra."

I frown. Is that why he's doing this? Has he been trying to pit me against the God of War from the start? "You have something against Widengra?"

"Not specifically," Shirasil admits. "Despite his general lack of imagination. Some gods are *terribly* dull."

"Then what do you want with me?" I demand, trying to keep up. I'm so disoriented. It's too much to process all at once. "Why do the gods want me dead?"

"Oh, child, we don't want you dead," Shirasil insists. He attempts a reassuring smile, but his teeth are sharp, and his eyes are empty, and the resulting expression conjures the image of a demon in my mind. "Well, not *all* of us," he amends. "Some are just a bit more... *shortsighted* than the rest. Now that I can prove gods like Widengra are behaving so impulsively, I should be able to wrangle the rest in line to pressure him and his ilk into compliance. Truly, I'm here to help."

"You didn't help before," I say. "When I nearly died a dozen different times. When Talia was killed."

"Unfortunate, that," Shirasil admits. "She could have been useful. But you must understand, stepping in to save you defeats the whole point. I've many footbirds in this race, and you're just the one who pulled ahead. How will you get stronger if I have to rescue you every time the going gets tough? What makes you worth betting on if you end up getting yourself killed the second my back is turned? No, no. I'm here to help. I want to see you thrive. But you will live or die by your own choices."

"So, what," I demand. "You just wanted me to stay alive long enough to kill Maru? That's it?"

Shirasil laughs. "Of course not! That would be so silly. Consider Maru a practice round. A way to dip your toes in. A preliminary test—which you passed with flying colors! Oh, Widengra never saw it coming."

"No thanks to you," I snap. He'd been up in the rafters watching as Lisari the whole time, and he didn't even lift a finger.

Thoughts of Lisari sting me with hurt. I'd liked her. I'd almost started to consider her a friend. But she wasn't even real. Just some... some *character* used to manipulate me. The loss I feel for this person who never even existed hurts almost as much as the betrayal.

Shirasil splays his fingers helplessly. "Even the gods have limits. To be caught working directly against another god would be... problematic. Which is why we have our proxies to do mortal work for us. Frankly, even the little help I've contributed so far has crossed many lines. It would be in both of our interests for this mutual accord to remain covert."

I continue to edge back. The door is only a dozen feet behind me. Maybe if I can get out of here, if I can get around other people, that same reluctance to reveal himself publicly will stop Shirasil from pursuing. With the threat of Widengra just above us, I might be able to slip away.

I'll just have to hope it's not out of the frying pan and into the fire.

"So, what, I'm just some kind of pawn to you?" I demand, trying to buy myself time. "A disposable piece to use in some cosmic game?"

"Oh, that's got a nice ring to it." Shirasil chuckles. "But everything's disposable, dear. *Everything*."

I turn and leap at the door. My still-bloodied hand slips over the knob, but I'm able to grapple for purchase, squeeze, turn—

It doesn't open.

"Please, I thought we were having a nice chat," Shirasil says, leaning against the door only inches away.

I stumble back, startled. I hadn't even seen him move.

"At least wait until I'm done," he continues, smiling like the Cheshire cat. "Aren't you even a little curious as to what I have to say? I've an offer you can't refuse."

"I'm not going to make deals with gods," I say. "You're all complicit. What Maru did—how Widengra ordered it. You all *let* that happen. You're sick."

"Yes!" Shirasil pushes off the door, gliding over the ground toward me as I quickly backpedal. "Yes, that's it exactly! It's a sickness. A stagnation. Things need to be shaken up. A change to the status quo. And you can be that catalyst. You, who would dare try what no one else will. Let me ask: where do you intend to go from here?"

The question catches me off guard. Where *do* I go from here? I killed Maru. I got my vengeance. But it doesn't fill me with the satisfaction I expected it would, and it doesn't feel like anything's really *changed.*

Before I can think of a response, Shirasil spins back toward the door.

"Look," he says, grabbing the doorknob.

I don't move.

"No tricks," he insists, throwing it all the way open. But something isn't right on the other side. Instead of showing the underbelly of the stadium, we're looking back into the spectator box. Widengra is at the other end of the box, seething as he looks down onto the stadium.

"Hurry up," Shirasil says, beckoning me over. "Look, but do not step through. Once you pass through, the way will be revealed, and if Widengra notices you, I won't intervene."

Hesitantly, I approach the door.

"Filth," Widengra hisses, and I pause for a moment, afraid he's spotted us. He looks up, but he doesn't turn our way. "I feel your meddling. I know you're somewhere nearby. It was a mistake to intervene.

When I find who you are, I will put you down, just as I've put down every other Tainted. Your efforts are for naught."

"Dramatic, isn't he?" Shirasil chuckles. "Given enough time, he might even be able to suss me out. However he's scheduled to return to the Heavenly Palace in a matter of minutes—which he will do, as he's such a stickler for the rules—and I'll need to depart before him so as not to be discovered."

Good, I think. If I can just play along for another few minutes, then he'll be gone. I can make it that long. Right?

Outside, Widengra shakes his head. "No matter. Whatever your machinations were, I will finish what I came here for today. Nothing has changed. I will simply have to ascend two champions instead of one."

Blood pools out from beneath Widengra's feet, melting into the surrounding gore of the room. His tattoos bleed out over his skin, entombing him in a red shell. Then he sinks into the puddle, and with a final ripple, the god vanishes.

My heart sinks, and Shirasil turns to look at me as if he can hear it.

"Again I ask you: where do you intend to go from here?" Shirasil says. "You killed one champion, yes, but two more will rise in her place. And you may certainly be able to kill them as well, if your luck continues, but the gods will only create more. What did your little quest of vengeance achieve? What has ultimately changed?"

I swallow around a knot in my throat. "I got justice for those Maru killed."

Shirasil scoffs. "An eye for an eye only perpetuates lack of foresight. Maru is dead. And so is Talia. And with her killer already slain by your enemy, how do you intend to get justice for her? What does any of this violence ultimately mean? It's a never-ending cycle."

Anger kindles in me at his words. "Then I will break that cycle."

"How?" Shirasil demands. "You are just a weak human, ignorant to our history and magic. You might have killed a demigod, but you also had help from Talia, and those kind innkeeps, and that naive little assassin boy. Not to mention, me. You couldn't even get your vengeance alone. What hope do you have of changing things? Of challenging the system? Of challenging the gods?"

Each of his words needle deeper and deeper beneath my skin, burrowing into my insecurities and frustrations. The worst part is that I'm not even sure if I can argue with what he's saying.

"If this were a game of stones, you'd be placing pieces one at a time, entirely unaware of the rest of the board. Meanwhile, your opponent is thinking four steps ahead. Yours aren't moves made with a plan or strategy in mind." Shirasil sneers. "Those are the plays of a child."

Something in me snaps. "I'm not a child." I plunge my hand into my bag of frost seeds. "And I'm not weak!"

I grab all the remaining frost seeds and throw them at Shirasil's eyes. In the same move I pull a shard of broken glass from my bandolier, dripping with orchid poison, and stab it toward his neck.

The seeds disintegrate into dust before they even touch him. The glass skips off his skin and goes spinning away. Frustration boiling over into tears, I throw a punch toward his head, and he catches my fist, almost dismissively.

[0 points of Slashing damage dealt.]

[0 points of Bludgeoning damage dealt.]

"You *are* weak," he says. "Come now, you don't think you could really hurt a god?"

I try to pull my hand away, and he lets me; it almost hurts more knowing that. "I know you're immortal," I growl. "I know you can't be killed. But I can't just do nothing. I won't just roll over and *let* things happen to me. I have to fight back. I have to try."

At this, Shirasil smiles. He leans in close to me, and I have to fight every instinct to not shove him back. He doesn't touch me, though. He only whispers in my ear.

"You're wrong."

Then he skips back, clasping his hands together like a child who's eagerly awaiting the reaction to some disclosed playground secret.

I frown. "Wrong about what?"

"About the gods," he says. "About immortality. What if I told you: the gods *can* be killed." Shirasil's grin grows even wider. "What if I told you we're not as immortal as we might seem?"

I eye him suspiciously. He can't be serious. If that's true, why would he even tell me? What would he stand to gain? "Everyone's said the gods are immortal."

"I suppose it's close enough to the truth, practically speaking," Shirasil says. "If everyone believes it, they'd have no reason to try to prove the theory wrong, now would they?"

He begins to circle around me, and I have to fight against every instinct to run for the door again. He's just playing with me. A cat with a bug.

But he doesn't want me dead. If he did, I already would be. I try to hold onto that as I force myself to stand up straight, shoulders back, defiant.

"Just because I said we *can* be killed doesn't mean it's easy," Shirasil says. "Surely you recognized Widengra wasn't even fazed by the little smoke bomb stunt that took down Maru. Champions only hold a fraction of the power of their gods. A borrowed strength; a spark of our fire. No, the idea that you could kill a god with all the world's poison is laughable. You're not strong enough." He pauses. "Not yet."

"You're saying I could become strong enough?" I ask, the possibilities spinning within my mind. Gods didn't exist on some unreachable mountain. They aren't immortal, which means they have vulnerabilities that can be exploited—vulnerabilities like Maru. And if the gods can be killed, then change is possible. Real change.

Assuming Shirasil's not lying.

"It's possible to gain enough strength to rival the gods?" I ask him.

"Oh yes," he says, and stops pacing, standing before me. "Very possible."

"How?" I demand.

Shirasil grins madly. "I was hoping you would ask that." He holds out a hand. "The first step is simple. Become my champion."

CHAPTER FORTY-THREE

CHAMPION OF CHAOS

I physically recoil. Become Shirasil's champion? "No! Never."

"Why not?" He splays his hands. "You want to challenge the gods, don't you? You want to change the system. I can help you do that. I can give you the power you need to get there."

I scoff. "Not if it means working *for* the gods. I won't be used by you. You yourself said the power champions have is only borrowed from their gods—that it's only a fraction of their strength. I won't be beholden to you, and I certainly don't want power that's only a fraction of yours." I lift my chin. "No. I'll get stronger my *own* way."

Shirasil giggles. "Sorry, sorry. It's just so refreshing to have a mortal speak to me this way! Hilarious." A growl creeps into his voice. "Oh, the others would kill you on the spot."

He's insane. Despite my bravado, shivers run up and down my back. Maybe he hadn't killed me before because he thought he could use me. But if I refuse, what motive does he have to keep me alive? That's why he told me about the gods' weakness, wasn't it? No god would simply let someone walk away after revealing something like that.

Shirasil chuckles to himself, passing a hand over his face. When he looks up at me, with those empty, soulless eyes, his expression is composed once more. The faintest smile tugs at the corner of his mouth.

"I understand your reluctance," he says. "After all, no one can be expected to make such a decision without all available information at their disposal, first, hm? Alright then. You think you stand any chance of challenging the gods without immortal aid? Let's look at the facts."

[Check,] Echo abruptly says, and stats appear over my vision.

[Name: Shirasil]

[Title: God]

[Class: Anarchic Alchemist]

[Level: 100]

[Attack: 2500]

[Agility: 750]

[HP: 10,000/10,000]

[Affinities: Wind, Shadow, Space]

[Role: The Inquisitor]

I blink as the numbers scroll past. Ten *thousand* hit points? But it's not infinite. Any number, no matter how big, can be brought to zero. And level one hundred is lower than I would have thought, for a god. But buried among the numbers, I notice something else.

"You have a Role?" I ask.

"We all have a role to play, dear," Shirasil says. "Now, as for your stats..." He flicks a finger in the air before him, and I feel Echo stir, pulling the values from my mind.

[Name: Sal]

[Class: Rogue (pending evolution)]

[Level: 20]

[Attack: 41]

[Agility: 27]

[HP: 90/90]

[Affinities: Poison]

[Role: Chef]

"What are you doing?" I demand, waving my hand in the air between us, as if I could interrupt his influence over Echo. "Stop it!"

"Too bad you hit 20 with Maru's death," Shirasil continues, staring off into space as if I'm no longer even there. "Should have gone up several more levels from the experience alone. There's a cap at each Class Evolution, however. But you see now the disparity you're working with? The mountain you'd need to summit within one human lifespan? Even Maru couldn't have achieved her level had the boon of being a champion not allowed her to live three hundred years—that's three hundred years of battle, training, and level ups. You're not even on the trail, yet." He tips his head toward me, which I can only interpret as a glance. "But you could be. Now let's see, what have we got to work with..."

[Class options available,] Echo says as the words scroll through my vision and mind.

[Rabid Blade: A small bladed-weapons class which specializes in "Death by a Thousand Cuts." Available skills often involve poisoned throwing knives and toxic hand-to-hand fighting. The user gains +20 to Accuracy with Bladed Weapons, and +10 to Efficacy with Poisons.]

"Not a bad option," Shirasil comments. "Rather fits your skillset, I think."

"Stop," I say, shaking my head as if to dislodge Shirasil's influence over Echo and my interface. But Echo continues regardless.

[Bane Alchemist,] Echo continues. [An alchemic class which specializes in brewing various spells in potion-form, specifically with respect to debuffs and status effects. +15 to Efficacy with Alchemic

Brewing, +5 Resistance to all debuffs, and +10 Damage to Poison related effects.]

"Ah, a class after my own heart," Shirasil says, laying a hand dramatically over his chest. "I would be remiss if I didn't encourage you to pick this one. It will make up quite a bit for your lack of innate magical ability."

For a moment I forget about Echo, too distracted by Shirasil's comment. Lisari is—was?—an alchemist. And Shirasil's class was some kind of alchemist, too. How much of Lisari was an act, and how much of her was real? How much of Lisari is still in Shirasil? Does he just have a soft spot for alchemy, or was there more to that whole charade?

Echo brings up the last Class Evolution option.

Shirasil laughs. "The System can seem to have quite the sense of humor, occasionally, doesn't it?"

[Culinary Rogue: A chef class which specializes in various cooking-related skills, including but not limited to: knifework, kitchen tool proficiency, cooking, baking, brewing, and ingredient identification and utilization. +25 to Accuracy with Kitchen-Related tools, +20 Efficacy to any consumables created with the assistance of heat, +10 Potency to any buff/debuff spells activated by the user, and +10 Resistance to temperature related debuffs.]

I frown at the last option. It's like the system *wants* me to be a chef, which makes me want to be one even less. Then again, Shirasil's nudging is similarly summoning an instinctive revulsion in me. Even if Alchemist is a good class, the fact that he wants me to pick it—that it would represent some interest or skill we have in common—inherently repulses me.

"Don't sleep too long on that," Shirasil says. "No matter what you pick, a class evolution will allow you to progress much more swiftly. Now, let's see here, what else have we got..."

The class skills vanish, and suddenly I'm looking at what appears to be a settings menu.

"You must make sure your interface is set to private," Shirasil says. "This should help keep you from being recognized by gods on the spot. Of course, I can't do anything about Widengra at this point, since he knows your face; avoiding him would be highly advisable."

[Privacy setting activated,] Echo says. [Role setting obscured.]

"Stop doing that!" I object. "Get out of my head!"

"Dear, if I were in your head, all of this would be far easier," Shirasil says. "I'm merely tampering with some display settings, as you haven't locked those down yet, and I have elevated permissions. That should be fixed now, however."

I shake my head. "What does that even mean?"

"It means no one will see your role unless you want them to," Shirasil says. "Really, you ought to be asking the System more questions. Learning how to use your interface to its utmost potential might become a life or death skill with the gods after you."

"System?" I repeat. "You mean Echo?"

He tips his head. "Echo?"

He doesn't know about Echo. Desperately holding onto that one nugget of privacy, I decide not to elaborate. "Why are you helping me with all of this anyway? I already told you I won't work for you."

"Well that's a matter of perspective, isn't it?" Shirasil says. "You want the gods dead. I want to see a shake up in the heavens. You don't have to work for me to be doing work for me. You see?"

Not really. "But you're a god. Why would you want your own kind killed?"

He laughs. "You might be the only one who would ask that. Do you recall what I am the god of?"

I frown, trying to remember the lines from the textbook he—Lisari—had shared with me. "The god of chaos. Destruction."

"Ah, yes," he says with a bitter chuckle. "That is what they think, isn't it? That it's my nature to want to break things; to dismantle order; to disturb peace."

I hesitate, but he rounds on me before I have a chance to respond.

"Wrong!" he seethes, towering over me.

There's a madness etched across his features, a wild danger to his stance. Again, out of nowhere, I feel that imminent sense of doom washing over me. This unpredictable insanity. He could snap at any moment, and I would never see it coming.

"I'm not some exterminator who revels in death, like Widengra," he insists. "I'm not some prophet who tries to control the fate of everything she can See, like Lorata." He draws himself up. "I am Curiosity. I am questions. I am the insatiable appetite to know, to seek out, to go prodding dragons just so I can observe the explosive consequences. *That* is my nature, you understand? I can't stand stagnation. It itches at me like beetles beneath the skin. I must usher in change even if it's painful. Even when it requires sacrifice. Oh, and we have been brackish, stewing in complacency, for far too long."

He spins around, grinning madly. "And then you all appeared! Something new. Something unexpected. Something fresh."

"All?" I ask, my heart skipping a beat. "What do you mean? Are there more like me?"

He takes my arm and gives me a reassuring pat. "There's no one quite like you, Sal. But that's enough chit chat. Time is running short. First we need to do something about this." He holds up my maimed hand.

Shirasil *tsks* to himself, turning it over in his grasp. It still aches dully, and I try to pull away, but his hold on my wrist only tightens.

"The system would have healed it properly on its own," he says. "Shame they interfered by using healing magic on it first. No matter. Nothing your ascension can't take care of!"

My heart lurches in my chest. "No!" I try to jerk back, but his grip is like a vice. "I won't!"

"Even after everything I've told you?" Shirasil wonders, mild surprise in his voice. "After all the evidence I've presented? Surely you understand this is the only way to achieve your goals."

"I don't care," I snarl. "I won't be your champion."

Shirasil laughs. "You really *haven't* been listening to anything I've said, have you?" He waggles a finger, the picture of teacherly patience. "I told you as Lisari, but perhaps it bears repeating." He smiles. "When the gods expect something from mortals, it's never an ask. It's a promise."

His grip goes white-hot as magic punches through me.

Chapter Forty-Four

Gift of the Gods

Fire burns through my bones. It pours through my arm like lava, sluggishly spilling into my chest and dripping through my limbs in an intense, concentrated heat. Shirasil lets go of me, and I sink to the ground, squeezing my wrist as if I can cut off the burning sensation that's crawling up my arm.

But it doesn't hurt. Like the fire that had fueled my revenge, this heat is blinding and fierce, yet also empowering. A lifeforce of its own. I grit my teeth against the intense sensation, turning my hand over to look at the spot Shirasil had held. There's a black brand there: a spell circle like the one Maru had marked me with. I rub my thumb over it, as if that can smear the lines away. At my touch, the spell circle illuminates with the green light of my magic, and the heat within the rest of me dims, coalescing at my wrist. A green mist spills from Shirasil's mark like one of my smoke bombs. Instead of dissipating into the room, however, it hovers before my hand. No, in the *shape* of a hand.

[Noxious Gauntlet activated,] Echo says.

A ghostly green claw is layered over what's left of my hand. Two glowing fingers of mist encircle my thumb and pinkie like a glove, while three more ethereal claws float in the space where my lost fingers should be. The fire under my skin dies down to a flickering heat. I flex my hand in awe, and the wispy hand flexes, too. I imagine squeezing the hand into a fist, and the mist obeys.

I shake my head. *Deactivate*, I think, and the hand vanishes. The warmth vanishes from my bones, leaving them feeling cold and numb. Only Shirasil's mark still glows with a faint, tempting warmth.

"See? Not so bad!" Shirasil says. "My, you can be so dramatic."

"I don't want this," I croak.

"Please, it's a *gift*," Shirasil insists, as if speaking to a child. "Given freely. Think of it as a present from a friend."

I hold my arm to my chest, glaring at him. "We're not friends."

"Oh," he says with a grin. "I think you'll come around."

I slump in defeat, looking at my hands. Am I still human? What did he do to me? I Check myself over, but there's only two changes to my stat sheet:

[Title: Demigod]

[Allegiance: Shirasil]

"Whoops," Shirasil says, chuckling to himself. He flicks a finger my way. "Let's set that one to Private as well. Can't have Widengra realizing I was the one interfering with his champion, after all."

[Allegiance set to private,] Echo reports.

I glare up at him. "I won't do this. I won't be your puppet."

He snorts. "I should hope not. That wouldn't be any fun!"

"I'll go back to the Starlight Inn," I say. "Live a quiet life. I won't use your gifts or become your weapon."

The smile vanishes from Shirasil's face. "Is that what you want?"

"Maybe," I say.

"You'd be happy cooking simple meals in a simple inn the rest of your days?" he asks. "Becoming a slave to your Role?"

"Better than a slave to you," I shoot back.

"Hm." He looks displeased, which I count as a victory. "Alright then. I'm willing to call that bluff. Make your choice."

He walks toward the study's double doors, hands clasped behind his back. "You've four minutes left until Widengra leaves. I'll be taking mine now. But don't expect the gods and their champions to ignore your existence just because you've decided to throw in the towel. You're involved, whether you like it or not. For your sake, and for my entertainment, try not to die."

Instead of pushing the doors open, Shirasil simply steps *through* them. They ripple, like the surface of a lake momentarily disturbed by a skipped stone, then shudder back into stillness once more. I wait another ten heartbeats, but he doesn't come back.

I gasp in a shuddering breath, shaking from fear and anger. My mind is a whirlwind of thoughts, unable to settle on anything that's happened within the last half hour. Lisari. Talia. Jules. Maru. Widengra. Shirasil. And now I'm his *champion?* What does that even mean? What will he make me do?

It all devolved so quickly.

I take a couple of steadying breaths. Shirasil is gone. Maru is dead. And I'm still alive. At least there's that. At least I can still walk out of here today.

I look up at the door. Is it safe to venture back outside? Shirasil's last warning rings in my ears. Widengra is still out there, and now he knows my face.

Weariness sinks into me all at once. I just want to lie down, pull a blanket over my head, and shut myself away from the world. I just want to be somewhere warm and quiet and safe. I want to be back at the Starlight Inn. I want to be in Iski and Gugora's embrace. And maybe I still can. But first, I need to make it out of here.

With a tired groan, I push myself to my feet, heading for the same doors Shirasil vanished through. I grimace, leaning against the frame. I'm out of potions. Weaponless. I'll have to hope I can find a crowd to blend into. Despite all of Shirasil's warnings and 'help,' I feel woefully unprepared. Still, staying hidden in a storage closet all day only delays the inevitable. I push on the door.

At my touch, they both swing open. Only, what's on the other side isn't the underbelly of the Stadium. I blink rapidly and take a step back, trying to make sense of the double-vision I'm presented with.

On the left is the stadium—the seats of the stadium, as if I'm already sitting in the bleachers. A stir of whispers and unnerved murmurs is rustling through the crowd.

"The guards are saying there's been an attack," a dryad tells their companion.

"Someone in the spectator box was killed," another says.

"What? Impossible. The champion is up there."

"Sabotage."

"A coup."

"Rumors. Merely rumors."

"What's going on?"

This last voice I know, and my heart leaps when I pick the goblin out of the crowd.

"Are we too late?" Iski asks. "Why aren't the fights happening?"

"Sal," Gugora says. "A young girl. Have you seen her?"

The nearby spectators shrug at their questions, disinterested. "One of the candidates damaged the field; they're repairing it. Should be starting back up again soon."

"But a girl," Gugora asks in desperation. "One of the candidates. Is she…"

"I don't recall," the spectator says, waving him away. "Say, did you hear anything about what's happening with the guards?"

I nearly step through the image. Something about the vision tells me that if I do, I'll be there, outside, able to sweep Iski and Gugora into a hug. And I yearn for that comfort and safety.

At the same time, an image appears in the doorway on the right. This setting is more dimly lit, and I immediately recognize the underbelly of the stadium. A shadow moves along the lattice: Cyros. The dryad moves silently, his wooden surroundings ushering him along and bending to assist his climb. There's a gash in the stadium floor ahead of him: he's making for the nearly-repaired hole.

For a moment, I'm confused by his presence. So much has happened in the last hour. Then I recall his promise before I was pulled into the tournament: he's here to help me.

I scowl at the sights. There's only one way out of this room, and Shirasil has made his message clear: I need to pick which way I'll be leaving.

"Ass," I mutter, glancing between the options.

Cyros will be fine. I don't know what his plan is, but he can take care of himself. Gugora and Iski need to know I'm okay. The choice is clear.

The room shakes, a layer of dust snowing down from the rafters. Gugora and Iski whip around, while Cyros looks up. Everyone stops in their tracks.

"You all."

I hear the words twice, first from Cyros's side, and a moment later echoed through Iski and Gugora's door. It's coming from somewhere on the stadium field: from Widengra.

From Iski and Gugora's side, I can make out a new figure on the arena field. The god is looming over the candidates still gathered there. In a panic, I touch my forehead, but Maru's mark is gone. I'm safe.

But no one out there is.

"So you're the pathetic excuse for candidates Maru could scrape together," Widengra says. He doesn't seem to be speaking loudly, but his voice reaches everywhere. A stir goes through the crowd. First it's only a few, then it's dozens, hundreds, nearly all of them: the crowd throws themselves to their feet, bowing before the deity. Even Gugora and Iski are on their knees, heads tucked low. Cyros doesn't bow; beneath the stadium floor, he doesn't dare move.

I grind my teeth. If Shirasil is right that not all gods are the same, that some are worth the worship they receive—well, Widengra's certainly not one of them.

Several of the candidates on the field have also prostrated themselves. A handful seem unsure.

"Disappointing," Widengra says. "I'd expected more."

His blood whips out, almost too fast to track, then all the still-standing candidates collapse to the ground. On Cyros's side, blood begins to drip between the boards in the ceiling. Even then, he doesn't twitch a muscle.

If Widengra realizes he's down there eavesdropping and not bowing reverently, what would he do?

Nothing good.

I glance again at Gugora and Iski. They came here looking for me. They don't owe me anything—they've barely known me for two months—but they still wanted to help.

A big part of me wants to go to them. To follow through on Shirasil's challenge. To really just give all this up and live a quiet, happy life at the Starlight Inn, with new friends, who might not be a new family, but could become one.

But Shirasil and I both know that's just a fantasy. I won't do it, not while there's gods like Widengra out there who will kill me on sight. Not while unjust gods like him are still breathing.

That said, I don't have to play Shirasil's game either. Pick a side? No. I don't have to pick just one.

"Hold on," I tell Iski and Gugora. "Just a little longer."

Then I turn to Cyros and jump through.

CHAPTER FORTY-FIVE

PLENTY OF TIME TO DIE

Shirasil's mark flares with a pulse of warmth against my skin as I pass through the doorframe. I step out onto a branch, which bows beneath my feet. The movement shakes my balance, and I instinctively grab a nearby branch. But it's with the wrong hand—my injured fingers slip off, and I nearly topple over, only managing to save myself as I throw my other arm around one of the crossbeams, leaning on it heavily.

Cyros's eyes widen at my appearance. "Where—"

I put a finger to my lips, jerking my head upward, lifting my gaze. Cyros snaps his mouth shut and glances up toward Widengra as well.

"The rest of you have an opportunity to prove your worthiness," Widengra's voice drifts down to reach us. "Additionally, due to a recent opening, I will be selecting two of you to become champions. However, I require proof of your commitment. I will not accept anyone as soft as Maru turned out to be. Therefore, the qualifications are this: whoever brings me the most heads in the next two minutes will become my champion."

Ice pours through me. He can't be serious, can he? No one can be that cruel and senseless.

Except the god of blood.

And there's plenty of blood to be harvested here. A whole stadium full of it—including Iski and Gugora's.

I can see the horror dawning over Cyros's face, too. I hold my hand out to him.

"And... begin!" Widengra says.

"Hurry!" I urge Cyros.

He takes my hand. I pivot on my heels, pulling Cyros back toward the door.

Wood explodes around us. Slivers shoot through the air, and light spills across our perch. My foot slips from the branch, and I'm going down. I snatch for a crossbeam, but once again my maimed hand slips away.

I activate the Noxious Gauntlet. The misty claw appears, and the hand latches around the beam. My weight falls onto my arm at the same moment, nearly yanking my shoulder from its socket. I let out a cry, but the gauntlet holds.

"What's this?" Widengra's voice chases us from above, and terror seizes my chest. "Two little mice, listening in."

Cyros springs around me, vines jumping into place around his feet. He heaves me upright by my good arm. I use the moment to stumble forward and toward Shirasil's door. I feel Cyros's arm go taut behind me, stuttering to an uncertain stop, but I yank him after me anyway.

"Don't stop!" I cry.

"But what's—"

"Whoever brings me that girl's head will become my first champion," Widengra says.

I dive through the door, dragging Cyros after me. "No time!"

I hit the floor of the storage room, and a thud tells me Cyros has, too. I leap to my feet and spin around. Cyros is looking around, bewildered, but it's the forest that has my attention. A woman has dropped down from the stadium floor and is dashing along the tree branches. A moment later, another candidate joins her.

I rush forward, grabbing the door and slamming it shut. The door rattles in its frame, then goes still.

"What was that!" Cyros demands, spinning around. "Where are we? How did that door appear! What's going on?"

"A trick of the gods," I tell him, cautiously watching the door. The closed side remains shut. I'll just have to hope it's no longer accessible on Widengra's side. The left half of the door is open, however, still displaying a view of the crowd and, more importantly, Iski and Gugora.

Shirasil had known about them, that's clear. He must have been following me and learning about my life for the last month at least. But does Widengra know they mean something to me? Will he go after them?

It doesn't matter; as long as they're out there with the god and his candidates, they aren't safe.

"Come on," I say, beckoning Cyros toward the open door. "We don't have much time. Help me!"

"What is going on?" Cyros repeats, bewildered. Even so, he follows me hesitantly toward the door. "A trick of the gods? Sal, your hand!"

I look down at the Noxious Gauntlet, which I still have activated. I consider turning it off then and there, disgusted with myself for already relying on Shirasil's 'gift.' But as much as I hate who it came from, I need it to help Iski and Gugora. I'll deal with the consequences of that choice when we're not fighting for our lives.

"I'll explain later," I tell him. "Right now, we've got about three minutes until Widengra leaves. In that time, his candidates might slaughter everyone in the stadium. You can stay here, but I have people I need to help. You in, or what?"

Cyros sobers. "Tell me what to do."

"Come on." I jump through the open door, and out into the stadium.

Sound erupts around me once more, this time the chaos of a stadium screaming instead of cheering, full of fear instead of excitement. I glance back to see Cyros jump through as well. The door doesn't disappear; it stays open, half embedded in one of the seats. Hopefully, until I need to close it, it'll stay that way.

"Iski!" I call, rushing over to them. "Gugora!"

They turn in surprise, and I'm not sure if it's the fact that I'm alive or that I'm soaked head-to-toe in blood that's causing their shocked looks. Maybe both.

"Sal!" Iski says, relieved. "We thought—"

"We need to get out of here," I cut her off. "Widengra's candidates—"

"We know," Gugora says. "We have to get to shelter."

"This way," I say, gesturing them back with me. "Through the door!"

Her eyes widen. "What is that? Where did it come from?"

"No time," I say. "It's a way out. No one can get through once you close the door. Hurry, both of you!"

"But what about everyone else?" Iski says.

"We'll get as many to come through with us as we can," Gugora says.

I want to scream. Of course they'd want to help others. "It won't matter if one of the candidates follows you through! Then no one will be safe."

"I can help guard the door," Cyros offers. "I should be able to stop anyone who gets too close. At least while I have the element of surprise on my side." He pulls his cloak tighter around himself, obscuring the weapons at his waist. Acting wide-eyed and fearful like everyone else, no one would know he was an assassin.

And I don't have time to argue.

"Fine," I relent. "Be careful. Hurry!" I turn to leave.

"Wait," Gugora calls after, even as Iski is jumping through the crowd like an antelope, directing people toward the strange doorway. "Where are you going?"

"To slow them down," I say. It's me Widengra wants. And if I can draw some of the candidates away from Iski and Gugora, all the better.

Echo, how much longer until Widengra's time limit is up? I ask.

[That information is not publicly available,] she replies.

I grind my teeth. *Well how much time has elapsed since Shirasil left?*

[Eighty-two seconds.]

And Shirasil had said Widengra only had four minutes left before he'd be forced to leave the mortal realm.

Subtract eighty-two seconds from four minutes and start a timer, I tell Echo.

[Starting a 158 second timer,] Echo says.

The numbers blink to life in the corner of my vision: that will have to do. But those numbers are much too high; anything could happen in half the time.

"I need a weapon," I say, looking around.

All I can make out is the panicked chaos of the crowd. Across the stadium there's a wave of people scattering in every direction—like ants fleeing from a drop of rain—which is where one of the candidates must have landed in the audience. I'll just have to hope they stay over there as long as possible. But that doesn't account for the other candidates. There's still too much time left. Way too much time.

I dodge through the crowd, scaling the benches three at a time as I leap between the fleeing audience and make my way quickly to the top. I keep an eye out for any weapons that might have been dropped, but belatedly realize I'm heading in the wrong direction; there are far more likely to be weapons beneath the stadium, in the practice rooms or with the other candidates (dead or alive).

Up here, various booths sprinkle the canopy of the stadium, selling food and drinks and souvenirs. Certainly no weapons shops. But—wait—

I dash over to a noodle stall where a vendor seems to have been halfway through chopping up a large cooked bird with a butcher cleaver before the chaos broke out. He's presently hesitating behind the counter, half ducked down and clearly unsure if he should hide or run. I glance at the cleaver, stuck into the chopping block on the counter, and inwardly groan.

"Sorry," I say, jumping behind his cart.

"Hey!" the dryad protests. "You can't be—"

"I'll pay you back!" I promise, ripping the knife from the block.

"Hey!" he cries again, this time angry.

I don't stick around to hear what he says after that.

The knife feels heavy and unbalanced in my grasp. Most of the knives in the Starlight were smaller and used for chopping vegetables. But it's a knife, so my Knifework skill still applies, and right about now I'd be willing to take a fork and whisk if offered.

Something rockets into the benches nearby, exploding into shards of ice. I duck, shielding my face, realizing I'm doing so with the Noxious Gauntlet and can see right through it.

A candidate stands halfway down the stands, spiky spheres of hail floating above each hand. She lobs another crystal into the audience, and it shatters on impact, spraying the surrounding crowd with shards of ice, leaving dozens injured and screaming.

She's also heading in the direction of Iski and Gugora's door.

I leap down the stadium, feeling stronger, more energized, more resilient than ever. I don't know if that's the adrenaline, the level up, or whatever the hell Shirasil did, but I do know I need to seize the moment before the feeling passes. I don't have any potions left; I don't have any spells or magic swords. Just this knife in my hand and the hate in my heart.

The candidate notices me when I'm nearly on top of her. I guess she hadn't been expecting anyone to challenge her, and the surprise on her face makes me smile. She throws an arm out toward me, and a spear of ice races in my direction.

I dodge to the side, slashing at the attack with the cleaver. The spear shatters into dozens of harmless shards as I continue my advance. She summons two more spheres of ice and launches them at me as well. My knife smashes through the first, but I'm too slow to bring it around and block the second; it crashes into my shoulder, spinning me around and knocking a gasp from my lungs.

[4 points of Bludgeoning damage sustained.]

[Status Effect sustained: Frozen]

A prickling sensation begins to radiate from my shoulder, spreading across my chest and down my arm. The knife slips from my hand as my fingers grow tingly and cold, and I scramble to pick it up with the Noxious Gauntlet instead. I awkwardly hold it in front of me. I'm not used to wielding with my offhand—let alone with a hand that's made of some weird kind of mist. Too close to back off now, however. All I can do is press forward.

The candidate smiles. Probably because of my fumble, but I can still hope she's just generally arrogant. I dash forward, and she raises a shield of ice between us. I slash across the surface, carving away a spray of frost, but my knife sticks in the material and lurches to a stop.

I try to yank it out, but my gauntlet slips from the handle. I grab it with both hands next, but I can't even feel anything with my frozen hand anymore.

The ice spears around my knife and toward my grip. It passes through the Noxious Gauntlet as if it were truly as insubstantial as mist, but grabs the real fingers underneath. An icy chill lances up my arm. I let out an alarmed cry and try to pull back. My frozen arm comes free, but for the gauntlet arm, it's too late: the ice already has its hold on me.

I smash at the ice with my free hand, but the growing crystalline structure is already too thick to break. Panic wells up inside me as I realize I'm pinned: a sitting duck.

I Check Echo's timer: 73 seconds. Still plenty of time to die.

I need another weapon. I need magic. I need to be stronger—something, anything that can help me!

A notification blinks in the corner of my vision: the class evolution. I still haven't made a choice. Could it help me here? Is it the power-up I need to live another day?

My mind races as I consider the options. Rabid Blade, Bane Alchemist, Culinary Rogue. The first two could help me in this fight. They're what Shirasil recommended.

The Blade class would give me +20 to Accuracy with Bladed Weapons, which could help me here. The Alchemist class was mostly focused on magic and brewing potions, but its +5 Resistance to debuffs would help raise my defense against things like this ice status effect. Maybe enough for me to break free.

And then there's the Culinary Rogue. Shirasil had dismissed it as a bad joke. So had I. But with a +25 to Accuracy with Kitchen-Related tools, and +10 Resistance to any temperature related debuffs, this class can become more powerful than the other two combined in very specific situations.

Like the situation I'm in now.

The ice user steps out behind her wall, grinning as she sees me caught in her trap.

No time for me to deliberate. I mentally make my choice.

Echo, activate my class evolution, I hurriedly think. *Now. Quick!*

A warmth washes over me.

[Evolving Class.]

Chapter Forty-Six

GOD'S BLESSING

[Debuff canceled.]

[Relevant Skills upgraded.]

[New Ability gained: Mana Steal]

[Class Evolution complete. You are now a Culinary Rogue.]

The cold evaporates from my arm like it was never even there. With a surge of energy, I twist the knife and yank my arm away. The ice shatters in a hail of fragments, and the candidate stumbles back in surprise.

I flex my wrist, looking down at the cleaver. It no longer feels awkward and unbalanced in my grasp. It feels familiar. Solid. Like I've been using it for years. I toss the knife in the air and catch it with my right hand, then flip it back. I grin.

The candidate raises her hands, forming several more spheres of ice. I jump at her before she's even finished, slashing the knife through each accruing block of ice. She snaps her hands away before my weapon can cleave them off, and the ice falls to the ground, shattering on impact. I press my attack, rushing after the woman even as she stumbles back. Suddenly, our roles are reversed. I'm the one on offense, and she's the one fighting for her life.

We dance up the steps, the crowd scrambling out of the way of our fight. Elation courses through me as I rush after her, reveling in my heightened reflexes and skills. I'm so buoyed by these feelings, I almost don't stop to consider what I even want to achieve here. I want to stop the candidate from hurting others, of course. But what's my end goal? Do I hurt her? *Kill* her? There's been so much death today already; does another person need to die?

Maybe. She wants to be one of Widengra's champions, after all. She's the same ilk as him. Killing her would be removing one more senseless worshiper of death from the world. And it might level me up. It would make me stronger.

The thought startles me even as it passes through my mind. Is that the kind of person I want to be? I might want to kill the gods, but would I stoop to killing other people to climb that mountain?

Would that be exactly what Shirasil wants?

I hesitate, faltering as I swing my blade. The woman notices and seizes the opportunity, launching several balls of ice my way. I flick my wrist, blocking two of them with the flat of my blade. The third catches the edge and deflects at a bad angle, sending a spray of ice into my face. I rapidly blink the melting shards away as the woman spreads her hands wide, opening herself to an attack, but summoning dozens of shards of ice in the air before her. If I hesitate, she'll unleash a volley of blades onto me. It's me or her.

I take aim and snap my wrist forward, launching the cleaver at her chest.

The air between us cracks. My knife flies off to the side, embedding itself in the wood benches, as I'm blown back. My back strikes a seat, sending a shock up and down my spine.

[8 points of Bludgeoning damage sustained.]

I gasp in a breath, rolling onto my side as my ribs throb with each pained inhale. Widengra stands where I'd previously been, a bloody whip around the candidate's wrist. She's looking up at him with a shocked expression. Behind him is a second candidate, also being dragged along by one of Widengra's living red tassels.

[Timer expired,] Echo reports.

"Congratulations," Widengra says to the candidate. "You have secured one of the two open positions to become my champion by default. It seems the other candidates were not worthy."

The woman starts to say something, but Widengra ignores her, turning to me instead. The two candidates are dragged behind him as he steps down the stadium seats and I scramble to my feet.

I raise my fists, and one of his tassels snaps out to grab my wrist—then stops at the last moment, hovering before my Noxious Gauntlet. His nose flares in distaste.

"What's this?" he demands. "Who gave this to you?"

Seeing as I'm not dead yet, I use the opportunity to back away.

"That blessing," he says. "Which god bestowed it?"

"Screw you," I say. As much as I hate Shirasil using me, I hate Widengra a whole hell of a lot more.

His eyes narrow, and then I feel a familiar mental tweak. [Check,] Echo says as my stats abruptly appear in my vision.

Widengra visibly balks at what he finds. "Champion?! When did this occur and who—they've obscured it." His voice has devolved into a growl, his tassels of blood snapping back and forth with his mounting rage. "How dare they. This is sedition against the gods!"

He storms toward me as I flinch back, raising the Noxious Gauntlet defensively before me. Once more, his tassels falter before they land the killing blow.

"You are lucky, mortal," he seethes. "Extremely lucky. If I were a less honorable god, who did not respect the pantheon's code as rigorously as I do, you would already be dead."

"Go to hell," I spit.

Widengra's mouth splits into a snarl, then he takes in a breath, and to my surprise, takes a step back.

"You are in a unique position to assist the pantheon," he says. The aggression isn't gone from his stance and voice, but now it's more controlled. "You do not understand the weight of the consequences your kind has brought into this world. If you cooperate and tell me which god has given you this gift, I will be merciful."

I grit my teeth. Why do I remain unconvinced of Widengra's capacity for mercy?

As much as I hate Shirasil using me like some kind of chess piece, I'm not about to do Widengra any favors either. And if Shirasil really is the only thing stopping Widengra from smiting me on the spot, there's no way I'm going to give him what he wants.

"But make no mistake, mortal," Widengra continues when I remain silent. "Just because I am forbidden from slaying a champion doesn't mean your allies share such restrictions. So this will be the only chance I give you. To which god are you loyal?"

At that, I can't help but laugh. "Loyal? I'm not loyal to any of them."

Widengra's mouth twists into a displeased grimace. "Is that your final answer?"

I bare my teeth at him. "No, my final answer is *fuck you.*"

Widengra's mouth curls in distaste. "It is unwise to speak to your betters that way. Best hope your blade is half as sharp as your tongue when my champions find you again."

He glances away suddenly, as if someone invisible is speaking to him. Then he hoists his two champion candidates from their feet as casually as a boy snatching up kittens. His tassels come alive, swirling around him like dozens of writhing centipede legs.

"My time in the mortal realm has expired," he says. "You have chosen your allegiances poorly, child."

"I'm not allied with anyone!" I object.

The tassels close around him and his champions, encasing them in a shell of red. The bloody sphere swirls, and I raise a hand to the mist that threatens to spray me as it grows smaller, spinning faster, with every passing moment. It shrinks to the size of a bush, then a melon, then a marble, until it quietly blinks out of existence entirely.

And with that, Widengra is gone.

A hush goes through the stadium. The previous screams have died out, replaced by a confused and concerned murmuring. Then shouts for help. Calls for a healer. Sure, *now* they aren't a fan of bloodshed.

I groan, sinking back against the seats as I *thunk* my head on a wooden bench. The sting of Shirasil's mark still pulses against my wrist. I hold up my hand, and mentally deactivate the Noxious Gauntlet, faintly disgusted with myself that I started using it almost immediately after telling Shirasil I'd never become his pawn. Am I really so easily manipulated by desperation? Are my convictions so meaningless?

What happens when the next god comes along to make demands of their own?

I stare up at the sky, exhausted, irritated, defeated.

"Just leave me alone!" I shout.

The gods don't answer.

Chapter Forty-Seven

ONWARD AND UPWARD

The storage room is subdued as healers tend to everyone's wounds. The same healers who were happy to stand by and watch as we slaughtered each other in the stadium. I guess it's different when it's your friends and family who are fighting for their lives.

Hypocrites.

"Sal?" Gugora asks again.

I look up. "Sorry. What?"

Gugora is sitting cross-legged on the floor, Iski standing on his knee to reach his shoulder, which she's patching with strips of fabric. The healers are ignoring those with lighter wounds, currently only addressing those in critical condition.

"I asked if you were alright," Gugora says. His brows are pinched in a concerned frown.

"Sure," I say, distracted. Even though the gods are gone, even though the killing is over, my mind is still running a mile a minute. Will Shirasil and Widengra be coming back for me? Will Shirasil be able to find and track me through his 'gift?' Will Widengra be sending his newly ascended champions to come torture the name of my Patron god out of me? Can I run from them? Do I even want to? "Yeah. I'm fine."

"No, you're not," Iski says sharply, her words cutting me out of my thoughts. "Talk to us. What happened here today?"

I open my mouth, and I shut it. I'm not even sure where to begin. I look at my maimed hand. The mark of Shirasil is like a shackle on my wrist. I think of Talia. Of all the blood. So much blood.

"Sal? You're alive!" Cyros hurries over. "Gods, I can't believe it. I saw you with Widengra and feared the worst."

"I'm fine," I say again, automatically. Given the hollow, numb sensation that seems to have replaced any capacity I once had for emotions, I might even believe it.

Gugora glances between us questioningly.

"A friend," I say, too tired to explain.

"Well, a friend of Sal is a friend of ours," Iski says. "I saw you out there helping the others. Thank you."

Cyros appears dismayed. "You *saw* me?"

I smile weakly at his disappointment. Nieve would surely give him an earful later for doing something so visible.

Cyros's gaze flicks over me, settling almost instantly on Shirasil's mark. He puts a hand on my arm. "Oh, no. What's this?"

I sigh, holding up my wrist. Honestly, he asks a good question.

Echo, Check.

[Mark of the gods,] Echo says. [This mark provides the user with the ability Noxious Gauntlet, which acts as an enhanced limb, and additionally allows the user's Affinity to be channeled through the mist when activated.]

Will people be able to tell it's from Shirasil by looking at it? I wonder.

[Negative.]

Will they know I am a champion?

[While activated, the user will display physical traits consistent with that of a champion.]

I grimace. *Can I remove it?*

[Negative.]

Probably should have seen that one coming.

"A god gave it to me," I tell the others. "Apparently I've got some kind of toxic magic mist hand now."

The others stare at me. Not with the obvious horror I was expecting, but rather with some kind of awe.

"You were given a blessing by the gods?" Cyros asks.

Iski seems similarly amazed. "Which one? Widengra?"

I sort of miss Lisari's candid dismissal of reverence for the gods—of course, I have to remind myself, she *was* one.

"I have to leave," I say, ignoring their questions. My gaze is unfocused. My head feels like it's full of cotton. I'm so tired, yet a restless anxiety is clawing at me.

Gugora slowly nods. "We need to get out of here. You've done more than enough to help. We can still make it back to the Inn by nightfall."

"Or you could stay with me if you need to rest," Cyros offers. "It sounds like there's a lot you need to—"

"No," I say, forcefully focusing my vision. I look at Gugora and Iski. "I can't stay with you two anymore. Widengra will find me there, and you won't be safe. Actually, I don't think it's safe for me to stay in this city."

"Why?" Iski asks, bewildered. "What are you talking about?"

"He's coming for me," I say. "Or at least his champions might be." I clench my jaw. "But not if I come for them first."

Iski shakes her head. "Not this again. You can't—"

"I don't have a choice," I say, raising my arm pointedly. "I can't just choose to stay uninvolved. I don't fully understand what the gods want with me, but I don't have the luxury to sit back and pretend like they don't exist. I can be their puppet, or I can grow strong enough to cut the strings."

"Why you?" Cyros asks. "I know you seem to be tangled in their plans but... Why?"

I think back on everything the gods have said to me. Everything Maru and Shirasil and even Widengra intentionally or inadvertently revealed.

"I don't think it's just me," I say. "I think there may be more out there like me who the gods are also looking for." Whether to kill, collect, or manipulate, I'm unsure. And how many of them could be anyone's guess. But if there are other people from Earth out there, they could use a helping hand—especially if the gods are after them. What other chance do we have if we don't stick together?

"I have to leave," I repeat, this time looking at Cyros. "To learn more. To get stronger. Can the Guild help me with that?"

"Guild?" Gugora asks, suspicious.

Cyros glances uncomfortably at Gugora and Iski, but nods. "There are branches in other cities. Nieve can find something for you."

"Other cities?" Iski objects. "Now, hold on. We should think this through. You don't have to make any rash decisions. You hardly know anything about this world, still."

"World?" Cyros asks.

I grimace. Another person put at risk of the gods' wrath for having knowledge they shouldn't. "I'll explain later," I tell him. "And we can talk about my future while we head back to the Inn," I add to Iski and Gugora. "I'll need to grab my things from there anyway."

Neither of them look happy. Cyros looks concerned. I guess I'm a mix of both. More than anything, though, I just want to find a small, quiet corner somewhere out of the way where I can curl up and sleep.

When we finally make it back to the Starlight Inn, I do, eventually, get my sleep. It's past sunset when we arrive, and I collapse into my bed without even kicking off my boots.

It's dark when I wake up. Iski tells me I slept an entire day. I spend the evening chopping vegetables to fulfill my ever-persistent Role Requirement. Though we hardly exchange three words, I think Iski enjoys the company.

The mood is subdued at the Starlight Inn. Gugora and Iski return to their typical duties, though they seem to be hovering somewhere nearby every time I turn around. I spend several hours soaking in a hot tub of water Iski draws for me. I spend even longer trying to scrub the blood out of my clothes and hair. Then, I pack.

I lay everything out on the floor of my workroom. All my potions, empty bottles, ingredients, cauldrons, chalk, utensils, and tools. Then I get to work strapping them all together. I undo my two bandoliers and sew one to the other and add more strips of leather to create a checkerboard of belts pockmarked by dozens of straps, hooks and knots. One by one, I tightly secure each of my belongings to the leather mat.

If I am going to survive on my own, if I am going to be facing the gods themselves, I can't afford to waste a single advantage, and my inventory will be the ticket to ensuring I am never parted from my weapons again. I'll be losing the ability to keep a single knife or potion on hand for a quick surprise, but the tradeoff of being able to bring everything I own with me is more than worth it. Of course,

I'll need a large space to be able to withdraw this complex binding of supplies all at once. No matter. I'll make myself new bandoliers. I'll figure out a better system through trial and error. The most important thing is the freedom to pick up and move at a moment's notice. I'll never worry about leaving anything behind. I'll never be tied down anywhere again.

A shadow falls over the doorframe. "I never taught you how to use that bow," Gugora says.

I sit back from the supplies I was bent over, wiping the sweat from my brow. Knotting the twine is giving me trouble since I'm not used to doing so one-handed.

I haven't turned the Noxious Gauntlet back on since the tournament.

"That's okay," I say, standing and stretching with a relieved sigh. "I don't think I would have been very good at it. Knives seem to be my specialty now, anyway."

Gugora hardly appears comforted by the explanation. "Speaking of which." He draws a knife from his belt and turns it around, offering me the handle. "Your knife. You should take it with you."

Gingerly, I take it. This knife and I have been through a lot the last month. Yet, it almost feels unnatural in my grip now. I Check it.

[Simple Hunting Knife,] Echo reports. [One-handed bladed weapon.]

Not a Chef knife, then. Not something my class would give me a bonus for using. I hand it back to Gugora.

"Thanks, but I think it's better served in your hands," I say. "However, if you've a set of kitchen knives to spare, I'd be grateful to borrow a few."

Gugora takes the knife, smiling softly. "Iski would love that."

I decide it's best not to mention the cutlery are unlikely to be used for food.

I go back to tying down the last of my supplies, and Gugora wordlessly kneels down next to me to help.

"You don't have to," I object.

"I want to," the orc grumbles.

I tighten down a strap. "I need the practice. Not used to working with my hand like this."

Gugora puts a finger down on the twine as I pull it tight. There's a span of silence as we work through the last three empty glass bottles, securing each one to my supply mat.

"I'm sorry about your fingers," he finally says.

I shrug. "It's inconvenient, but it's fine. They're not really me."

"Who?" Gugora asks, confused.

"The fingers," I say. "They were a part of my body, but they're not *me*. No more than my body is me. Your body is just... something your mind is stuck in."

"Is that how you see yourself?" His tone sounds sad.

I bristle. "It's just facts." I tighten the last knot, then brush Gugora's hand away, going over every one of my belongings in turn, making sure each object is secured. Finally, when I'm satisfied, I add the whole contraption to my inventory. The entire display vanishes.

[Apothecary added to inventory.]

It worked. I allow myself a satisfied smile.

The two of us stand up, surveying the now empty room.

"I guess you'll have your butcher shed back," I say.

"I guess so."

I ignore the sting of sadness that follows me as I turn my back on the room and leave it for the last time.

Iski cooks me a large lunch. She doesn't call it a goodbye meal, but we all know it is. I eat every bite, even though I'm not hungry. When Gugora brings up my request for cooking knives, Iski happily obliges with what I strongly suspect is her best set. I add them to my Apothecary.

Nieve and Cyros appear not long after that.

I raise an eyebrow at Cyros. "I didn't think you were coming."

"You're new to the Guild," Cyros says. "Even if you're not my apprentice, since I brought you into the fold, I'm responsible for you. Which means I'm coming with."

"You are?" I ask, surprised. "I'm sorry, I—I didn't know. I don't want to be a burden for you."

Cyros snorts. "You're a lot things, but you're not a burden."

"But your home," I object.

"It's already decided," he interrupts. Then he smiles. "You can't get rid of me that easily."

I still feel a little guilty. But somehow, I also feel relieved.

"Ready?" Nieve asks me as I linger outside the Starlight.

Even though I've only been on this planet for a few short months, this inn has started to feel like home. Probably for the best that I'm leaving, then.

"Yeah," I say, turning to face Gugora and Iski.

Dark looks cloud the innkeeps' faces.

"Thank you," I tell them. "I've truly appreciated your hospitality. You treated me better than I deserved and I don't know how I can—"

"Oh, come here," Iski says, yanking my scarf down so she can wrap her arms around my neck in a hug. When she lets go, I only have enough time to straighten up before Gugora's arms engulf me in a second one. A familial yearning wells up inside me. An overwhelming desire to stay here, where I'm accepted, where I have people who care about me.

But I think of the gods, and Talia, and my parents, and I know this is a door I have to shut.

"Sorry," I say, blinking back tears.

"What have you got to apologize for?" Iski snaps.

I shake my head, unsure why I'd even said it.

"Be careful," Gugora says, releasing me from his grasp. "Stay safe."

"And don't forget to sharpen those knives," Iski adds. "Nothing more dangerous than a dull knife."

"I will," I promise her.

"And oil!" she adds. "Don't let them rust!"

This time I chuckle. "I won't."

Gugora squeezes my shoulder one last time. "Come back some day." He smiles lopsidedly. "Just so we know you're alive."

I return the smile. "Okay," I promise.

He drops his hand from my shoulder and doesn't say anything else. He doesn't need to.

Finally, reluctantly, I turn away. I join Nieve and Cyros on the road, and we begin to walk. It will take a couple weeks by foot to reach the next major city. Apparently, there's a branch of the Blackcloaks that's active there, where I should be able to find work easily enough.

"You're leaving behind quite a bounty," Nieve remarks. "Most would not find it so easy to turn away from such a life."

"It's not easy," I say, though the irony isn't lost on me. I'd wanted to join an adventuring guild, learn weapons and magic, and go off traveling the world since the first moment I arrived here. Now I'm getting all that, and I wish I didn't have to.

What would have happened if I'd just accepted the role I'd been given? If I never tried to force a magical affinity? If I'd never gone to

Fairwood, or joined the Blackcloaks, or sought revenge? Would I be happier, or filled with resentment?

Even now I don't know.

"But I know what I have to do," I say. "I need to learn more about the gods. I need to get stronger. Develop my magic and fighting abilities." Investigate the hints that there's others out there like me.

If I'm going to storm the heavens, if I want to seek justice for the wrongs the gods have inflicted on us—if I want to kill a god—I'll need all the help I can get.

Determination simmers in my gut. Just reminding myself of why I'm leaving boils away the last lingering feelings of regret. The injustices that still need to be answered for. The indignation that the gods think they can play with my life like I'm a mere toy. I let my resolve fan the warm anger that's spreading through me.

"The Guild is a good place to start," Nieve says, pulling me from my thoughts. "You will find many resources at your disposal there. If it's power you seek, climbing the Guild's ranks will open many doors for you."

"Good," I say shortly. "What's the highest rank you can achieve?"

"S class missions," Nieve says.

"How long does it take to get there?" I ask.

"What?" Cyros says. "Sal, don't even think about it."

"It varies greatly by individual," Nieve replies anyway. "Some are content only to pursue low rank jobs their entire lives. Others are eager to gamble on the more lucrative and dangerous tasks. I unlocked S rank missions after working for the Guild for three years."

Three years is too long. I need to get stronger faster. And with Echo and the System on my side, I should be able to do just that. "I'll do it in half that time."

Cyros groans, but Nieve smiles approvingly. "I look forward to witnessing your progress."

I squeeze my hand into a fist.

So do I.

CHAPTER FORTY-EIGHT

EPILOGUE

Shirasil feigned mild curiosity as the gods blinked into the room, one at a time, answering Widengra's emergency summons. The God of War paced angrily about the central pedestal, while others hung back, eyes averted and whispering amongst themselves in an attempt to avoid drawing the god's attention—or wrath.

Yua Tin and their champion—well, ex-champion—were also appeared nearby, draped as always in robes of white and blue, hair tied back with gold ribbons. They were already engaged in quiet conversation with one another as Shirasil drifted casually over to them.

"Resplendent as always, God of Starlight," he said to Yua Tin. "And you, Lord Blair. It's good to see you in the hall of the gods."

Blair's cat ears twitched at his words, but she otherwise did not acknowledge his greeting.

"Shirasil." Yua Tin spread their hands welcomingly. "You speak with the sweetness of a sugar snake. Do you also come bearing its fangs?"

Shirasil held up his hands in defense. "I merely came to make small talk. I don't suppose either of you have any insight into why Widengra called us here today?"

"No," Blair said, "but I suspect you might."

Shirasil grinned. "And what about your newly acquired insight? Any progress on finding this Kanin individual?"

The felis's tail whipped back and forth. "If I did, you would not be the first to learn of it."

Shirasil laughed. "The suspicion is understandable, given the circumstances. However I promise, I only intend to help."

"I believe you do," Yua Tin says. "Though *who* you intend to help is an enigma sure to remain shrouded in uncertainty."

Shirasil placed a hand on his chest, as if wounded. "Then allow me to be blunt: the safety of the Travelers is my top priority. All that I ask—"

"I will not pledge my loyalty to you, Shirasil," Yua Tin said.

Disappointing. "I would never presume that you would." He needed to take another approach. "Do our centuries of friendship mean nothing?"

Yau Tin smiled faintly. "Of course."

He tipped his head. "Of course, they mean nothing? Or of course, our friendship counts for something?"

"Yes." They laughed lightly, taking Blair's arm. "Come, friend, we shall continue our conversation in private."

"Blair doesn't belong to you, anymore," Shirasil said, perhaps a little more shortly than he intended. He turned to Blair. "They may have trained you, but you don't owe anyone anything. You can make your own choices."

"I am *choosing* to depart with Yua Tin," Blair replied shortly. "But thank you for your concern."

"Just keep me in mind," he added as the pair turned away. "I'm on your side."

The gods wandered off, leaving Shirasil alone. Well, he could have handled that better. But those two knew something, he was sure of it, and he just *hated* being left out when schemes were afoot. Shirasil skimmed the room, searching for anyone else that might be holding interesting information, and found the company depressingly lacking. Lorata saved him from having to make a second attempt at small talk when she abruptly appeared in the hall with a flash of light.

"Finally," Widengra growled. "To think you'd be the last to show."

"I am somewhat busy with many other pressing matters," Lorata snapped, striding up to the pedestal. "This better be worth my while."

Widengra *almost* wilted beneath her scorn; but he was equipped with more spite than sense, and the former quickly won out. "I would not have called a meeting if it wasn't. There is a betrayer in our midst."

Several audible groans drifted through the room, and Shirasil had to stifle a laugh. He'd been making such claims for half a century at least, and the other gods were beginning to tire of the accusations.

Not that it mattered that this time he was right.

Lorata pressed her mouth into a displeased line. "Explain."

"My champion was slain by a Traveler," Widengra said, and this *did* get a stir from the room. "Then, she was made into a champion herself."

Many gods spoke at once in response to this. It took Lorata nearly a minute to quiet them all.

"A champion?" she repeated, skeptical. "To which god?"

Widengra faltered. "That information was obscured to me."

"Do you have evidence to support this claim?" Lorata asked. She turned to the room. "Unless anyone would care to step forward and explain?"

The hall went dead silent.

"It's true," Widengra insisted. "I saw her myself. Sal was her name."

Several gods' eyes glazed over as they checked the information logged on System users. They wouldn't find much, though. Just basic information on her name, level, and class.

"There does appear to be someone of that name in the list," Lorata said after a moment. "But this claim is difficult to believe. Making a Traveler into a champion would be rash. Hiding them from the pantheon, more so. And she only appears to be level 20. How could she have bested one of your champions? What motive would she have had?"

"Revenge," Widengra snarled. "She used poison and trickery to target my champion and enact a ploy to assassinate her."

"Why?" Blair spoke up. "Revenge for what?"

Ah, Shirasil loved it when someone else did his work for him.

Widengra scowled. "Maru initially failed to exterminate the aberration when she first appeared on our world."

"Exterminate?" Lorata repeated, horrified.

"She was dangerous!" Widengra snarled. "The fact that she managed to kill my champion proves it!"

"And remind me," Shirasil finally spoke up. "This Traveler attacked your champion before or after she was attacked first?"

Widengra rounded on Shirasil, his blood tattoos lashing with rage. His eyes narrowed.

Oops. This was one dragon he probably shouldn't be prodding, as entertaining as it was. "Tell me this," Shirasil continued, before Widengra had a chance to say anything intelligent. "If this Traveler really did kill your champion, why'd you let her go? Why not bring her back here to show the rest of us and have her face justice?"

"Laying a hand on another god's champion is forbidden," Widengra snaps. "But of course *you* of all people would suggest breaking such customs."

"Well, yes." Shirasil shrugged, looking around at all the other gods. "I would. Of course. This sounds like extremely extenuating circumstances."

It was a risky move. The laws of the gods protected Sal the last time she encountered Widengra, but pushing for an exception to the rules would mean it wouldn't save her in any encounters going forward.

But it was a price Shirasil was willing to pay for shifting suspicion off of him. Afterall, why would he be advocating for his own champion to be caught?

Lorata sighed, rubbing her temple. "I agree with Shirasil. Finding and monitoring these Travelers is top priority. If it's true she was made a champion, that would be even more reason to bring her before us."

Briefly, Shirasil caught Blair watching him. He inclined his head a fraction of an inch, his mouth twitching with a ghost of a smile. She held the look for a moment, then glanced away.

"The way we are currently handling the situation is insufficient," Lorata continued. "We do not have enough champions to be everywhere at once. And killing the Travelers should be a last resort," she added, turning to Widengra. "We stand to learn more about the situation and how we can bring it under control through apprehension, not murder. That shouldn't be difficult for a god of your abilities."

Widengra ground his teeth. "This one is dangerous. And I deserve justice for my champion."

"If you can find her and bring her here, I will be the judge of that," Lorata said.

"But—"

"Enough," she snapped, the light in the room flickering with her words. Lorata took a steadying breath, then turned back to the rest of the gods. "If anyone can find this supposed Traveler champion, you are to bring her here—alive. And if I find out it is true, whichever one of you behaved so rashly will be stripped of their champions and face the possibility of demotion."

Alarmed murmurs whispered through the room.

"Further," Lorata continued, "I will be creating a rotating schedule for visits to the mortal realm. If you have fewer than three champions, now will be your opportunity to take on more acolytes. The sooner we can account for all Travelers, the better."

Now that *was* a surprise. Not an unwelcome one, however. Shirasil wouldn't turn up his nose at a legitimate excuse to be in the mortal realm.

"Additionally, *all* Travelers are to be brought to me alive," Lorata said. "If your champions are unable to do so, then I expect you to step in in their place. Eliminating a Traveler should only occur under situations where they may also possess a remnant, and even then only if containment is deemed impossible." Lorata shot a look at Widengra. "Is that all?"

The god glowered at her. "Yes."

"Good." Lorata turned away, flicking a hand over her shoulder. "Dismissed."

Shirasil briefly considered approaching Lorata to further ingrain his innocence before thinking better of it. This had been an extremely fruitful day, and he didn't need to push his luck. He had a new, promising champion, Widengra's judgement was in question, he had more opportunities to visit the mortal realm, and on top of it all, Lorata had blatantly ordered the gods to stop killing Travelers.

Of course, that wasn't going to stop gods with an ax to grind, like Widengra, but it now would hilariously put Shirasil in Lorata's good graces when he intervened. Rewarded for more meddling. Fantastic!

Shirasil was about to leave as Blair caught his eye. He paused, but she continued to walk as she passed him.

"One chance to prove your integrity," she said, already moving away. "Then we'll talk."

Ah, how Shirasil loved the young ones. So quick to sing a different tune. It always made dealings with them interesting.

As he left the Hall of the Gods, his surroundings blinked out of existence, and when they blinked back in, the tangible weight of reality settled around him. He was in a forest, not far from a town he'd visited centuries ago. Perhaps he was overdue for another visit.

"Now, let's see here," he said, a wind stirring about his feet as he walked. His garb began to leak its black hue, gradually fading to shades of white and green. His hair grew out, and he plucked a pair of dark glasses from the air to rest on his face. "Where shall we visit next?" There were tales of a floating castle in the south. A war brewing in the east. Trouble in Valenia's capital. So many options—so many areas of interest. How many were likely to involve a Traveler?

Lisari adjusted her clothes and ran a hand through her hair, smiling as the sun warmed her skin. "I suppose it doesn't matter where I start," she said. "Either way, it's bound to be fun."

Acknowledgements

First off, I want to thank my editor, Justine Manzano, for tolerating my adoration of em-dashes and polishing my story into something resembling a real book. I also can't express how much I love the amazing cover art that Vexdye designed for me. It captured Sal so perfectly!

Huge thanks goes out to my critique partners and beta readers for reading the early drafts of this story and helping me to realize that Sal should *definitely* become a Champion of Chaos at the end of this book. Your insight is as valuable to me as our friendship.

And last but certainly not least, thank you, thank you, thank you to all of my readers from RoyalRoad and Patreon. I couldn't have done this without all of your support and motivation.

BOOKS BY KIA LEEP

A Little Salty is part of the NPSeeds Saga. Four different book series all take place in this universe. If you enjoyed *A Little Salty,* you might enjoy *Glass Kanin*, which answers how Sal got to this world in the first place. You can check them out below!

Glass Kanin
Friendly Fyre
Nyte in Shining Armor

Flip the page for a sneak peek at the first two chapters of *Friendly Fyre.*

FRIENDLY FYRE

NPSeeds SAGA

KIA LEEP

FRIENDLY FYRE CHAPTER 1

SNEAK PEEK

So this is what dying feels like, I think.

There's no fear. No sadness. Just clinical observation as the pain fades from my chest, and the surrounding cubicle walls are consumed by the darkness of my tunneling vision.

Died at my desk, was it? They always said I would. Ah, well. It was a good run. Over fifty years. Not as long as I would have liked, but longer than some. My life doesn't flash before my eyes as my consciousness fades, but I do think about the big moments. Marriage. Divorce. The nurse placing my daughter in my arms.

It's only then that sorrow crashes through me. Becoming a father was my greatest joy, and my greatest failure. I would have liked to have seen her one last time.

As sight, sound, and sensation leave me, all I can do is heave a mental sigh of regret. I suppose now comes The Great Mystery. Afterlife or oblivion? Reincarnation, or something inconceivable? It will be interesting to finally know, if nothing else.

Abruptly, malice closes around me. It licks at my essence like acid, faintly eating away at my mind. I try to flinch away from this new, horrific sensation, but it seems to be everywhere, and the more I struggle, the more I can't make sense of where I am, or what I'm experiencing. I spiral with disorientation, all comprehension of time and space slipping away from me. All I understand is that this is bad—existentially bad—and I need to escape.

As the biting void whirls around me, I encounter a tiny, fragile grain of kindness suspended in the enmity, like the faint glow of a candle in the dark. I try to move toward it, and surprisingly find I'm able to. I huddle close and begin to notice other small flickering lights nearby as well. I can't see them, exactly, but I can *feel* them there. Other... *presences.*

I'm sorry. The words come from the small spark of warmth. *I didn't mean for this to happen. I'm sorry.*

Hello? I try to reply. The other lights—people?—are also emitting confusion, fear, curiosity. *What's wrong?* I ask. *Where are we? What can we do?*

If the light hears me, it doesn't respond. I'm not sure how I can tell, but I can sense it struggling to not go out. Struggling to not be swallowed by the hunger. Its attention is elsewhere—external? I try to cast my mind outward as well and am rewarded with a chaotic tangle of sensations. A blur of colors, the stinging smell of the sea, a distant roar like a waterfall, and feelings of hatred and famine that aren't mine, pounding at me from every angle. I—my mind—my soul?—begins to ache.

"...hoping you'd forgotten about me..."

With a surge of anger, an impression of movement passes through me. Time and space feel more concrete again. I'm being lurched around even as the darkness continues to eat at me, like I'm slowly being digested in the belly of a giant beast.

Something is happening outside. A struggle. The hungry dark is exuding a sense of triumph—which suddenly shifts to hesitation, then alarm, then everything is illuminated with a burst of light.

The world careens around me once more, and now the maelstrom of emotions are injured, upset, desperate. I can almost feel myself slipping from the grasp of the dark cloud of hunger. I can feel its viscosity thinning. Then—

Pain slams through me. For a moment, the acidic corrosion magnifies a thousand fold, stripping my essence away.

It's going to eat me, I realize. And there's nothing I can do to stop it.

Then, just as abruptly, it evaporates. The other minds are gone. That single spark of warmth has vanished. I'm left alone with the lingering pain of an intangible wound as I fade into the world.

. . .

I take in a shuddering breath, the cold of my surroundings immediately digging its claws into my skin. I blink my eyes rapidly, but can see nothing. This isn't the same nothing I'd previously experienced, however—that was a true absence of sight. This is just dark. Pitch black. Like I'm in the bowels of a cave.

What even was that? Was it real? A strange dream? I thought I had died. I touch a hand to my chest, recalling the moment I felt my heart stop. My fingers run over something soft, like a downy blanket, but beneath it I can feel the steady beat of my pulse. Well. I seem to be alive now. But where am I?

I groan, rolling onto my side as the cold, hard ground grinds against my hip bone. Maybe I am in a cave. There's freezing stone beneath my hands, and I still can't see anything. My body feels strange and clunky, as if each movement is not exactly what I intend it to be. A shiver runs through me, cold prickling all over my body. Am I going numb? I might be experiencing early stages of hypothermia. If I don't do something to warm up soon, I'll be in trouble.

[New user established. Populating stats.]

I tip my head at the feminine voice. Not a human voice, though. Vaguely mechanical, like something out of an arcade.

"Hello?" I call. I clear my throat. My voice doesn't sound right. "Is someone there?"

Definitely not right. My voice has always been quiet and slightly croaky—like I had a cold I couldn't quite get rid of. The words coming out of my mouth presently are the same low alto they've always been, but now they're warm and smooth, like all the roughness has been sanded away.

Also, they're distinctly feminine.

"What…" I trail off, touching my throat. Something soft and skin-tight is covering my neck as well. The covering ruffles as I run my fingers over it, but doesn't come away. What's happening? Where am I? There's too many questions to process at once.

[Compilation complete. Role assigned. Displaying stats.]

[Name: Faber]

[Species: Harpy]

[Subspecies: Phoenix]

[Class: Psion]

[Level: 20]

[HP: 100/100]

[Mana: 200/200]

[Role: The Dark Lord]

My mind spins as words abruptly appear in the dark. I reach a blind hand out, but no light reflects onto my skin. Somehow I instinctively recognize the words, like the voice, are not physical, but inside my own head.

I'd think this were a dream if it didn't all feel so real. The stone is hard and cold beneath me, and my breathing echoes in the cave around me. I shudder against the freezing air, and I suspect if I could see, my breath would be fogging. Whatever strange thing is happening, whomever this voice is and however I got here, one thing is clear enough: I'm in danger of perishing if I don't find shelter soon.

I push myself up onto my hands and knees, the feeling of acute physical strangeness persisting with the motion. It's not numbness, I can tell that now. Something is different. My limbs keep getting in the way of each other, bending oddly, my feet scraping strangely across the floor. I reach a hand back to try to feel what's going on, and I bump into my arm. But it's not my arm. What's this?

I stretch my limbs out, then flinch, hissing in a startled breath as six limbs respond to the instinct.

"What's happening?" I wonder in that warm, unfamiliar voice.

Tentatively, I reach back again, touching the extra set of limbs that shouldn't be there. My fingers encounter soft resistance, skimming across a series of velvety... well, I know what they are just from touch, but it's difficult to bring myself to believe it.

Feathers?

I trace the wing down to my back, where the limb appears to be fixed along my lower spine, just above the hips.

Harpy. The word comes to me unbidden as my attention flickers back to those strange words fixed in the corner of my vision. Phoenix.

I huff out a disbelieving laugh. This might not be a dream, but it certainly can't be coherent, sane thought. A hallucination? Drugs, or a concussion, or...

I shiver. Death?

The heart attack was so vivid. I was so sure I had died, and maybe I had.

A faint pressure of anxiety squeezes around my heart. I take in a shuddering breath, and let it out slowly. No, I can't let myself panic. Fear impedes reason. I have to keep myself together. Think through all this rationally. There's a logical explanation for everything—even if that explanation is one I won't like.

Like being dead.

But even if that's true, it doesn't make what I'm experiencing any more sensible. "I'm not *really* a harpy, am I?"

[Affirmative.]

I freeze. Did the voice just respond to me?

[Affirmative.]

In my mind, too! Unless it was only a coincidence. I decide to test that hypothesis. *Can you really hear me?* I think.

[Affirmative,] the voice repeats.

I shake my head at the absurdity of it all. But at least I have someone to speak to—someone who might be able to give me answers.

What are you? I think, deciding that's less unsettling than hearing my new voice. *Are you a person? A program?*

[This unit is a clone of the unit designated Echo,] Echo says. [This audiovisual display acts as the interface between your neuromagical pathways and the extraplanar arcane network which governs select users' metaphysical evolution within the System.]

That's a lot of interesting words. *There's other users in this... System?*

[Affirmative.]

How many? I ask. *Are there any nearby?*

[This unit does not have access to that data,] Echo says.

Can you ping anyone? I wonder. *Escalate a service request?*

[Command not recognized.]

I smile slightly to myself. Well, it was worth a shot.

Alright, then, Echo. How else can you help me? I shift into a more comfortable sitting position, blinking against the black, uncomfortably trying to ignore the existence of my wings. *Don't suppose you can summon a blanket to warm me up?*

[Negative,] Echo says, which pulls a small, unsurprised chuckle from me. But then she says something that is surprising. [However, the user may create a source of warmth via spell activation.]

I blink. "Spell?"

[List of user's known spells,] Echo recites.

[Spark: Summon a small flame maintained above the caster's hand. Mana cost: 1 per minute. Required affinity: Fire.]

[Blaze: Summon a flame of variable size and shape capable of moving with the caster's intent. Mana cost: 10 per cubic yard per second. Required affinity: Fire.]

[Psionic Touch: Communicate telepathically with any thinking entity while maintaining physical contact with the target. Required Class: Psion. Mana cost: 1 mana per 5 seconds.]

I reel with this new information. She can't mean *magic*? I can't do magic. I'm an engineer!

Or, was.

I struggle to wrap my mind around what Echo is saying. Magic flies against everything I've ever known. Everything I've ever studied, and every assumption I've ever made in my career.

Then again, magic is just a word. Perhaps there is a rational system here, merely hiding beneath the veneer of mysticism. I suppose whichever way the coin falls, there's only one way to find out. Even if my well-being didn't hinge on the immediate need to find a source of warmth, my curiosity wouldn't allow me to dismiss all this out of hand.

Alright, Echo, I think, trying to suppress my skepticism. *How do I go about casting Spark?*

[The user may activate the relevant arcanum simply by envisioning the spell, though audio cues typically assist in concentration.]

Sounds a bit wishy-washy to me. But I won't knock it until I try it. I hold my hand out in front of me, still invisible in the complete darkness. I imagine a fire there, hovering in my palm, warming my shivering body, and I say, "Spark."

Light flares into existence. I jerk my head away and squeeze my eyes shut as the light stabs into my skull, and a white sphere is burned into my vision. But the warmth that kisses my face, hand, and arms is unmistakable.

Cautiously, I peek an eye back open. There, nestled in the palm of my hand, the size of a peach, is a flickering orange flame. I stare at it in awe. I made this? This came from me?

It's too close to my hand, I realize. Practically resting on my skin. Yet, it only feels pleasantly warm. A wonderful, soothing warmth that's already spreading down my arm and driving the fangs of cold away. I bring it closer to my chest to try to warm the rest of my body as well. *Why isn't it burning me?* I ask Echo.

[In addition to providing the Fire Affinity, harpies with the sub-species of "phoenix" are allotted Fire Damage and Burn Effect resistance,] Echo says.

I snort at that. Clearly. Of course.

But I'm only fire resistant, I note. Not fireproof. Good to remember as I use this ability to stave off hypothermia.

I gingerly bring my other hand close to warm over the fire, then pause as light spills over my arm. It's covered in a layer of delicate feathers, and my fingers are sharpened into claws. It's such a bizarre sight. I can't really be a harpy now, can I? How does that even happen? What's caused all this?

Questions neither I nor Echo, it seems, have an answer to. Instead, I move my cupped hand of fire up and down my limbs in fascination, warming myself as I get my first look at this strange new body.

The feathers are all the colors of a sunrise. Purple, red, orange, pink, yellow. A burst of warm colors to rival the flames in my fingers. The feathers are shorter on my arms and longer on my main body. And longest, of course, on my wings. I timidly stretch one out: The tip vanishes into the darkness, but even then I can tell it's around six feet long. I frown. A wingspan of twelve feet? That shouldn't be nearly enough to produce sufficient lift for flight. How much do I weigh, at any rate? I don't feel like I have the hollow bones of a bird.

[Weight: 45 kg,] Echo reports.

Hm. Handy. *Are there other numbers you can display?*

[Most physical or quantifiable attributes can be displayed.]

Interesting. But there you have it: I might have lost a little weight, but I'm still much too heavy for flight. At least, according to aerodynamics.

Carefully and awkwardly folding the wing back in, I catch a glimpse of my fire reflecting off something near my feet. Upon closer inspection, I find the light is reflecting off my feet themselves. If they can be called feet.

Each of my legs end in an eagle-like talon—three clawed toes in the front, one thumb-like claw in the rear. I flex the digits, and am rather disturbed by their immediate response, as if I'd somehow been expecting them to be false boots concealing my actual toes. But they're real. As real as the wings.

I take a steadying breath in, and slowly let it out. A breathing exercise I'd been doing as long as I could remember. This is all very strange, but it's manageable. I can work with these new... accessories, at least as long as I need to in order to find out what's going on and how I ended up in this state.

It's even a bit fitting—or perhaps, ironic is the better term. I spent my whole life obsessed with planes, learning aeronautics, dreaming about flight as birds passed overhead. And now I am one, of a sort.

As I finish examining my feet, the firelight illuminates yet another change in my body parts—or rather, the lack of one.

My eyebrows shoot up as I double check my body. That can't be right. I run a hand down my chest, which feels rather flat, I think—though I suppose that wouldn't be surprising for a bird. Coupled with my voice, and a specific lack of equipment...

Echo, I ask. *Am I a woman?*

[Sex: Female]

[Gender: Undetermined]

I stare at the word Female printed over the top of my vision. Harpies were always women in mythology, weren't they? It shouldn't be surprising. It makes sense. I suppose I should have put it all together right away.

I lean back, trying to process this newest bit of information. My mind chews on it, forces it down the gullet, and reluctantly starts to digest.

I died. I was reborn. I'm in the body of a harpy. I can do fire magic. And I'm a woman.

I try to find the words to sum up my feelings on the subject. "Well this is all just... rather unexpected, isn't it?"

FRIENDLY FYRE CHAPTER 2

SNEAK PEEK

"Unexpected" feels like a bit of an understatement. I am certainly surprised. More than a little disbelieving. Yet the proof is in the pudding, as they say, and I cannot deny the reality of this new body simply by deciding it is not so.

"Alright then," I say, allowing myself to listen to my new, unfamiliar voice. I suppose I should try to get used to it. "What to do from here?"

As much as I desire answers about this body and how I got here, my immediate needs are clear: food, water, shelter.

I cup my flame between both hands, bringing it closer to my chest as I revel in its warmth and marvel at its existence. I suppose shelter is partially covered. At least I'm no longer at risk of freezing to death in this place. But what is this place?

Cautiously, I gather my taloned feet beneath me and stand. I immediately stumble backward and threaten to fall over, overbalancing from the unexpected weight of my wings. I flap them instinctively, like pinwheeling arms on a tightrope, the gusts of which threaten to snuff out my wildly flickering flame. Hunching forward, wings spread to either side, I recover.

"This will certainly be an experience," I mutter.

Glancing to my left, I watch and feel my wing flex with no small amount of awe. The feathers are a fiery display of colors, starting with the deepest maroon at the base and brightening to an intense yellow at the tips. I splay the wings wide, arcing them up above me as high as I can reach. These things really are a part of me. I'm controlling them.

The feathers at my wingtips brush against something in the dark. I lift my fire above my head, but its small shell of illumination isn't enough to light the roof overhead. I suppose I'll need a bigger flame for that.

Hadn't Echo mentioned something along those lines?

"Echo," I say, folding my wings back in to tuck the long leading-edge feathers behind my back (and away from my flames). "I had another fire spell I could use, didn't I?"

[Affirmative,] Echo says. [Blaze: Summon a flame of variable size and shape capable of moving with the caster's intent. Mana cost: 10 per cubic yard per second.]

"And how much mana do I have to work with?"

[Check,] Echo says, my stats reappearing from where they'd slowly faded from my vision and mind. [Mana: 199/200]

That missing point must be from the Spark spell I currently have going.

Ten mana per second is a lot if I only have two-hundred altogether. A resource I'm hesitant to burn through if it's the only thing keeping me from descending into hypothermia.

"Is there a way to recover mana?" I ask.

[Affirmative. Various spells and items may replenish a target's mana pool. Additionally, this user passively recovers mana at a rate of 1 per minute.]

That's convenient.

"If memory serves, doesn't the Spark spell deplete mana at a rate of one per minute?"

[Affirmative.]

Then I can effectively keep it going forever. That's one small comfort. In that case, one large burst of flame to get an idea of where I am won't hurt anything.

"Let's try one of those Blaze spells then," I say, focusing on the fire in my hands. If this works how the previous one did, all I have to do is envision it, right? I mentally push on the fire, imagining it growing larger, brighter.

[Blaze spell activated,] Echo says.

The flame swells to the size of a watermelon. Alarmed, I hold my hands out at arm's length, but the flame doesn't engulf them as I'd feared. Instead it seems to be moving exactly as I intend it to, staying carefully away from my fingers.

In the corner of my vision, my mana starts to tick away.

Right. No time to marvel now.

I pull my hands back, and the fire continues to hover before me. I shape it larger, pushing it higher in the air as the heat begins to sting my face. Larger. Larger. In just a few seconds it's the size of a kitchen table. My mana plummets, so I mentally throw the ball of fire as high into the air as I can manage, then disperse it in the shape of an expanding ring, the fire racing away from me like a pulse of radar. I quickly spin around, taking in my surroundings. The room momentarily bursts with color, as bright as sunlight. Then my fire collides with the far walls, extinguishing itself, and I'm wisped back into darkness.

[Blaze spell ended.]

[Mana cost: 53]

For a brief moment, however, I caught a glimpse of my surroundings, and my heart squeezes in fear. I'm certainly in a cave, that much is clear. The cavern extends radially around me by about sixty feet, and is peppered with stalactites and stalagmites. More importantly, however, are the objects which litter the floor.

I breathe into the silence, ears ringing. The vision of the room lingers, burned into my retinas, like hundreds of grinning ghosts. Finally, I raise a hand.

"Spark."

The small flame reappears above my fingers. I crouch down to the smooth stone, running my free hand over the surface. Perfectly smooth. Spotless, too, like I'm at the epicenter of... *something* which blew everything else away.

Balancing like this in a crouch, my wings naturally unfold to either side, countering the slight tilts and shifts of my body. One of my wingtips, extended into the dark, brushes against something on the ground there, and I hear the wooden tinkling of small objects falling over one another. Like a cascade of pebbles. Only, from the glimpse I caught earlier, I know they're not pebbles.

I cautiously step toward the edge of the clearing I now know surrounds me. Beyond this flat bed of rock is rough slate, stalagmites, and...

I hold my light over the ground, the spots of white almost seeming to glow against the contrast of their dark surroundings.

...Bones.

Hundreds of bones. Maybe thousands. The skulls are easiest to pick out, round like stones. But they don't all appear human. Some have horns, while others are much too large or small, and squashed or stretched. I pick my way carefully around my small death-free island. Now that I'm really looking at the skeletons, only some of them seem to be human. A few have wing structures—possibly harpies, like me.

Others seem to be made of some material that's not quite bone and have... far, far too many legs. I suppress a shudder at these remains.

After making it all the way around the circle, it's clear I'll have to pick my way out. There's no clear path through the chilling graveyard I find myself in, and even if there was, I need to explore this cavern. Without water, I'll only be able to survive here a few days at most. Another bright light would help me explore the area, but—I Check my mana, and find the Blaze spell reduced it to 146. No, this little Spark will have to do for now.

"Sorry, friend," I murmur as I step carefully around the remains of the nearest skeleton. My talons slide and clatter noisily over the loose rock. My wings open once more to help balance me, and I try not to marvel at them, how instinctive they're becoming, as I focus on where to place my steps next.

Glints of metal shine occasionally among the stones and bones. Perhaps this was a battlefield from long, long before. The cave smells of must and earth rather than decay. That gives me hope that there must be some open-air passage out of here—and also fills me with concern that these remains have been left to be lost to time. Whomever fought here—would their people not have tried to reclaim their remains? If they made no attempt to lay them to rest, then why? Was this location too remote or inhospitable? If so, that doesn't bode well for me.

I make it to a wall without stepping on too many bones, cringing each time I feel them break beneath my talons, and then begin to trace it around the room. The quiet has become eerie, or perhaps that's just my imagination now that I know what surrounds me. I'm quite certain I'm alone, but even so it's hard to shake the unsettling feeling of being watched while lost in some ancient necropolis.

I trace the wall for what I estimate to be two-thirds of the way around the room before coming upon something unusual. The wall here is crumbly and loose instead of the smooth limestone I'd become accustomed to, and as I move my light over its surface, it's clear this space has been filled in, naturally or otherwise. Giant rocks and slabs of stone block what might have been a tunnel out of the cavern. Perhaps there's still a way around this rockslide. Searching the sealed exit, I'm not paying near enough attention to my feet, and trip over something on the floor. Alarm flashes through my mind. My wings shoot out to catch me. One of them immediately strikes the wall, which only serves to leverage me over and expedite the fall.

I collapse to the ground in an unruly heap, wincing as I check to make sure nothing's broken. The bones in my wings seem hardier than those of a bird, however, and in the end the only thing injured is my pride. I move my Spark over the ground, searching for what I'd tripped over.

Another skeleton is buried in the rubble. The lower half of their torso has been swallowed by the boulders, but their upper half is uncovered and largely preserved. Something glints in their hand.

A large blood-red gem rests atop the bones. Perhaps a garnet. But rests isn't entirely accurate. The jewel seems to have... seeped around the bones. Melted somewhat back into the rocks. Dozens of veins zigzag away from the gem, embedding themselves in the limestone floor like lines on a circuit board. How strange.

My fire flickers on the surface of the precious jewel as if a second fire burns within its depths. Staring into that light, I'm overcome with a strong sense of familiarity. Like I've seen this exact stone somewhere before. Like I know it.

The feeling is troubling. "What are you?" I ask the ruby. What made it so special that this person died clutching it?

[Check,] Echo says, as if I'd been asking her. [Dormant Dungeon Core. Psionic Touch available.]

"What?" I say.

[Dormant Dungeon Core,] Echo repeats. Apparently she isn't well versed in rhetorical questions. [Psionic Touch available.]

"That means it can think?" I ask. "You said Psionic Touch only worked with creatures that could think."

[Affirmative.]

A thinking rock. Of course. Why not?

What could a rock have to think about? And I suppose more to the point, would it know anything that could help me get out of here?

It's the first interesting thing I've come across so far. I suppose it can't hurt to try to speak with it. Perhaps it will know something about my circumstances. Still holding the fire in my right hand, I reach out my left to touch the stone. The surface is cold and hard, just like any other rock.

Psionic Touch, I think, willing myself to cast that spell. Triggering this one doesn't seem as intuitive as wishing a fire into existence, but mentally saying the name seems to do the trick.

[Psionic Touch activated.]

[Cost: 1 mana per 5 seconds.]

Oh right, I forgot about that part. I need to keep a closer eye on the costs of these spells. At this rate, it will eat up my remaining mana in roughly ten minutes. Which means I'll need to switch off my Spark if I want to stretch that number at all. Not a problem, just... an uncomfortable thought to be alone in a dark room full of bones while speaking to a strange entity in my mind. But I'll cross that bridge when I get to it. For now, I'll play it by ear.

At first, nothing happens. I'm just touching a rock, trying to mentally speak with it. The thought makes me laugh. How absurd this all is! But I give it a mental nudge anyway. *Hey there. Are you, um, alive?*

And then I feel it. Something *stirs* in my mind. A presence slowly unfolding. Sensations roll into me in abstract waves. It's tired. Confused, but curious. It's wondering what roused it from its slumber.

"That would be me," I say, amazed that I'm actually speaking with a gemstone. It really can think! Fascinating.

The Dungeon Core's mind shifts, noticing me. It's becoming more solid in my mind now, more alert, as if it's shaking off the vestiges of sleep.

Mana, I can feel it realize as it focuses on me. All at once, its budding consciousness swells into a storm of thoughts and emotions that crash into me. There's mana! Oh, it needs mana so bad. It's desperate. Disoriented. Eager. Ravenous—

I gasp, snapping my hand away, and the mental presence vanishes. [Spell ended.]

My mind spins as it tries to process the stone's words. It's nothing like speech with a person; my mind can only try to interpret it that way. But at its core, it's such a chaotic thing, a swirl of emotions and impulses, no clear structure to its turbulent thoughts. And for one fearful, irrational moment, I felt I was about to be swept up in them.

"Echo?" I ask, hesitant to touch the stone again. "You said this thing is a Dungeon Core. What precisely does that mean?"

[A Dungeon Core is an entity capable of infusing essence of itself into its surroundings, thereby gaining the ability to manipulate and transform the affected landscape into a sentient dungeon.]

I raise both eyebrows. I suppose I should be beyond feeling surprised by anything I learn at this stage. Nothing should be stranger than waking up in a new body, with feathers and wings and the ability to summon fireballs.

Although a stone which can create a living dungeon does stretch one's suspension of disbelief.

Curiosity draws my hand back to the stone, but practicality has me pulling it away once more. "It can't hurt me, can it? It's just thoughts." Then something else occurs to me. "Am I inside a living dungeon right now?"

[Negative. The Dungeon Core has expired its mana supply, and is therefore incapable of enacting its will on its surroundings.]

That's a relief. "So alive, but dormant," I surmise.

[Negative,] Echo says. [The targeted object does not meet minimum requirements to qualify as 'alive.']

"Rather, it's sentient," I correct myself.

[Affirmative.]

"And sapient?"

[The degree to which the Dungeon Core is capable of logic and reason could be debated.]

I chuckle at that. It did seem quite driven by its instincts. Pity. I thought maybe I could ask it to open a door or turn on a light or some such. I give the rock a sympathetic look. "Looks like you and I are stuck in here together."

Not in any hurry to experience the unsettling swirl of emotions that come from touching the Dungeon Core again, I decide to leave it be for now and continue to map my surroundings. My mana hasn't recovered from the earlier Blaze, as the Spark spell consumes mana at the same rate I recover it, but all it will take is enduring an hour or two in the darkness to restore that amount. For now, I rely on my Spark to finish my lap around the cave, careful to avoid tripping over any other precious and sentient jewelry.

There's not much more to uncover, however. The room is roughly circular, littered with bones, and, as far as I can tell, only has the one blocked exit I found. Briefly I entertain the idea of trying to fly to see if there are any exits higher up along the walls. Feeling rather self-conscious, I flap both of my wings, stirring up a wind and scattering some of the smaller bone fragments. I push harder, flapping them with all my strength, but my feet don't even begin to lift from the floor. I quickly stop the absurd endeavor, chastising my own foolishness; I knew that wouldn't work.

I'd rightfully identified the wings as too small to provide sufficient lift the moment I'd first laid eyes on them. Are they merely ornamental, then? A vestige of evolution in the process of generationally dwindling?

These are not useful things to be wondering about while stuck in a cave and at risk of gradually succumbing to dehydration.

[Spell Level Up,] Echo abruptly speaks, causing me to jump. [Spark: Level 2. Mana consumption reduced to 1 mana every 2 minutes.]

Well that's nice, if not a bit strange. Levels? I recall seeing something like that on the Stats Echo provided, now that I'm thinking about it. But in all my years of reading, I've never encountered a magic system that seems so quantifiable.

I think I like it.

Eventually, I make my way back over to the blocked exit, hoping to find a way to loosen the stones and clear a path through. I step carefully around the Dungeon Core as I search, tugging on rocks and shining my Spark through every crack and crevice. No luck, however. The collapse of this tunnel clearly happened a long time ago—judging by the skeleton half buried in the rubble, as well as all of these fallen warriors. The stones might as well be cemented in place. I look back toward the ceiling. If I can't fly up there, perhaps I could climb?

No, not up these smooth walls. I'm more likely to get myself hurt. Then what's the answer?

My gaze falls back to the Dungeon Core.

"Echo. You said that stone is dormant because it doesn't have any mana, correct?"

[Affirmative.]

"And gaining mana would reactivate it?"

[Affirmative.]

"And if it's activated, you said it can manipulate its environment?" I press further. "As in, shift the earth itself?"

[Among other influences, affirmative.]

I chew my bottom lip, having serious doubts about the soundness of this plan. I know nothing about this thinking rock. It could as easily be friend or foe. But given everything else at my disposal—which is to say, nothing—and the time ticking down to my inevitable demise, I'm not left with many alternatives.

I crouch beside the stone, hesitating before I touch it. I know it poses no physical threat, though a mental one remains yet to be determined. But if nothing else, I can always pull my hand away—and if for some reason I can't do that, the Psionic Touch spell will eventually end on its own anyway once my mana is extinguished. It should be safe to touch the thinking rock.

The thought makes me lean back, and I huff out a laugh. How peculiar it is that I'm already growing used to all this strangeness. Yet, how intriguing! The mystery of all these new things sends a thrill through me. When was the last time I felt so excited to explore, to learn something new, to solve a problem?

If only my life didn't hang in the balance!

Even so, I can't help but grin as I reach for the Core, my fingers buzzing in anticipation.

[Psionic Touch activated.]

Once more, some *thing* springs into my mind, whirling with a dozen thoughts and instincts at once. Elation, suspicion, hunger, urgency—I push back, imagining a wall between us, and surprisingly, this works. The Core's mind suddenly feels distant and muted. Cautiously, I shift the form of my imaginary wall into that of a screen: a filter through which its mind can pass. This time, instead of the foreign thoughts blinking through my mind in a turbulent mess, the flow becomes more laminar.

Can you hear me? I think toward the Core. *Can you understand?*

There's a spark of recognition. Yes, it understands me. Its mind eagerly presses toward me, and I can sense it sensing my own mana. Starved. It is starving!

I know, I tell it. *I can help with that.* I pause. *At least, I think I can.*

The Core swells with elation. Yes! It needs mana. Any mana. Now, give it now!

"Bit demanding, aren't we?" I chuckle.

I will, I tell it. *But I need your help. If I give you mana, would you be able to open a way out of here for me?*

The Core hungrily accepts. Easy! Trivial. Effortless. It can shape mountains, with enough mana to power it. It will show me! I will be so impressed.

I smile at its enthusiasm. At least it's cooperative. And it doesn't seem to have any ill intent. More like a starved animal than a calculating predator. But I haven't actually established that I can hold up my end of the bargain.

"Echo?" I prompt. "Can I lend mana to this Dungeon Core?"

[Negative,] Echo says, and I grimace in disappointment. I should have thought to ask this sooner. [You do not have the correct class or skills to disseminate mana to other targets, living or otherwise. However,] she adds, [this entity is capable of forming a Pact with another creature.]

"Pact?" I ask.

[A Pact involves sharing resources between two targets,] Echo explains. [In this instance, the Dungeon Core would gain access to the user's mana reserves, while the user would gain access to several of the Dungeon Core's skills and abilities.]

Seems like a fair trade, not that I'm in any position to bargain. I can mentally feel the Dungeon Core's presence pacing at the edge of my mind, like a dog impatiently waiting for its bowl to be set down.

Well, why not? There's no other way out of here that I can see. And I'm sure this sentient rock is just as eager to leave this place as I am.

"Alright, then," I tell the stone, mentally echoing the thought. "Let's form a Pact."

The Core perks up at those words, practically vibrating with anticipation. I can feel it extend a portion of itself toward me, and I bridge the gap, completing the mental handshake. The moment our minds touch, an electric thrill passes through me, and my perception of the Core abruptly shifts.

For a moment—just a fraction of a second—a pane of reality seems to shift. Like a mask slipping away. Like briefly conceiving a three-dimensional cube for the four-dimensional tesseract it truly is. The Dungeon Core is a small, tiny jewel—and then it's a vast canyon of unfathomable depth. A black hole of bottomless hunger. Fractaling shards of existence threatening to pull me into its infinite potential.

And then it's merely a gem once more.

My mind reels with shock. But before I have a moment to process all this—or voice any newly raised concerns—Echo speaks up.

[Pact initiated.]

About the Author

Kia Leep is a young adult cancer survivor, who specializes in writing comedic, quirky, queer fantasy. When not roller skating or sending people to the Moon, they can be found at home with a cup of tea working on any of their dozens of in-progress books.

You can find more about their projects on their website: www.KiaLeep.com